Brendan & Erc in Exile
Volume 2

THE BIG PICTURE

Catholic Answers
Press

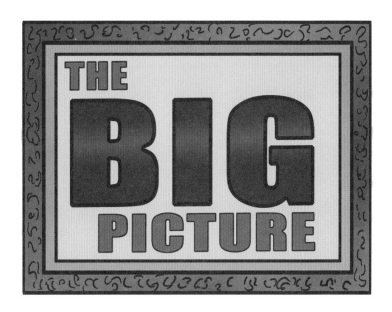

Imprimi Potest: ✠ Right Reverend William J. Driscoll, M.M.A.
Abbot of Most Holy Trinity Monastery

Nihil Obstat: Reverend Robert E. Nortz, M.M.A., S.T.L.
Censor Deputatus

Imprimatur: ✠ The Most Reverend Gregory J. Mansour, S.T.L.
Bishop of the Eparchy of Saint Maron of Brooklyn
Feast of the Immaculate Conception, 2015

The *Nihil Obstat* and *Imprimatur* are official declarations that a book or pamphlet is free of doctrinal or moral error.
No implication is contained therein that those who have granted the *Nihil Obstat* or *Imprimatur* agree with the contents,
opinions, or statements expressed.

www.maronitemonks.org

Published by Catholic Answers, Inc.
2020 Gillespie Way
El Cajon, California 92020
1-888-291-8000 orders
619-387-0042 fax
catholic.com

ISBN 978-1-941663-73-8

Image of embryos on page 74 © Dr. Michael K. Richardson. Used with permission.
Images of the Trinity on pages 16 & 20 copied from Andrei Rublev's *Holy Trinity* icon.

FOR MOM AND DAD,
WHOSE LOVE BROUGHT ME INTO THIS GREAT STORY,
AND WHOM I CAN NEVER THANK ENOUGH.

INTRODUCTION

Most sequels spring out of a first part. In this case, it was just the opposite: *this* was the book that I set out to draw in the beginning, and the first volume sprang out of it by necessity.

It began like this: After reading a summary of salvation history in Tanqueray's book, *The Spiritual Life*, I was filled with a desire to share the joy of seeing the "big picture" of our Faith. But a question soon came to mind: why should anyone believe it? There are many stories and myths about the origins of the world, the human race, and the goal of our lives, each claiming to be more or less true and worthy of belief. Why should the "Catholic story" of salvation history be any better than the rest?

The answer to this important question was the subject of the first volume: *The Truth Is Out There*. That work laid the foundation for this book, which relates the story of God's love for our human race.

That first book was essentially a work of apologetics, attempting to remove obstacles to the Faith, whereas this book assumes that the reader already has faith in Christ and his Church, and explores the theology behind it. Also, since salvation history is a *history,* parts of its story appear before most chapters. These drawings were based on Scripture and Tradition, with some inspiration from the liturgy, the Fathers of the Church, writings of mystics, spiritual authors, and other pious works. In some sections the drawings use symbolism to communicate something that cannot be seen and so is impossible to draw. For example, in the story of creation, Adam and Eve are represented as adolescents before the Fall, symbolizing their state of innocence.

This book is a modest attempt to retell the greatest story ever told; one full of suspense and surprise, disappointments and victories, love and joy. It is the story of the battle between good and evil that surrounds our human race from beginning to end. Above all, this is the story of a

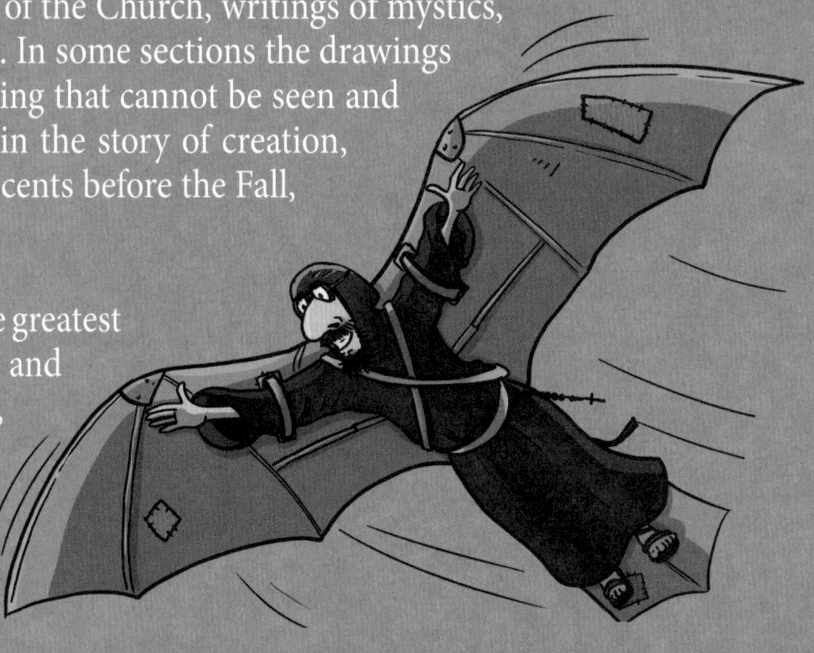

loving father, who takes no pleasure in the death of the wicked (Ezek. 18:23) but goes to great lengths to bring him back to his father's house. It is a love story, and one to which each of us belongs by our very existence. I hope that you will enjoy reading it and come away with a deep sense of gratitude to God, whose mercy endures forever (Psalm 118).

A word of thanks to the many good people who made this book possible, including: Our bishop Gregory, for all his kind encouragement; our abbot William, for all his support; all the members of my beloved community, especially Fr. Robert and Fr. Michael for ensuring that these pages were free from doctrinal (and, often, grammatical) errors; Fr. Elias for his thoughtful feedback; Br. Augustine for his technical and artistic aid, especially with word balloons; and Br. Maron for cheering me on. Thanks also to my family and friends for their ongoing interest in this book, and a willingness to sit through my long-winded explanations of theology; to everyone at Catholic Answers, especially Jon, Erik, Peggy and, above all, Todd, who worked relentlessly to make this a better book; to Ben Hatke, a true friend and mentor both in advice and example. Indeed, if this book is an improvement over the first, I owe much of it to him. And, finally, a special thank-you to everyone who, in one way or another, encouraged me to persevere. May God bless you all!

THE BIG PICTURE CONTENTS

PART I: GOD

PART II: ON ANGELS

PART III: THE CREATION OF MAN

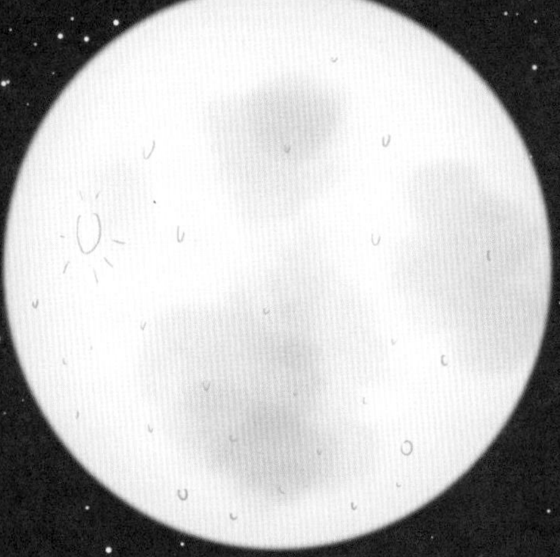

PART VI: CONSUMMATION AND FULFILLMENT

PART V: DAWN OF THE REDEEMER

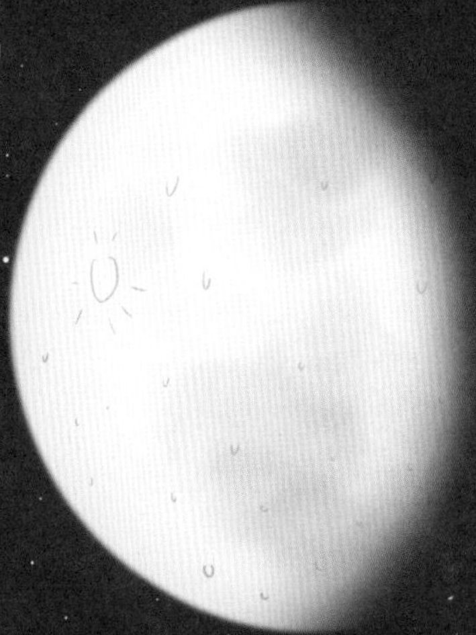

PART IV: THE FALL AND THE PROMISE

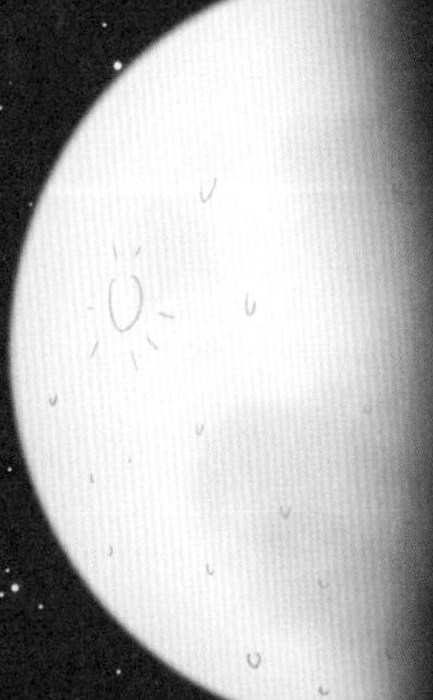

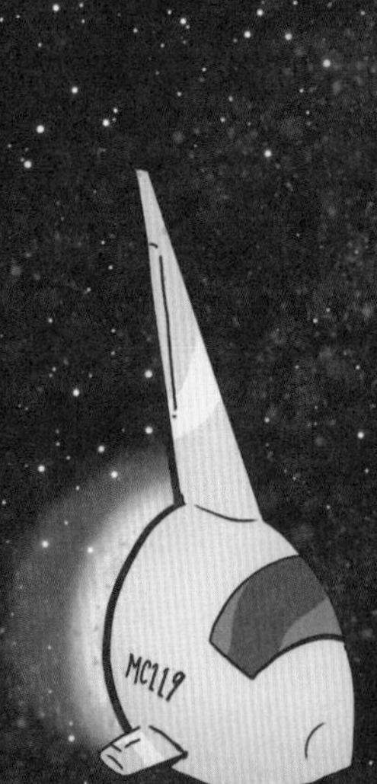
MC119

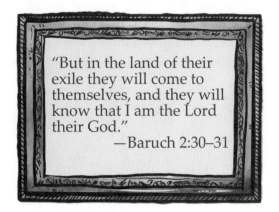

"But in the land of their exile they will come to themselves, and they will know that I am the Lord their God."
—Baruch 2:30–31

"For the Son of man came to seek and to save the lost."
—Luke 19:10

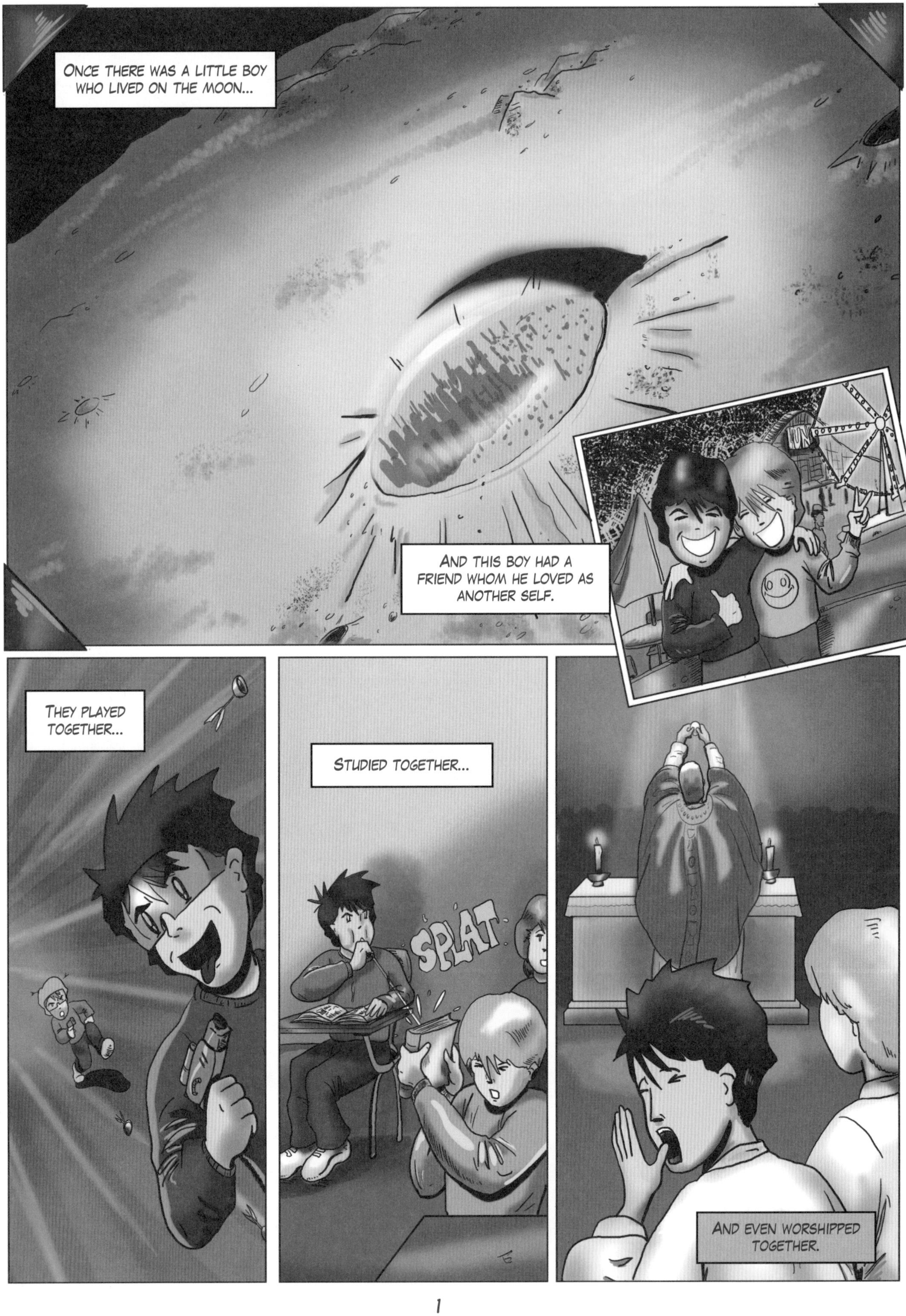
Once there was a little boy who lived on the moon...
And this boy had a friend whom he loved as another self.
They played together...
Studied together...
SPLAT
And even worshipped together.

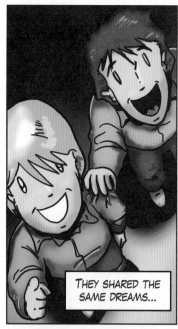

THEY SHARED THE SAME DREAMS...
SPACE FORCES GO HIGHER!
THE SAME SPORTS...
17
4
BEEEEP
CLAK
17
THE SAME GAMES.
KNOCKOUT!
AND AS THEY GREW OLDER, THEIR FRIENDSHIP ALSO GREW.
AND THEIR DREAMS CAME TRUE.

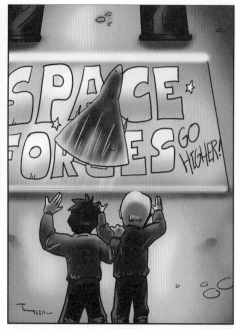

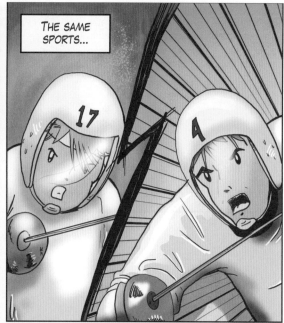

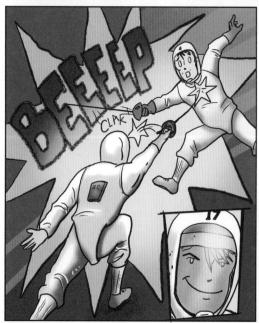

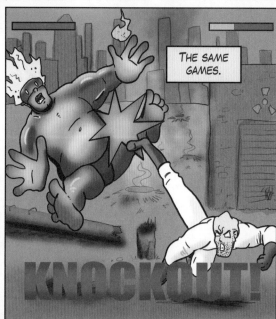

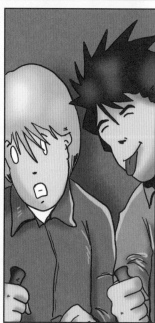

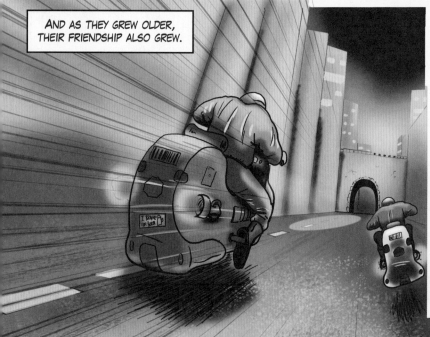

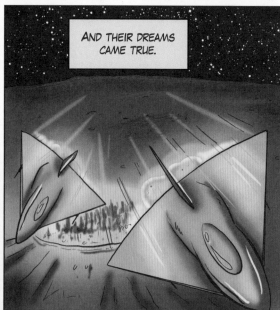

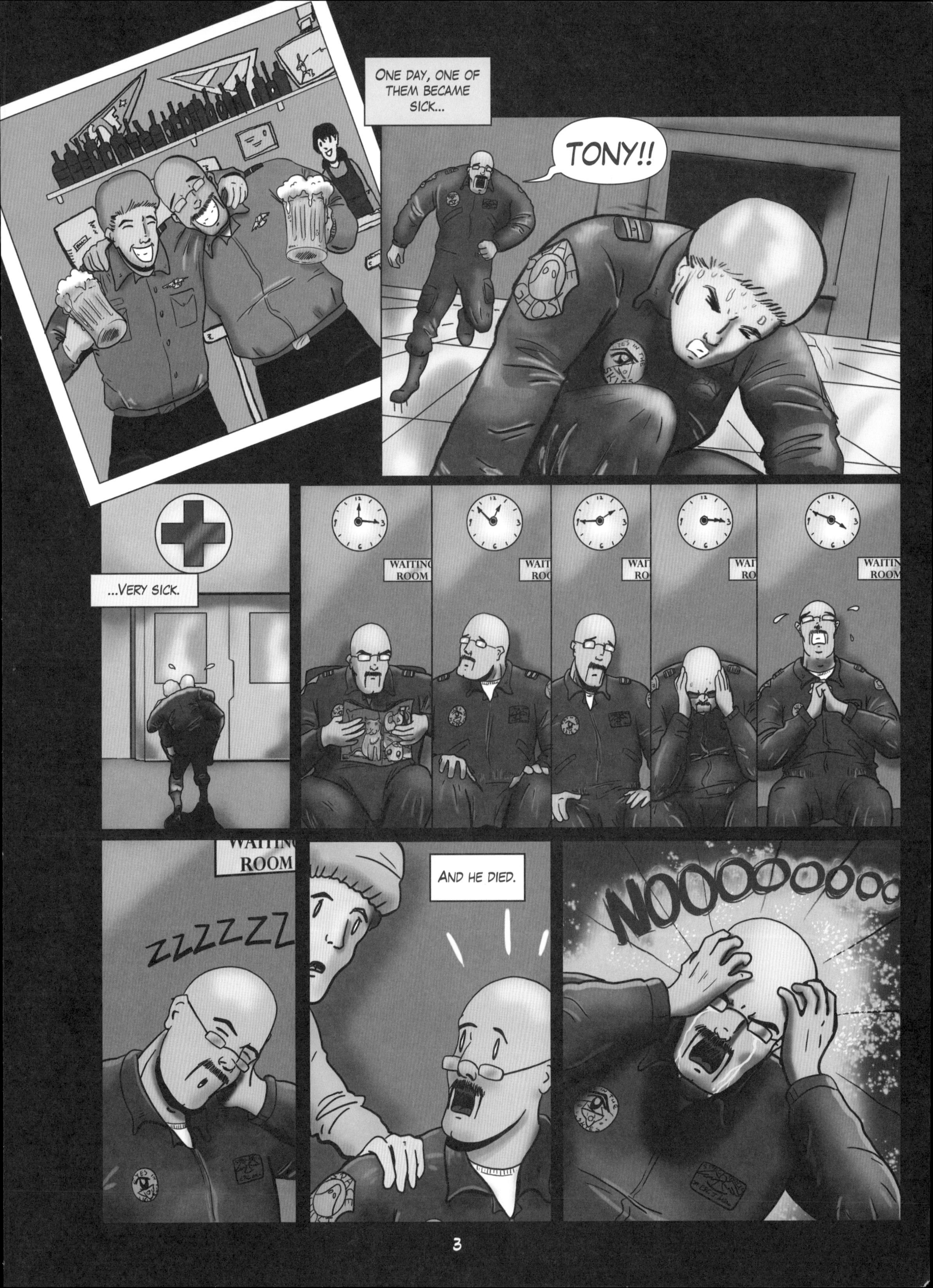
ONE DAY, ONE OF THEM BECAME SICK...
TONY!!
...VERY SICK.
WAITING ROOM
ZZZZZZ
AND HE DIED.
NOOOOOOOOO

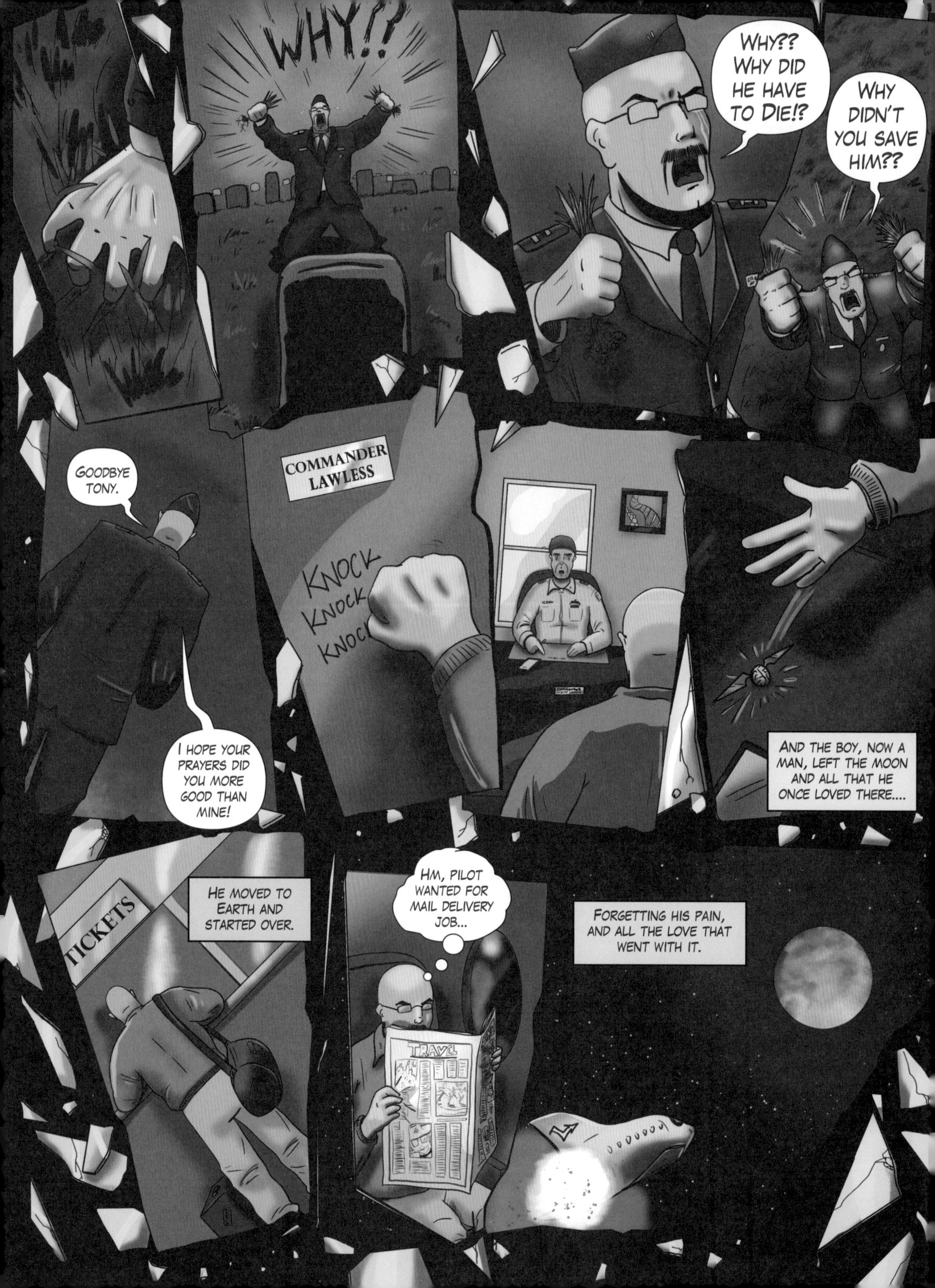
WHY!?
WHY?? WHY DID HE HAVE TO DIE!?
WHY DIDN'T YOU SAVE HIM??
GOODBYE TONY.
I HOPE YOUR PRAYERS DID YOU MORE GOOD THAN MINE!
COMMANDER LAWLESS
KNOCK KNOCK KNOCK
AND THE BOY, NOW A MAN, LEFT THE MOON AND ALL THAT HE ONCE LOVED THERE....
TICKETS
HE MOVED TO EARTH AND STARTED OVER.
HM, PILOT WANTED FOR MAIL DELIVERY JOB...
TRAVEL
FORGETTING HIS PAIN, AND ALL THE LOVE THAT WENT WITH IT.

PART I: GOD

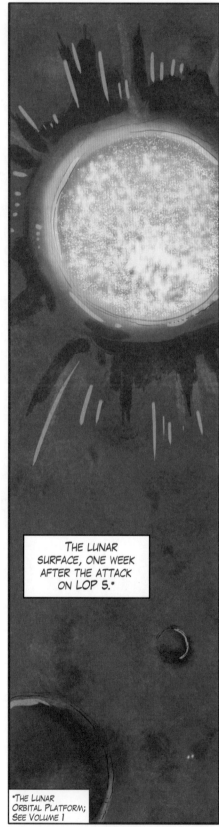

THE LUNAR
SURFACE, ONE WEEK
AFTER THE ATTACK
ON LOP 5.*

*THE LUNAR
ORBITAL PLATFORM;
SEE VOLUME 1

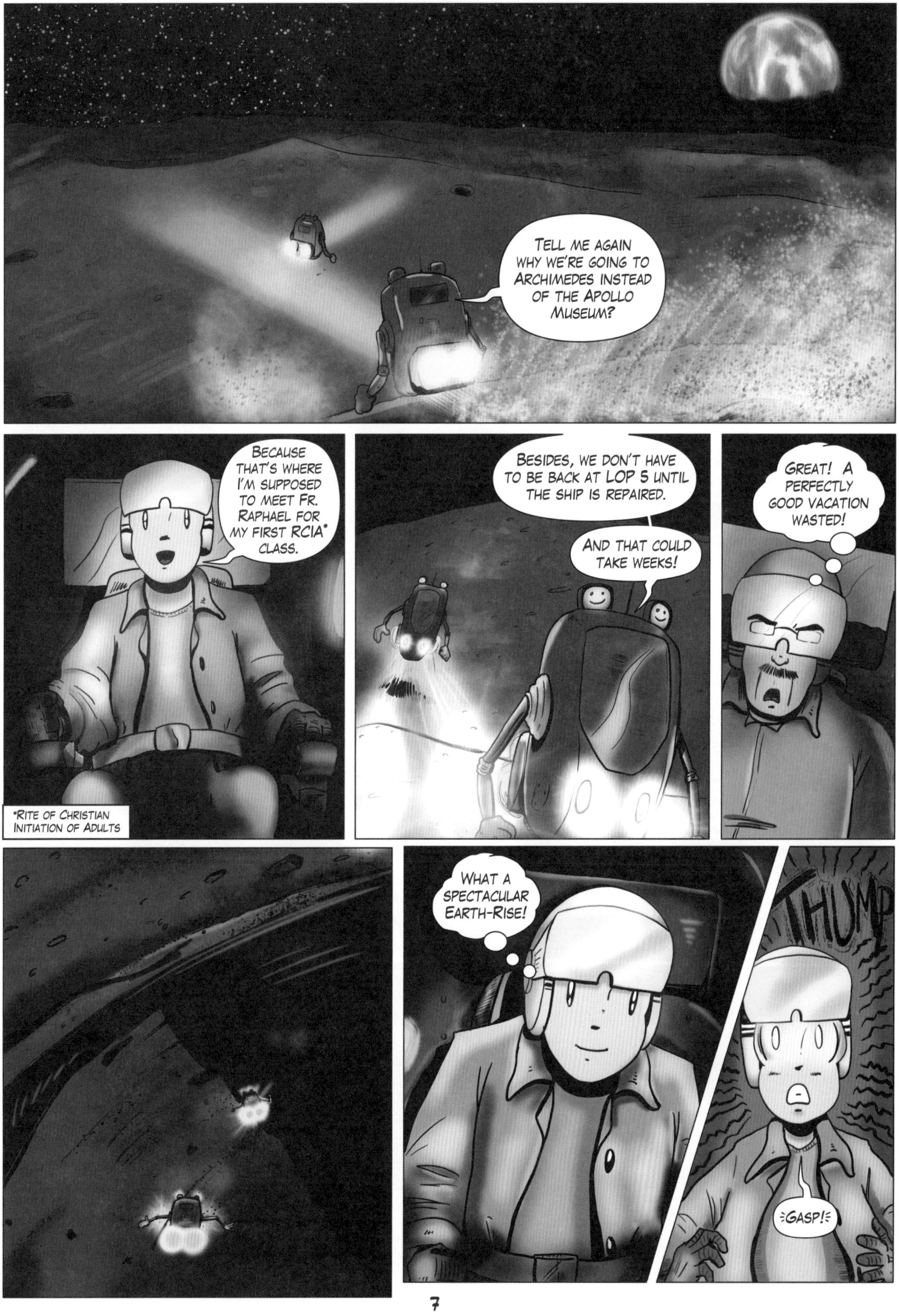
Tell me again why we're going to Archimedes instead of the Apollo Museum?
Because that's where I'm supposed to meet Fr. Raphael for my first RCIA* class.
*Rite of Christian Initiation of Adults
Besides, we don't have to be back at LOP 5 until the ship is repaired.
And that could take weeks!
Great! A perfectly good vacation wasted!
What a spectacular Earth-Rise!
THUMP
Gasp!

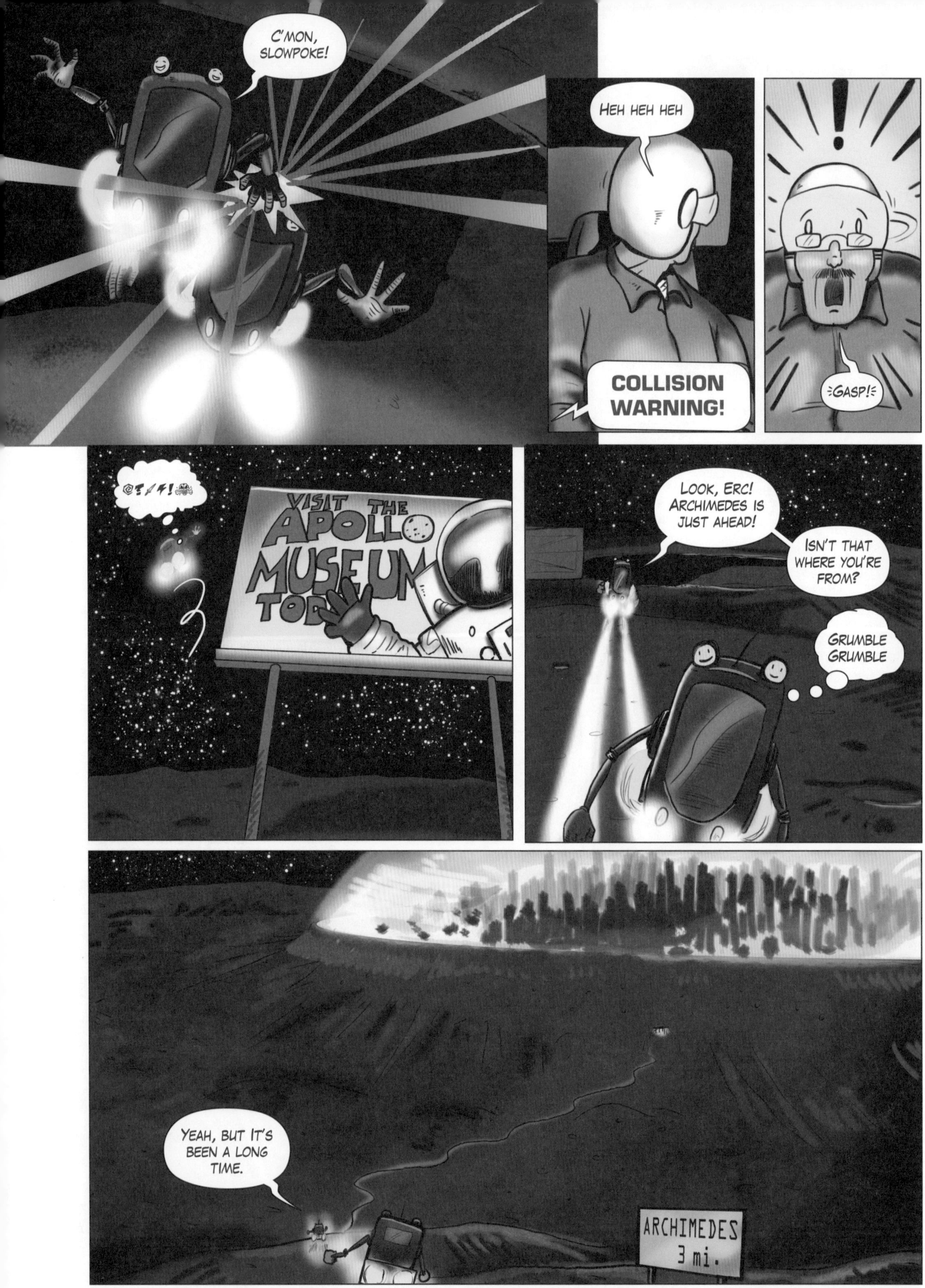
C'MON, SLOWPOKE!
HEH HEH HEH
COLLISION WARNING!
GASP!
VISIT THE APOLLO MUSEUM TOD
LOOK, ERC! ARCHIMEDES IS JUST AHEAD!
ISN'T THAT WHERE YOU'RE FROM?
GRUMBLE GRUMBLE
YEAH, BUT IT'S BEEN A LONG TIME.
ARCHIMEDES 3 mi.

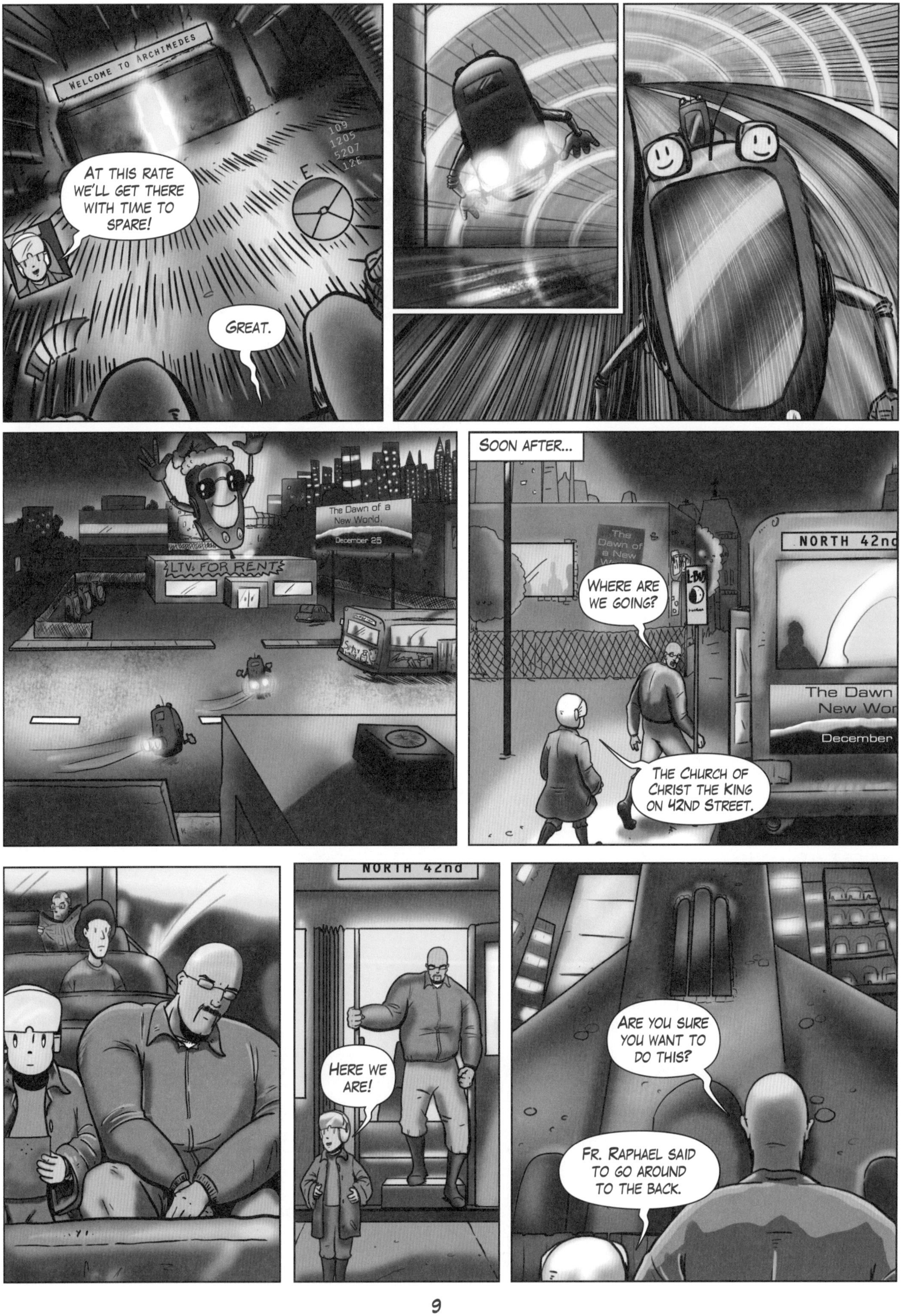

WELCOME TO ARCHIMEDES
AT THIS RATE WE'LL GET THERE WITH TIME TO SPARE!
GREAT.
LTV FOR RENT
The Dawn of a New World. December 25
SOON AFTER...
NORTH 42nd
WHERE ARE WE GOING?
THE CHURCH OF CHRIST THE KING ON 42ND STREET.
The Dawn New Wor December
NORTH 42nd
HERE WE ARE!
ARE YOU SURE YOU WANT TO DO THIS?
FR. RAPHAEL SAID TO GO AROUND TO THE BACK.

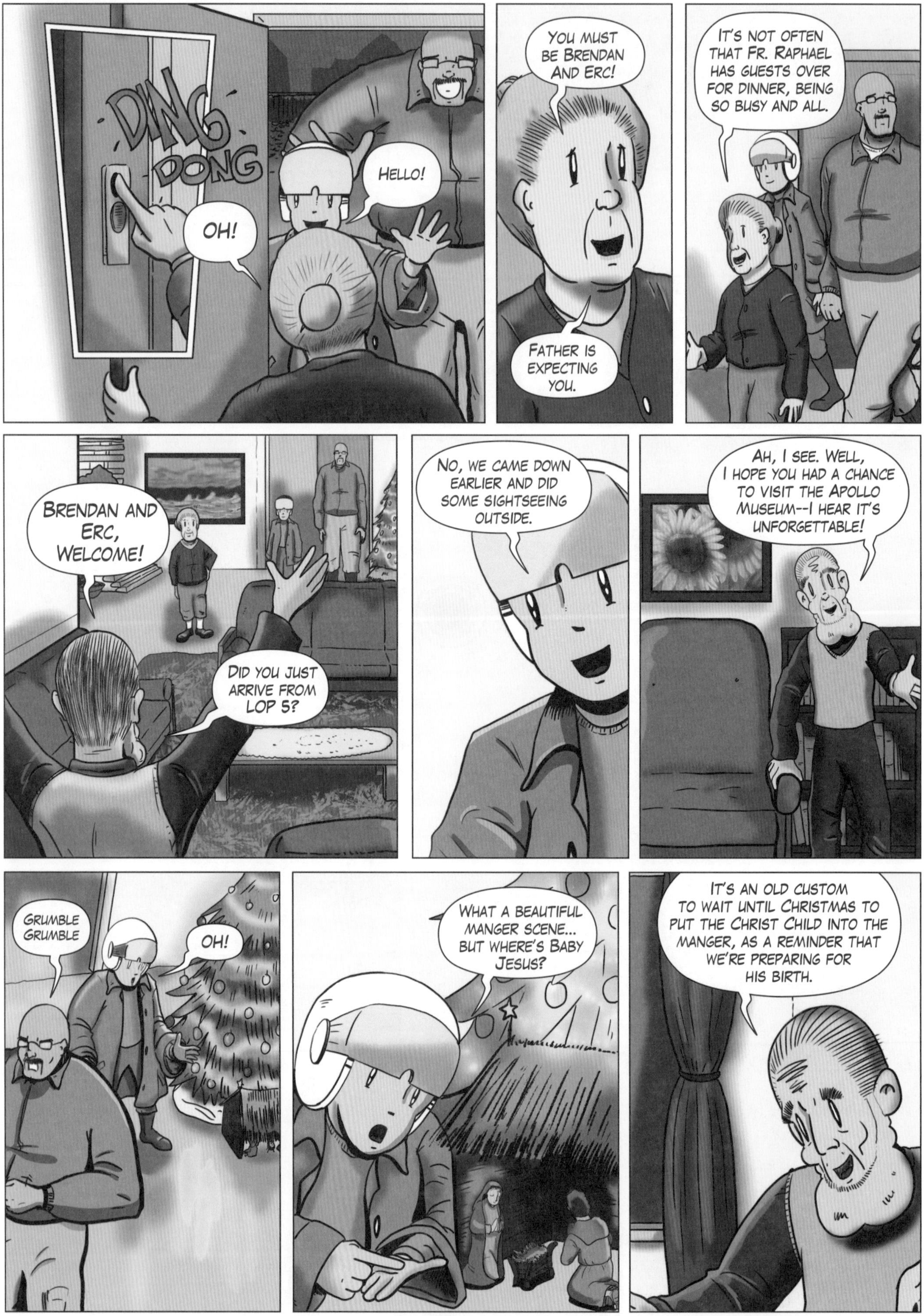
DING DONG
Hello!
Oh!
You must be Brendan and Erc!
Father is expecting you.
It's not often that Fr. Raphael has guests over for dinner, being so busy and all.
Brendan and Erc, welcome!
Did you just arrive from LOP 5?
No, we came down earlier and did some sightseeing outside.
Ah, I see. Well, I hope you had a chance to visit the Apollo Museum--I hear it's unforgettable!
Grumble Grumble
Oh!
What a beautiful manger scene... but where's Baby Jesus?
It's an old custom to wait until Christmas to put the Christ Child into the manger, as a reminder that we're preparing for his birth.

HERE'S DOTTIE WITH OUR DRINKS. PLEASE, HAVE A SEAT.

THANK YOU.

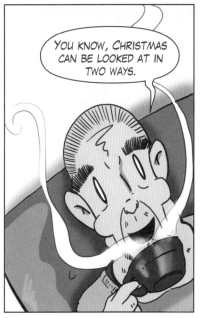

YOU KNOW, CHRISTMAS CAN BE LOOKED AT IN TWO WAYS.

IN ONE WAY, IT'S AT THE BEGINNING OF A STORY—THAT OF CHRISTIANITY.

BUT IN ANOTHER WAY, THE BIRTH OF OUR LORD IS ALSO PART OF A MUCH BIGGER STORY...

THAT OF OUR SALVATION!

A STORY FULL OF ACTION, SUSPENSE, LOVE, AND MYSTERY...

LIKE A GREAT MOVIE, WHERE EACH OF US PLAYS A PART!

WOULD YOU LIKE TO HEAR IT?

YES!

DO WE HAVE A CHOICE?

VERY WELL, THEN, LET'S START AT THE TOP... THE VERY TOP!

11

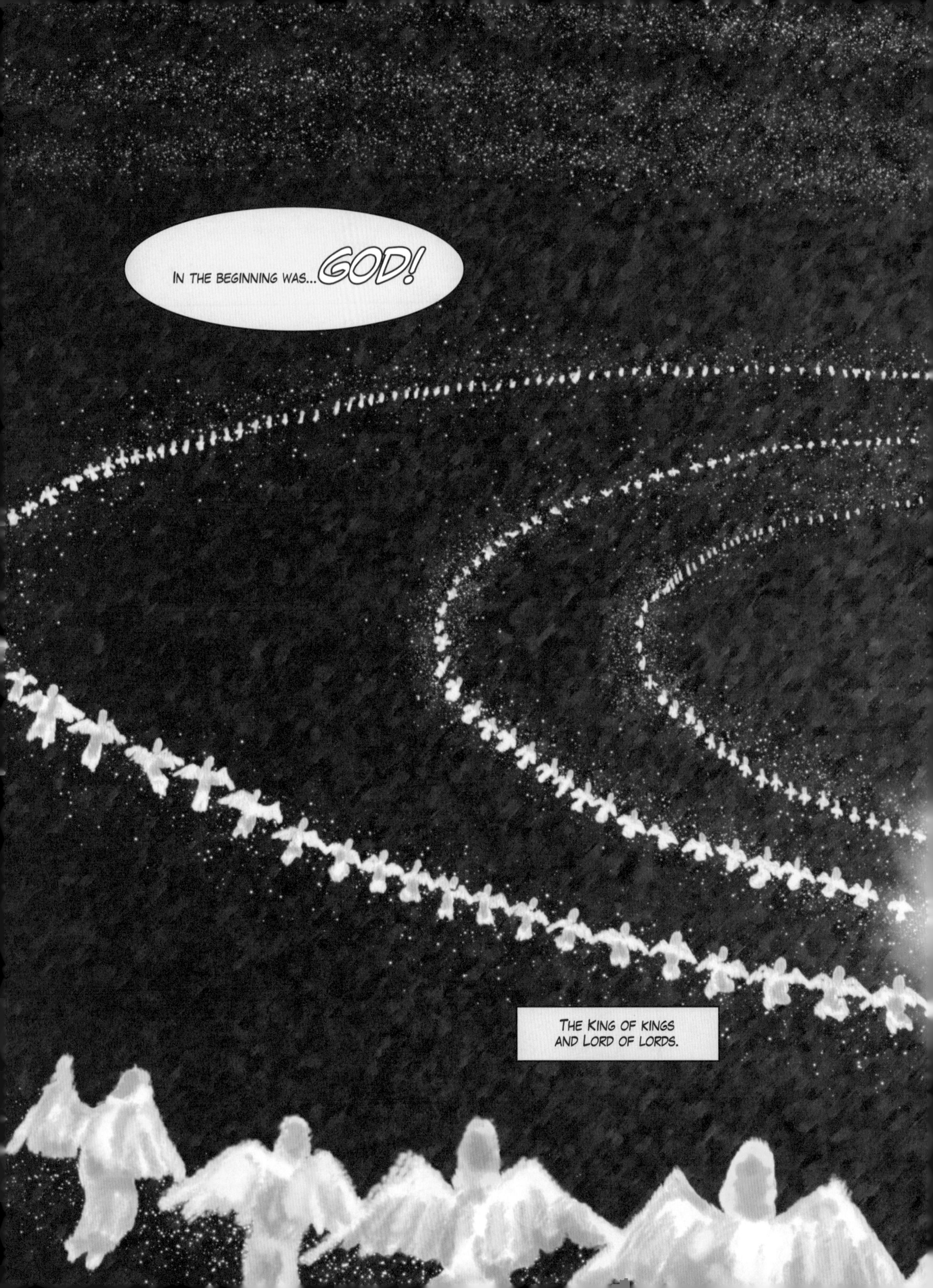
In the beginning was...GOD!
The King of kings and Lord of lords.

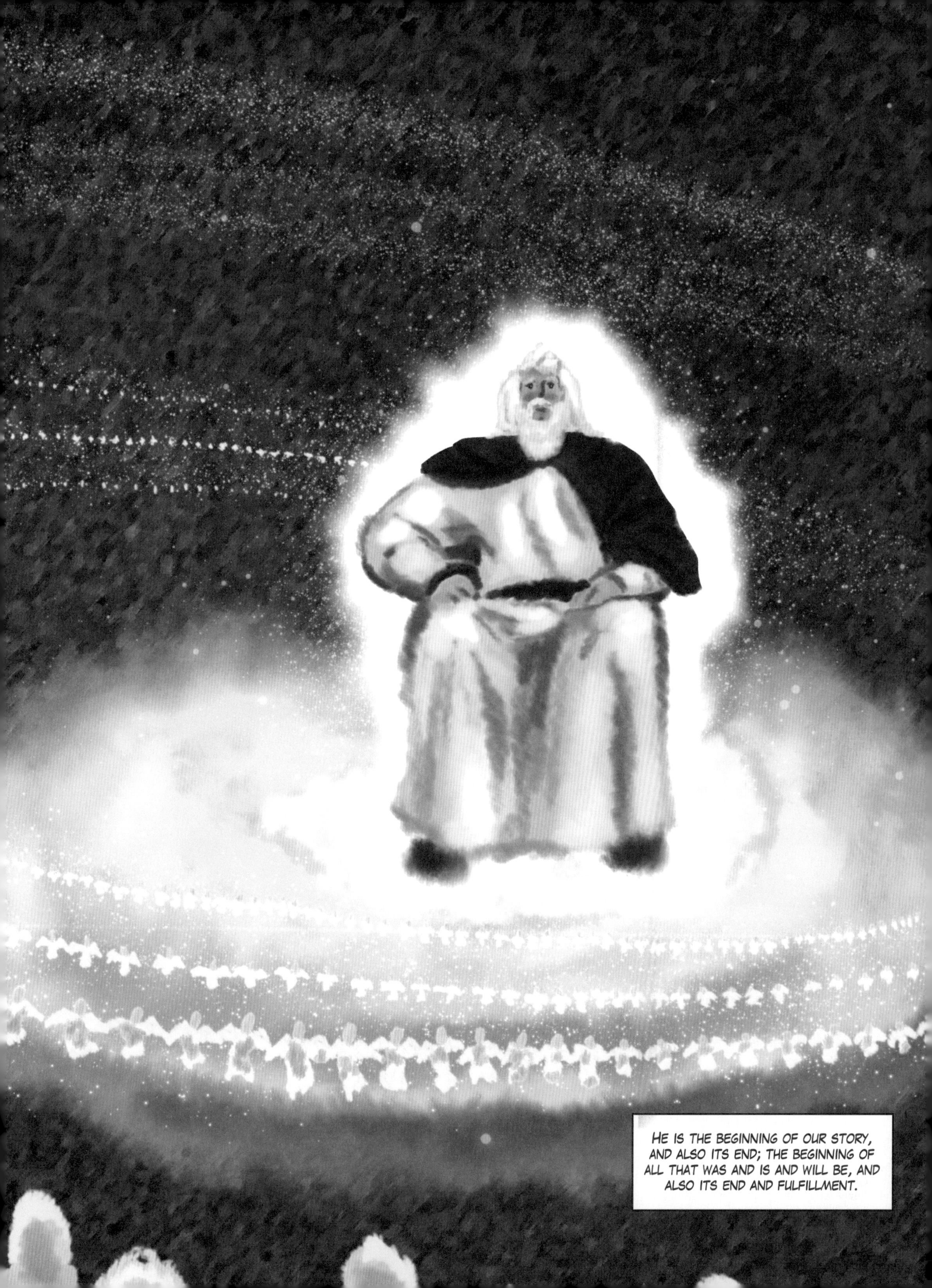
HE IS THE BEGINNING OF OUR STORY, AND ALSO ITS END; THE BEGINNING OF ALL THAT WAS AND IS AND WILL BE, AND ALSO ITS END AND FULFILLMENT.

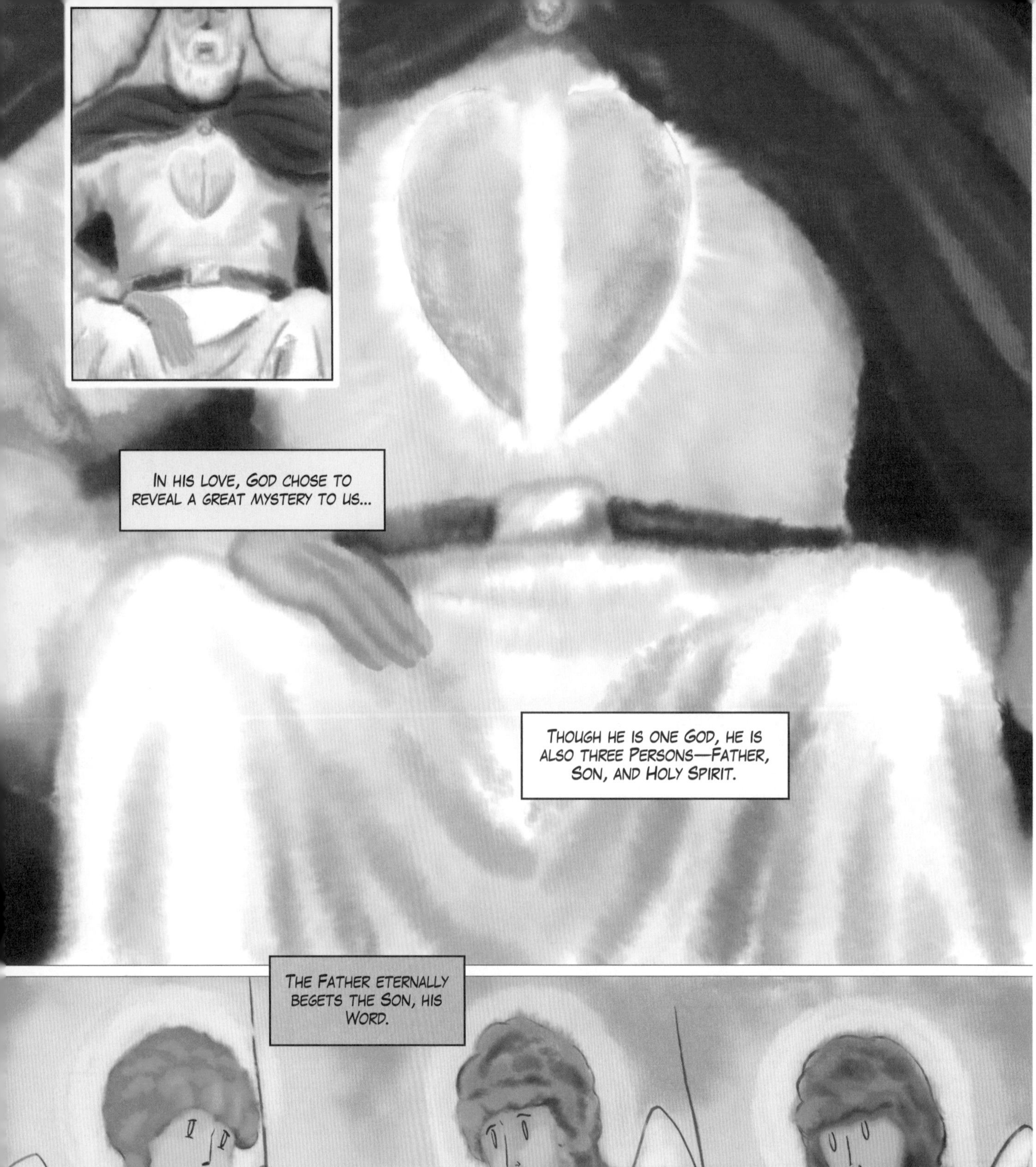
In his love, God chose to reveal a great mystery to us...
Though he is one God, he is also three Persons—Father, Son, and Holy Spirit.

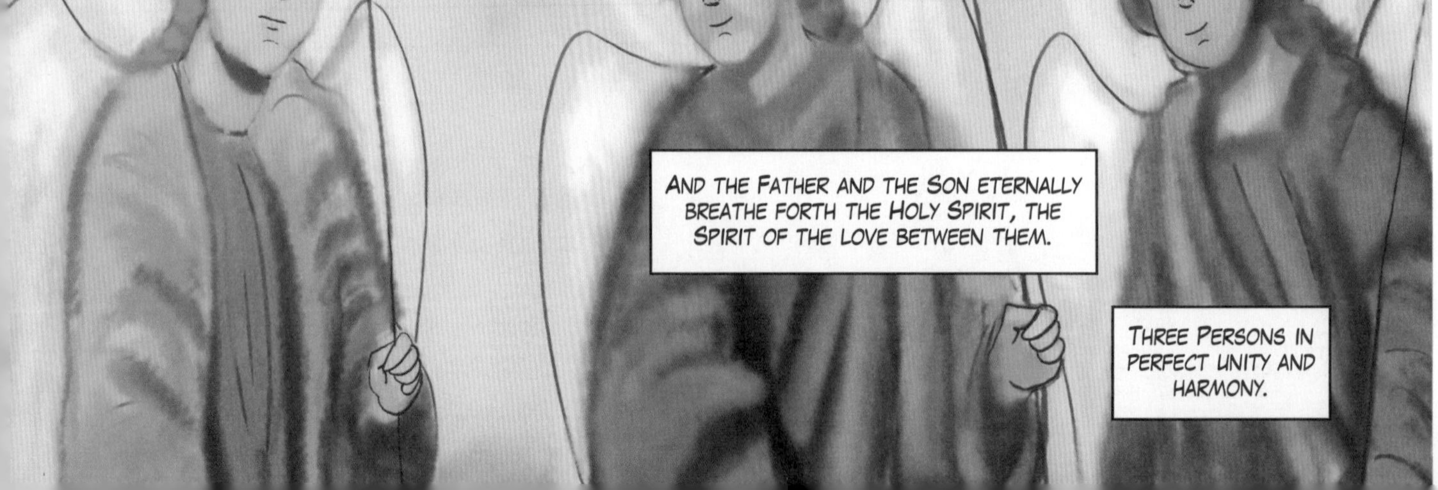
The Father eternally begets the Son, his Word.
And the Father and the Son eternally breathe forth the Holy Spirit, the Spirit of the love between them.
Three Persons in perfect unity and harmony.

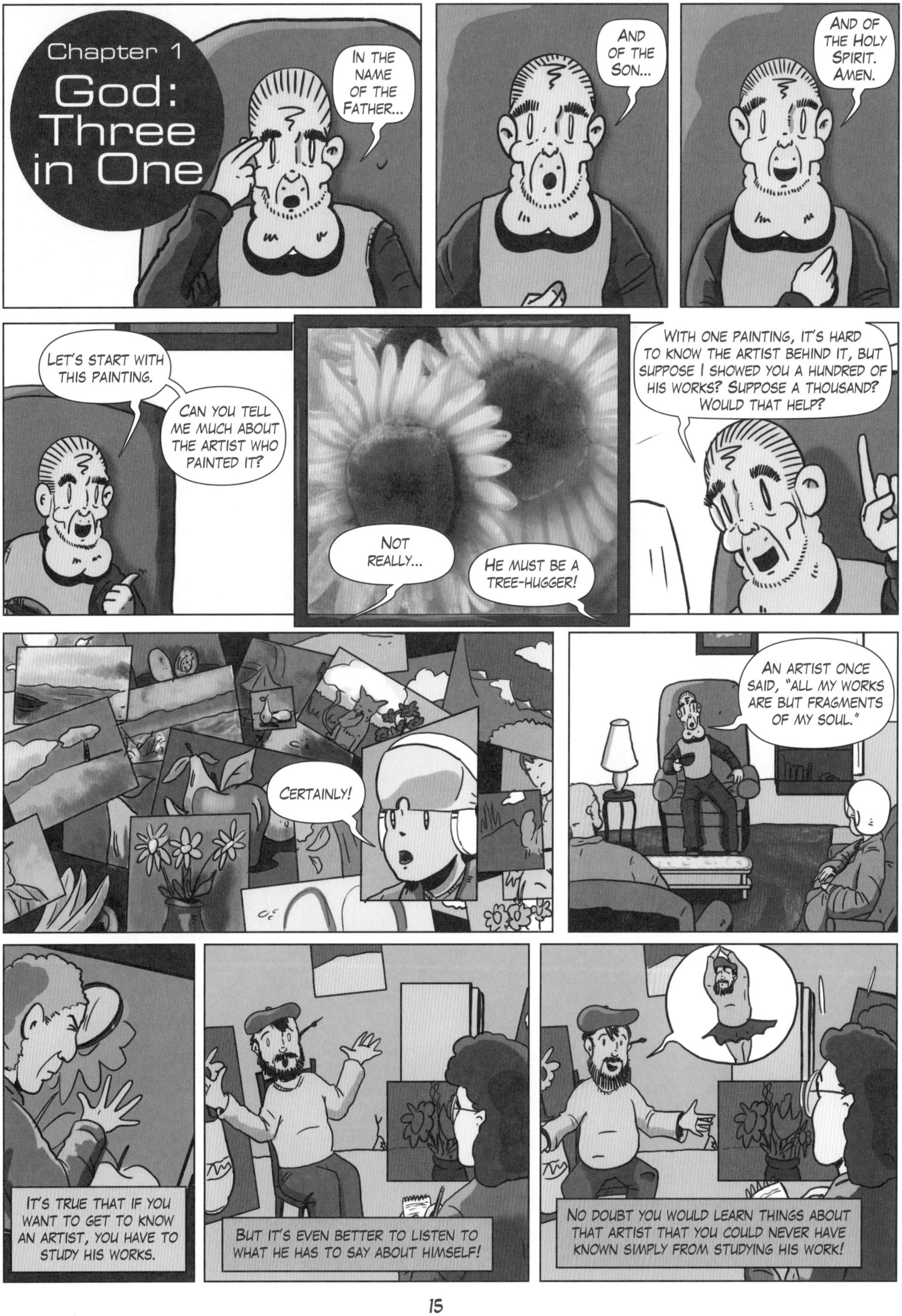
Chapter 1
God: Three in One
In the name of the Father...
And of the Son...
And of the Holy Spirit. Amen.
Let's start with this painting.
Can you tell me much about the artist who painted it?
Not really...
He must be a tree-hugger!
With one painting, it's hard to know the artist behind it, but suppose I showed you a hundred of his works? Suppose a thousand? Would that help?
Certainly!
An artist once said, "All my works are but fragments of my soul."
It's true that if you want to get to know an artist, you have to study his works.
But it's even better to listen to what he has to say about himself!
No doubt you would learn things about that artist that you could never have known simply from studying his work!

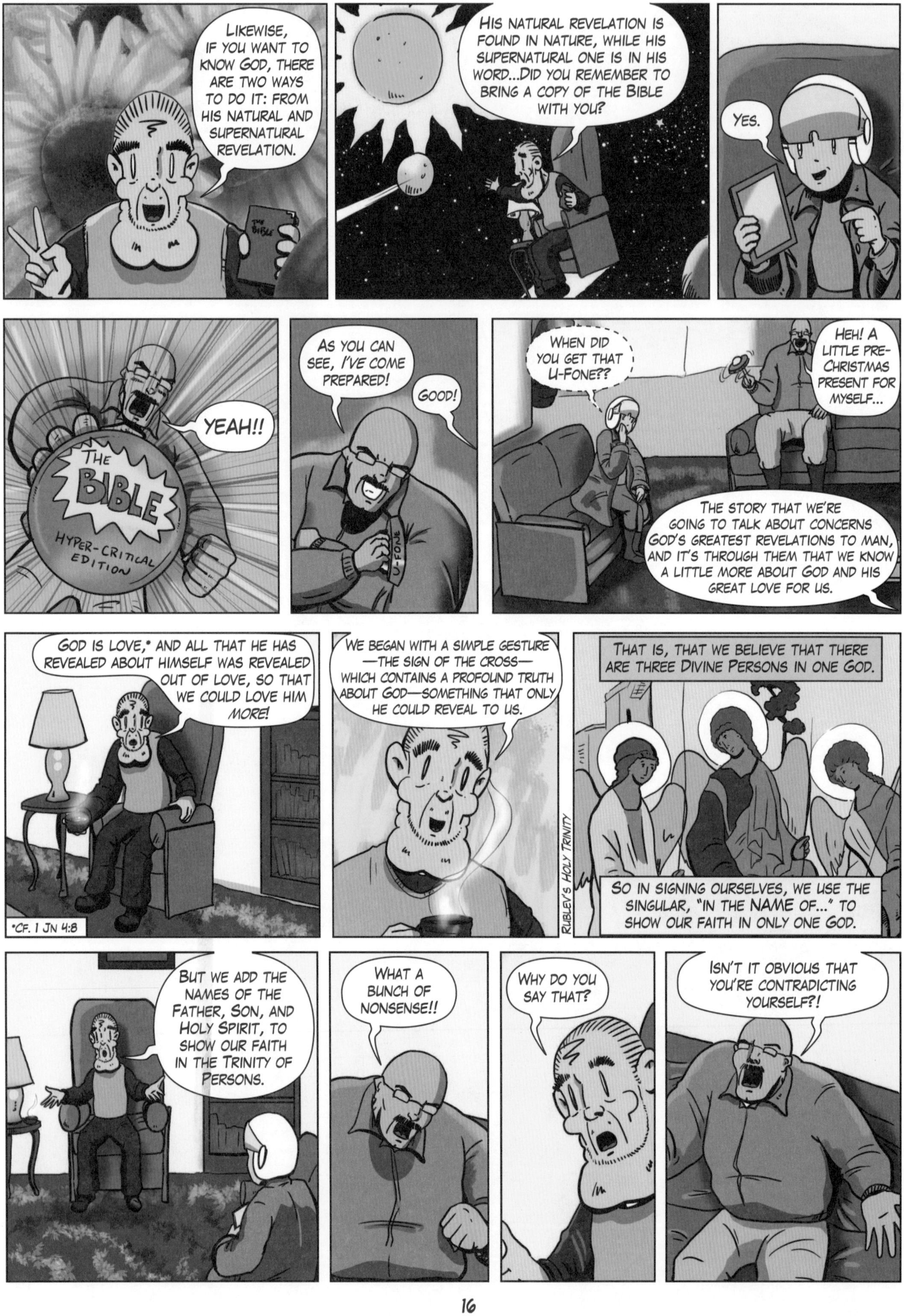

LIKEWISE, IF YOU WANT TO KNOW GOD, THERE ARE TWO WAYS TO DO IT: FROM HIS NATURAL AND SUPERNATURAL REVELATION.
THE BIBLE
HIS NATURAL REVELATION IS FOUND IN NATURE, WHILE HIS SUPERNATURAL ONE IS IN HIS WORD...DID YOU REMEMBER TO BRING A COPY OF THE BIBLE WITH YOU?
YES.
YEAH!!
THE BIBLE HYPER-CRITICAL EDITION
AS YOU CAN SEE, I'VE COME PREPARED!
GOOD!
U-FONE
WHEN DID YOU GET THAT U-FONE??
HEH! A LITTLE PRE-CHRISTMAS PRESENT FOR MYSELF...
THE STORY THAT WE'RE GOING TO TALK ABOUT CONCERNS GOD'S GREATEST REVELATIONS TO MAN, AND IT'S THROUGH THEM THAT WE KNOW A LITTLE MORE ABOUT GOD AND HIS GREAT LOVE FOR US.
GOD IS LOVE,* AND ALL THAT HE HAS REVEALED ABOUT HIMSELF WAS REVEALED OUT OF LOVE, SO THAT WE COULD LOVE HIM MORE!
*CF. 1 JN 4:8
WE BEGAN WITH A SIMPLE GESTURE —THE SIGN OF THE CROSS— WHICH CONTAINS A PROFOUND TRUTH ABOUT GOD—SOMETHING THAT ONLY HE COULD REVEAL TO US.
RUBLEV'S HOLY TRINITY
THAT IS, THAT WE BELIEVE THAT THERE ARE THREE DIVINE PERSONS IN ONE GOD.
SO IN SIGNING OURSELVES, WE USE THE SINGULAR, "IN THE NAME OF..." TO SHOW OUR FAITH IN ONLY ONE GOD.
BUT WE ADD THE NAMES OF THE FATHER, SON, AND HOLY SPIRIT, TO SHOW OUR FAITH IN THE TRINITY OF PERSONS.
WHAT A BUNCH OF NONSENSE!!
WHY DO YOU SAY THAT?
ISN'T IT OBVIOUS THAT YOU'RE CONTRADICTING YOURSELF?!

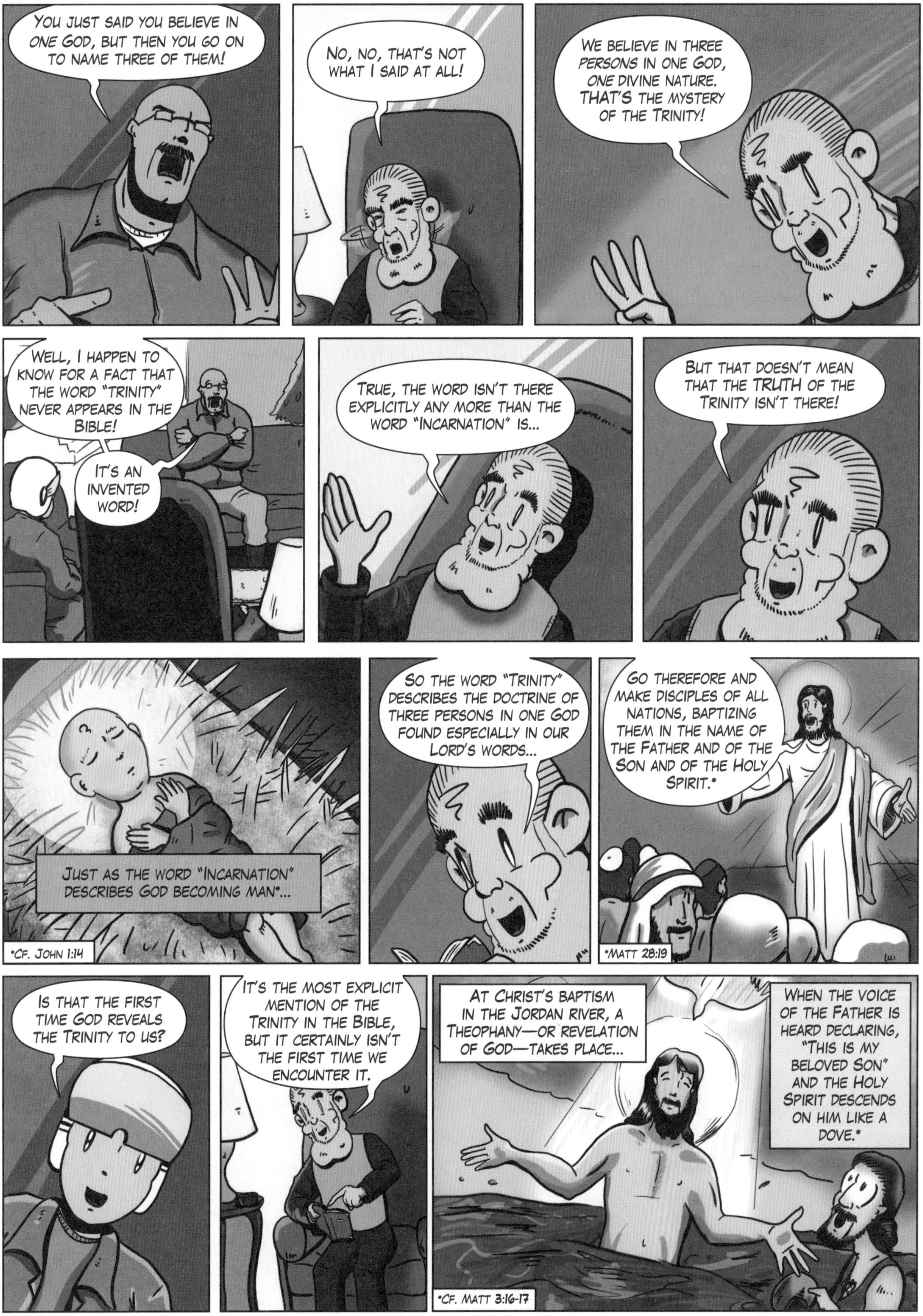

You just said you believe in one God, but then you go on to name three of them!
No, no, that's not what I said at all!
We believe in three persons in one God, one divine nature. THAT'S the mystery of the Trinity!
Well, I happen to know for a fact that the word "Trinity" never appears in the Bible!
It's an invented word!
True, the word isn't there explicitly any more than the word "Incarnation" is...
But that doesn't mean that the TRUTH of the Trinity isn't there!
Just as the word "Incarnation" describes God becoming man*...
*Cf. John 1:14
So the word "Trinity" describes the doctrine of three persons in one God found especially in our Lord's words...
Go therefore and make disciples of all nations, baptizing them in the name of the Father and of the Son and of the Holy Spirit.*
*Matt 28:19
Is that the first time God reveals the Trinity to us?
It's the most explicit mention of the Trinity in the Bible, but it certainly isn't the first time we encounter it.
At Christ's baptism in the Jordan river, a Theophany—or revelation of God—takes place...
When the voice of the Father is heard declaring, "This is my beloved Son" and the Holy Spirit descends on him like a dove.*
*Cf. Matt 3:16-17

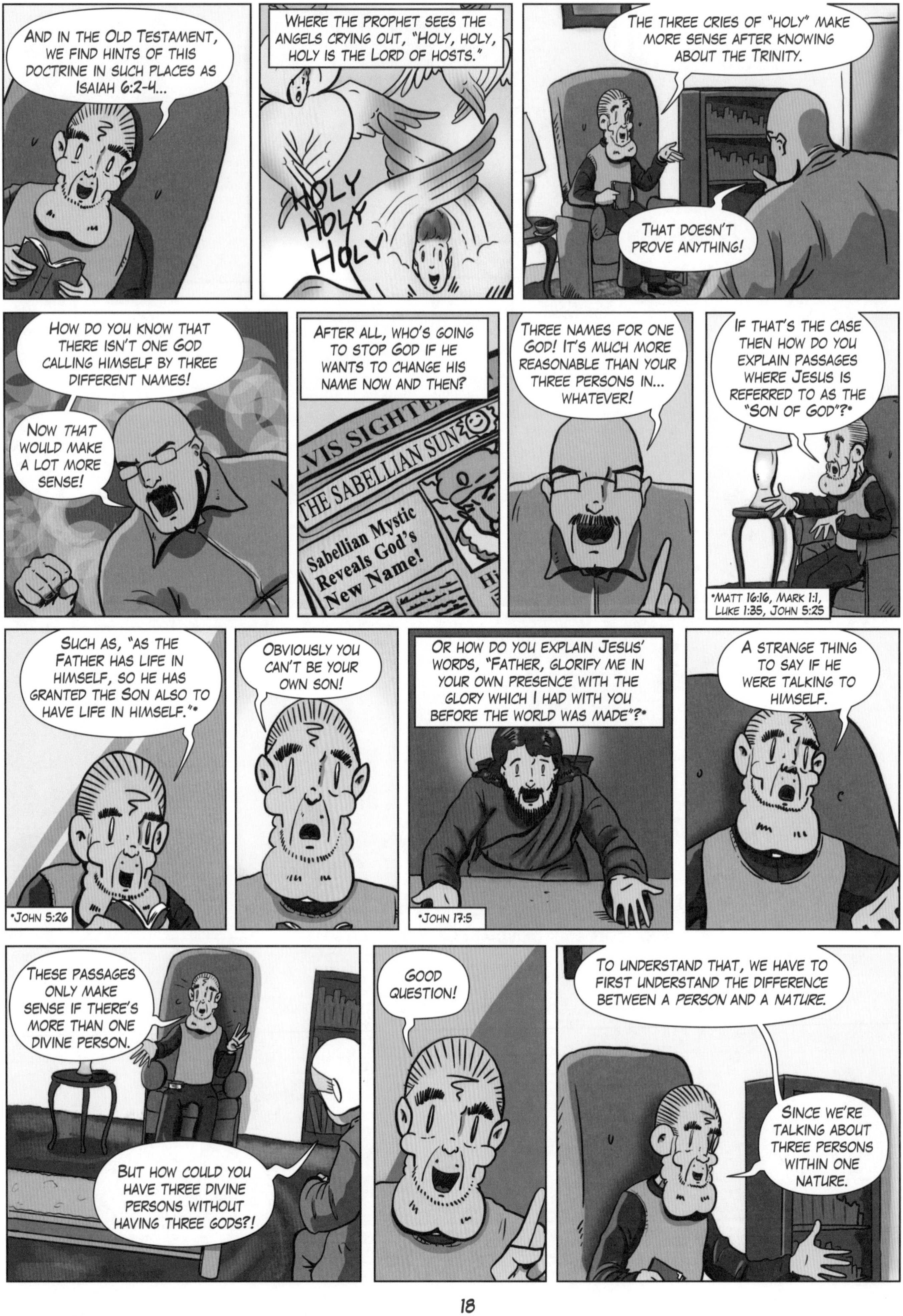
AND IN THE OLD TESTAMENT, WE FIND HINTS OF THIS DOCTRINE IN SUCH PLACES AS ISAIAH 6:2-4...
WHERE THE PROPHET SEES THE ANGELS CRYING OUT, "HOLY, HOLY, HOLY IS THE LORD OF HOSTS."
HOLY HOLY HOLY
THE THREE CRIES OF "HOLY" MAKE MORE SENSE AFTER KNOWING ABOUT THE TRINITY.
THAT DOESN'T PROVE ANYTHING!
HOW DO YOU KNOW THAT THERE ISN'T ONE GOD CALLING HIMSELF BY THREE DIFFERENT NAMES!
NOW THAT WOULD MAKE A LOT MORE SENSE!
AFTER ALL, WHO'S GOING TO STOP GOD IF HE WANTS TO CHANGE HIS NAME NOW AND THEN?
LVIS SIGHTE
THE SABELLIAN SUN
Sabellian Mystic Reveals God's New Name!
THREE NAMES FOR ONE GOD! IT'S MUCH MORE REASONABLE THAN YOUR THREE PERSONS IN... WHATEVER!
IF THAT'S THE CASE THEN HOW DO YOU EXPLAIN PASSAGES WHERE JESUS IS REFERRED TO AS THE "SON OF GOD"?*
*MATT 16:16, MARK 1:1, LUKE 1:35, JOHN 5:25
SUCH AS, "AS THE FATHER HAS LIFE IN HIMSELF, SO HE HAS GRANTED THE SON ALSO TO HAVE LIFE IN HIMSELF."*
*JOHN 5:26
OBVIOUSLY YOU CAN'T BE YOUR OWN SON!
OR HOW DO YOU EXPLAIN JESUS' WORDS, "FATHER, GLORIFY ME IN YOUR OWN PRESENCE WITH THE GLORY WHICH I HAD WITH YOU BEFORE THE WORLD WAS MADE"?*
*JOHN 17:5
A STRANGE THING TO SAY IF HE WERE TALKING TO HIMSELF.
THESE PASSAGES ONLY MAKE SENSE IF THERE'S MORE THAN ONE DIVINE PERSON.
BUT HOW COULD YOU HAVE THREE DIVINE PERSONS WITHOUT HAVING THREE GODS?!
GOOD QUESTION!
TO UNDERSTAND THAT, WE HAVE TO FIRST UNDERSTAND THE DIFFERENCE BETWEEN A PERSON AND A NATURE.
SINCE WE'RE TALKING ABOUT THREE PERSONS WITHIN ONE NATURE.

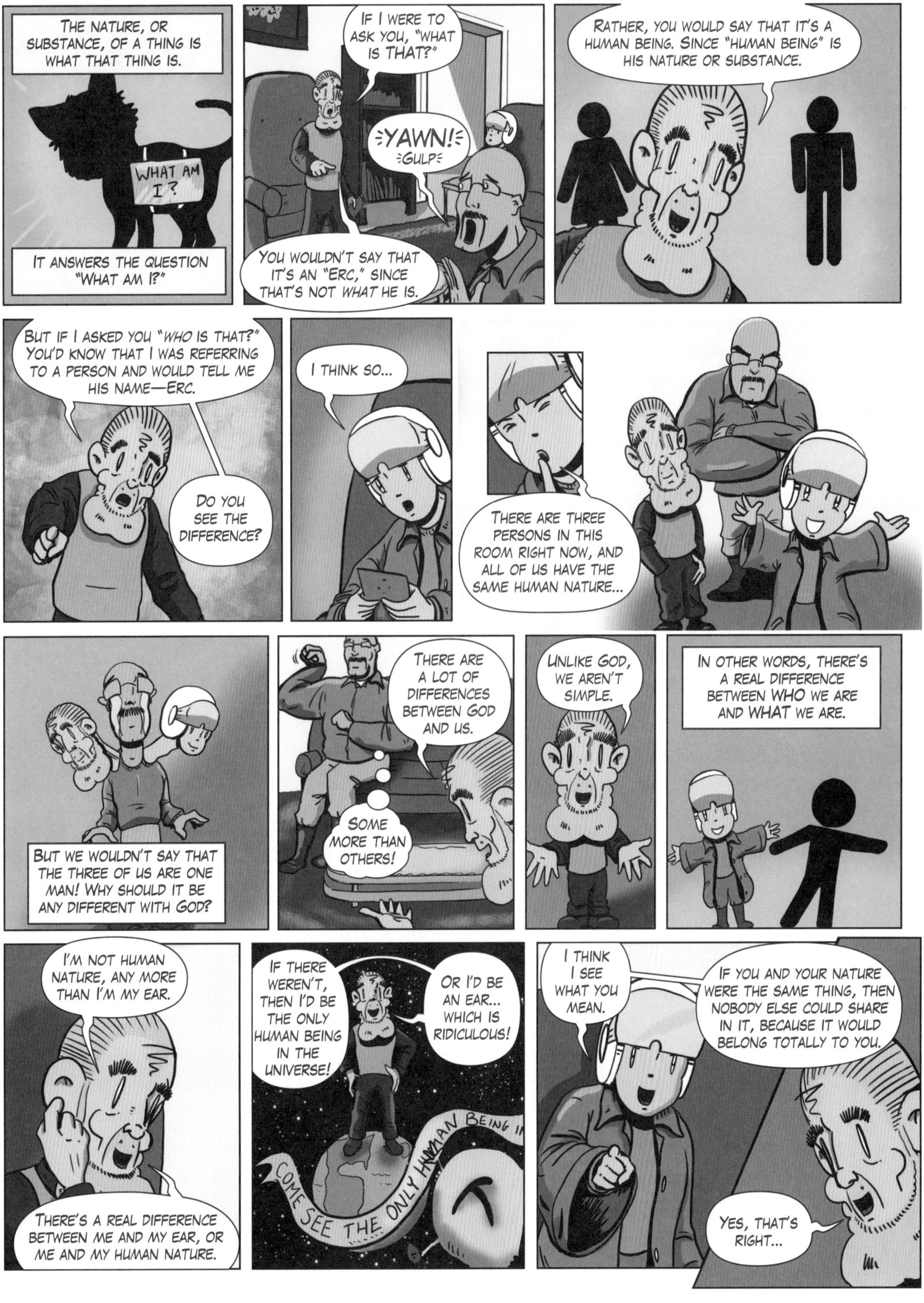

THE NATURE, OR SUBSTANCE, OF A THING IS WHAT THAT THING IS.
WHAT AM I?
IT ANSWERS THE QUESTION "WHAT AM I?"
IF I WERE TO ASK YOU, "WHAT IS THAT?"
YAWN!
GULP
YOU WOULDN'T SAY THAT IT'S AN "ERC," SINCE THAT'S NOT WHAT HE IS.
RATHER, YOU WOULD SAY THAT IT'S A HUMAN BEING. SINCE "HUMAN BEING" IS HIS NATURE OR SUBSTANCE.
BUT IF I ASKED YOU "WHO IS THAT?" YOU'D KNOW THAT I WAS REFERRING TO A PERSON AND WOULD TELL ME HIS NAME—ERC.
DO YOU SEE THE DIFFERENCE?
I THINK SO...
THERE ARE THREE PERSONS IN THIS ROOM RIGHT NOW, AND ALL OF US HAVE THE SAME HUMAN NATURE...
BUT WE WOULDN'T SAY THAT THE THREE OF US ARE ONE MAN! WHY SHOULD IT BE ANY DIFFERENT WITH GOD?
THERE ARE A LOT OF DIFFERENCES BETWEEN GOD AND US.
SOME MORE THAN OTHERS!
UNLIKE GOD, WE AREN'T SIMPLE.
IN OTHER WORDS, THERE'S A REAL DIFFERENCE BETWEEN WHO WE ARE AND WHAT WE ARE.
I'M NOT HUMAN NATURE, ANY MORE THAN I'M MY EAR.
THERE'S A REAL DIFFERENCE BETWEEN ME AND MY EAR, OR ME AND MY HUMAN NATURE.
IF THERE WEREN'T, THEN I'D BE THE ONLY HUMAN BEING IN THE UNIVERSE!
OR I'D BE AN EAR... WHICH IS RIDICULOUS!
COME SEE THE ONLY HUMAN BEING IN
I THINK I SEE WHAT YOU MEAN.
IF YOU AND YOUR NATURE WERE THE SAME THING, THEN NOBODY ELSE COULD SHARE IN IT, BECAUSE IT WOULD BELONG TOTALLY TO YOU.
YES, THAT'S RIGHT...

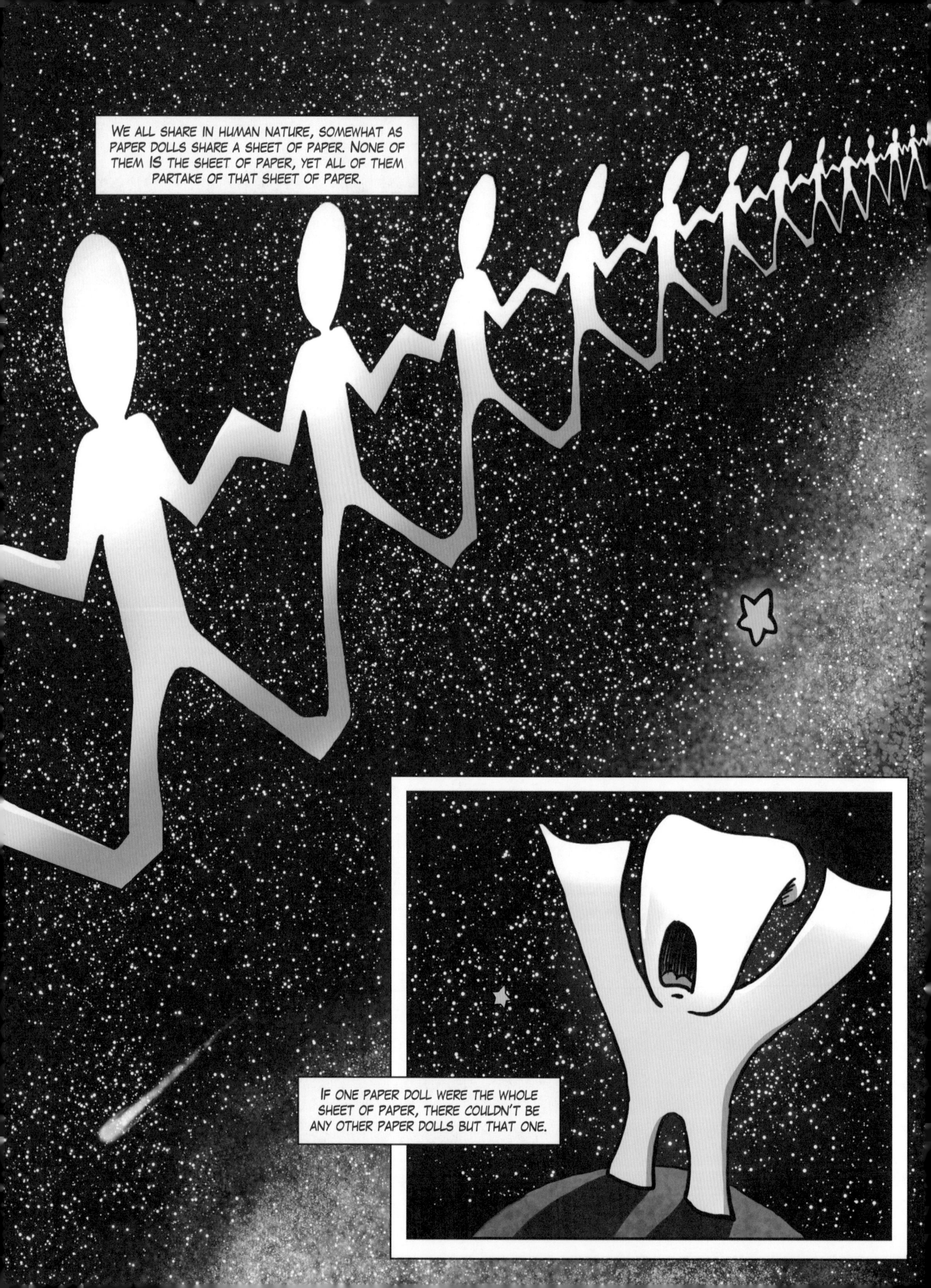
WE ALL SHARE IN HUMAN NATURE, SOMEWHAT AS PAPER DOLLS SHARE A SHEET OF PAPER. NONE OF THEM IS THE SHEET OF PAPER, YET ALL OF THEM PARTAKE OF THAT SHEET OF PAPER.
IF ONE PAPER DOLL WERE THE WHOLE SHEET OF PAPER, THERE COULDN'T BE ANY OTHER PAPER DOLLS BUT THAT ONE.

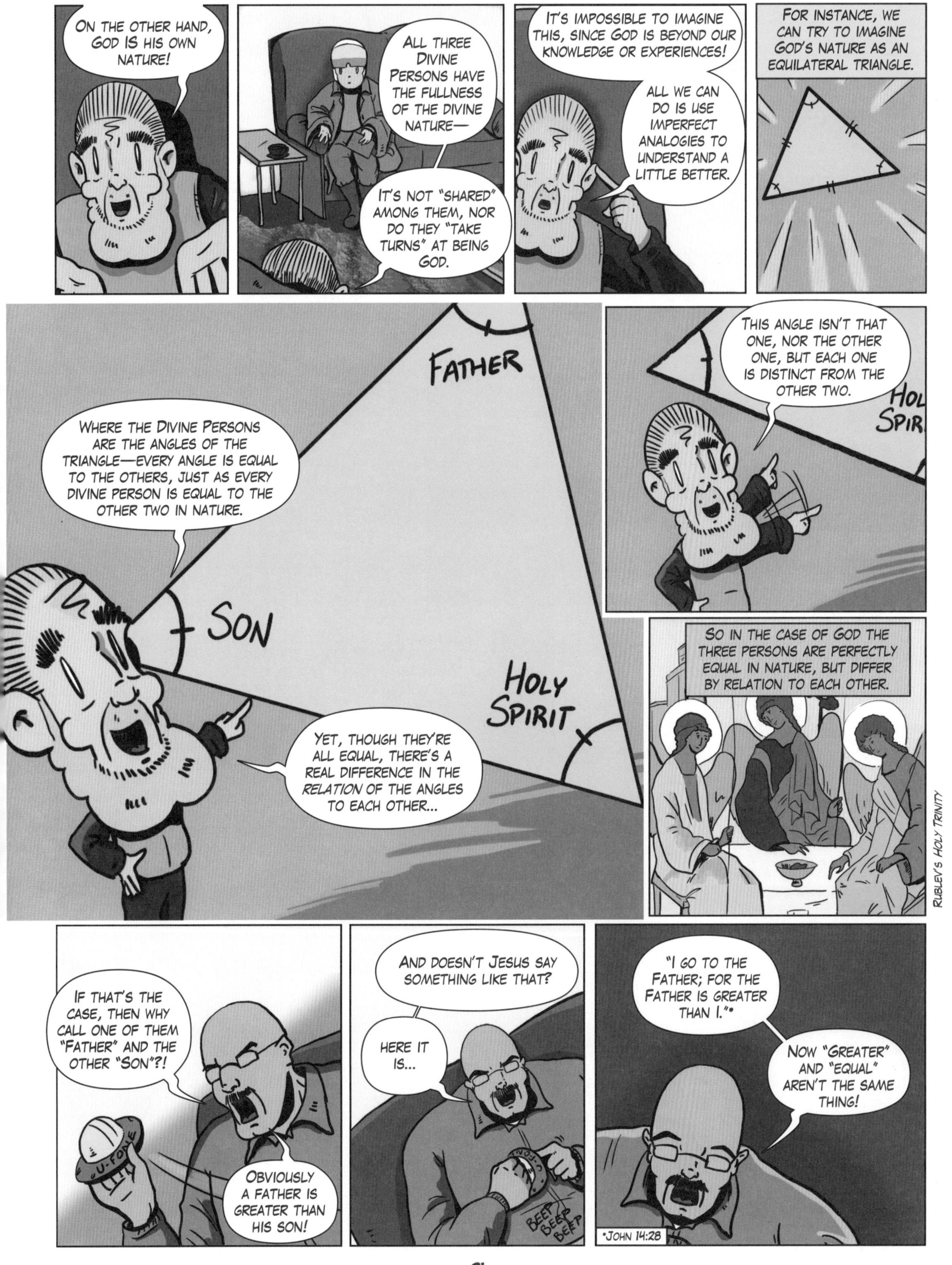

On the other hand, God IS his own nature!
All three Divine Persons have the fullness of the divine nature—
It's not "shared" among them, nor do they "take turns" at being God.
It's impossible to imagine this, since God is beyond our knowledge or experiences!
All we can do is use imperfect analogies to understand a little better.
For instance, we can try to imagine God's nature as an equilateral triangle.
Father
Where the Divine Persons are the angles of the triangle—every angle is equal to the others, just as every divine person is equal to the other two in nature.
Son
Holy Spirit
Yet, though they're all equal, there's a real difference in the *relation* of the angles to each other...
This angle isn't that one, nor the other one, but each one is distinct from the other two.
So in the case of God the three persons are perfectly equal in nature, but differ by relation to each other.
Rublev's *Holy Trinity*
If that's the case, then why call one of them "Father" and the other "Son"?!
U-Fone
Obviously a father is greater than his son!
And doesn't Jesus say something like that?
Here it is...
Beep Beep Beep
"I go to the Father; for the Father is greater than I."*
Now "greater" and "equal" aren't the same thing!
*John 14:28

ACCORDING TO ST. THOMAS AQUINAS, OUR LORD IS SPEAKING ABOUT THE FATHER BEING GREATER THAN HE IS IN HIS HUMAN NATURE... BUT WE CAN TALK ABOUT THAT LATER...

AS FOR THE WORD "FATHER" VERSUS "SON," YOU'RE RIGHT: THERE IS A SIGNIFICANCE TO THESE NAMES!

BUT IT CAN'T BE THAT ONE IS BEFORE THE OTHER IN TIME, AS IT IS WITH US, SINCE GOD IS ETERNAL AND OUTSIDE OF TIME.

RATHER, AS FIRE FROM THE MOMENT IT'S IGNITED EMITS BOTH LIGHT AND HEAT...

SO FROM ALL ETERNITY THERE WAS GOD THE FATHER, GOD THE SON, AND GOD THE HOLY SPIRIT.

THE NAME "SON" SHOWS THAT HE HAS THE SAME NATURE OR SUBSTANCE AS THE FATHER, THAT HE'S GOD TOO, "CONSUBSTANTIAL" WITH HIS FATHER.

JUST AS THE SON OF A MAN IS ALSO A MAN, NOT A CAT OR A DOG OR A MONKEY.

IT ALSO SHOWS THE RELATION BETWEEN THE FATHER AND THE SON, SINCE THE SON PROCEEDS FROM THE FATHER.

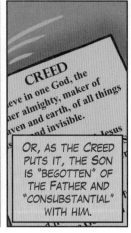

CREED
...eve in one God, the
...er almighty, maker of
...aven and earth, of all things
...and invisible.

OR, AS THE CREED PUTS IT, THE SON IS "BEGOTTEN" OF THE FATHER AND "CONSUBSTANTIAL" WITH HIM.

BUT IF THE SON IS BEGOTTEN OF THE FATHER, THEN WOULDN'T HE BE A SEPARATE BEING?

JUST AS WHEN A CHILD IS BORN HE'S NO LONGER UNITED TO HIS MOTHER.

THAT WOULD BE TRUE FOR US, BUT NOT FOR GOD.

REMEMBER THAT THE SON HAS ANOTHER NAME IN SCRIPTURE— THE "WORD"!

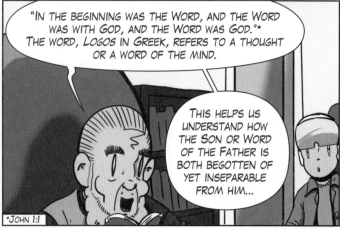

"IN THE BEGINNING WAS THE WORD, AND THE WORD WAS WITH GOD, AND THE WORD WAS GOD."* THE WORD, LOGOS IN GREEK, REFERS TO A THOUGHT OR A WORD OF THE MIND.

THIS HELPS US UNDERSTAND HOW THE SON OR WORD OF THE FATHER IS BOTH BEGOTTEN OF YET INSEPARABLE FROM HIM...

*JOHN 1:1

SINCE THOUGHTS STAY IN THE MIND OF THE THINKER!

IN OUR CASE, OUR THOUGHTS AREN'T THE SAME AS OURSELVES. BUT, AS I SAID, GOD IS PERFECTLY SIMPLE, AND THERE'S NO DIFFERENCE BETWEEN WHAT GOD IS AND WHAT HE HAS.

SO THE WORD OR THOUGHT OF GOD IS ALSO GOD, AND ANOTHER PERSON OF THE TRINITY.

AND I SUPPOSE GOD HAD ANOTHER THOUGHT AND CALLED HIM THE HOLY SPIRIT?

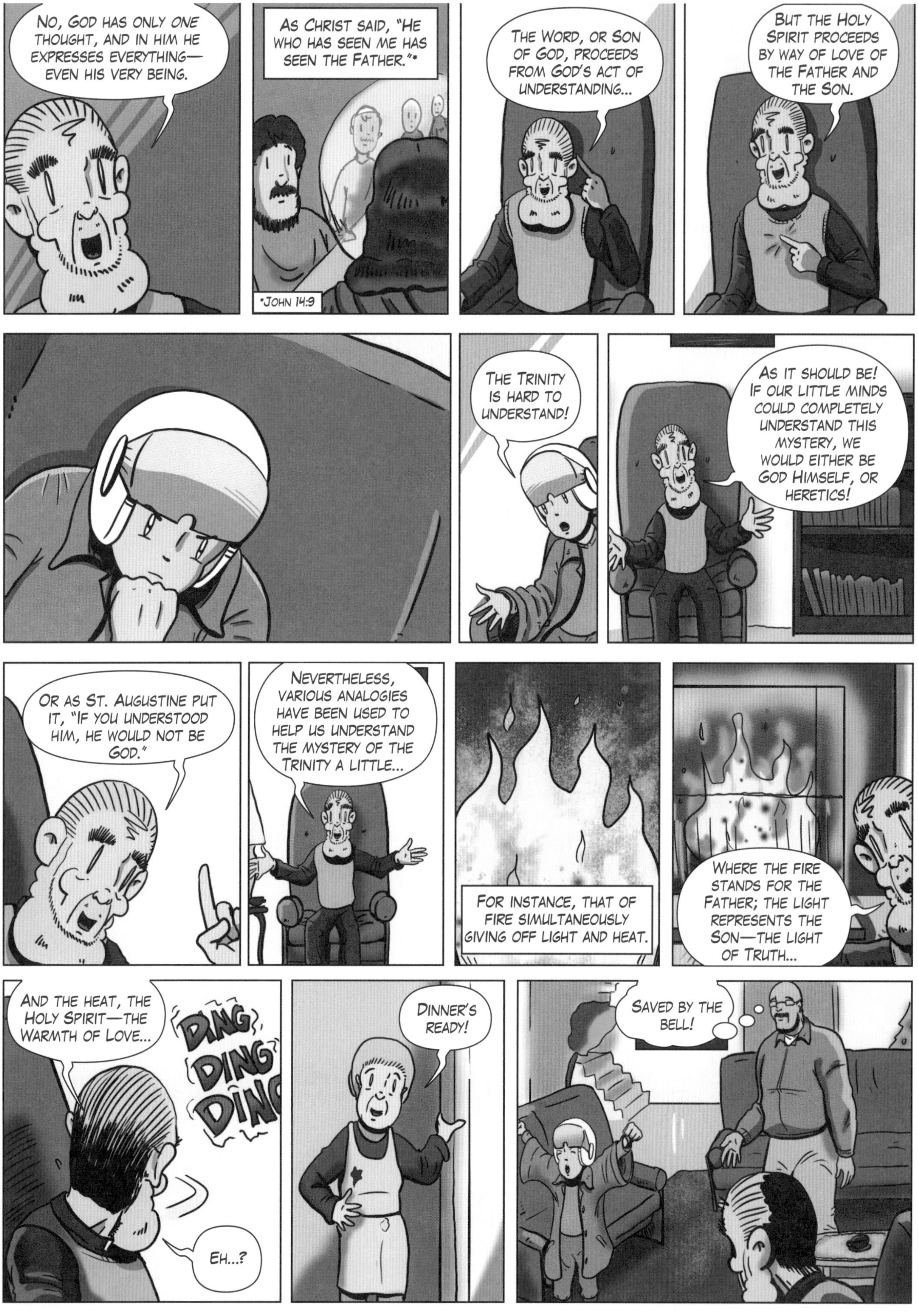
No, God has only one thought, and in him he expresses everything—even his very being.
As Christ said, "He who has seen me has seen the Father."*
*John 14:9
The Word, or Son of God, proceeds from God's act of understanding...
But the Holy Spirit proceeds by way of love of the Father and the Son.
The Trinity is hard to understand!
As it should be! If our little minds could completely understand this mystery, we would either be God Himself, or heretics!
Or as St. Augustine put it, "If you understood him, he would not be God."
Nevertheless, various analogies have been used to help us understand the mystery of the Trinity a little...
For instance, that of fire simultaneously giving off light and heat.
Where the fire stands for the Father; the light represents the Son—the light of Truth...
And the heat, the Holy Spirit—the warmth of Love...
DING DING DING
Eh...?
Dinner's ready!
Saved by the bell!

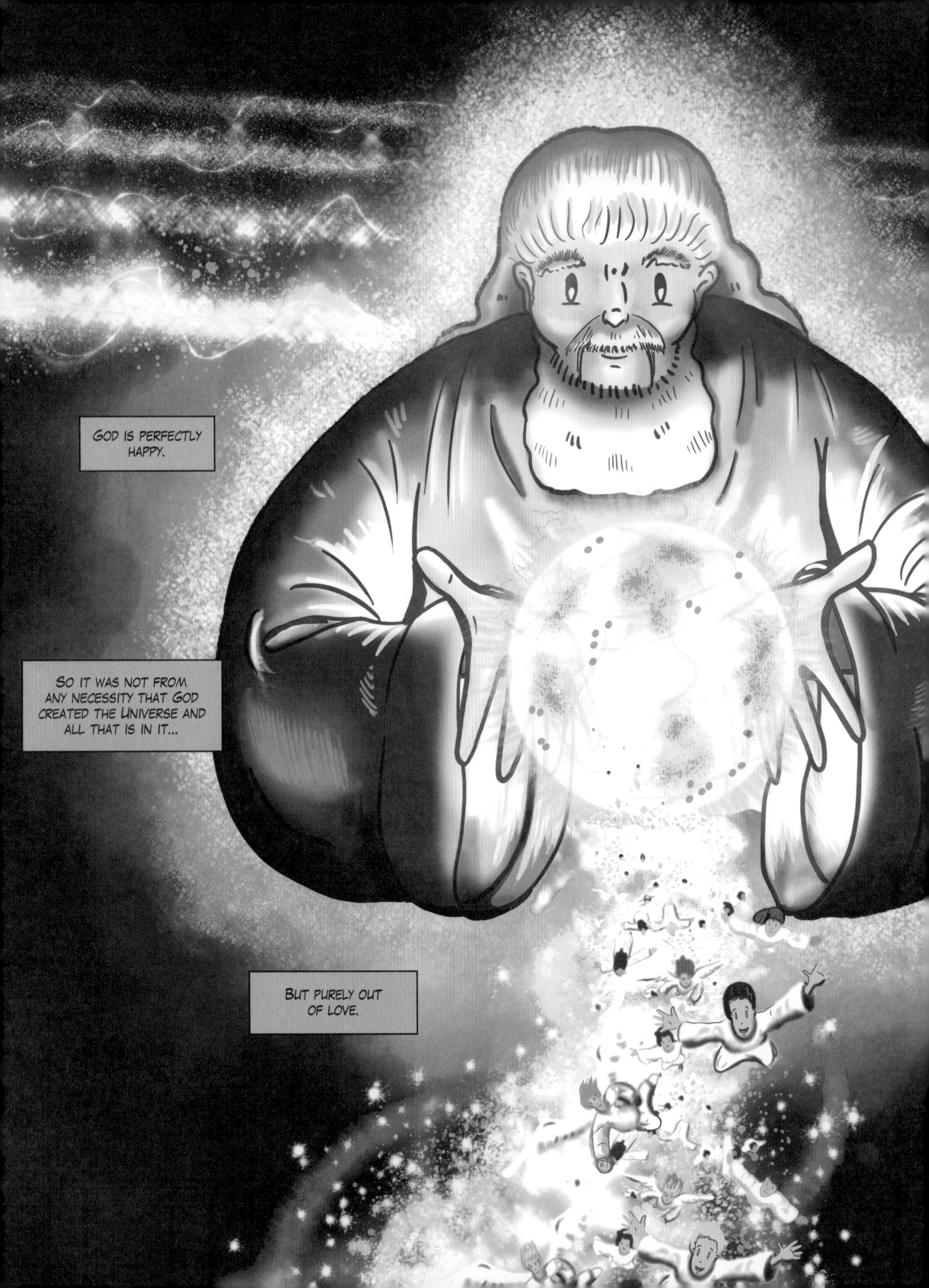
GOD IS PERFECTLY HAPPY.
SO IT WAS NOT FROM ANY NECESSITY THAT GOD CREATED THE UNIVERSE AND ALL THAT IS IN IT...
BUT PURELY OUT OF LOVE.

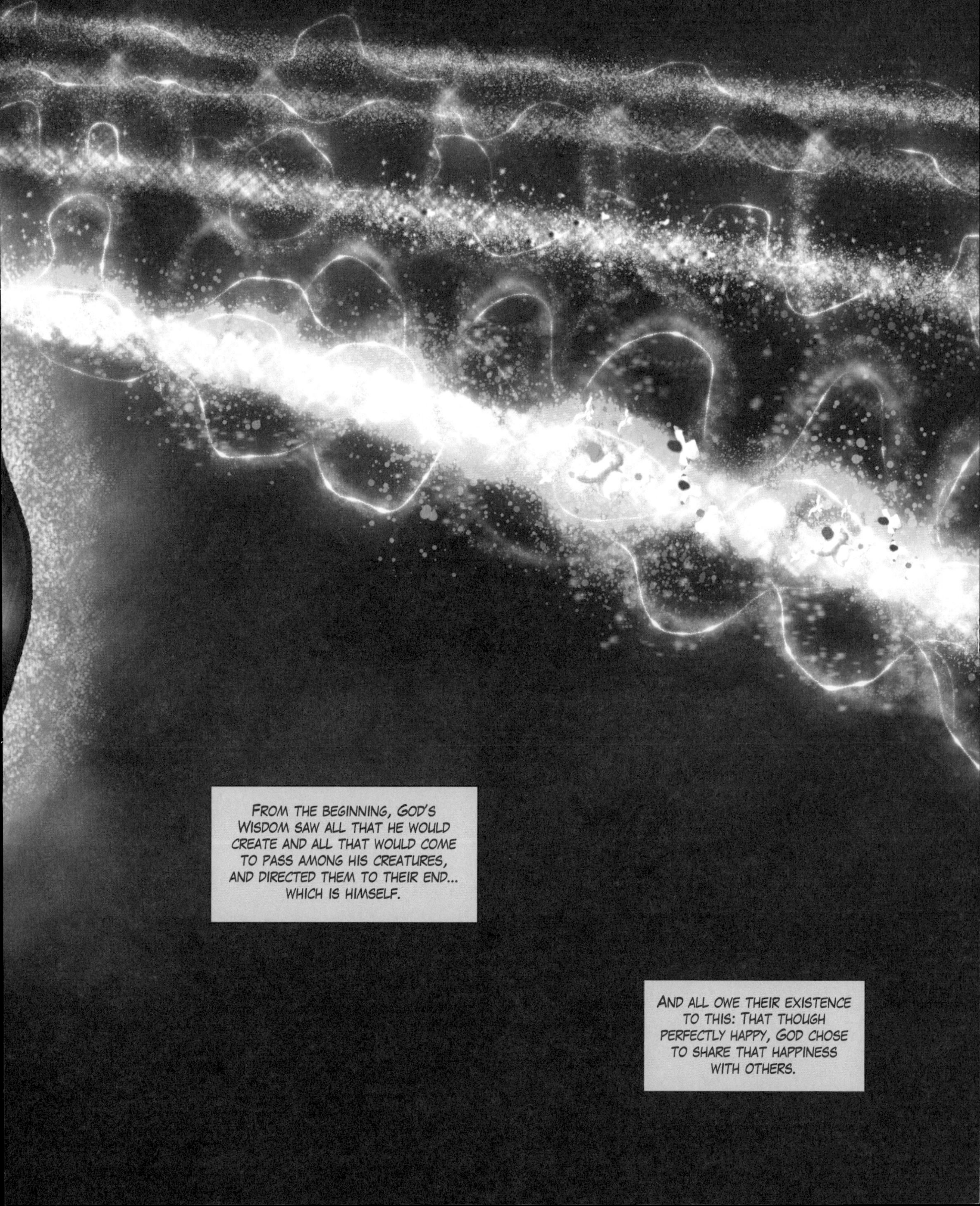
FROM THE BEGINNING, GOD'S WISDOM SAW ALL THAT HE WOULD CREATE AND ALL THAT WOULD COME TO PASS AMONG HIS CREATURES, AND DIRECTED THEM TO THEIR END... WHICH IS HIMSELF.
AND ALL OWE THEIR EXISTENCE TO THIS: THAT THOUGH PERFECTLY HAPPY, GOD CHOSE TO SHARE THAT HAPPINESS WITH OTHERS.

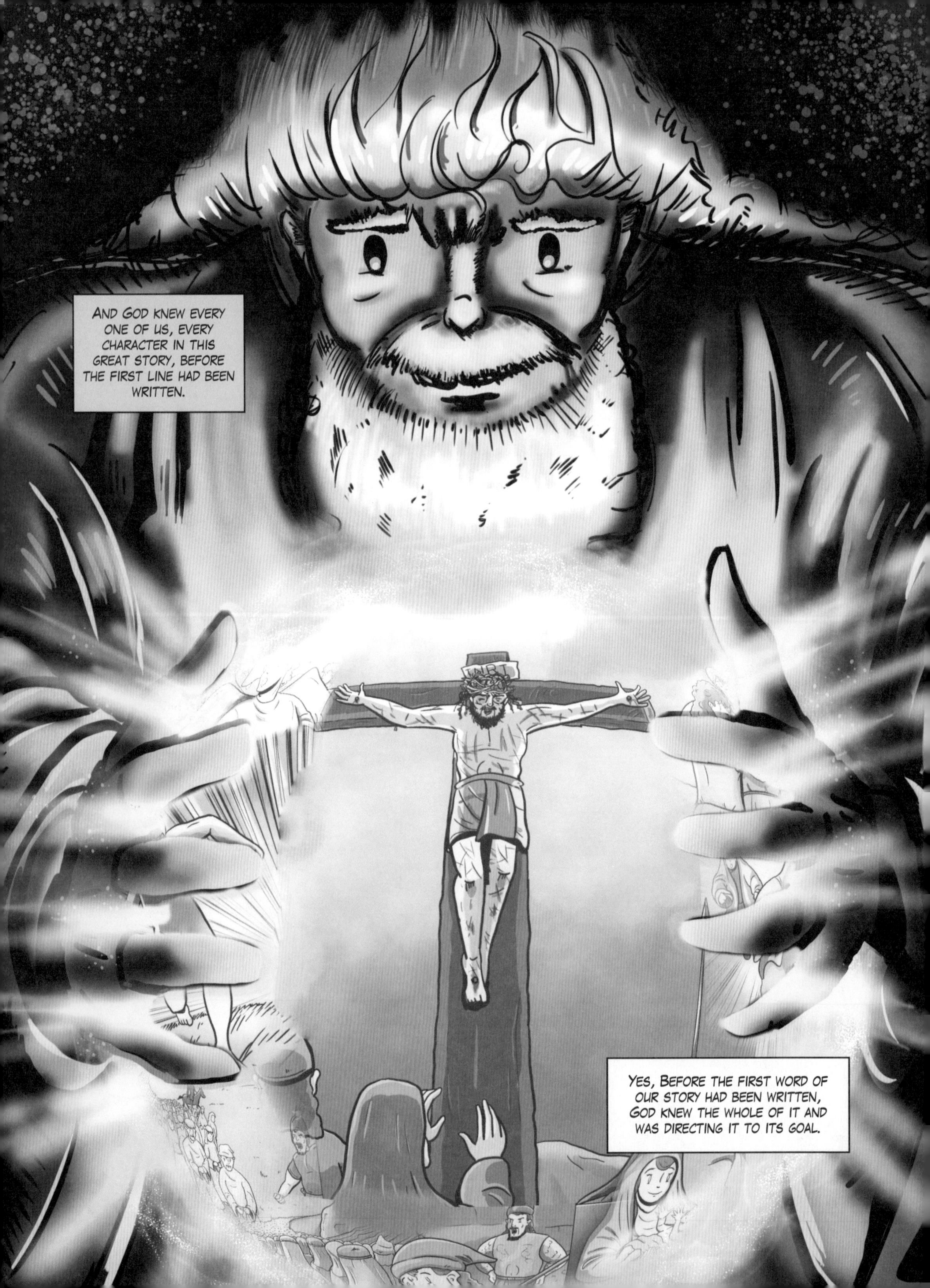
AND GOD KNEW EVERY ONE OF US, EVERY CHARACTER IN THIS GREAT STORY, BEFORE THE FIRST LINE HAD BEEN WRITTEN.
YES, BEFORE THE FIRST WORD OF OUR STORY HAD BEEN WRITTEN, GOD KNEW THE WHOLE OF IT AND WAS DIRECTING IT TO ITS GOAL.

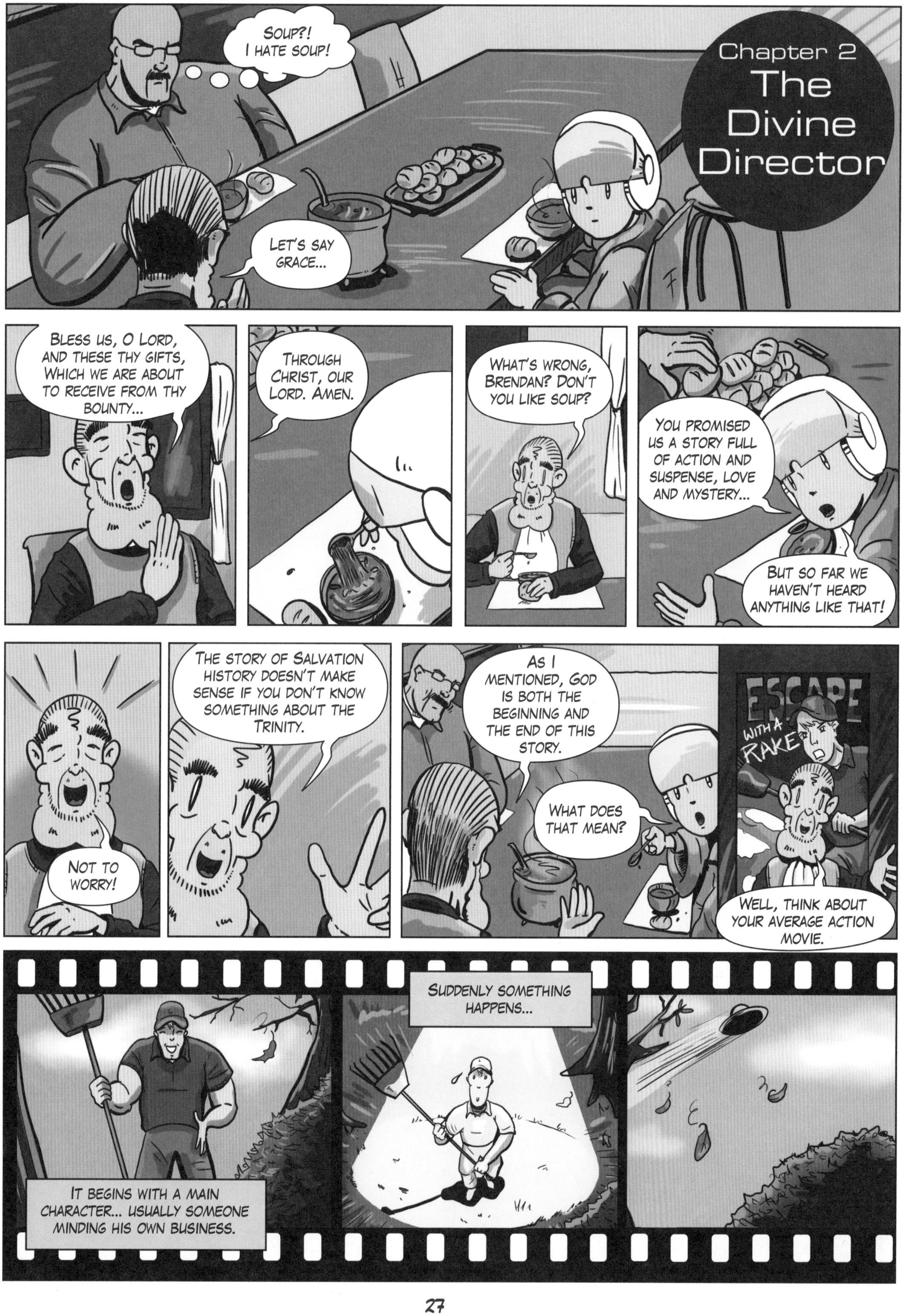
SOUP?!
I HATE SOUP!
Chapter 2
The Divine Director
LET'S SAY GRACE...
BLESS US, O LORD, AND THESE THY GIFTS, WHICH WE ARE ABOUT TO RECEIVE FROM THY BOUNTY...
THROUGH CHRIST, OUR LORD. AMEN.
WHAT'S WRONG, BRENDAN? DON'T YOU LIKE SOUP?
YOU PROMISED US A STORY FULL OF ACTION AND SUSPENSE, LOVE AND MYSTERY...
BUT SO FAR WE HAVEN'T HEARD ANYTHING LIKE THAT!
NOT TO WORRY!
THE STORY OF SALVATION HISTORY DOESN'T MAKE SENSE IF YOU DON'T KNOW SOMETHING ABOUT THE TRINITY.
AS I MENTIONED, GOD IS BOTH THE BEGINNING AND THE END OF THIS STORY.
WHAT DOES THAT MEAN?
ESCAPE WITH A RAKE
WELL, THINK ABOUT YOUR AVERAGE ACTION MOVIE.
IT BEGINS WITH A MAIN CHARACTER... USUALLY SOMEONE MINDING HIS OWN BUSINESS.
SUDDENLY SOMETHING HAPPENS...

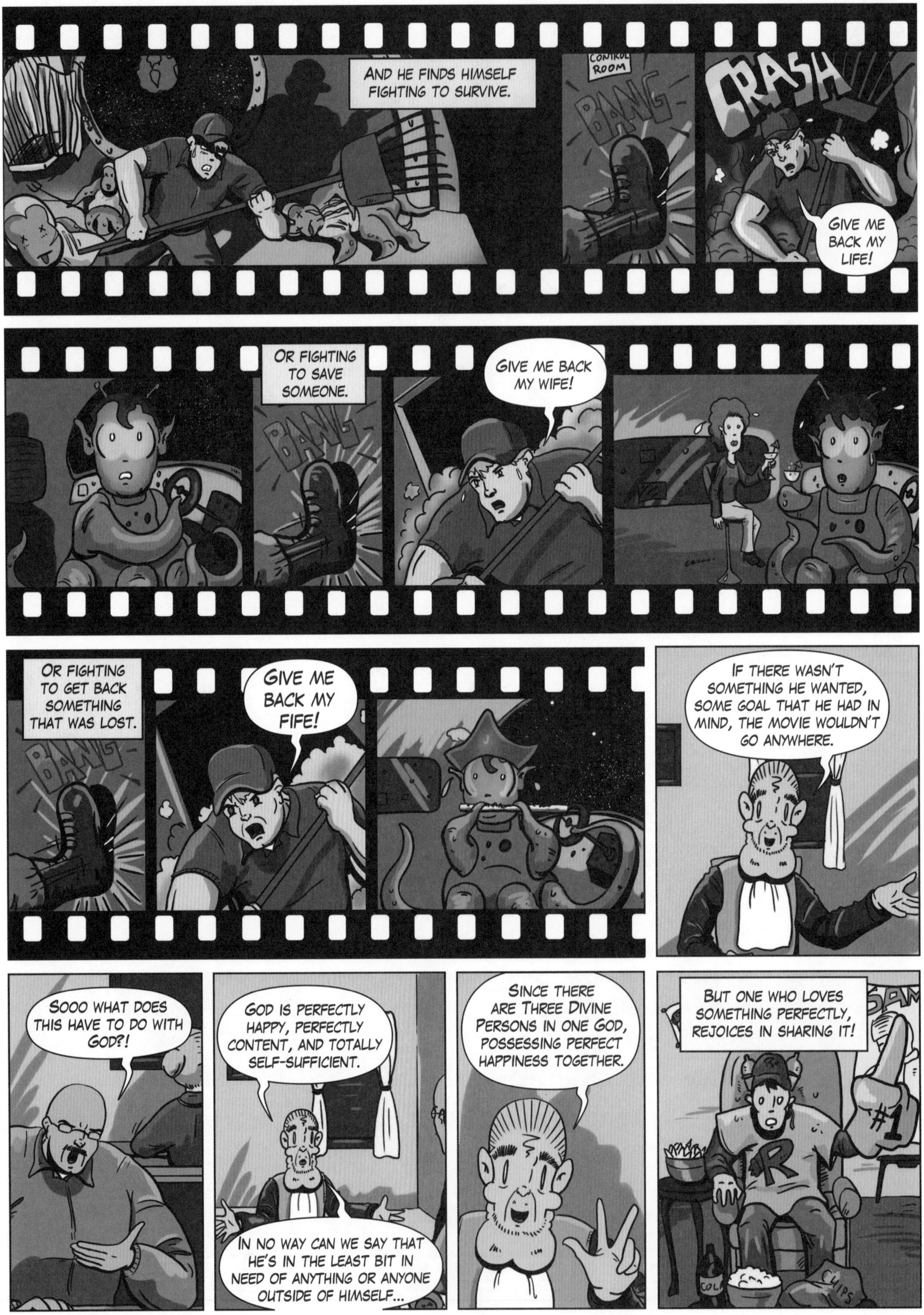
AND HE FINDS HIMSELF FIGHTING TO SURVIVE.
CONTROL ROOM
BANG
CRASH
GIVE ME BACK MY LIFE!
OR FIGHTING TO SAVE SOMEONE.
BANG
GIVE ME BACK MY WIFE!
OR FIGHTING TO GET BACK SOMETHING THAT WAS LOST.
BANG
GIVE ME BACK MY FIFE!
IF THERE WASN'T SOMETHING HE WANTED, SOME GOAL THAT HE HAD IN MIND, THE MOVIE WOULDN'T GO ANYWHERE.
SOOO WHAT DOES THIS HAVE TO DO WITH GOD?!
GOD IS PERFECTLY HAPPY, PERFECTLY CONTENT, AND TOTALLY SELF-SUFFICIENT.
IN NO WAY CAN WE SAY THAT HE'S IN THE LEAST BIT IN NEED OF ANYTHING OR ANYONE OUTSIDE OF HIMSELF...
SINCE THERE ARE THREE DIVINE PERSONS IN ONE GOD, POSSESSING PERFECT HAPPINESS TOGETHER.
BUT ONE WHO LOVES SOMETHING PERFECTLY, REJOICES IN SHARING IT!
#1
CHIPS

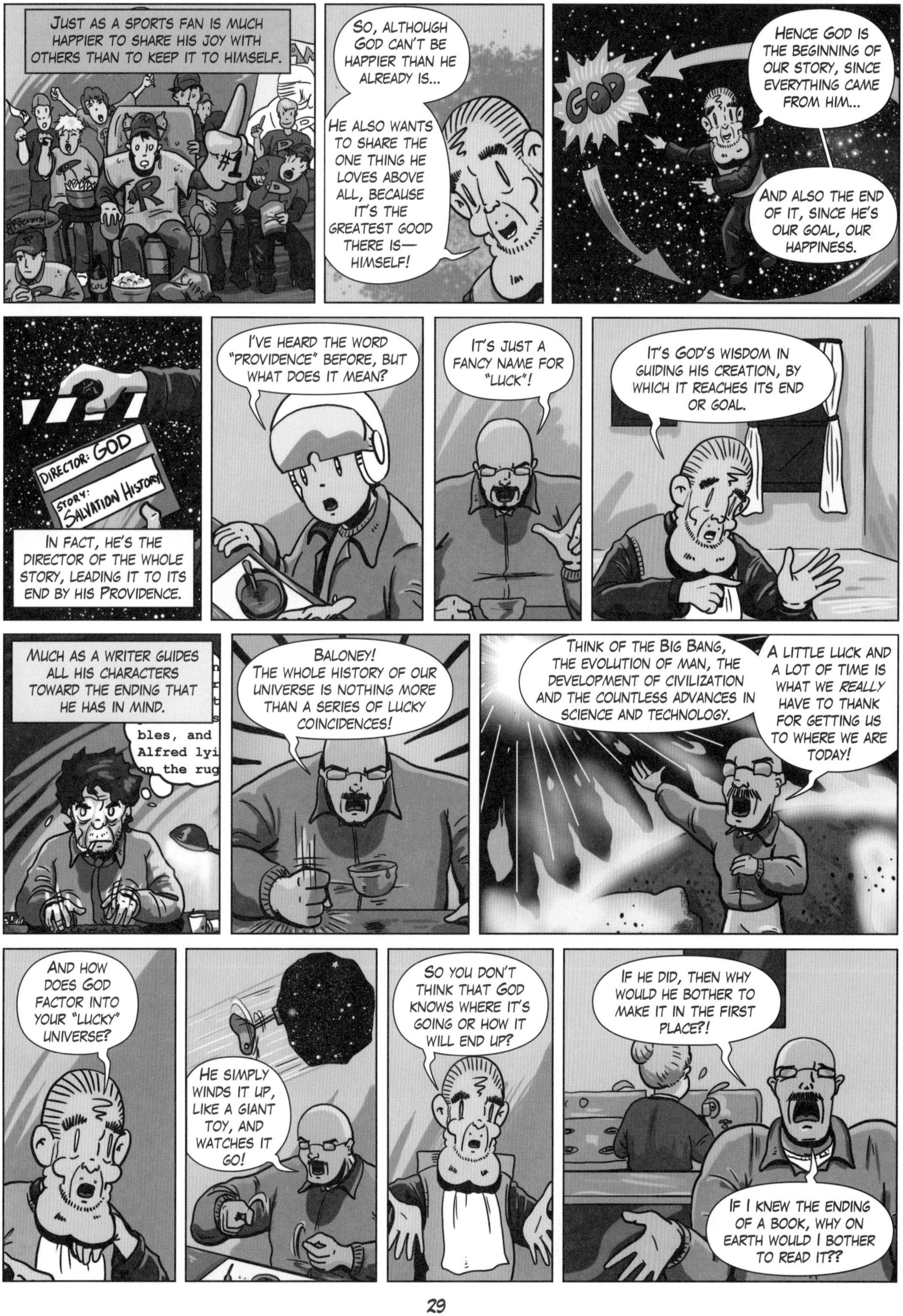
Just as a sports fan is much happier to share his joy with others than to keep it to himself.
So, although God can't be happier than he already is...
He also wants to share the one thing he loves above all, because it's the greatest good there is—himself!
GOD
Hence God is the beginning of our story, since everything came from him...
And also the end of it, since he's our goal, our happiness.
Director: GOD
Story: Salvation History
In fact, he's the director of the whole story, leading it to its end by his Providence.
I've heard the word "providence" before, but what does it mean?
It's just a fancy name for "luck"!
It's God's wisdom in guiding his creation, by which it reaches its end or goal.
Much as a writer guides all his characters toward the ending that he has in mind.
bles, and Alfred lyi on the rug
Baloney! The whole history of our universe is nothing more than a series of lucky coincidences!
Think of the Big Bang, the evolution of man, the development of civilization and the countless advances in science and technology.
A little luck and a lot of time is what we *really* have to thank for getting us to where we are today!
And how does God factor into your "lucky" universe?
He simply winds it up, like a giant toy, and watches it go!
So you don't think that God knows where it's going or how it will end up?
If he did, then why would he bother to make it in the first place?!
If I knew the ending of a book, why on earth would I bother to read it??

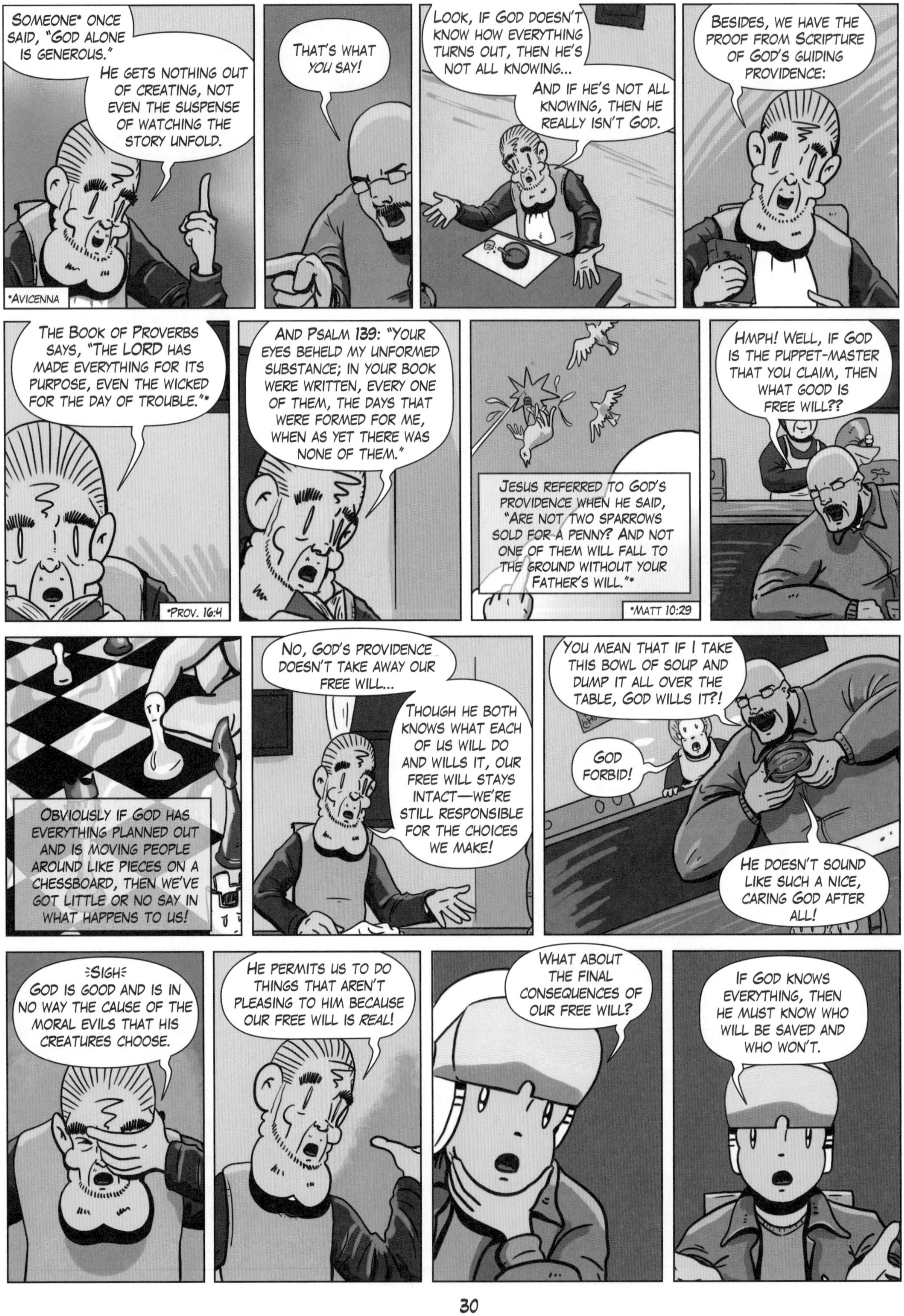
SOMEONE* ONCE SAID, "GOD ALONE IS GENEROUS."
HE GETS NOTHING OUT OF CREATING, NOT EVEN THE SUSPENSE OF WATCHING THE STORY UNFOLD.
*AVICENNA
THAT'S WHAT *YOU* SAY!
LOOK, IF GOD DOESN'T KNOW HOW EVERYTHING TURNS OUT, THEN HE'S NOT ALL KNOWING...
AND IF HE'S NOT ALL KNOWING, THEN HE REALLY ISN'T GOD.
BESIDES, WE HAVE THE PROOF FROM SCRIPTURE OF GOD'S GUIDING PROVIDENCE:
THE BOOK OF PROVERBS SAYS, "THE LORD HAS MADE EVERYTHING FOR ITS PURPOSE, EVEN THE WICKED FOR THE DAY OF TROUBLE."*
*PROV. 16:4
AND PSALM 139: "YOUR EYES BEHELD MY UNFORMED SUBSTANCE; IN YOUR BOOK WERE WRITTEN, EVERY ONE OF THEM, THE DAYS THAT WERE FORMED FOR ME, WHEN AS YET THERE WAS NONE OF THEM."
JESUS REFERRED TO GOD'S PROVIDENCE WHEN HE SAID, "ARE NOT TWO SPARROWS SOLD FOR A PENNY? AND NOT ONE OF THEM WILL FALL TO THE GROUND WITHOUT YOUR FATHER'S WILL."*
*MATT 10:29
HMPH! WELL, IF GOD IS THE PUPPET-MASTER THAT YOU CLAIM, THEN WHAT GOOD IS FREE WILL??
OBVIOUSLY IF GOD HAS EVERYTHING PLANNED OUT AND IS MOVING PEOPLE AROUND LIKE PIECES ON A CHESSBOARD, THEN WE'VE GOT LITTLE OR NO SAY IN WHAT HAPPENS TO US!
NO, GOD'S PROVIDENCE DOESN'T TAKE AWAY OUR FREE WILL...
THOUGH HE BOTH KNOWS WHAT EACH OF US WILL DO AND WILLS IT, OUR FREE WILL STAYS INTACT—WE'RE STILL RESPONSIBLE FOR THE CHOICES WE MAKE!
YOU MEAN THAT IF I TAKE THIS BOWL OF SOUP AND DUMP IT ALL OVER THE TABLE, GOD WILLS IT?!
GOD FORBID!
HE DOESN'T SOUND LIKE SUCH A NICE, CARING GOD AFTER ALL!
SIGH
GOD IS GOOD AND IS IN NO WAY THE CAUSE OF THE MORAL EVILS THAT HIS CREATURES CHOOSE.
HE PERMITS US TO DO THINGS THAT AREN'T PLEASING TO HIM BECAUSE OUR FREE WILL IS *REAL*!
WHAT ABOUT THE FINAL CONSEQUENCES OF OUR FREE WILL?
IF GOD KNOWS EVERYTHING, THEN HE MUST KNOW WHO WILL BE SAVED AND WHO WON'T.

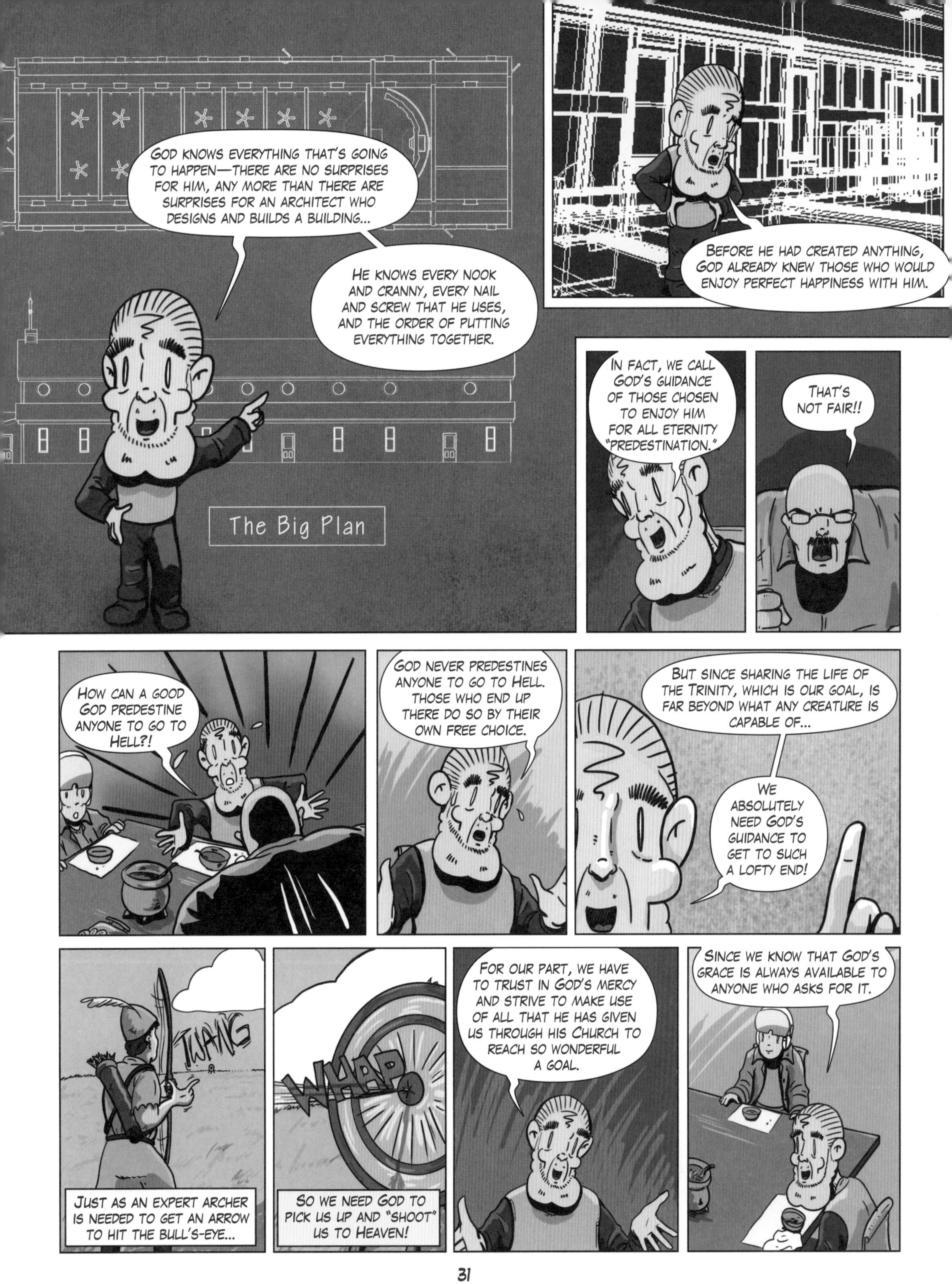
God knows everything that's going to happen—there are no surprises for him, any more than there are surprises for an architect who designs and builds a building...
He knows every nook and cranny, every nail and screw that he uses, and the order of putting everything together.
The Big Plan
Before he had created anything, God already knew those who would enjoy perfect happiness with him.
In fact, we call God's guidance of those chosen to enjoy him for all eternity "predestination."
That's not fair!!
How can a good God predestine anyone to go to Hell?!
God never predestines anyone to go to Hell. Those who end up there do so by their own free choice.
But since sharing the life of the Trinity, which is our goal, is far beyond what any creature is capable of...
We absolutely need God's guidance to get to such a lofty end!
TWANG
Just as an expert archer is needed to get an arrow to hit the bull's-eye...
WHAP
So we need God to pick us up and "shoot" us to Heaven!
For our part, we have to trust in God's mercy and strive to make use of all that he has given us through his Church to reach so wonderful a goal.
Since we know that God's grace is always available to anyone who asks for it.

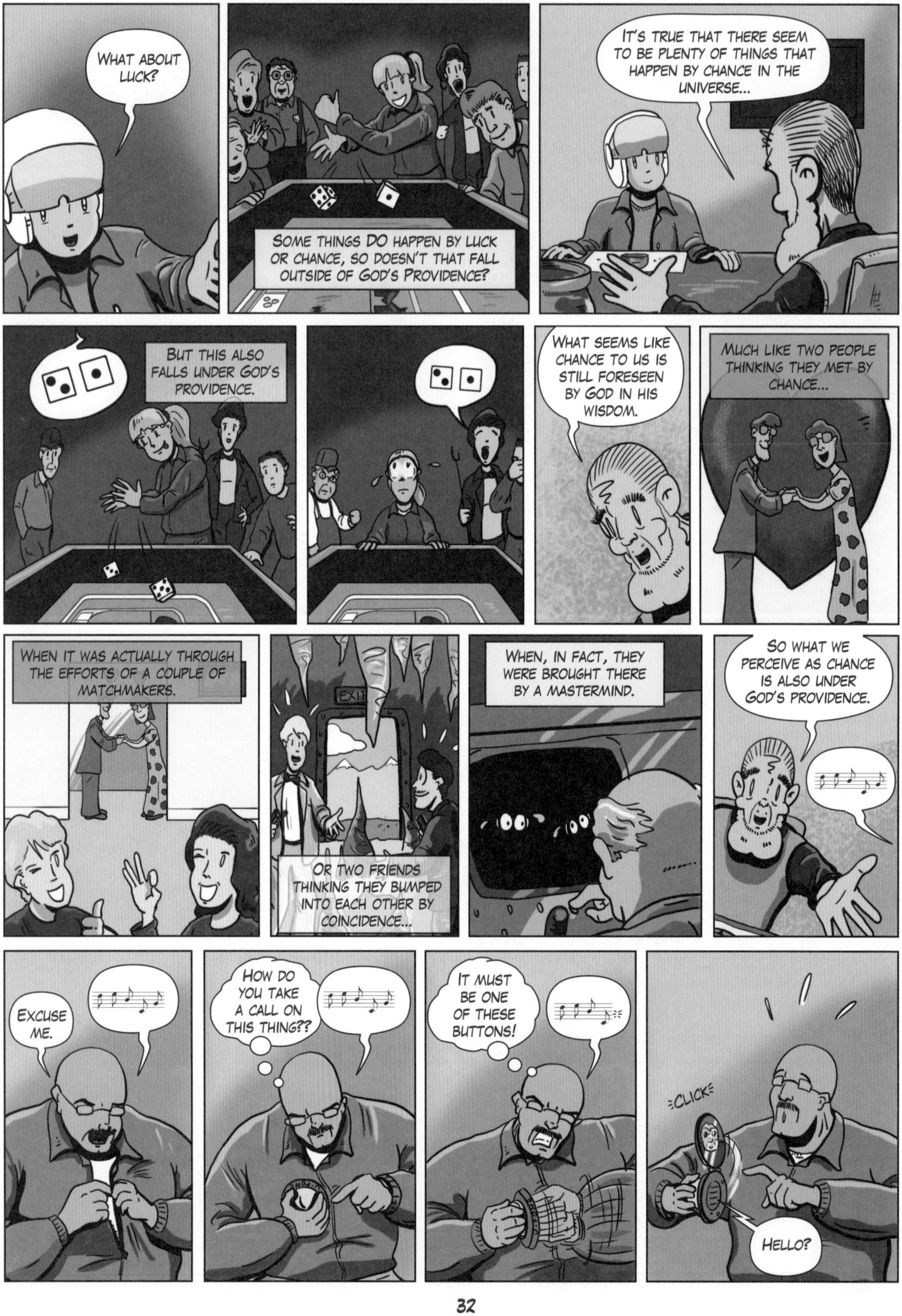
WHAT ABOUT LUCK?
SOME THINGS DO HAPPEN BY LUCK OR CHANCE, SO DOESN'T THAT FALL OUTSIDE OF GOD'S PROVIDENCE?
IT'S TRUE THAT THERE SEEM TO BE PLENTY OF THINGS THAT HAPPEN BY CHANCE IN THE UNIVERSE...
BUT THIS ALSO FALLS UNDER GOD'S PROVIDENCE.
WHAT SEEMS LIKE CHANCE TO US IS STILL FORESEEN BY GOD IN HIS WISDOM.
MUCH LIKE TWO PEOPLE THINKING THEY MET BY CHANCE...
WHEN IT WAS ACTUALLY THROUGH THE EFFORTS OF A COUPLE OF MATCHMAKERS.
EXIT
OR TWO FRIENDS THINKING THEY BUMPED INTO EACH OTHER BY COINCIDENCE...
WHEN, IN FACT, THEY WERE BROUGHT THERE BY A MASTERMIND.
SO WHAT WE PERCEIVE AS CHANCE IS ALSO UNDER GOD'S PROVIDENCE.
EXCUSE ME.
HOW DO YOU TAKE A CALL ON THIS THING??
IT MUST BE ONE OF THESE BUTTONS!
CLICK
HELLO?

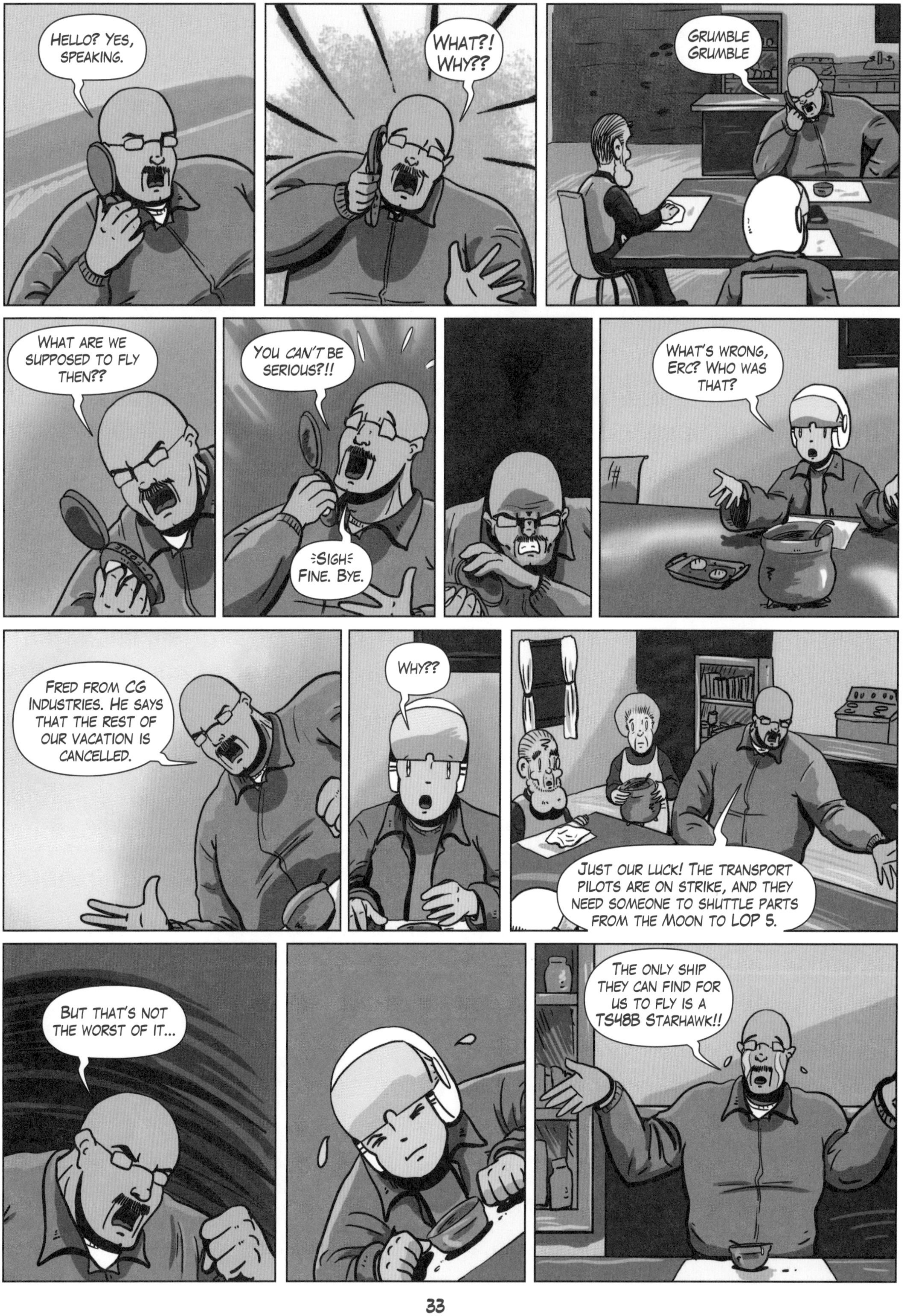
HELLO? YES, SPEAKING.
WHAT?! WHY??
GRUMBLE GRUMBLE
WHAT ARE WE SUPPOSED TO FLY THEN??
YOU CAN'T BE SERIOUS?!!
SIGH FINE. BYE.
WHAT'S WRONG, ERC? WHO WAS THAT?
FRED FROM CG INDUSTRIES. HE SAYS THAT THE REST OF OUR VACATION IS CANCELLED.
WHY??
JUST OUR LUCK! THE TRANSPORT PILOTS ARE ON STRIKE, AND THEY NEED SOMEONE TO SHUTTLE PARTS FROM THE MOON TO LOP 5.
BUT THAT'S NOT THE WORST OF IT...
THE ONLY SHIP THEY CAN FIND FOR US TO FLY IS A TS48B STARHAWK!!

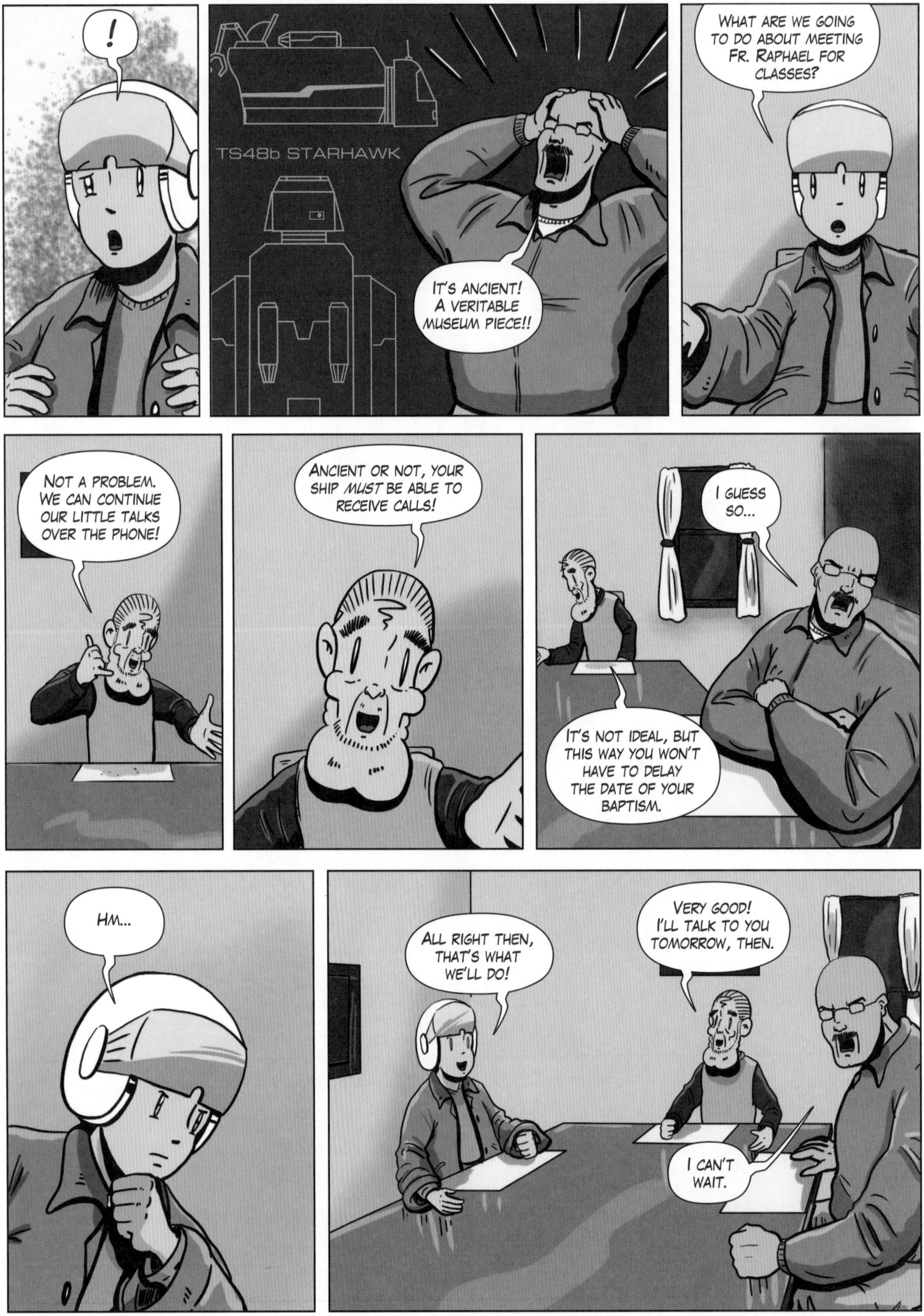
!
TS48b STARHAWK
IT'S ANCIENT! A VERITABLE MUSEUM PIECE!!
WHAT ARE WE GOING TO DO ABOUT MEETING FR. RAPHAEL FOR CLASSES?
NOT A PROBLEM. WE CAN CONTINUE OUR LITTLE TALKS OVER THE PHONE!
ANCIENT OR NOT, YOUR SHIP *MUST* BE ABLE TO RECEIVE CALLS!
I GUESS SO...
IT'S NOT IDEAL, BUT THIS WAY YOU WON'T HAVE TO DELAY THE DATE OF YOUR BAPTISM.
HM...
ALL RIGHT THEN, THAT'S WHAT WE'LL DO!
VERY GOOD! I'LL TALK TO YOU TOMORROW, THEN.
I CAN'T WAIT.

PART II: ON ANGELS

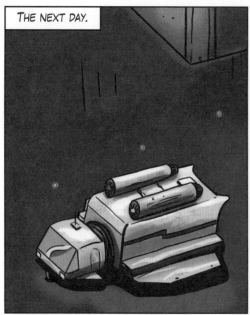

THE NEXT DAY.

I CAN'T BELIEVE I'M STUCK FLYING A STARHAWK!

WHERE DID THEY DIG THIS THING UP, ANYWAY?! A TAR PIT?!

THIS IS ALMOST AS HUMILIATING AS THE TIME I PLAYED A DAISY IN THE MIDDLE-SCHOOL CHRISTMAS PLAY.

IT CAN'T GET ANY WORSE THAN THIS!

LOOK, ERC, IS THAT A TAPE DECK??

AAAAAHHH!!!

WAS IT SOMETHING I SAID?

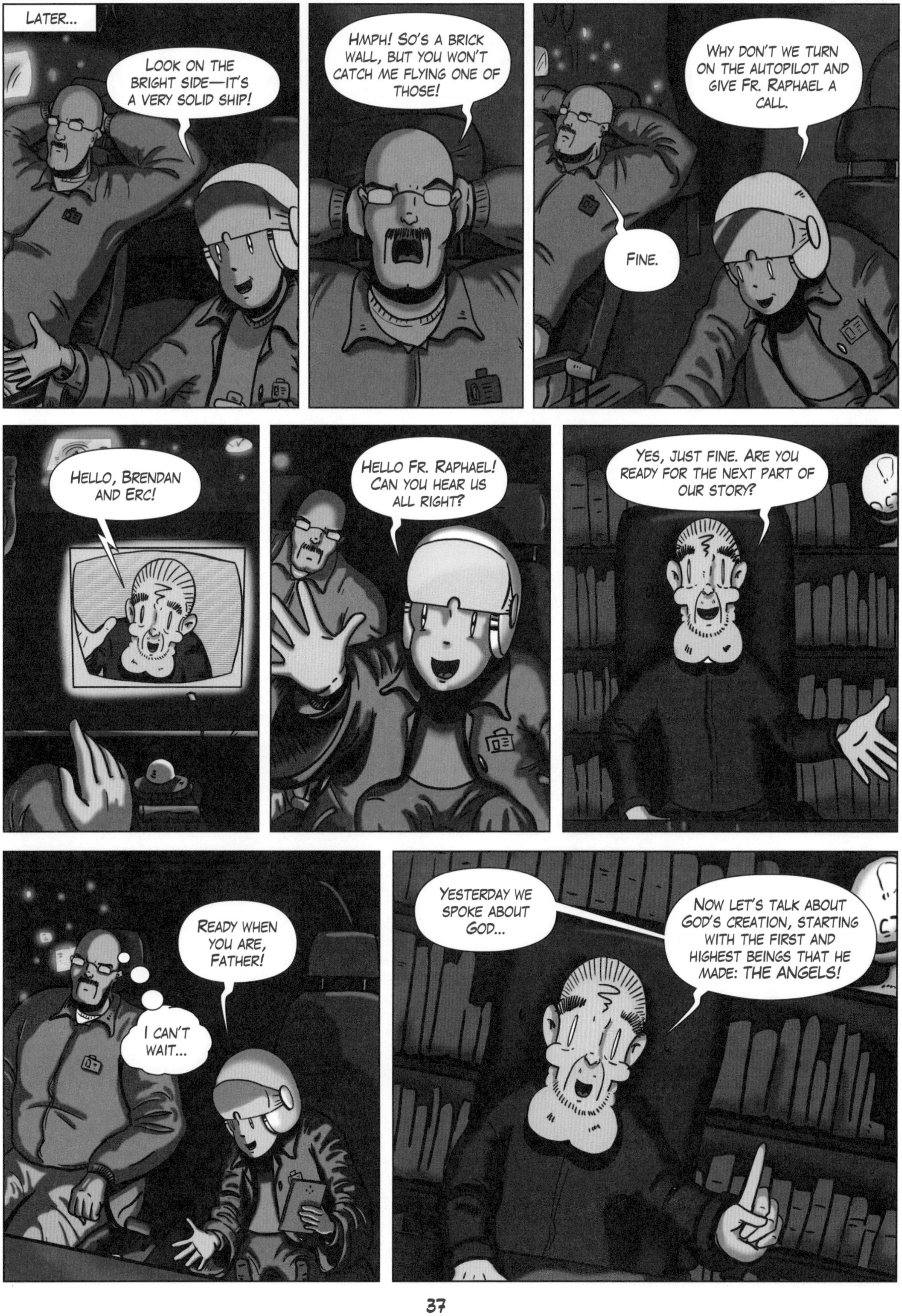
LATER...
LOOK ON THE BRIGHT SIDE—IT'S A VERY SOLID SHIP!
HMPH! SO'S A BRICK WALL, BUT YOU WON'T CATCH ME FLYING ONE OF THOSE!
WHY DON'T WE TURN ON THE AUTOPILOT AND GIVE FR. RAPHAEL A CALL.
FINE.
HELLO, BRENDAN AND ERC!
HELLO FR. RAPHAEL! CAN YOU HEAR US ALL RIGHT?
YES, JUST FINE. ARE YOU READY FOR THE NEXT PART OF OUR STORY?
READY WHEN YOU ARE, FATHER!
I CAN'T WAIT...
YESTERDAY WE SPOKE ABOUT GOD...
NOW LET'S TALK ABOUT GOD'S CREATION, STARTING WITH THE FIRST AND HIGHEST BEINGS THAT HE MADE: THE ANGELS!

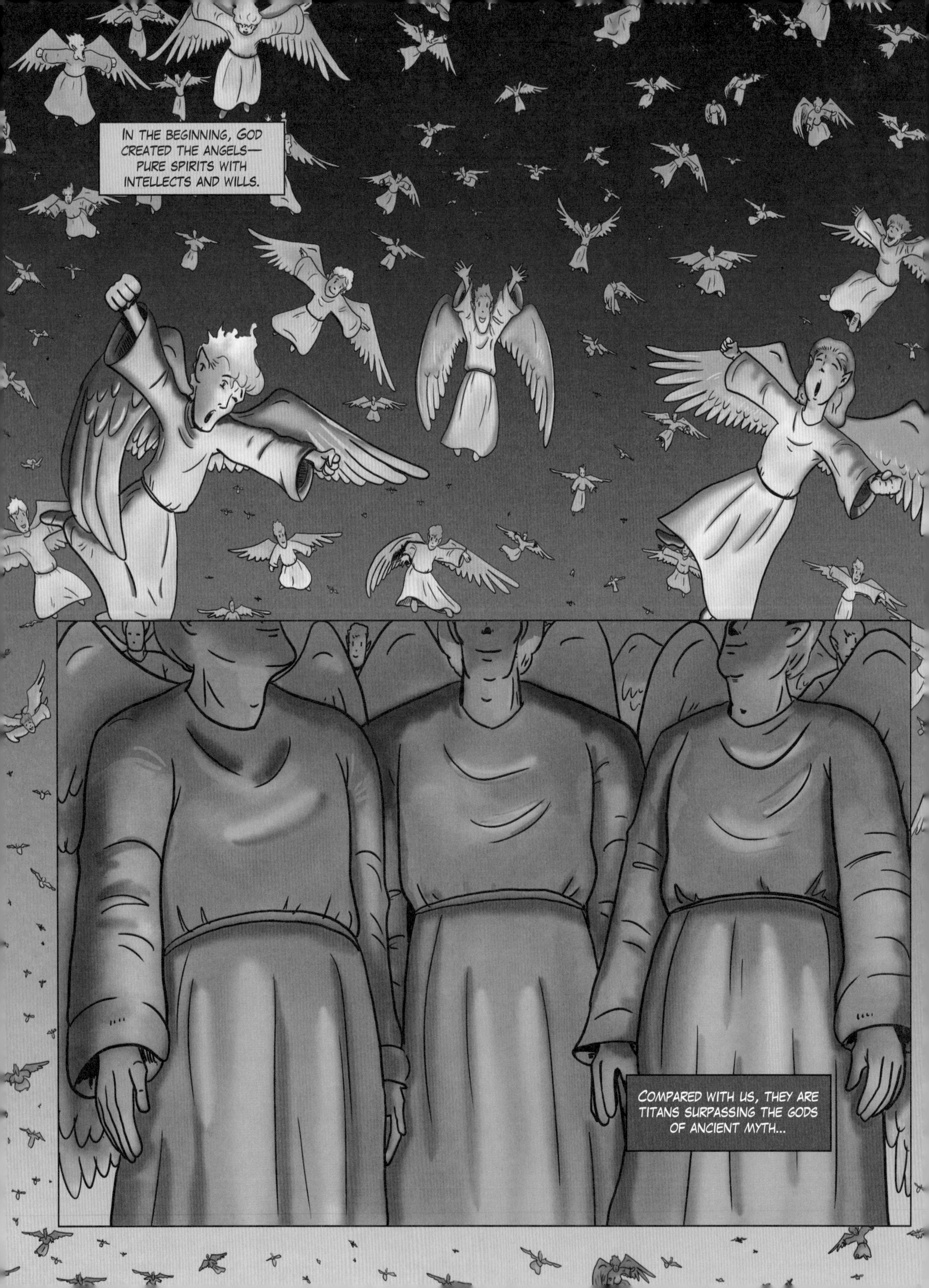
In the beginning, God created the angels— pure spirits with intellects and wills.
Compared with us, they are titans surpassing the gods of ancient myth...

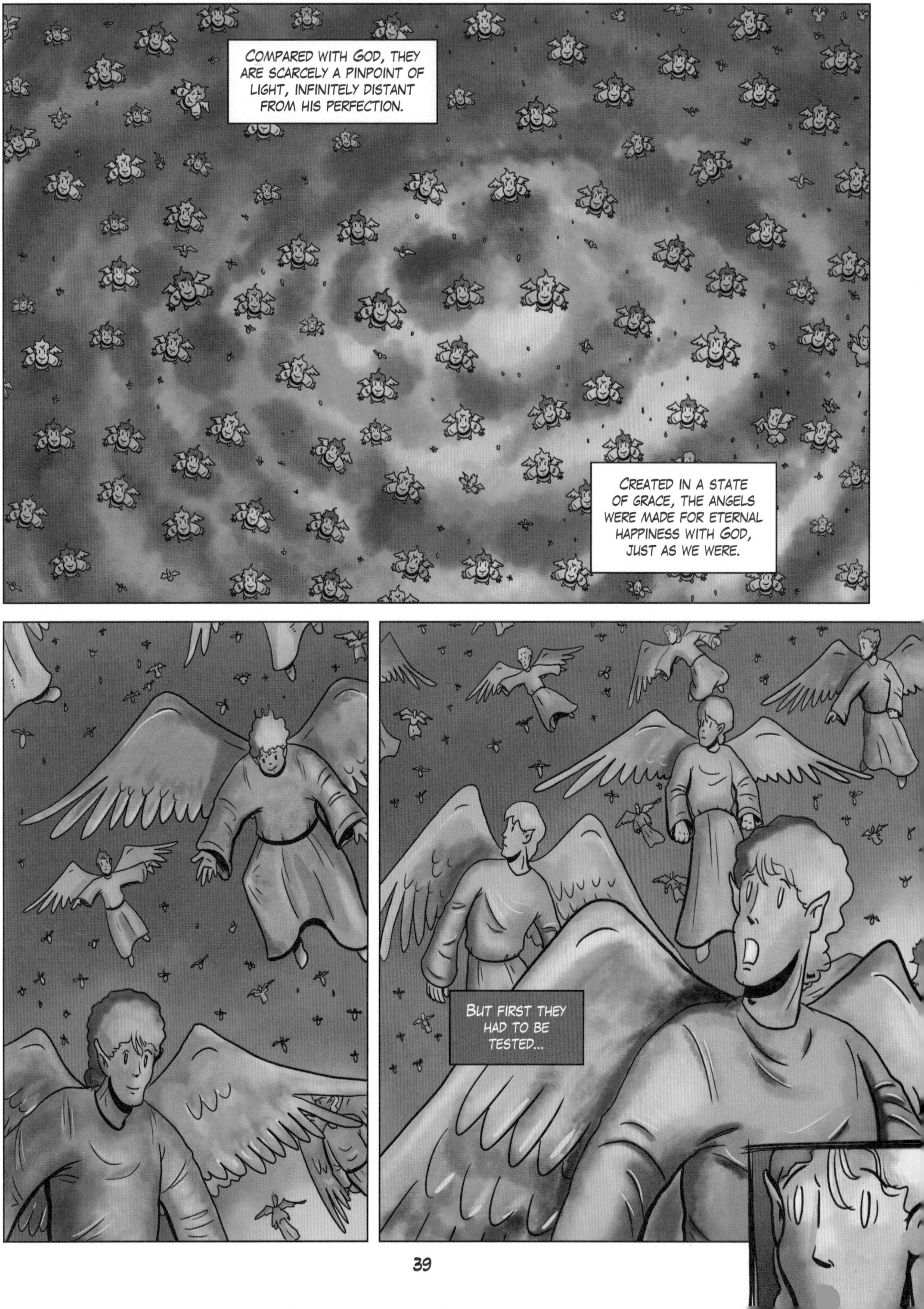
COMPARED WITH GOD, THEY ARE SCARCELY A PINPOINT OF LIGHT, INFINITELY DISTANT FROM HIS PERFECTION.
CREATED IN A STATE OF GRACE, THE ANGELS WERE MADE FOR ETERNAL HAPPINESS WITH GOD, JUST AS WE WERE.
BUT FIRST THEY HAD TO BE TESTED...

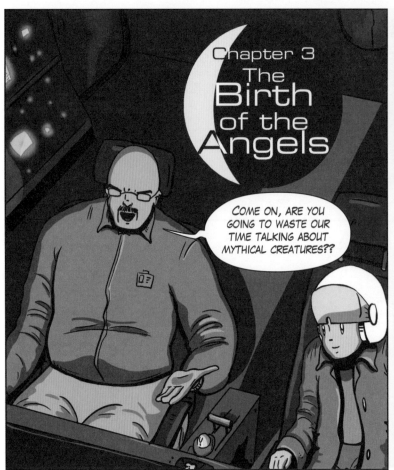

Chapter 3
The **Birth** of the **Angels**

COME ON, ARE YOU GOING TO WASTE OUR TIME TALKING ABOUT MYTHICAL CREATURES??

WHY NOT INCLUDE FAIRIES AND UNICORNS WHILE YOU'RE AT IT!!

THEY'RE ALL JUST AS REAL!!

BWHAHAHAHA

WHAP

?!?

POOF

ANGELS ARE MORE REAL THAN YOU THINK!

IN FACT, THEY'RE MORE REAL THAN YOU ARE!

?

WHAT DO YOU MEAN?

I MEAN THAT OF ALL THE CREATURES THAT GOD MADE, ANGELS RESEMBLE HIM MOST.

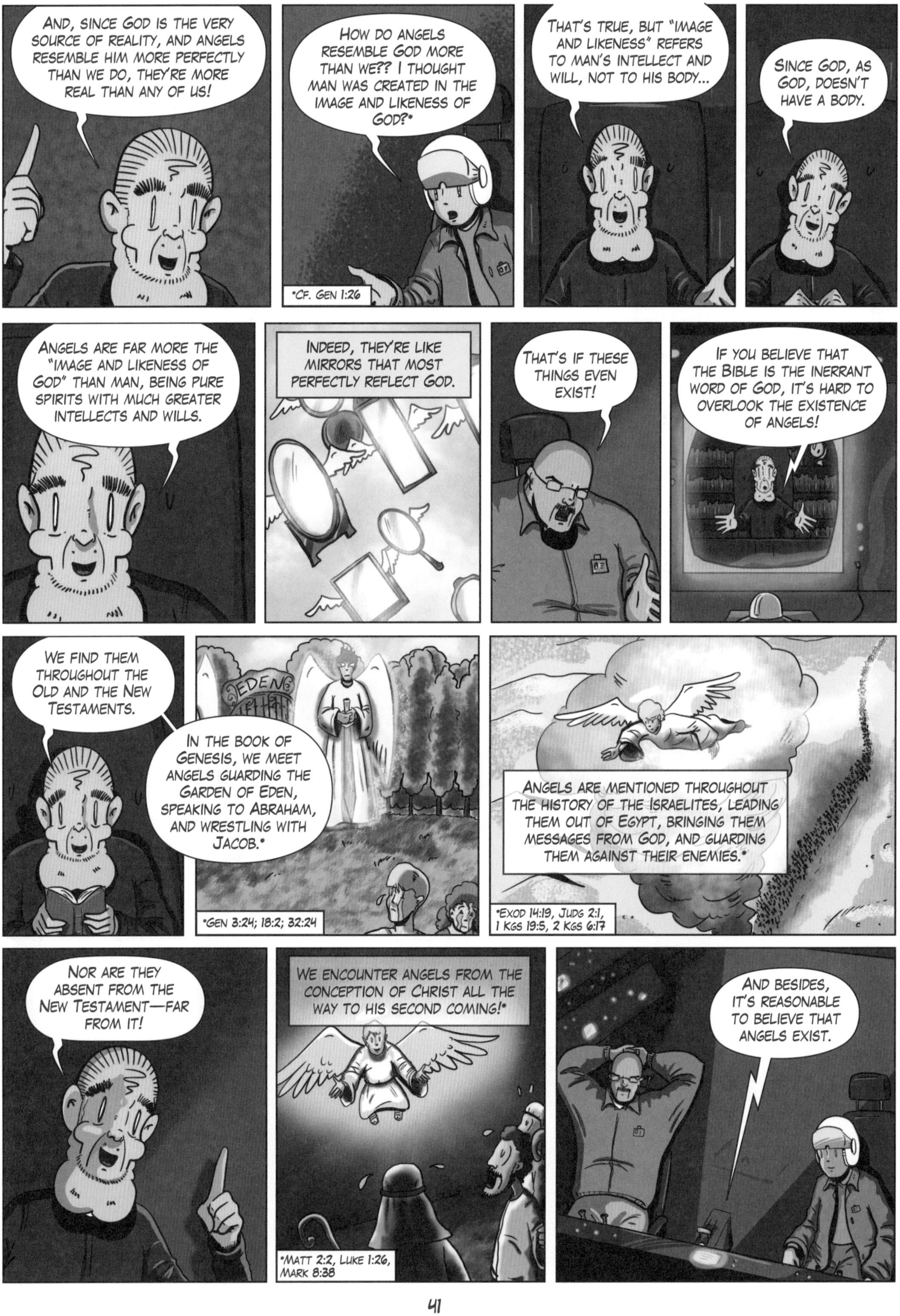

And, since God is the very source of reality, and angels resemble him more perfectly than we do, they're more real than any of us!
How do angels resemble God more than we?? I thought man was created in the image and likeness of God?*
*Cf. Gen 1:26
That's true, but "image and likeness" refers to man's intellect and will, not to his body...
Since God, as God, doesn't have a body.
Angels are far more the "image and likeness of God" than man, being pure spirits with much greater intellects and wills.
Indeed, they're like mirrors that most perfectly reflect God.
That's if these things even exist!
If you believe that the Bible is the inerrant word of God, it's hard to overlook the existence of angels!
We find them throughout the Old and the New Testaments.
In the book of Genesis, we meet angels guarding the Garden of Eden, speaking to Abraham, and wrestling with Jacob.*
EDEN
*Gen 3:24; 18:2; 32:24
Angels are mentioned throughout the history of the Israelites, leading them out of Egypt, bringing them messages from God, and guarding them against their enemies.*
*Exod 14:19, Judg 2:1, 1 Kgs 19:5, 2 Kgs 6:17
Nor are they absent from the New Testament—far from it!
We encounter angels from the conception of Christ all the way to his second coming!*
*Matt 2:2, Luke 1:26, Mark 8:38
And besides, it's reasonable to believe that angels exist.

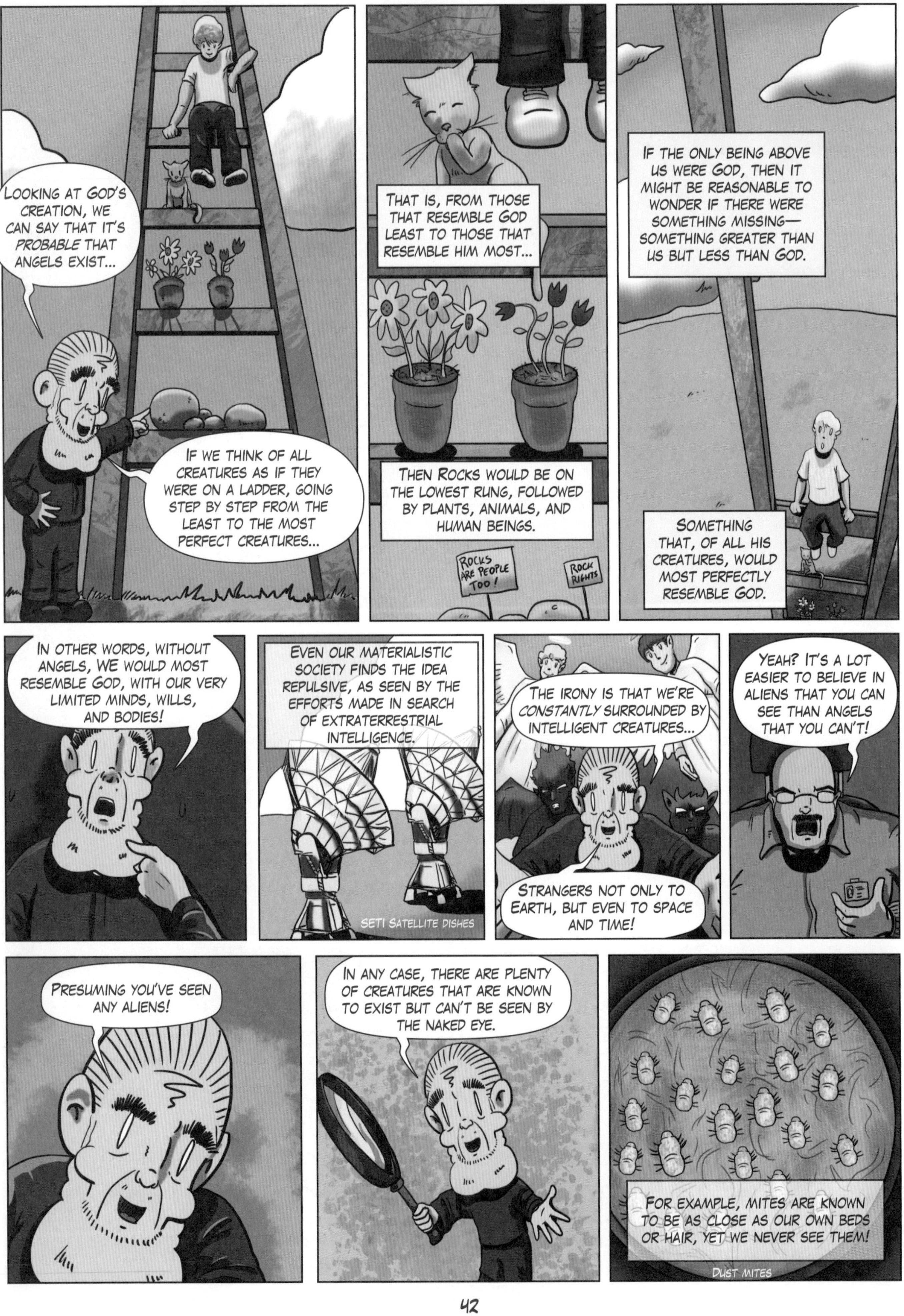
Looking at God's creation, we can say that it's *probable* that angels exist...
If we think of all creatures as if they were on a ladder, going step by step from the least to the most perfect creatures...
That is, from those that resemble God least to those that resemble him most...
Then rocks would be on the lowest rung, followed by plants, animals, and human beings.
Rocks are people too!
Rock rights
If the only being above us were God, then it might be reasonable to wonder if there were something missing—something greater than us but less than God.
Something that, of all his creatures, would most perfectly resemble God.
In other words, without angels, WE would most resemble God, with our very limited minds, wills, and bodies!
Even our materialistic society finds the idea repulsive, as seen by the efforts made in search of extraterrestrial intelligence.
SETI Satellite dishes
The irony is that we're *constantly* surrounded by intelligent creatures...
Strangers not only to Earth, but even to space and time!
Yeah? It's a lot easier to believe in aliens that you can see than angels that you can't!
Presuming you've seen any aliens!
In any case, there are plenty of creatures that are known to exist but can't be seen by the naked eye.
For example, mites are known to be as close as our own beds or hair, yet we never see them!
Dust mites

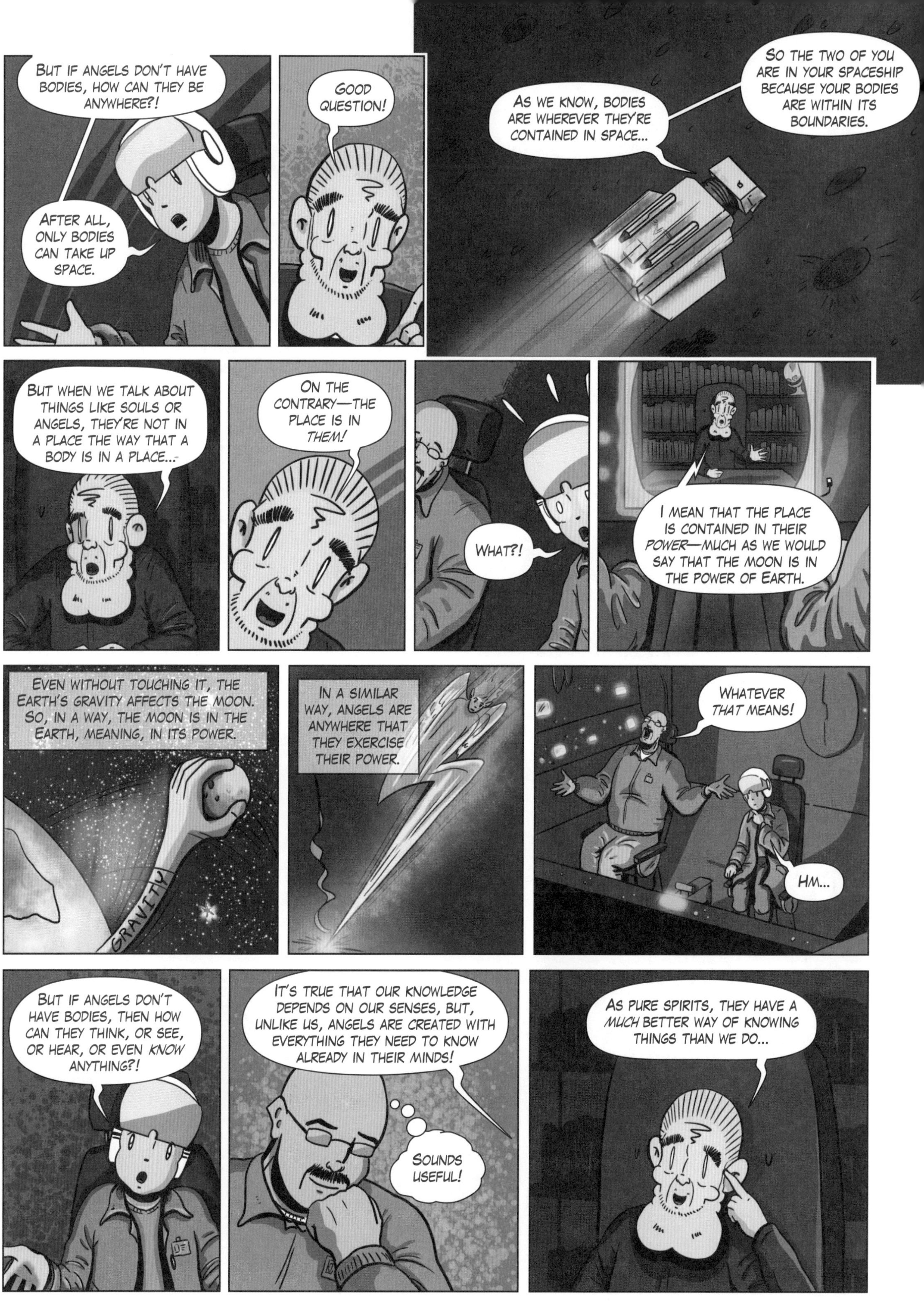

But if angels don't have bodies, how can they be anywhere?!
After all, only bodies can take up space.
Good question!
As we know, bodies are wherever they're contained in space...
So the two of you are in your spaceship because your bodies are within its boundaries.
But when we talk about things like souls or angels, they're not in a place the way that a body is in a place...
On the contrary—the place is in *them!*
What?!
I mean that the place is contained in their *power*—much as we would say that the moon is in the power of Earth.
Even without touching it, the Earth's gravity affects the moon. So, in a way, the moon is in the Earth, meaning, in its power.
Gravity
In a similar way, angels are anywhere that they exercise their power.
Whatever *that* means!
Hm...
But if angels don't have bodies, then how can they think, or see, or hear, or even *know* anything?!
It's true that our knowledge depends on our senses, but, unlike us, angels are created with everything they need to know already in their minds!
Sounds useful!
As pure spirits, they have a *much* better way of knowing things than we do...

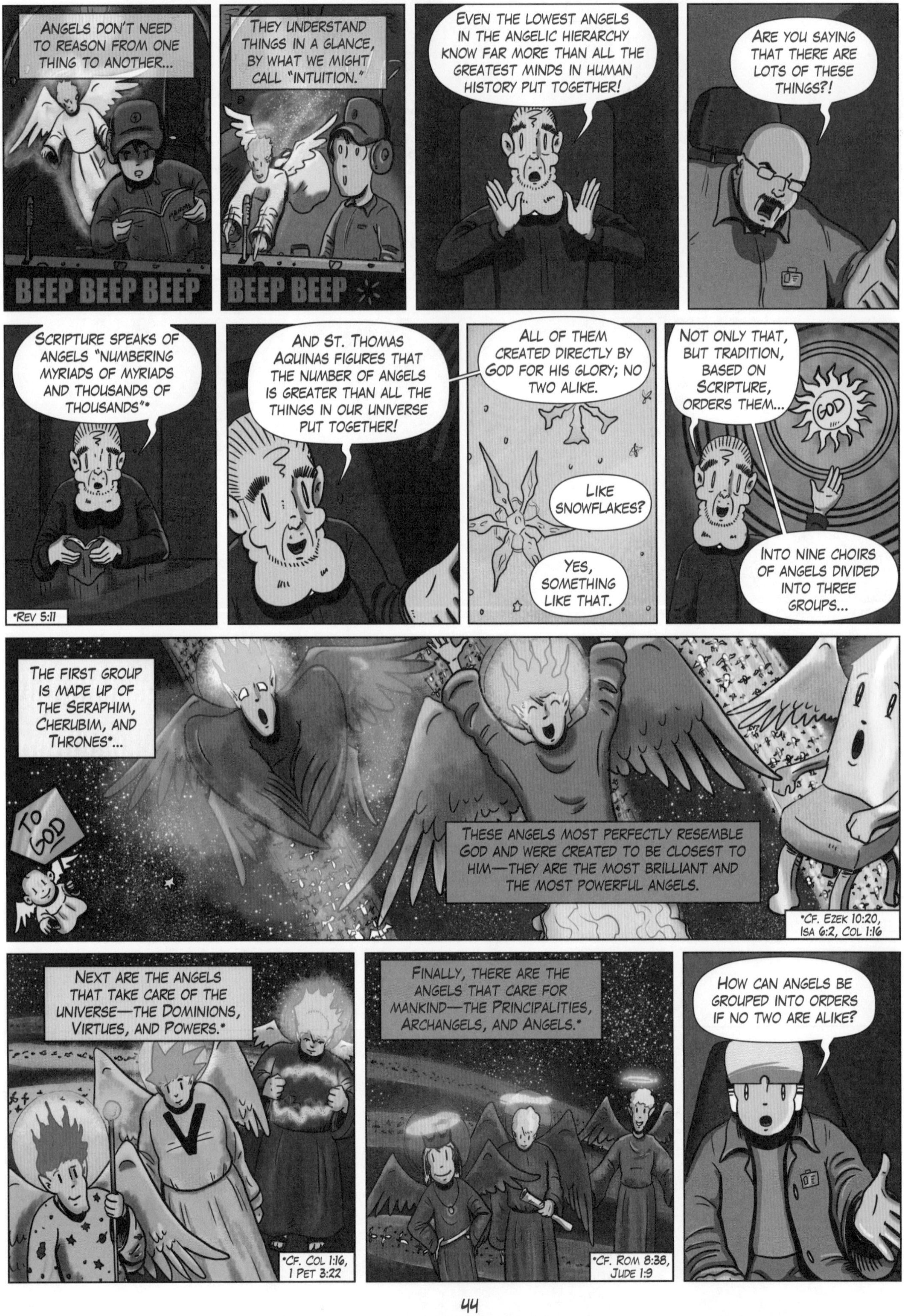
ANGELS DON'T NEED TO REASON FROM ONE THING TO ANOTHER...
BEEP BEEP BEEP
THEY UNDERSTAND THINGS IN A GLANCE, BY WHAT WE MIGHT CALL "INTUITION."
BEEP BEEP
EVEN THE LOWEST ANGELS IN THE ANGELIC HIERARCHY KNOW FAR MORE THAN ALL THE GREATEST MINDS IN HUMAN HISTORY PUT TOGETHER!
ARE YOU SAYING THAT THERE ARE LOTS OF THESE THINGS?!
SCRIPTURE SPEAKS OF ANGELS "NUMBERING MYRIADS OF MYRIADS AND THOUSANDS OF THOUSANDS"*
*REV 5:11
AND ST. THOMAS AQUINAS FIGURES THAT THE NUMBER OF ANGELS IS GREATER THAN ALL THE THINGS IN OUR UNIVERSE PUT TOGETHER!
ALL OF THEM CREATED DIRECTLY BY GOD FOR HIS GLORY; NO TWO ALIKE.
LIKE SNOWFLAKES?
YES, SOMETHING LIKE THAT.
NOT ONLY THAT, BUT TRADITION, BASED ON SCRIPTURE, ORDERS THEM...
GOD
INTO NINE CHOIRS OF ANGELS DIVIDED INTO THREE GROUPS...
THE FIRST GROUP IS MADE UP OF THE SERAPHIM, CHERUBIM, AND THRONES*...
TO GOD
THESE ANGELS MOST PERFECTLY RESEMBLE GOD AND WERE CREATED TO BE CLOSEST TO HIM—THEY ARE THE MOST BRILLIANT AND THE MOST POWERFUL ANGELS.
*CF. EZEK 10:20, ISA 6:2, COL 1:16
NEXT ARE THE ANGELS THAT TAKE CARE OF THE UNIVERSE—THE DOMINIONS, VIRTUES, AND POWERS.*
*CF. COL 1:16, 1 PET 3:22
FINALLY, THERE ARE THE ANGELS THAT CARE FOR MANKIND—THE PRINCIPALITIES, ARCHANGELS, AND ANGELS.*
*CF. ROM 8:38, JUDE 1:9
HOW CAN ANGELS BE GROUPED INTO ORDERS IF NO TWO ARE ALIKE?

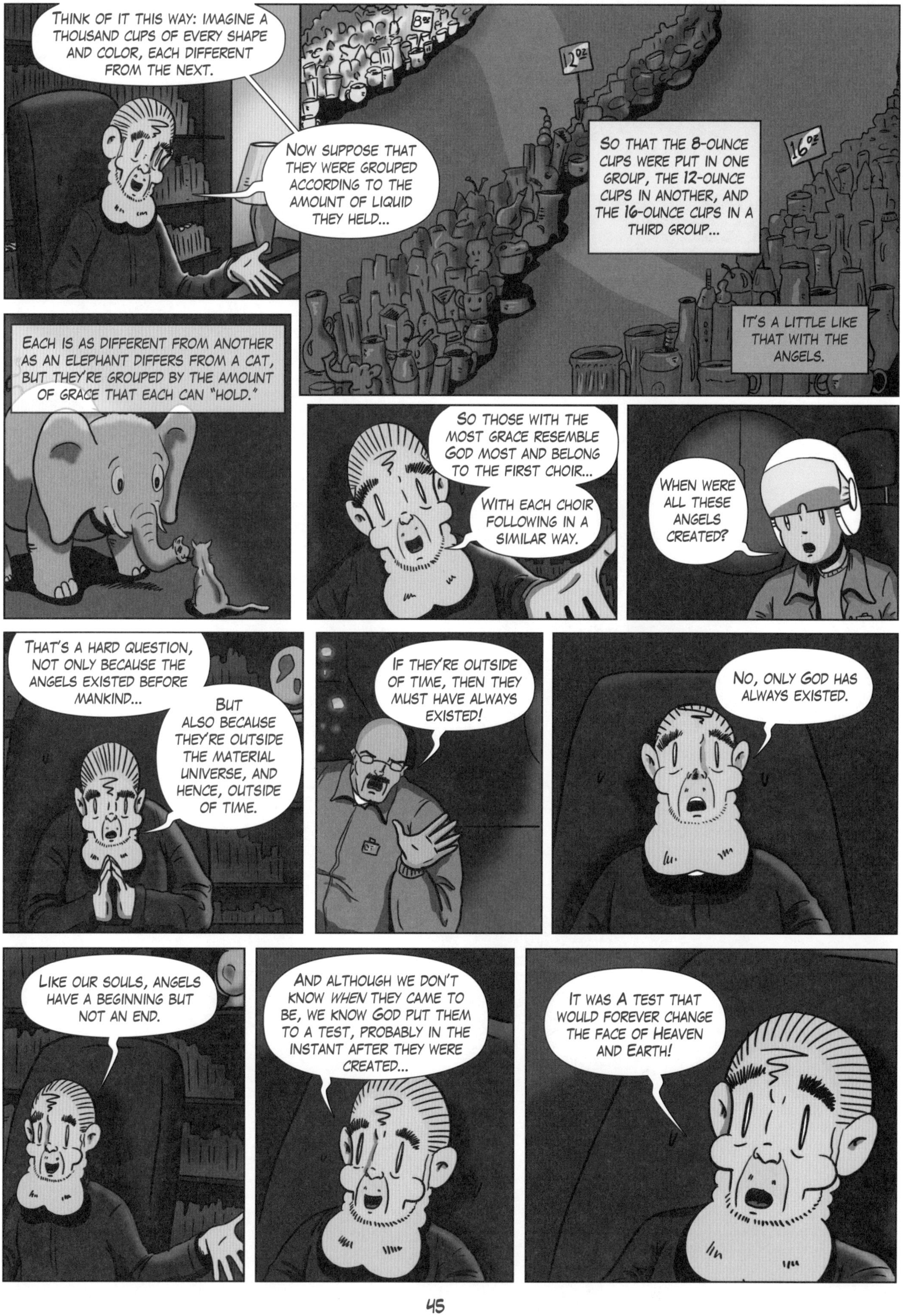
THINK OF IT THIS WAY: IMAGINE A THOUSAND CUPS OF EVERY SHAPE AND COLOR, EACH DIFFERENT FROM THE NEXT.
NOW SUPPOSE THAT THEY WERE GROUPED ACCORDING TO THE AMOUNT OF LIQUID THEY HELD...
8oz
12oz
16oz
SO THAT THE 8-OUNCE CUPS WERE PUT IN ONE GROUP, THE 12-OUNCE CUPS IN ANOTHER, AND THE 16-OUNCE CUPS IN A THIRD GROUP...
IT'S A LITTLE LIKE THAT WITH THE ANGELS.
EACH IS AS DIFFERENT FROM ANOTHER AS AN ELEPHANT DIFFERS FROM A CAT, BUT THEY'RE GROUPED BY THE AMOUNT OF GRACE THAT EACH CAN "HOLD."
SO THOSE WITH THE MOST GRACE RESEMBLE GOD MOST AND BELONG TO THE FIRST CHOIR...
WITH EACH CHOIR FOLLOWING IN A SIMILAR WAY.
WHEN WERE ALL THESE ANGELS CREATED?
THAT'S A HARD QUESTION, NOT ONLY BECAUSE THE ANGELS EXISTED BEFORE MANKIND...
BUT ALSO BECAUSE THEY'RE OUTSIDE THE MATERIAL UNIVERSE, AND HENCE, OUTSIDE OF TIME.
IF THEY'RE OUTSIDE OF TIME, THEN THEY MUST HAVE ALWAYS EXISTED!
NO, ONLY GOD HAS ALWAYS EXISTED.
LIKE OUR SOULS, ANGELS HAVE A BEGINNING BUT NOT AN END.
AND ALTHOUGH WE DON'T KNOW *WHEN* THEY CAME TO BE, WE KNOW GOD PUT THEM TO A TEST, PROBABLY IN THE INSTANT AFTER THEY WERE CREATED...
IT WAS A TEST THAT WOULD FOREVER CHANGE THE FACE OF HEAVEN AND EARTH!

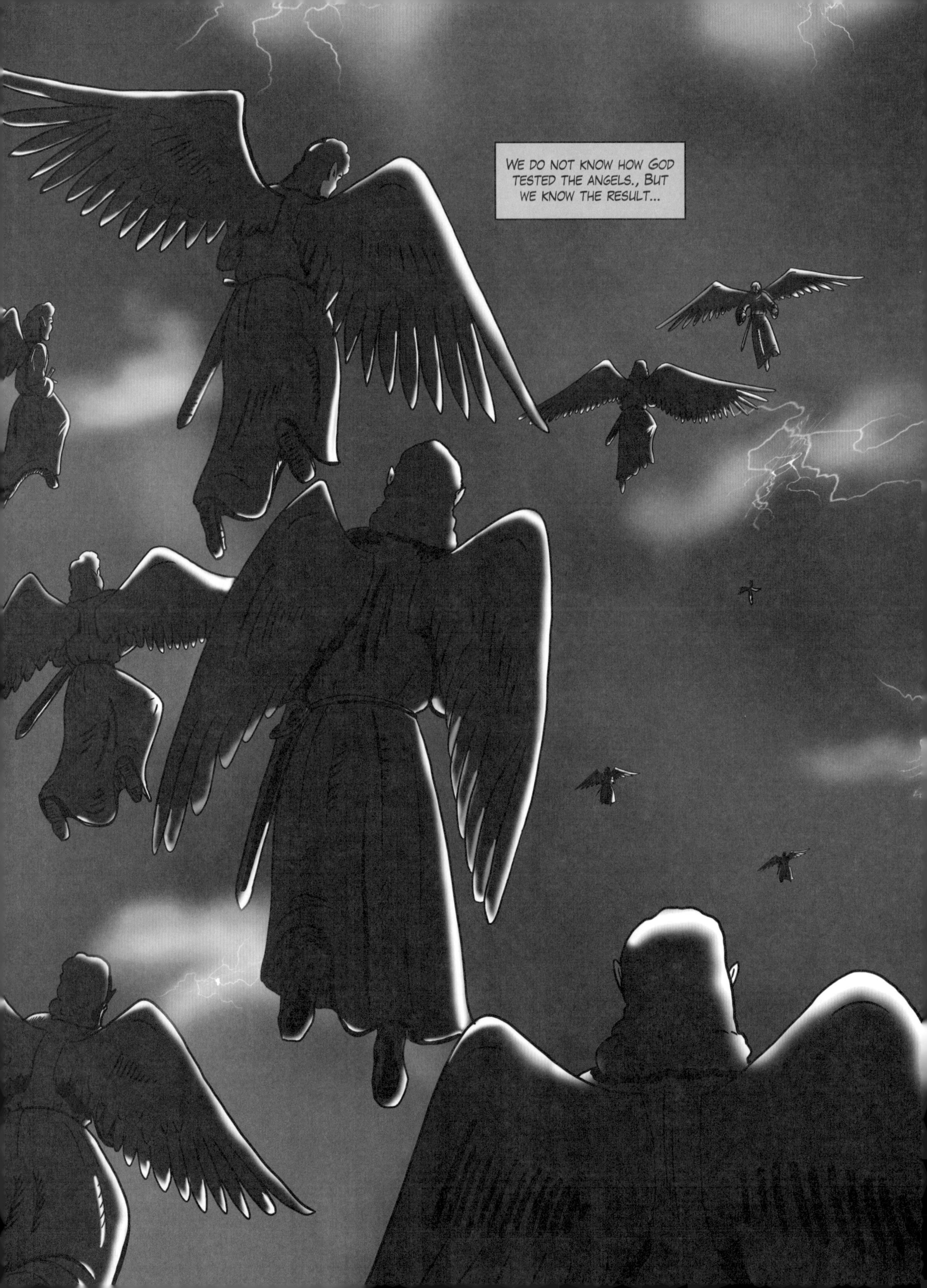
WE DO NOT KNOW HOW GOD TESTED THE ANGELS., BUT WE KNOW THE RESULT...

I WILL NOT SERVE!!
LUCIFER, OR "LIGHT-BEARER", WAS THE GREATEST AND MOST GOD-LIKE OF THE ANGELS...
IT WAS HE WHO FIRST REBELLED AND LED OTHERS IN REBELLION AGAINST GOD.

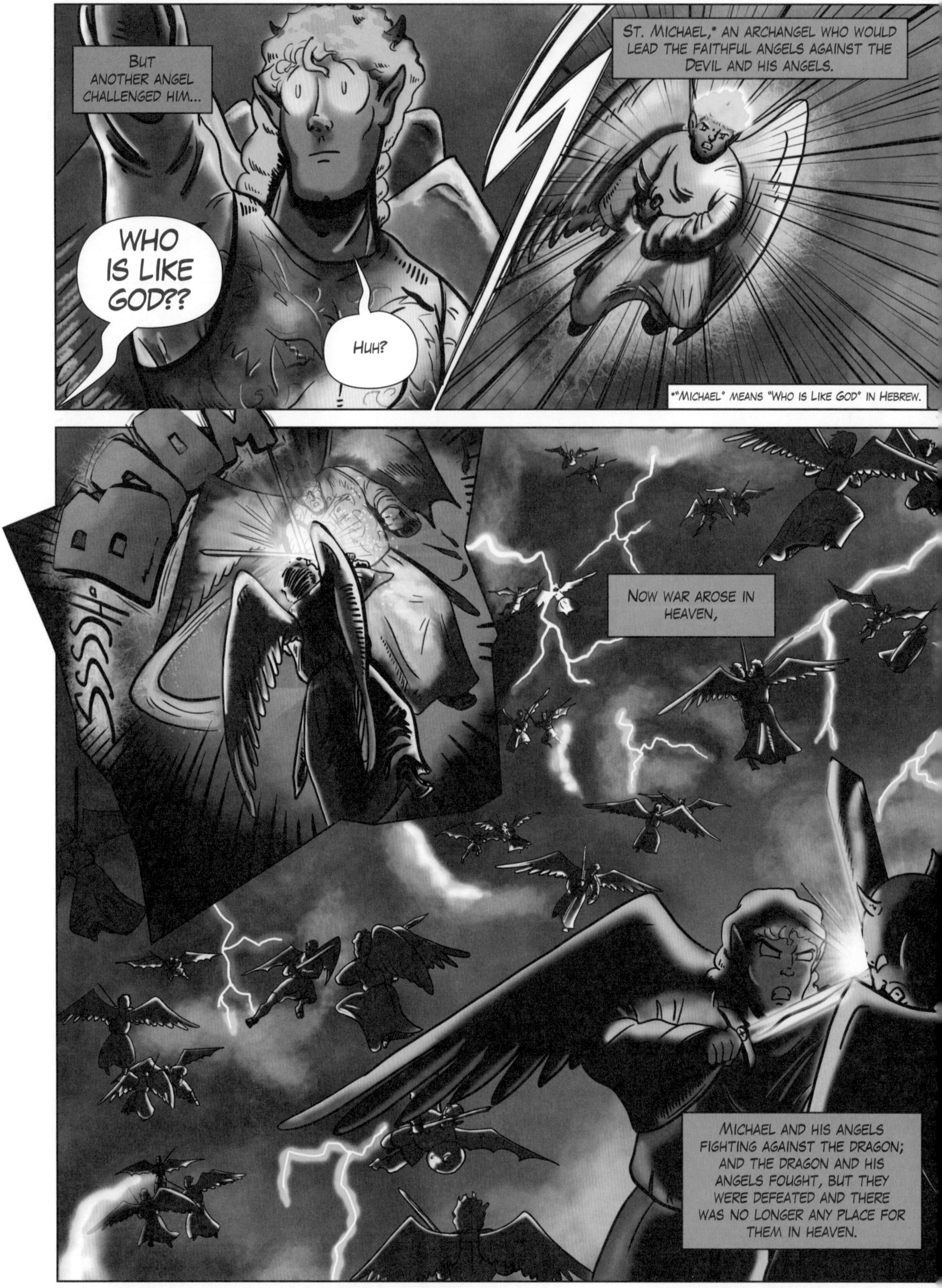
BUT ANOTHER ANGEL CHALLENGED HIM...
WHO IS LIKE GOD??
HUH?
ST. MICHAEL,* AN ARCHANGEL WHO WOULD LEAD THE FAITHFUL ANGELS AGAINST THE DEVIL AND HIS ANGELS.
*"MICHAEL" MEANS "WHO IS LIKE GOD" IN HEBREW.
BOOM
NOW WAR AROSE IN HEAVEN,
MICHAEL AND HIS ANGELS FIGHTING AGAINST THE DRAGON; AND THE DRAGON AND HIS ANGELS FOUGHT, BUT THEY WERE DEFEATED AND THERE WAS NO LONGER ANY PLACE FOR THEM IN HEAVEN.

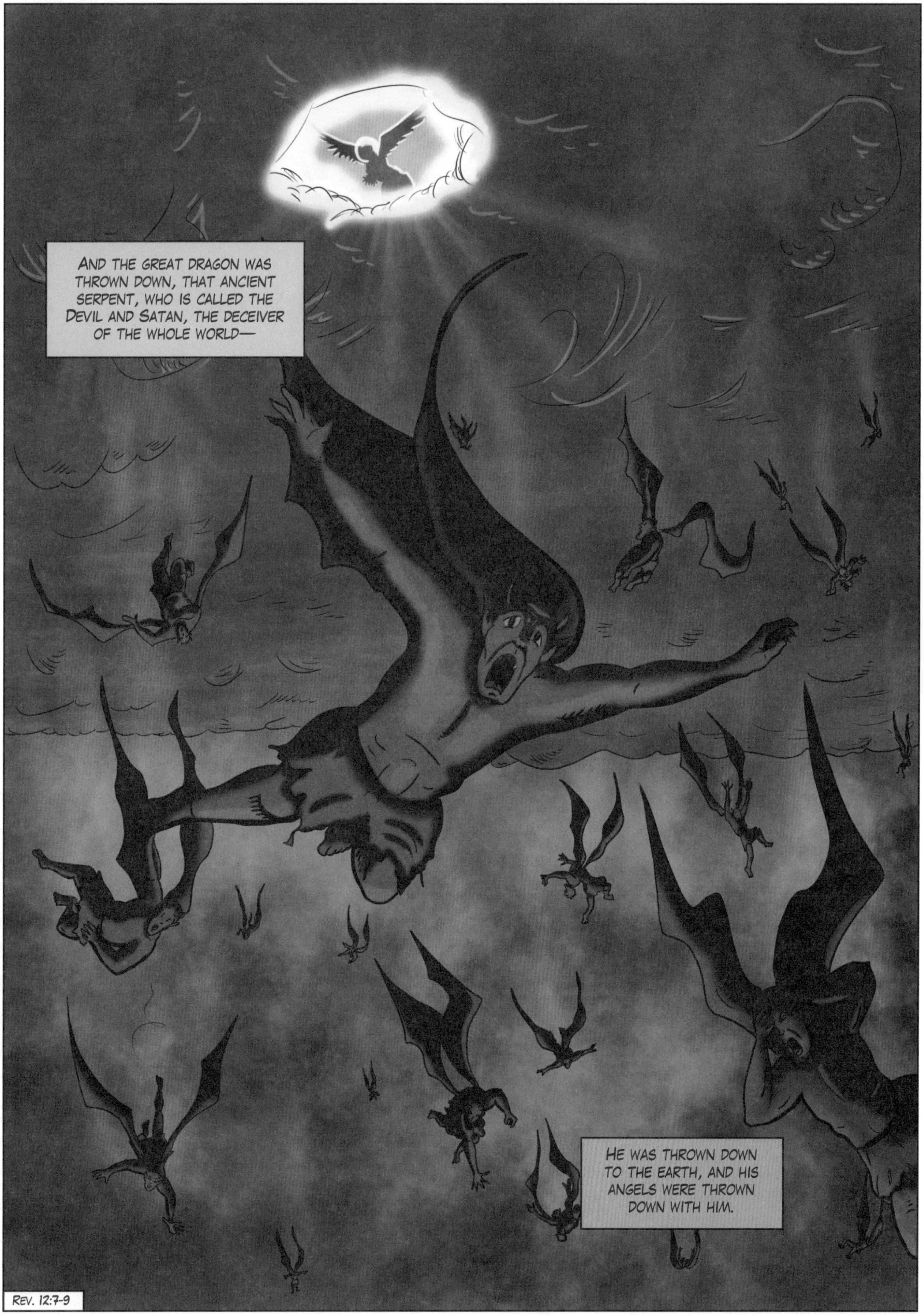
AND THE GREAT DRAGON WAS THROWN DOWN, THAT ANCIENT SERPENT, WHO IS CALLED THE DEVIL AND SATAN, THE DECEIVER OF THE WHOLE WORLD—
HE WAS THROWN DOWN TO THE EARTH, AND HIS ANGELS WERE THROWN DOWN WITH HIM.
REV. 12:7-9

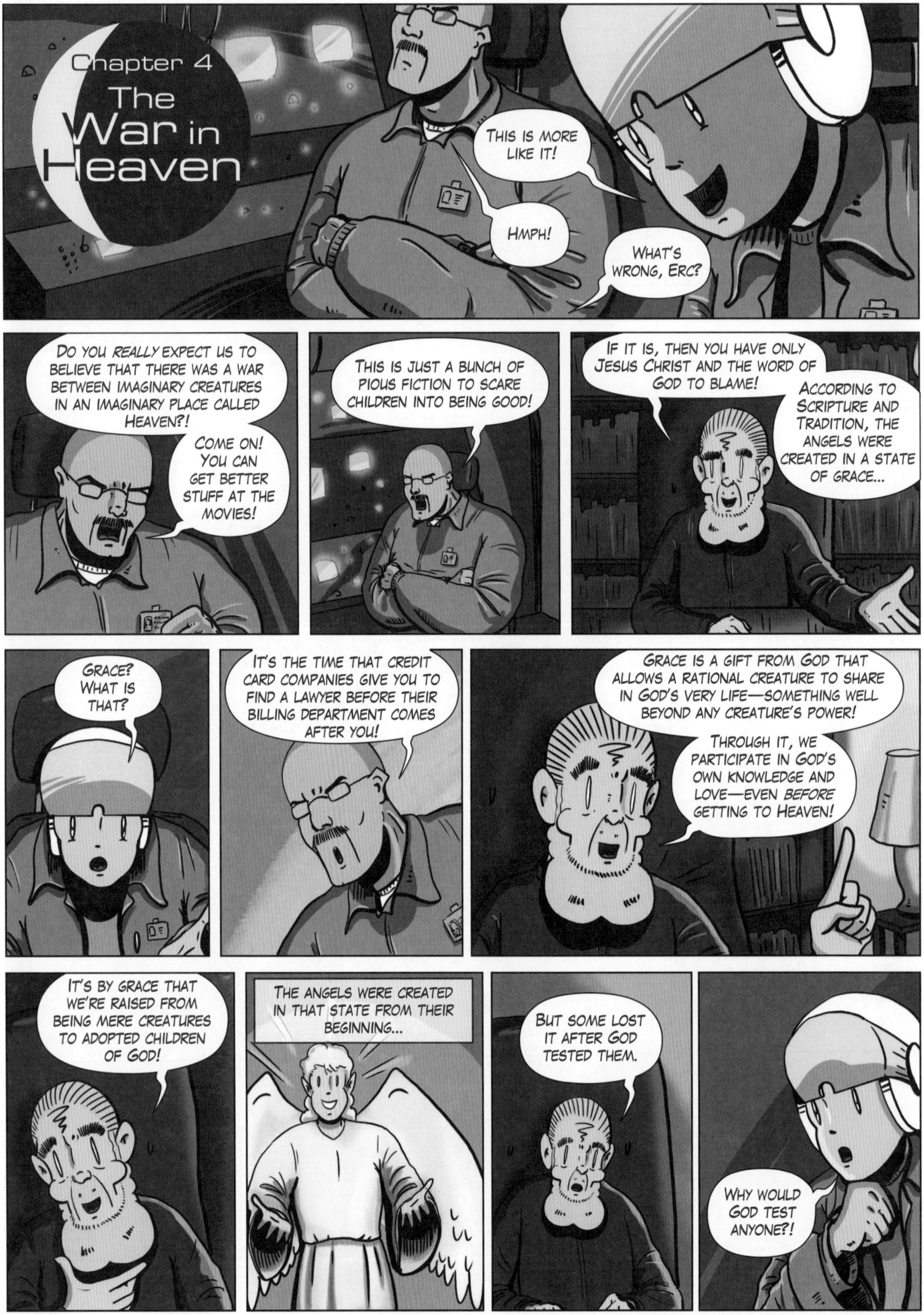

Chapter 4
The War in Heaven
This is more like it!
Hmph!
What's wrong, Erc?
Do you *really* expect us to believe that there was a war between imaginary creatures in an imaginary place called Heaven?!
Come on! You can get better stuff at the movies!
This is just a bunch of pious fiction to scare children into being good!
If it is, then you have only Jesus Christ and the word of God to blame!
According to Scripture and Tradition, the angels were created in a state of grace...
Grace? What is that?
It's the time that credit card companies give you to find a lawyer before their billing department comes after you!
Grace is a gift from God that allows a rational creature to share in God's very life—something well beyond any creature's power!
Through it, we participate in God's own knowledge and love—even *before* getting to Heaven!
It's by grace that we're raised from being mere creatures to adopted children of God!
The angels were created in that state from their beginning...
But some lost it after God tested them.
Why would God test anyone?!

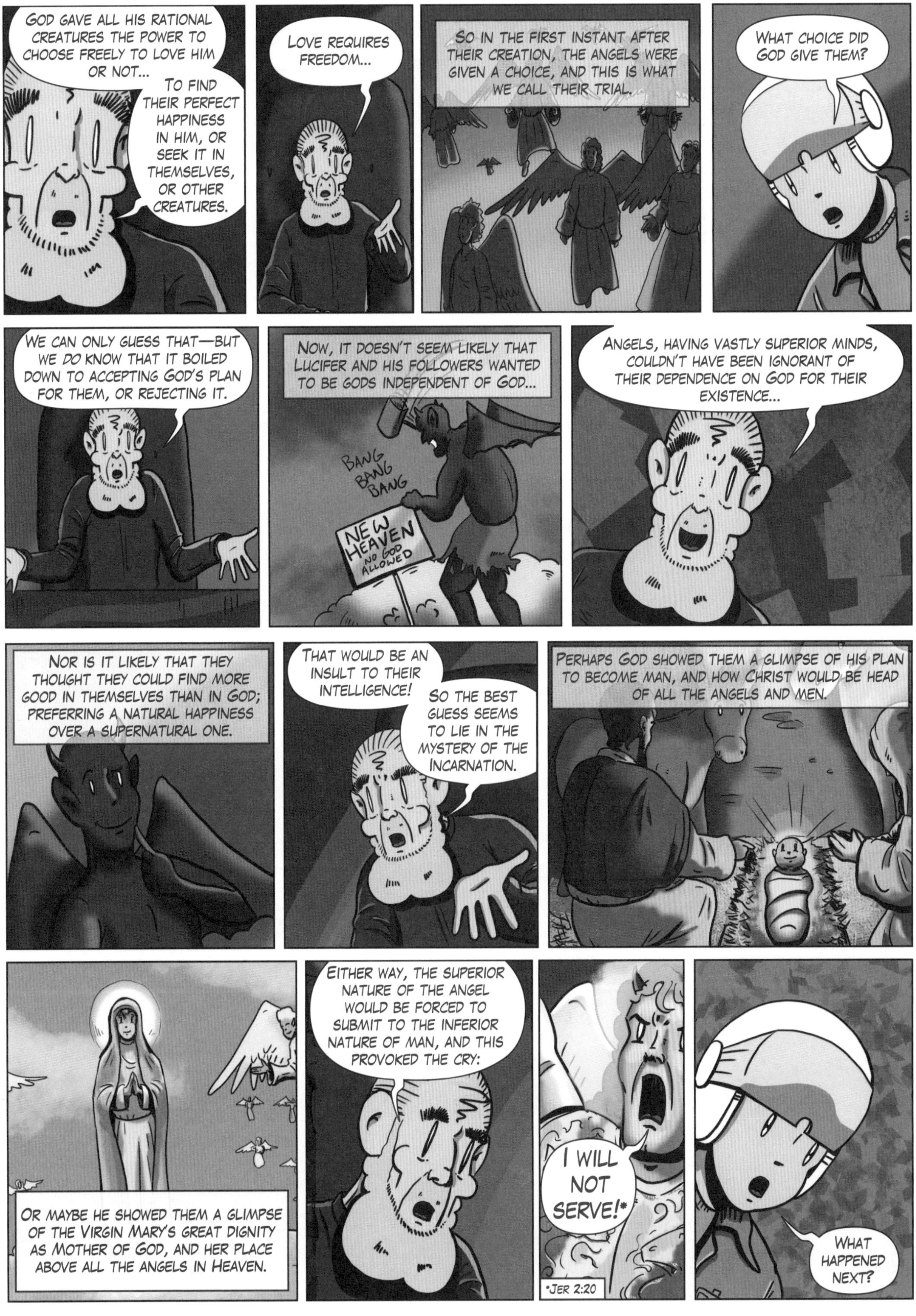

GOD GAVE ALL HIS RATIONAL CREATURES THE POWER TO CHOOSE FREELY TO LOVE HIM OR NOT...
TO FIND THEIR PERFECT HAPPINESS IN HIM, OR SEEK IT IN THEMSELVES, OR OTHER CREATURES.
LOVE REQUIRES FREEDOM...
SO IN THE FIRST INSTANT AFTER THEIR CREATION, THE ANGELS WERE GIVEN A CHOICE, AND THIS IS WHAT WE CALL THEIR TRIAL.
WHAT CHOICE DID GOD GIVE THEM?
WE CAN ONLY GUESS THAT—BUT WE *DO* KNOW THAT IT BOILED DOWN TO ACCEPTING GOD'S PLAN FOR THEM, OR REJECTING IT.
NOW, IT DOESN'T SEEM LIKELY THAT LUCIFER AND HIS FOLLOWERS WANTED TO BE GODS INDEPENDENT OF GOD...
BANG BANG BANG
NEW HEAVEN NO GOD ALLOWED
ANGELS, HAVING VASTLY SUPERIOR MINDS, COULDN'T HAVE BEEN IGNORANT OF THEIR DEPENDENCE ON GOD FOR THEIR EXISTENCE...
NOR IS IT LIKELY THAT THEY THOUGHT THEY COULD FIND MORE GOOD IN THEMSELVES THAN IN GOD; PREFERRING A NATURAL HAPPINESS OVER A SUPERNATURAL ONE.
THAT WOULD BE AN INSULT TO THEIR INTELLIGENCE!
SO THE BEST GUESS SEEMS TO LIE IN THE MYSTERY OF THE INCARNATION.
PERHAPS GOD SHOWED THEM A GLIMPSE OF HIS PLAN TO BECOME MAN, AND HOW CHRIST WOULD BE HEAD OF ALL THE ANGELS AND MEN.
OR MAYBE HE SHOWED THEM A GLIMPSE OF THE VIRGIN MARY'S GREAT DIGNITY AS MOTHER OF GOD, AND HER PLACE ABOVE ALL THE ANGELS IN HEAVEN.
EITHER WAY, THE SUPERIOR NATURE OF THE ANGEL WOULD BE FORCED TO SUBMIT TO THE INFERIOR NATURE OF MAN, AND THIS PROVOKED THE CRY:
I WILL NOT SERVE!*
*JER 2:20
WHAT HAPPENED NEXT?

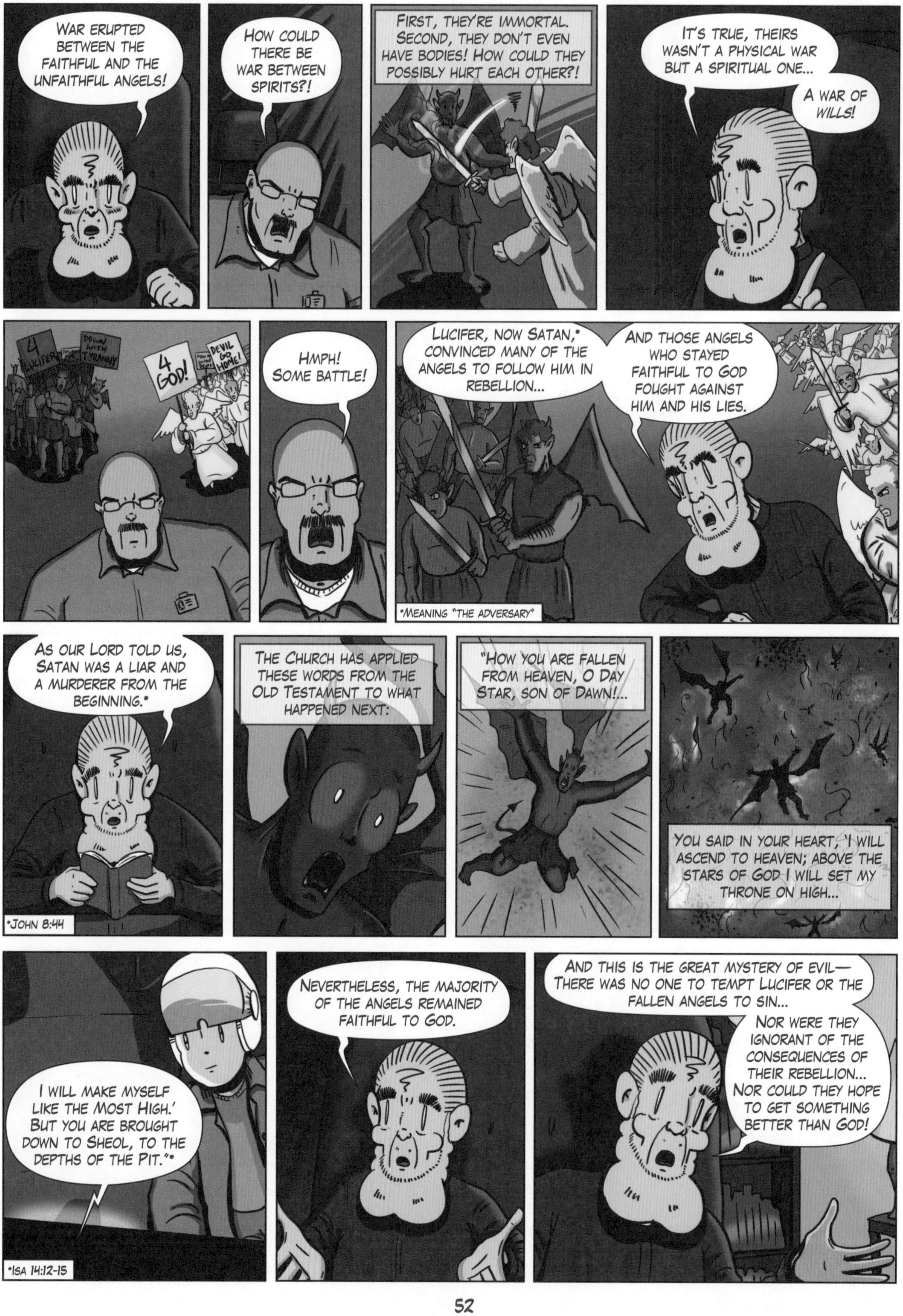
War erupted between the faithful and the unfaithful angels!
How could there be war between spirits?!
First, they're immortal. Second, they don't even have bodies! How could they possibly hurt each other?!
It's true, theirs wasn't a physical war but a spiritual one...
A war of wills!
4 Lucifer
Down with tyranny
Devil go home!
4 God!
Hmph! Some battle!
Lucifer, now Satan,* convinced many of the angels to follow him in rebellion...
And those angels who stayed faithful to God fought against him and his lies.
*Meaning "the adversary"
As our Lord told us, Satan was a liar and a murderer from the beginning.*
*John 8:44
The Church has applied these words from the Old Testament to what happened next:
"How you are fallen from heaven, O Day Star, son of Dawn!...
You said in your heart, 'I will ascend to heaven; above the stars of God I will set my throne on high...
I will make myself like the Most High.' But you are brought down to Sheol, to the depths of the Pit."*
*Isa 14:12-15
Nevertheless, the majority of the angels remained faithful to God.
And this is the great mystery of evil— There was no one to tempt Lucifer or the fallen angels to sin...
Nor were they ignorant of the consequences of their rebellion... Nor could they hope to get something better than God!

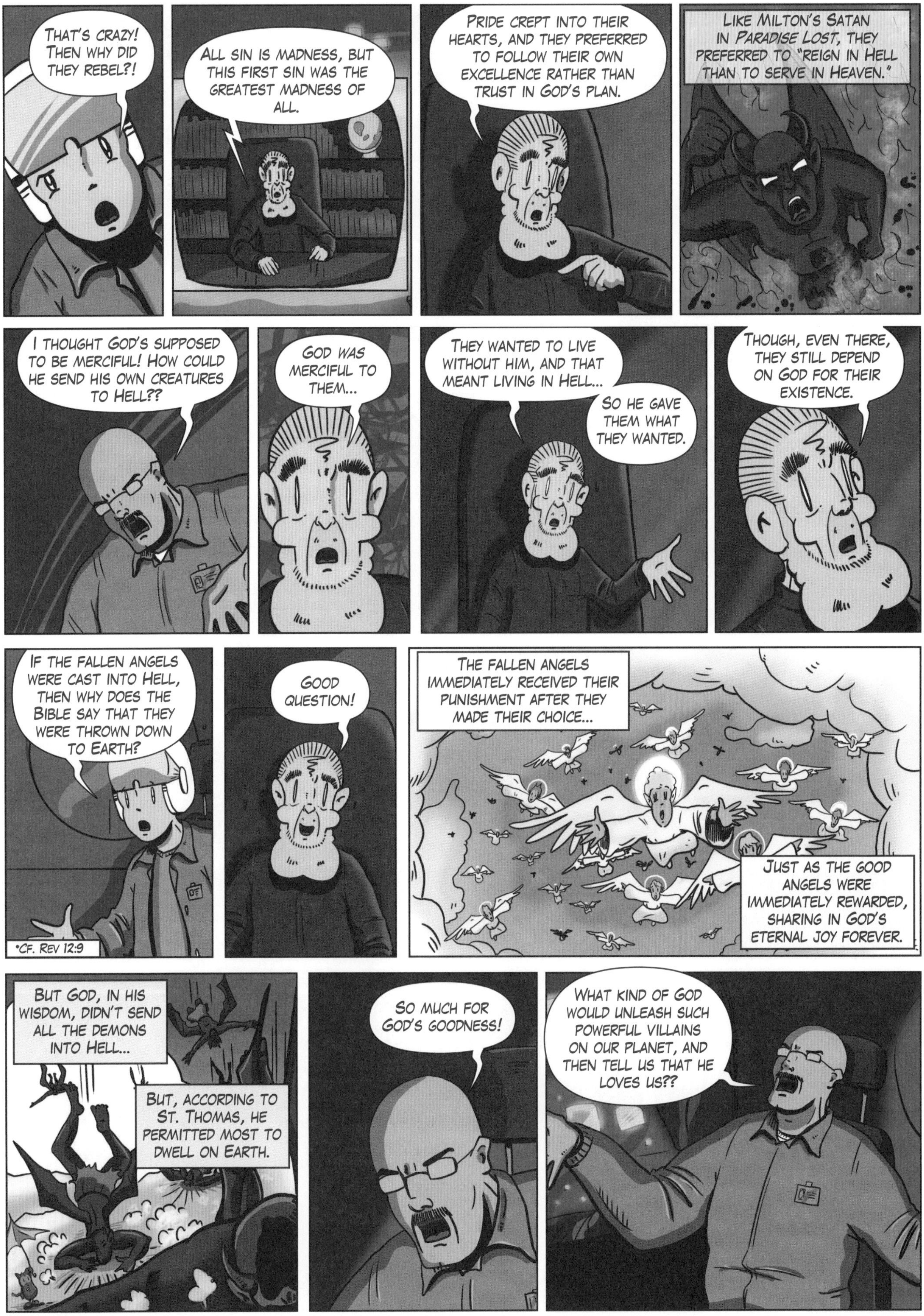
That's crazy! Then why did they rebel?!
All sin is madness, but this first sin was the greatest madness of all.
Pride crept into their hearts, and they preferred to follow their own excellence rather than trust in God's plan.
Like Milton's Satan in *Paradise Lost*, they preferred to "reign in Hell than to serve in Heaven."
I thought God's supposed to be merciful! How could he send his own creatures to Hell??
God was merciful to them...
They wanted to live without him, and that meant living in Hell...
So he gave them what they wanted.
Though, even there, they still depend on God for their existence.
If the fallen angels were cast into Hell, then why does the Bible say that they were thrown down to Earth?
*Cf. Rev 12:9
Good question!
The fallen angels immediately received their punishment after they made their choice...
Just as the good angels were immediately rewarded, sharing in God's eternal joy forever.
But God, in his wisdom, didn't send all the demons into Hell...
But, according to St. Thomas, he permitted most to dwell on Earth.
So much for God's goodness!
What kind of God would unleash such powerful villains on our planet, and then tell us that he loves us??

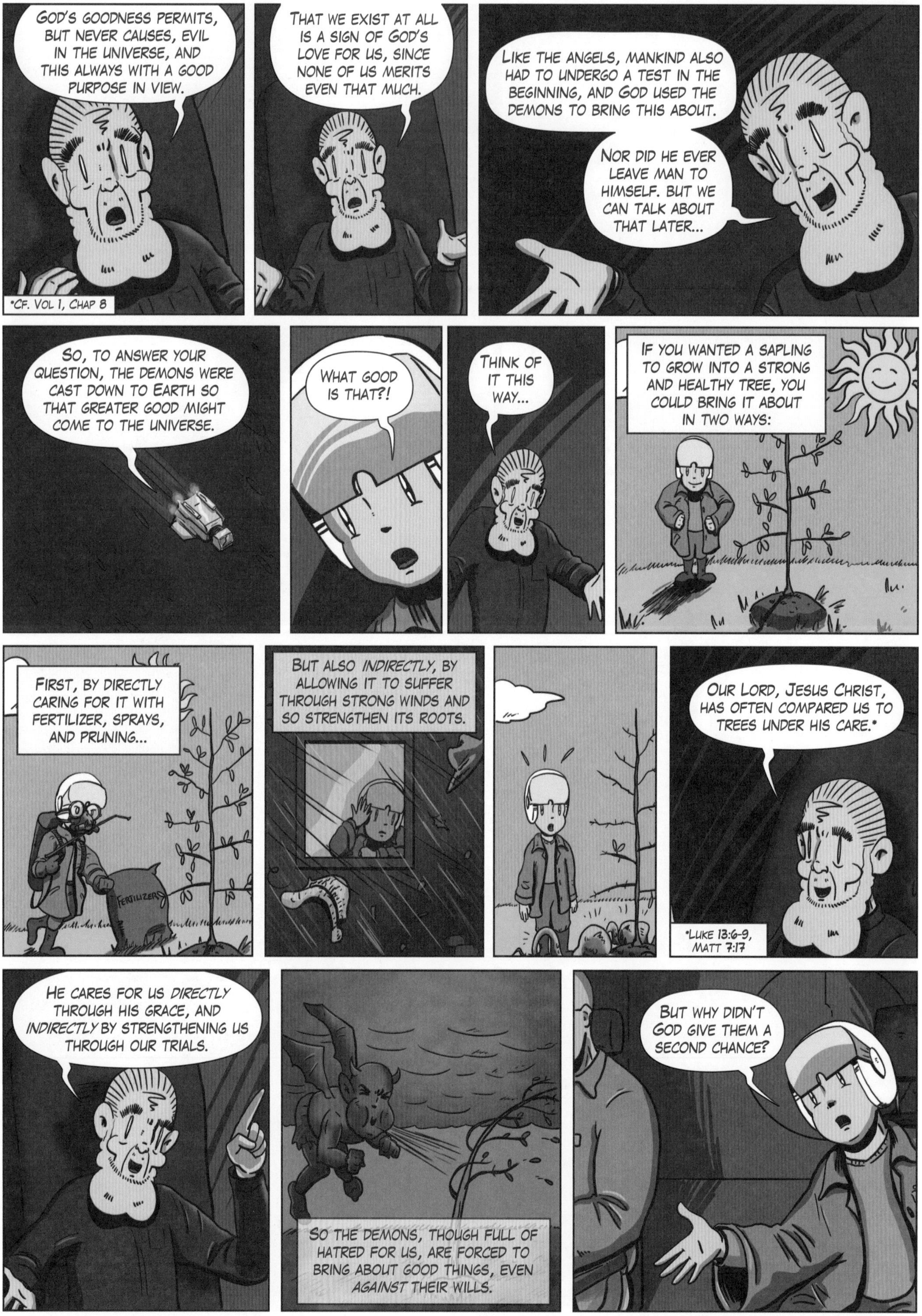
God's goodness permits, but never causes, evil in the universe, and this always with a good purpose in view.
*Cf. Vol 1, Chap 8
That we exist at all is a sign of God's love for us, since none of us merits even that much.
Like the angels, mankind also had to undergo a test in the beginning, and God used the demons to bring this about.
Nor did he ever leave man to himself. But we can talk about that later...
So, to answer your question, the demons were cast down to Earth so that greater good might come to the universe.
What good is that?!
Think of it this way...
If you wanted a sapling to grow into a strong and healthy tree, you could bring it about in two ways:
First, by directly caring for it with fertilizer, sprays, and pruning...
Fertilizer
But also indirectly, by allowing it to suffer through strong winds and so strengthen its roots.
Our Lord, Jesus Christ, has often compared us to trees under his care.*
*Luke 13:6-9, Matt 7:17
He cares for us directly through his grace, and indirectly by strengthening us through our trials.
So the demons, though full of hatred for us, are forced to bring about good things, even against their wills.
But why didn't God give them a second chance?

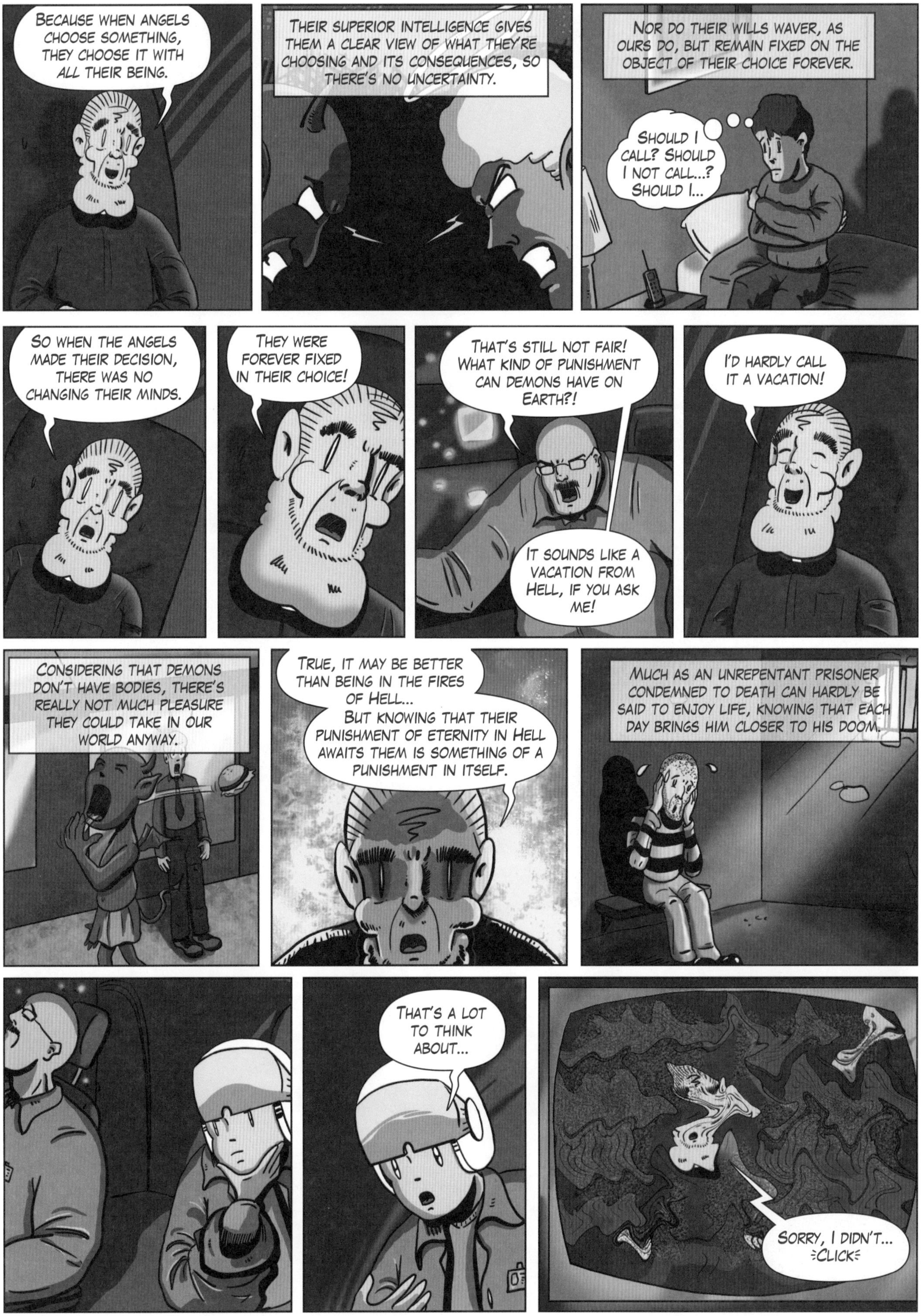

Because when angels choose something, they choose it with all their being.
Their superior intelligence gives them a clear view of what they're choosing and its consequences, so there's no uncertainty.
Nor do their wills waver, as ours do, but remain fixed on the object of their choice forever.
Should I call? Should I not call...? Should I...
So when the angels made their decision, there was no changing their minds.
They were forever fixed in their choice!
That's still not fair! What kind of punishment can demons have on Earth?!
It sounds like a vacation from Hell, if you ask me!
I'd hardly call it a vacation!
Considering that demons don't have bodies, there's really not much pleasure they could take in our world anyway.
True, it may be better than being in the fires of Hell...
But knowing that their punishment of eternity in Hell awaits them is something of a punishment in itself.
Much as an unrepentant prisoner condemned to death can hardly be said to enjoy life, knowing that each day brings him closer to his doom.
That's a lot to think about...
Sorry, I didn't...
Click

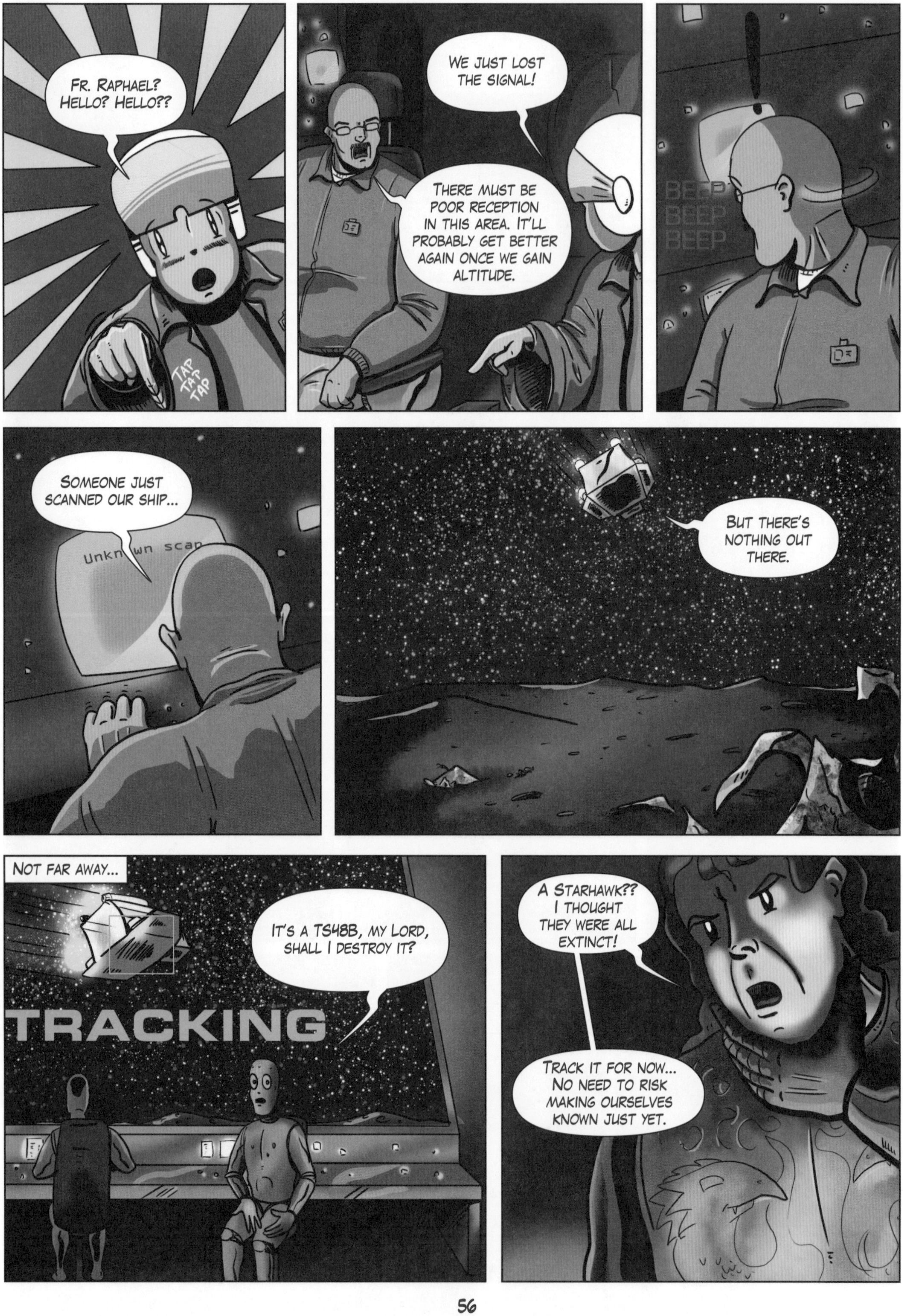
Fr. Raphael? Hello? Hello??
TAP TAP TAP
We just lost the signal!
There must be poor reception in this area. It'll probably get better again once we gain altitude.
!
BEEP BEEP BEEP
Someone just scanned our ship...
Unkn wn scan
But there's nothing out there.
Not far away...
It's a TS48B, my Lord, shall I destroy it?
TRACKING
A Starhawk?? I thought they were all extinct!
Track it for now... No need to risk making ourselves known just yet.

PART III:
THE CREATION OF MAN

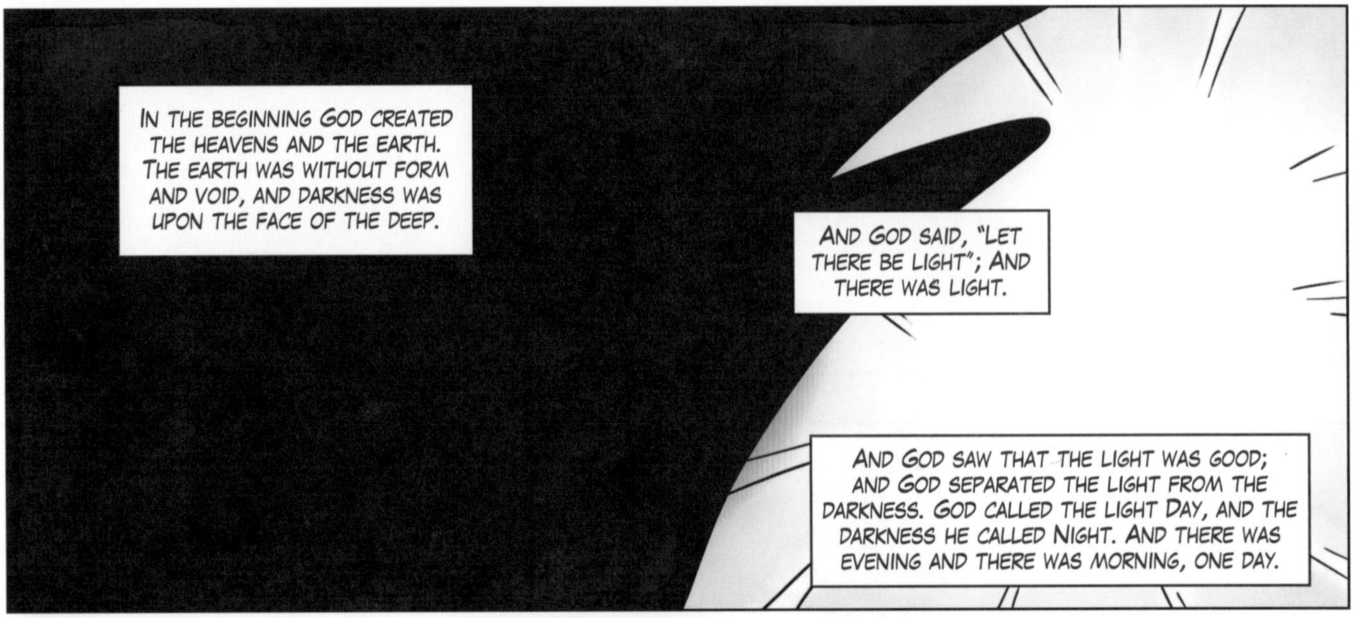
IN THE BEGINNING GOD CREATED THE HEAVENS AND THE EARTH. THE EARTH WAS WITHOUT FORM AND VOID, AND DARKNESS WAS UPON THE FACE OF THE DEEP.
AND GOD SAID, "LET THERE BE LIGHT"; AND THERE WAS LIGHT.
AND GOD SAW THAT THE LIGHT WAS GOOD; AND GOD SEPARATED THE LIGHT FROM THE DARKNESS. GOD CALLED THE LIGHT DAY, AND THE DARKNESS HE CALLED NIGHT. AND THERE WAS EVENING AND THERE WAS MORNING, ONE DAY.

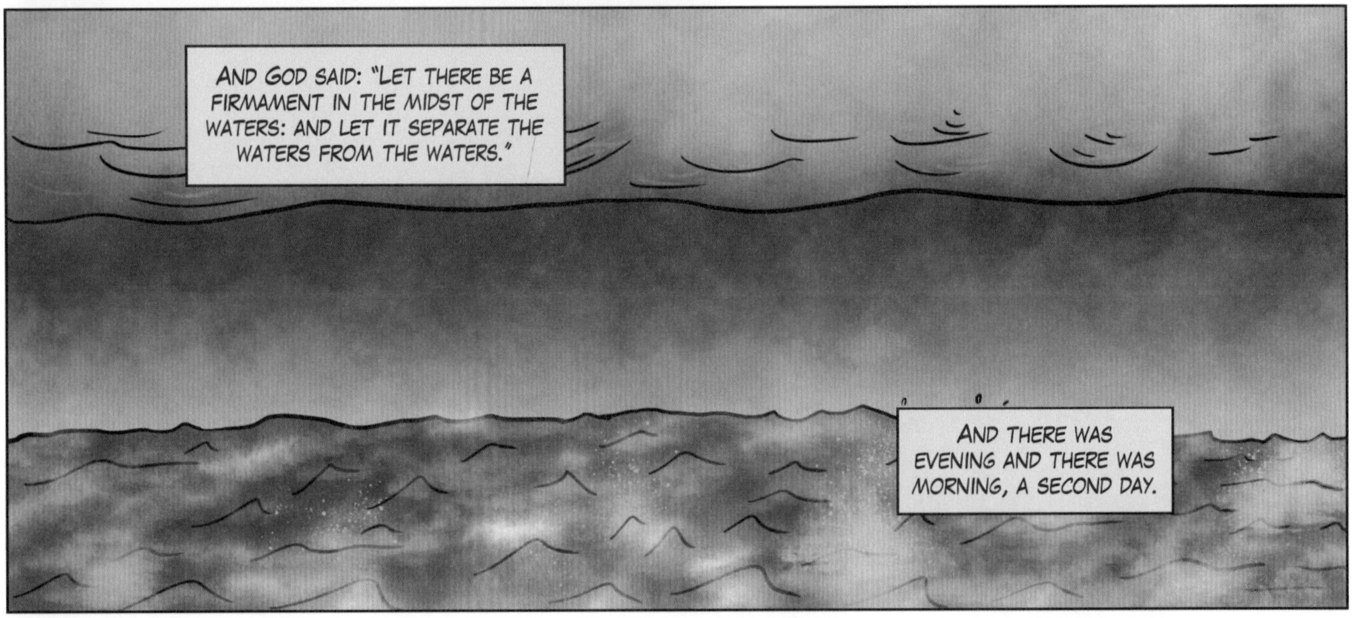
AND GOD SAID: "LET THERE BE A FIRMAMENT IN THE MIDST OF THE WATERS: AND LET IT SEPARATE THE WATERS FROM THE WATERS."
AND THERE WAS EVENING AND THERE WAS MORNING, A SECOND DAY.

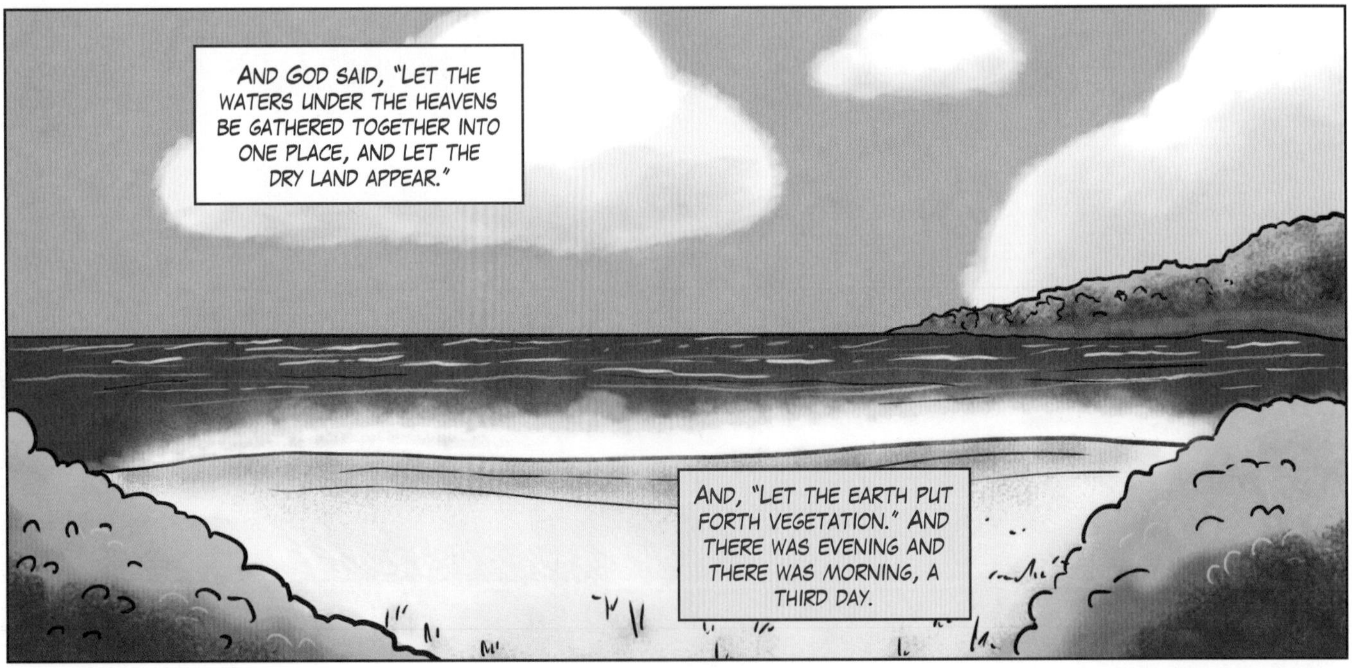
AND GOD SAID, "LET THE WATERS UNDER THE HEAVENS BE GATHERED TOGETHER INTO ONE PLACE, AND LET THE DRY LAND APPEAR."
AND, "LET THE EARTH PUT FORTH VEGETATION." AND THERE WAS EVENING AND THERE WAS MORNING, A THIRD DAY.

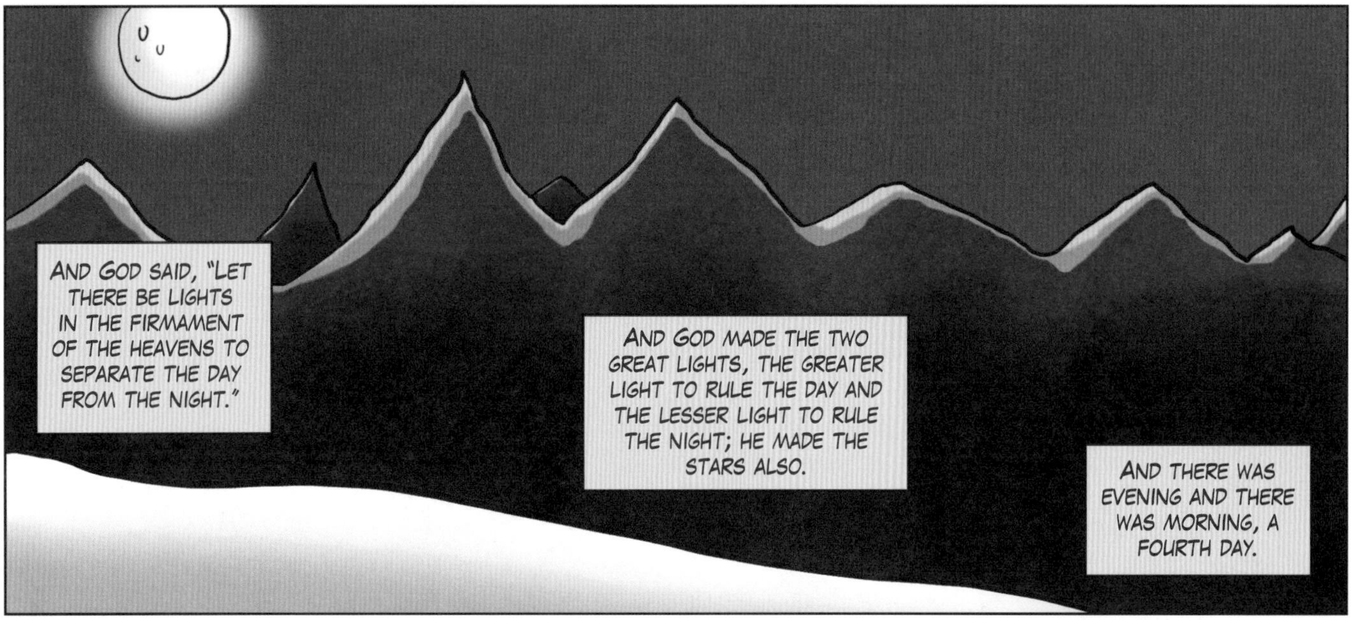
AND GOD SAID, "LET THERE BE LIGHTS IN THE FIRMAMENT OF THE HEAVENS TO SEPARATE THE DAY FROM THE NIGHT."
AND GOD MADE THE TWO GREAT LIGHTS, THE GREATER LIGHT TO RULE THE DAY AND THE LESSER LIGHT TO RULE THE NIGHT; HE MADE THE STARS ALSO.
AND THERE WAS EVENING AND THERE WAS MORNING, A FOURTH DAY.

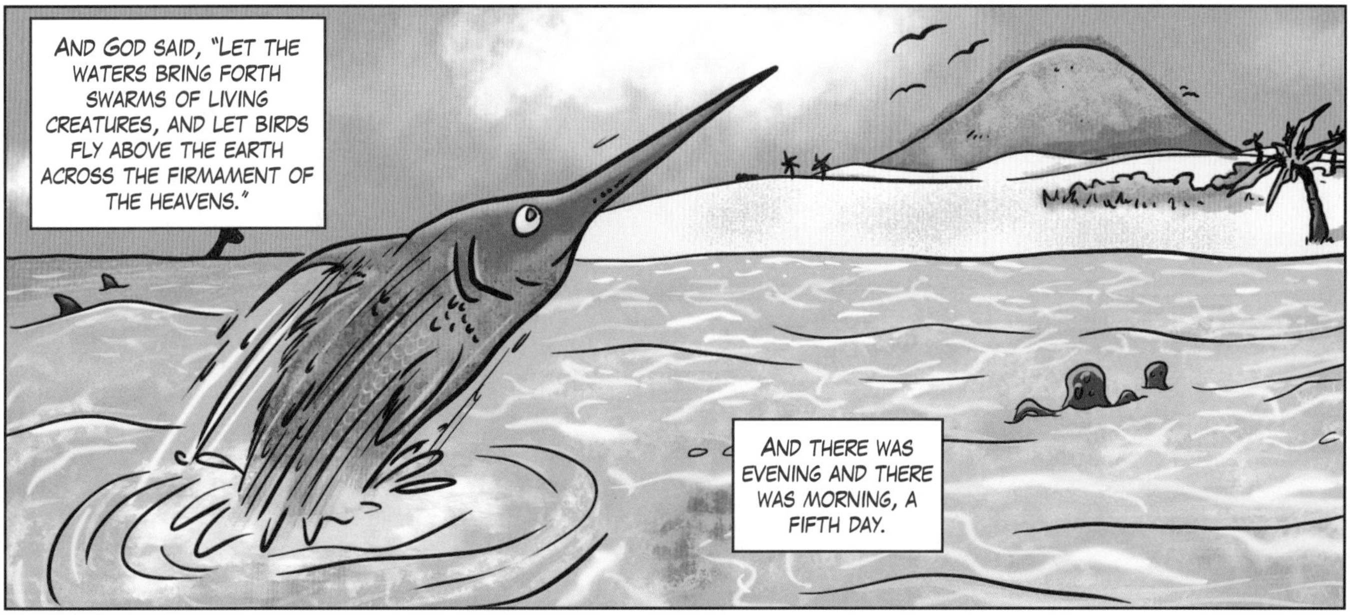
AND GOD SAID, "LET THE WATERS BRING FORTH SWARMS OF LIVING CREATURES, AND LET BIRDS FLY ABOVE THE EARTH ACROSS THE FIRMAMENT OF THE HEAVENS."
AND THERE WAS EVENING AND THERE WAS MORNING, A FIFTH DAY.

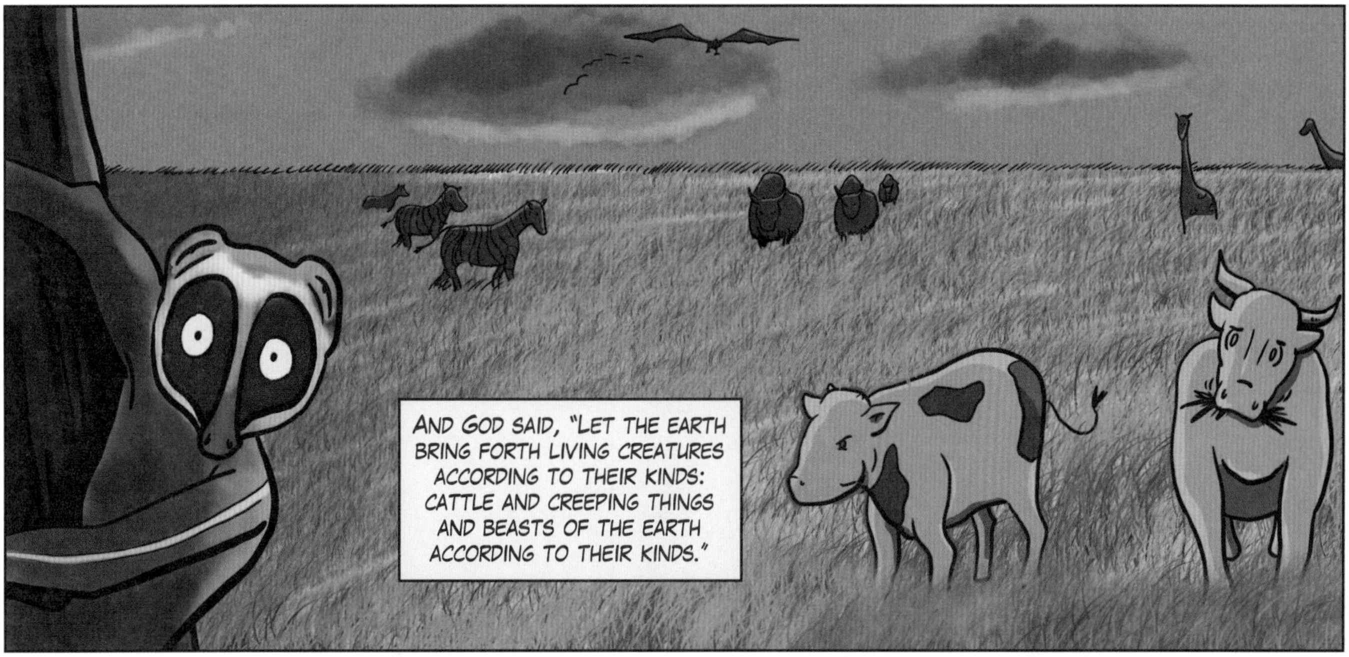
AND GOD SAID, "LET THE EARTH BRING FORTH LIVING CREATURES ACCORDING TO THEIR KINDS: CATTLE AND CREEPING THINGS AND BEASTS OF THE EARTH ACCORDING TO THEIR KINDS."

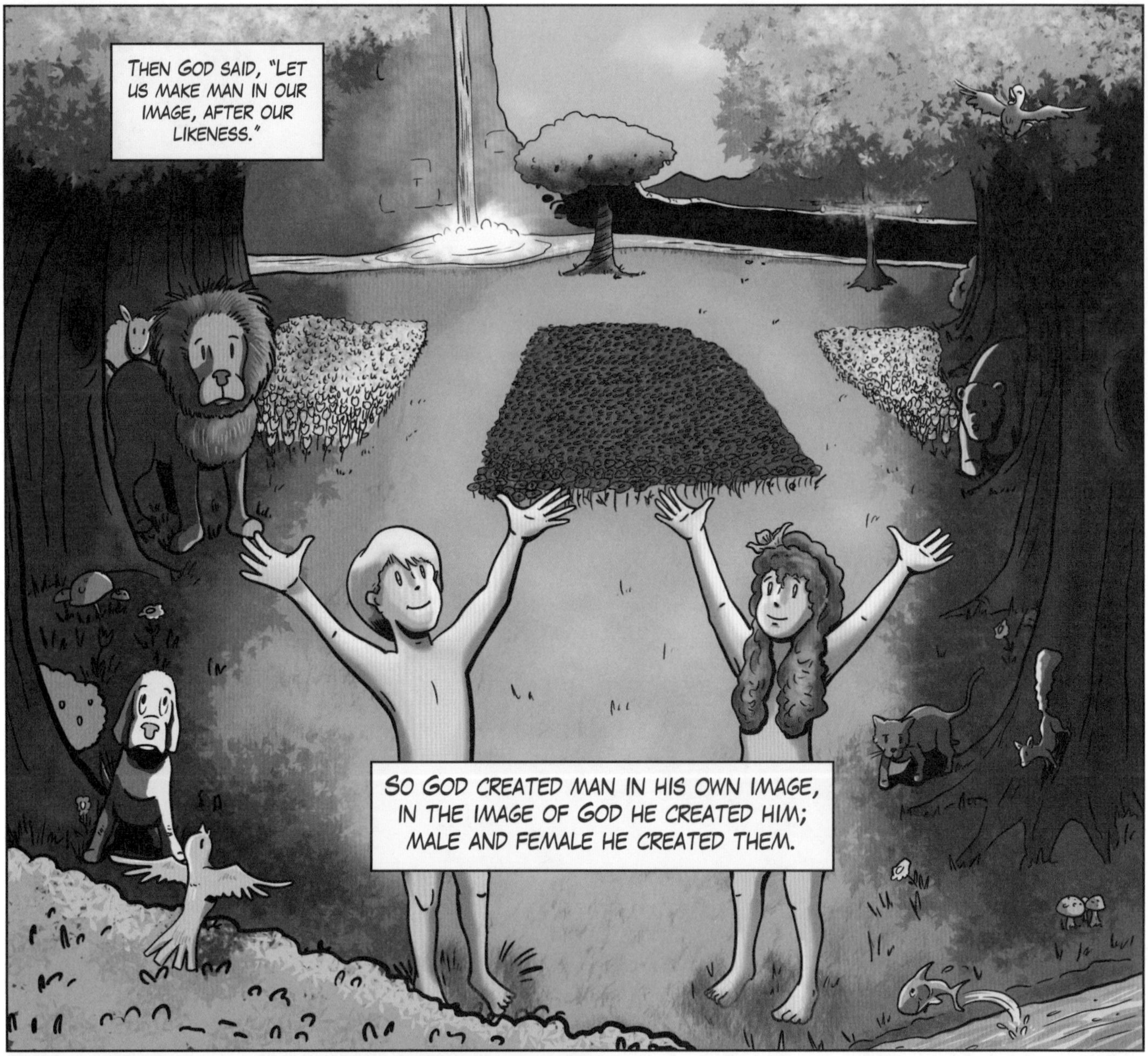
THEN GOD SAID, "LET US MAKE MAN IN OUR IMAGE, AFTER OUR LIKENESS."
SO GOD CREATED MAN IN HIS OWN IMAGE, IN THE IMAGE OF GOD HE CREATED HIM; MALE AND FEMALE HE CREATED THEM.

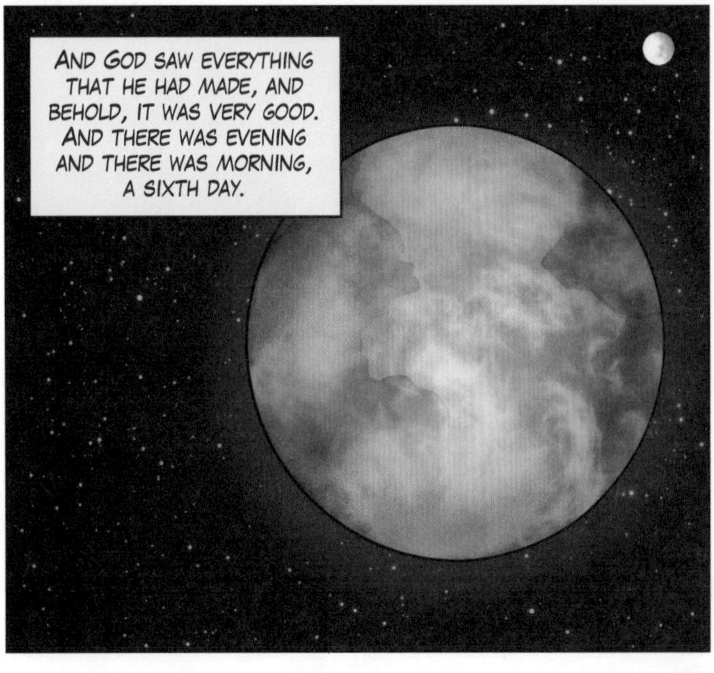
AND GOD SAW EVERYTHING THAT HE HAD MADE, AND BEHOLD, IT WAS VERY GOOD. AND THERE WAS EVENING AND THERE WAS MORNING, A SIXTH DAY.

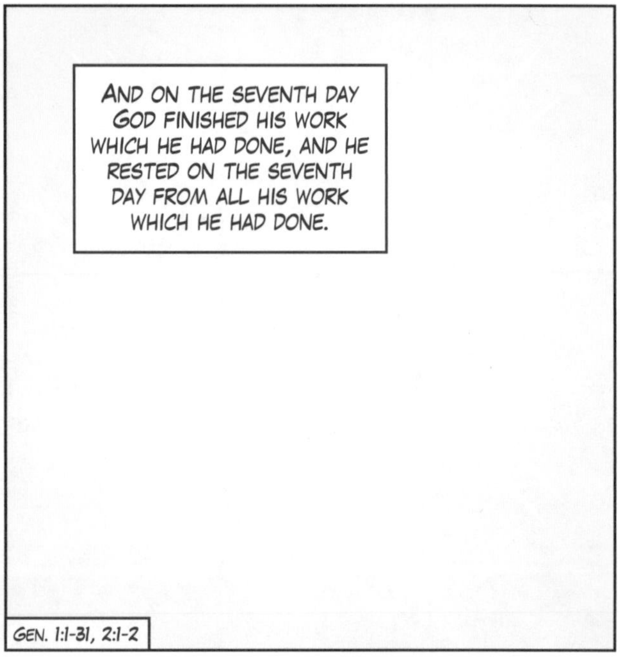
AND ON THE SEVENTH DAY GOD FINISHED HIS WORK WHICH HE HAD DONE, AND HE RESTED ON THE SEVENTH DAY FROM ALL HIS WORK WHICH HE HAD DONE.
GEN. 1:1-31, 2:1-2

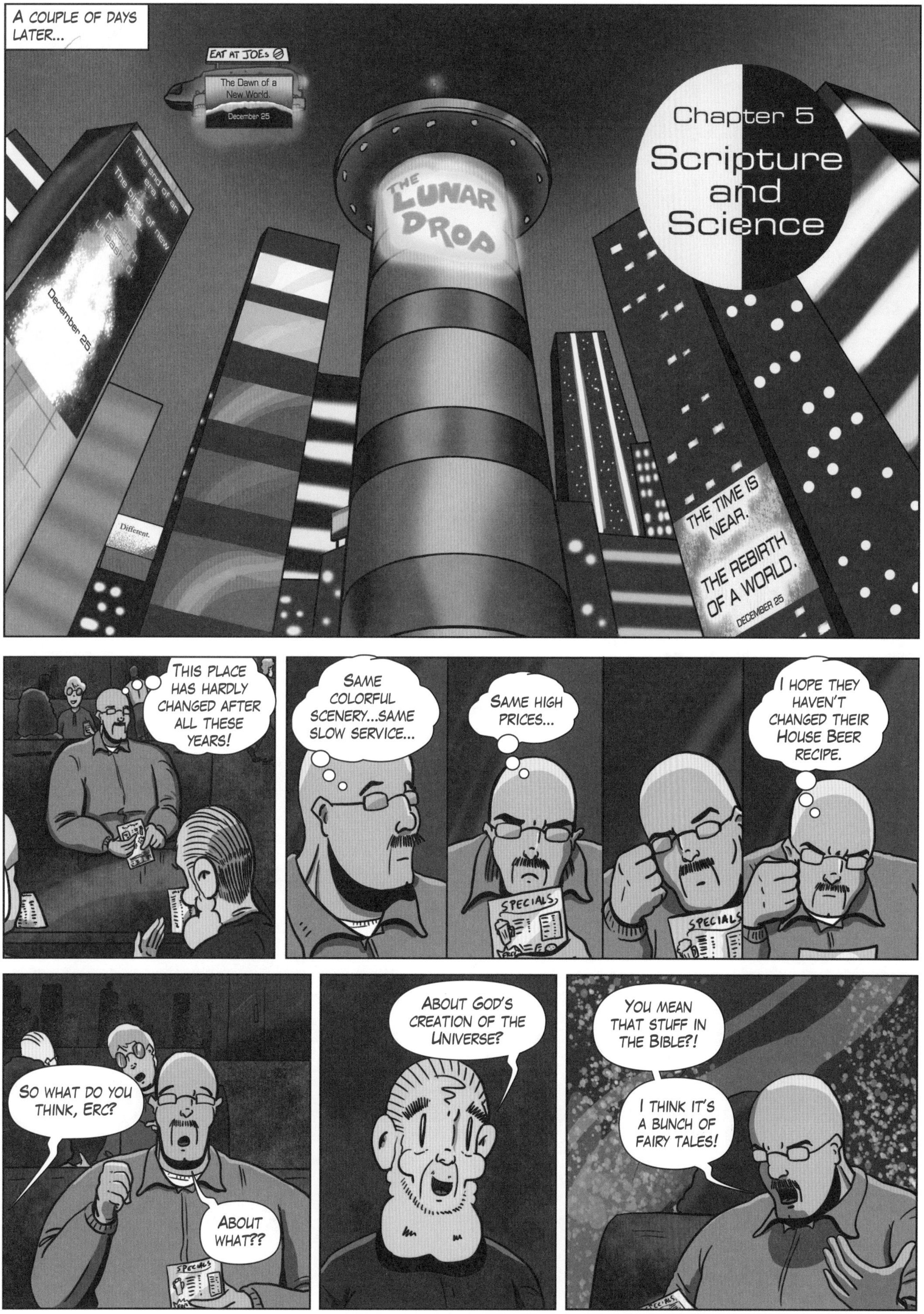
A COUPLE OF DAYS LATER...
EAT AT JOES
The Dawn of a New World.
December 25
The end of an era. The birth of new hope. Freedom Unleashed.
December 25
THE LUNAR DROP
Chapter 5
Scripture and Science
Different.
THE TIME IS NEAR.
THE REBIRTH OF A WORLD.
DECEMBER 25
THIS PLACE HAS HARDLY CHANGED AFTER ALL THESE YEARS!
SAME COLORFUL SCENERY...SAME SLOW SERVICE...
SAME HIGH PRICES...
SPECIALS
I HOPE THEY HAVEN'T CHANGED THEIR HOUSE BEER RECIPE.
SPECIALS
SO WHAT DO YOU THINK, ERC?
ABOUT WHAT??
SPECIALS
ABOUT GOD'S CREATION OF THE UNIVERSE?
YOU MEAN THAT STUFF IN THE BIBLE?!
I THINK IT'S A BUNCH OF FAIRY TALES!

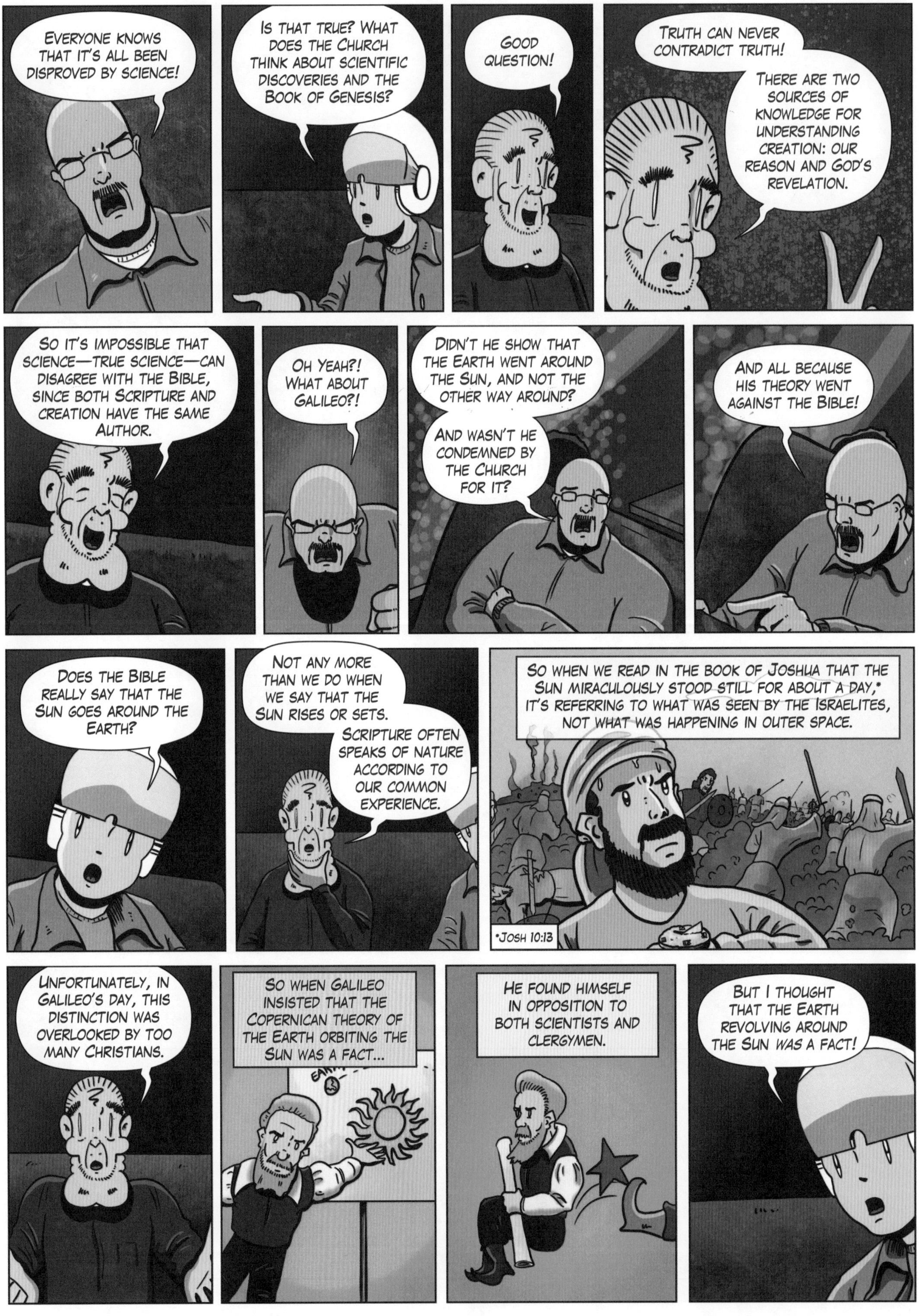

Everyone knows that it's all been disproved by science!
Is that true? What does the Church think about scientific discoveries and the Book of Genesis?
Good question!
Truth can never contradict truth!
There are two sources of knowledge for understanding creation: our reason and God's revelation.
So it's impossible that science—true science—can disagree with the Bible, since both Scripture and creation have the same Author.
Oh Yeah?! What about Galileo?!
Didn't he show that the Earth went around the Sun, and not the other way around?
And wasn't he condemned by the Church for it?
And all because his theory went against the Bible!
Does the Bible really say that the Sun goes around the Earth?
Not any more than we do when we say that the Sun rises or sets.
Scripture often speaks of nature according to our common experience.
So when we read in the book of Joshua that the Sun miraculously stood still for about a day,* it's referring to what was seen by the Israelites, not what was happening in outer space.
*Josh 10:13
Unfortunately, in Galileo's day, this distinction was overlooked by too many Christians.
So when Galileo insisted that the Copernican theory of the Earth orbiting the Sun was a fact...
He found himself in opposition to both scientists and clergymen.
But I thought that the Earth revolving around the Sun was a fact!

IT MAY WELL BE, BUT BACK THEN THEY LACKED THE INSTRUMENTS TO PROVE IT.

BOTH MODELS, THE GEOCENTRIC—WHERE THE EARTH IS THE CENTER OF THE UNIVERSE—AND THE HELIOCENTRIC—WHERE EVERYTHING REVOLVES AROUND THE SUN—COULD ACCOUNT FOR GALILEO'S OBSERVATIONS.

THIS WASN'T THE CAUSE OF GALILEO'S CONDEMNATION.

GEOCENTRIC

HELIOCENTRIC

HIS TROUBLE CAME ABOUT WHEN HE BEGAN TO TELL SCRIPTURE SCHOLARS THAT THE BIBLE HAD TO BE INTERPRETED FIGURATIVELY WHENEVER IT SPEAKS ABOUT THE EARTH STANDING STILL.*

*E.G., PSALM 104:5

ONCE AGAIN INSISTING THAT WHAT WAS STILL A THEORY SHOULD TO BE TAKEN AS A FACT.

IN THE END GALILEO WAS REBUKED FOR DISOBEDIENCE, NOT HERESY.

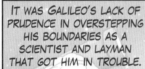

DEFENDANT

AS URBAN VIII, THE POPE THEN, ADMITTED THERE WAS NOTHING HERETICAL ABOUT THE COPERNICAN THEORY.

AND THOUGH HIS JUDGES SHOULD NEVER HAVE DECLARED THE COPERNICAN THEORY "FALSE AND ABSURD"...

IT WAS GALILEO'S LACK OF PRUDENCE IN OVERSTEPPING HIS BOUNDARIES AS A SCIENTIST AND LAYMAN THAT GOT HIM IN TROUBLE.

CONSIDERING THE MANY ADVANCES IN SCIENCE THAT THE CHURCH HAS ENCOURAGED, IT'S HARD TO ACCUSE IT OF BEING ANTI-SCIENTIFIC.

SO DOES THE CHURCH BELIEVE WHATEVER SCIENCE PROPOSES?

I'M NOT SURE THAT SCIENTISTS BELIEVE WHATEVER SCIENCE PROPOSES!

ON THE ONE HAND, THE CHURCH IS INTERESTED IN SCIENCE INASMUCH AS IT AFFECTS MAN AND HIS UNDERSTANDING ABOUT HIMSELF,

BUT IT ALSO REALIZES THAT SCIENTIFIC THEORIES COME AND GO.

SO ALTHOUGH REASON AND REVELATION CAN'T CONTRADICT EACH OTHER, IT'S IMPORTANT TO REMEMBER THAT GOD'S REVELATION IS MORE CERTAIN THAN WHAT CAN BE KNOWN BY REASON ALONE.

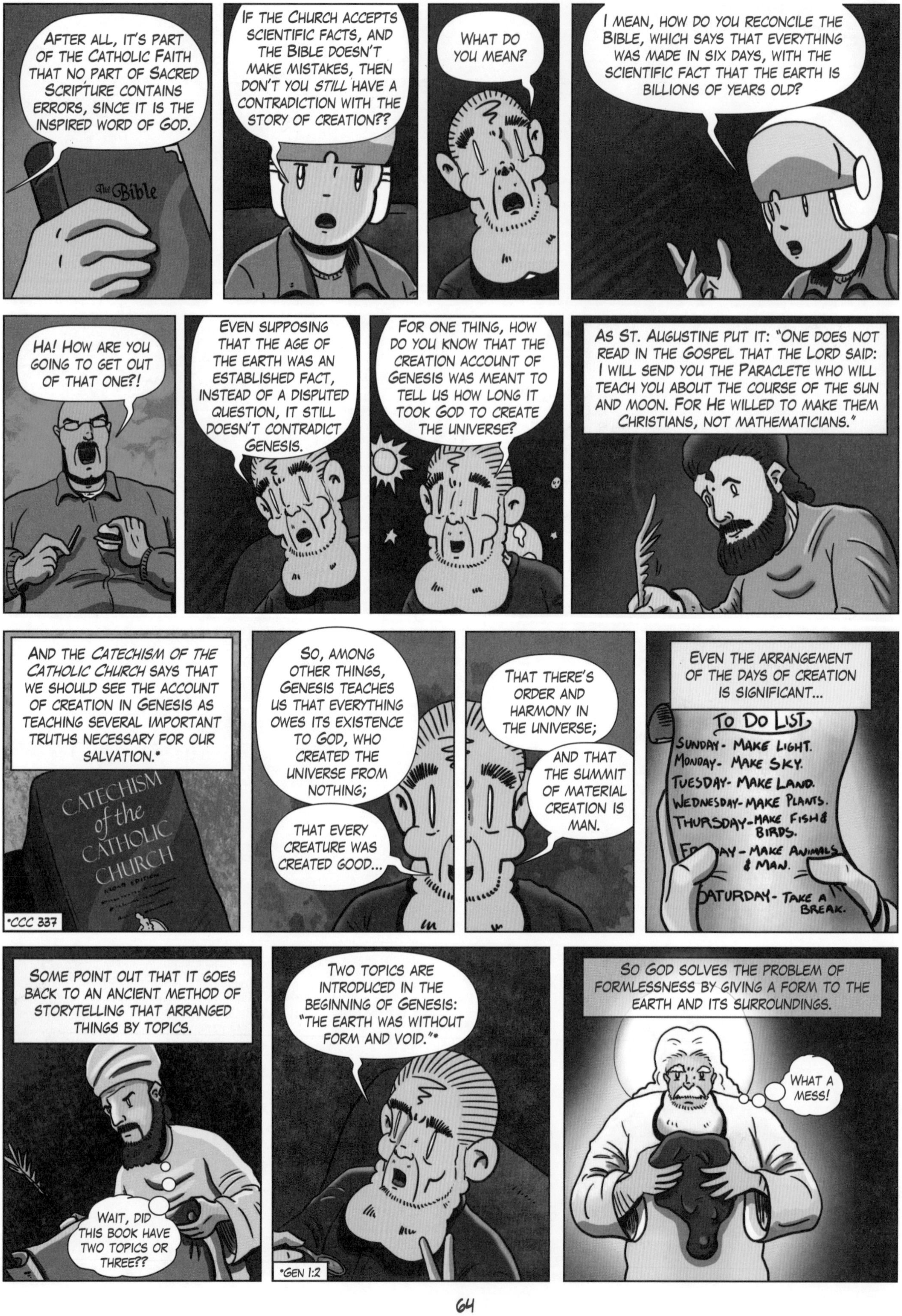

After all, it's part of the Catholic Faith that no part of Sacred Scripture contains errors, since it is the inspired word of God.
The Bible
If the Church accepts scientific facts, and the Bible doesn't make mistakes, then don't you *still* have a contradiction with the story of creation??
What do you mean?
I mean, how do you reconcile the Bible, which says that everything was made in six days, with the scientific fact that the earth is billions of years old?
Ha! How are you going to get out of that one?!
Even supposing that the age of the earth was an established fact, instead of a disputed question, it still doesn't contradict Genesis.
For one thing, how do you know that the creation account of Genesis was meant to tell us how long it took God to create the universe?
As St. Augustine put it: "One does not read in the Gospel that the Lord said: I will send you the Paraclete who will teach you about the course of the sun and moon. For He willed to make them Christians, not mathematicians."
And the *Catechism of the Catholic Church* says that we should see the account of creation in Genesis as teaching several important truths necessary for our salvation.*
Catechism of the Catholic Church
*CCC 337
So, among other things, Genesis teaches us that everything owes its existence to God, who created the universe from nothing;
That every creature was created good...
That there's order and harmony in the universe;
And that the summit of material creation is man.
Even the arrangement of the days of creation is significant...
To Do List
Sunday- Make Light.
Monday- Make Sky.
Tuesday- Make Land.
Wednesday- Make Plants.
Thursday- Make Fish & Birds.
Friday- Make Animals & Man.
Saturday- Take a Break.
Some point out that it goes back to an ancient method of storytelling that arranged things by topics.
Wait, did this book have two topics or three??
Two topics are introduced in the beginning of Genesis: "The earth was without form and void."*
*Gen 1:2
So God solves the problem of formlessness by giving a form to the earth and its surroundings.
What a mess!

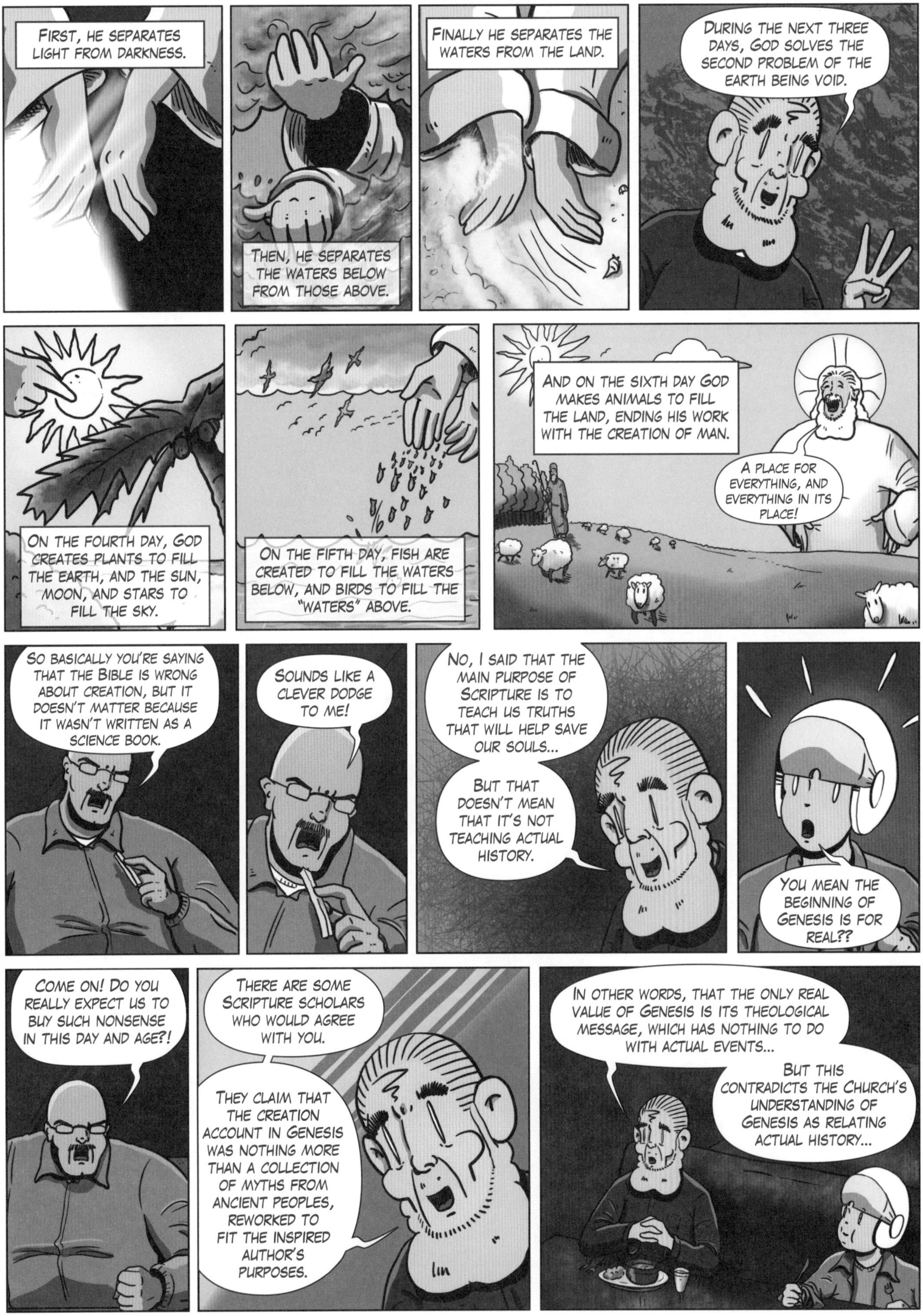

First, he separates light from darkness.
Then, he separates the waters below from those above.
Finally he separates the waters from the land.
During the next three days, God solves the second problem of the earth being void.
On the fourth day, God creates plants to fill the earth, and the sun, moon, and stars to fill the sky.
On the fifth day, fish are created to fill the waters below, and birds to fill the "waters" above.
And on the sixth day God makes animals to fill the land, ending his work with the creation of man.
A place for everything, and everything in its place!
So basically you're saying that the Bible is wrong about creation, but it doesn't matter because it wasn't written as a science book.
Sounds like a clever dodge to me!
No, I said that the main purpose of Scripture is to teach us truths that will help save our souls...
But that doesn't mean that it's not teaching actual history.
You mean the beginning of Genesis is for real??
Come on! Do you really expect us to buy such nonsense in this day and age?!
There are some Scripture scholars who would agree with you.
They claim that the creation account in Genesis was nothing more than a collection of myths from ancient peoples, reworked to fit the inspired author's purposes.
In other words, that the only real value of Genesis is its theological message, which has nothing to do with actual events...
But this contradicts the Church's understanding of Genesis as relating actual history...

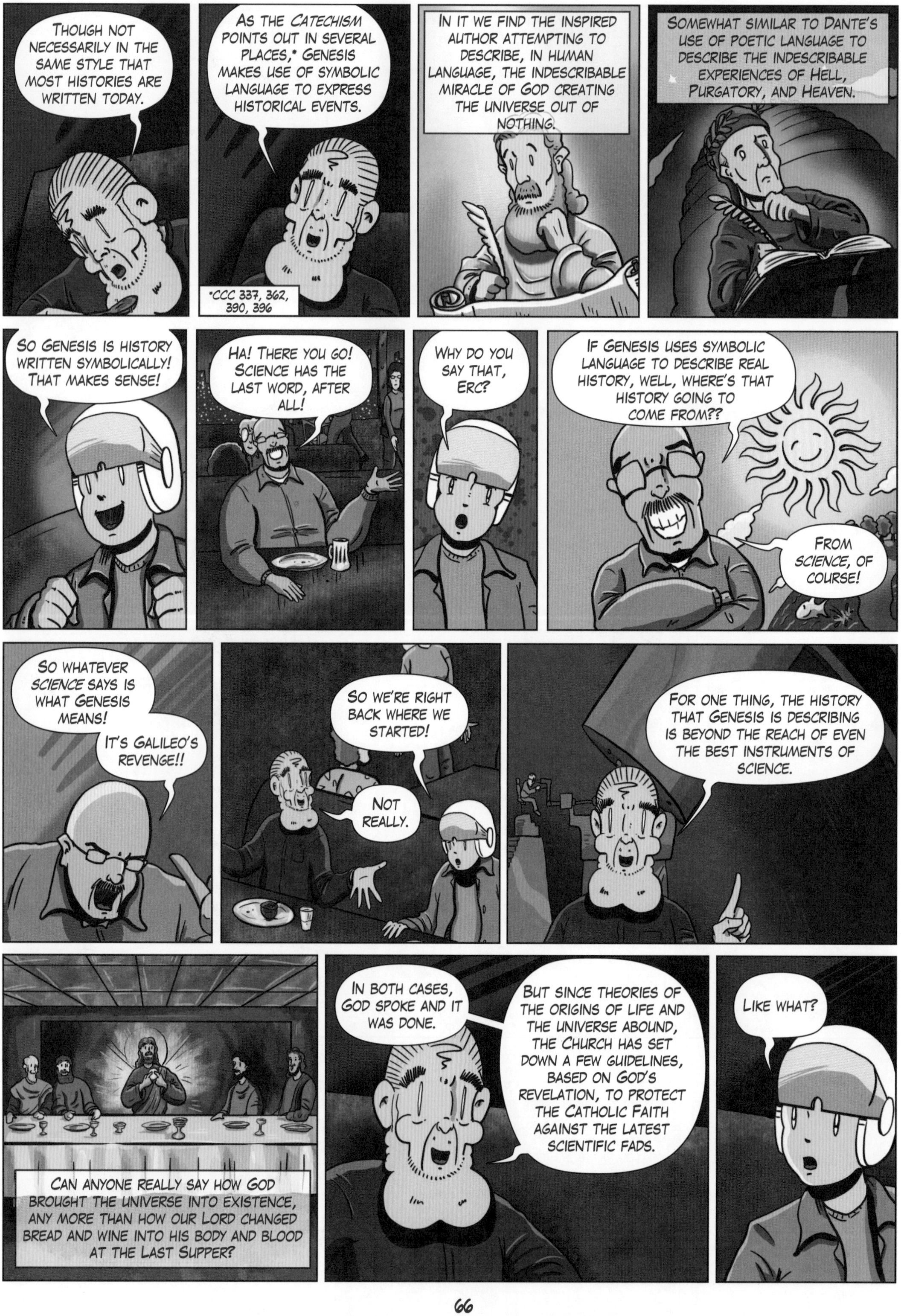
Though not necessarily in the same style that most histories are written today.
As the *Catechism* points out in several places,* Genesis makes use of symbolic language to express historical events.
*CCC 337, 362, 390, 396
In it we find the inspired author attempting to describe, in human language, the indescribable miracle of God creating the universe out of nothing.
Somewhat similar to Dante's use of poetic language to describe the indescribable experiences of Hell, Purgatory, and Heaven.
So Genesis is history written symbolically! That makes sense!
Ha! There you go! Science has the last word, after all!
Why do you say that, Erc?
If Genesis uses symbolic language to describe real history, well, where's that history going to come from??
From science, of course!
So whatever *science* says is what Genesis means!
It's Galileo's revenge!!
So we're right back where we started!
Not really.
For one thing, the history that Genesis is describing is beyond the reach of even the best instruments of science.
Can anyone really say how God brought the universe into existence, any more than how our Lord changed bread and wine into his body and blood at the Last Supper?
In both cases, God spoke and it was done.
But since theories of the origins of life and the universe abound, the Church has set down a few guidelines, based on God's revelation, to protect the Catholic Faith against the latest scientific fads.
Like what?

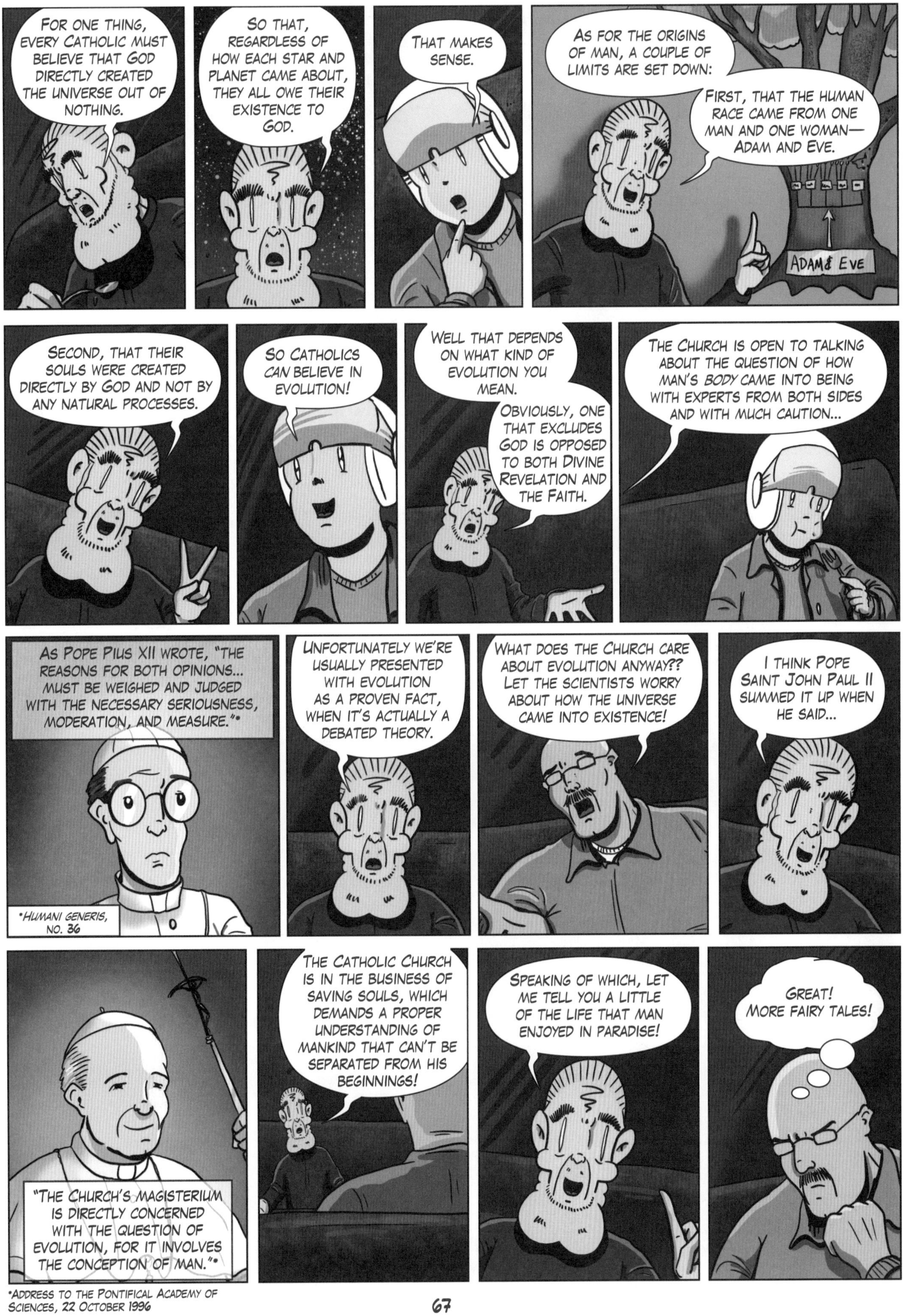
For one thing, every Catholic must believe that God directly created the universe out of nothing.
So that, regardless of how each star and planet came about, they all owe their existence to God.
That makes sense.
As for the origins of man, a couple of limits are set down:
First, that the human race came from one man and one woman— Adam and Eve.
Adam & Eve
Second, that their souls were created directly by God and not by any natural processes.
So Catholics can believe in evolution!
Well that depends on what kind of evolution you mean.
Obviously, one that excludes God is opposed to both Divine Revelation and the Faith.
The Church is open to talking about the question of how man's *body* came into being with experts from both sides and with much caution...
As Pope Pius XII wrote, "The reasons for both opinions... must be weighed and judged with the necessary seriousness, moderation, and measure."*
*Humani generis, no. 36
Unfortunately we're usually presented with evolution as a proven fact, when it's actually a debated theory.
What does the Church care about evolution anyway?? Let the scientists worry about how the universe came into existence!
I think Pope Saint John Paul II summed it up when he said...
"The Church's magisterium is directly concerned with the question of evolution, for it involves the conception of man."*
The Catholic Church is in the business of saving souls, which demands a proper understanding of mankind that can't be separated from his beginnings!
Speaking of which, let me tell you a little of the life that man enjoyed in paradise!
Great! More fairy tales!

*Address to the Pontifical Academy of Sciences, 22 October 1996

THEN THE LORD GOD FORMED MAN OF DUST FROM THE GROUND...

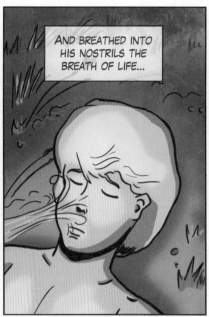

AND BREATHED INTO HIS NOSTRILS THE BREATH OF LIFE...

AND MAN BECAME A LIVING SOUL.

AND THE LORD GOD PLANTED A GARDEN IN EDEN, IN THE EAST; AND THERE HE PUT THE MAN WHOM HE HAD FORMED...TO TILL IT AND KEEP IT.

AND THE LORD GOD COMMANDED THE MAN, SAYING, "YOU MAY FREELY EAT OF EVERY TREE OF THE GARDEN; BUT OF THE TREE OF THE KNOWLEDGE OF GOOD AND EVIL YOU SHALL NOT EAT..."

"FOR IN THE DAY THAT YOU EAT OF IT YOU SHALL DIE."

THEN THE LORD GOD SAID, "IT IS NOT GOOD THAT THE MAN SHOULD BE ALONE; I WILL MAKE HIM A HELPER FIT FOR HIM."

SO OUT OF THE GROUND THE LORD GOD FORMED EVERY BEAST OF THE FIELD AND EVERY BIRD OF THE AIR, AND BROUGHT THEM TO THE MAN TO SEE WHAT HE WOULD CALL THEM...

UM, COW!

AND WHATEVER THE MAN CALLED EVERY LIVING CREATURE, THAT WAS ITS NAME.

ME?? A CHICKEN??

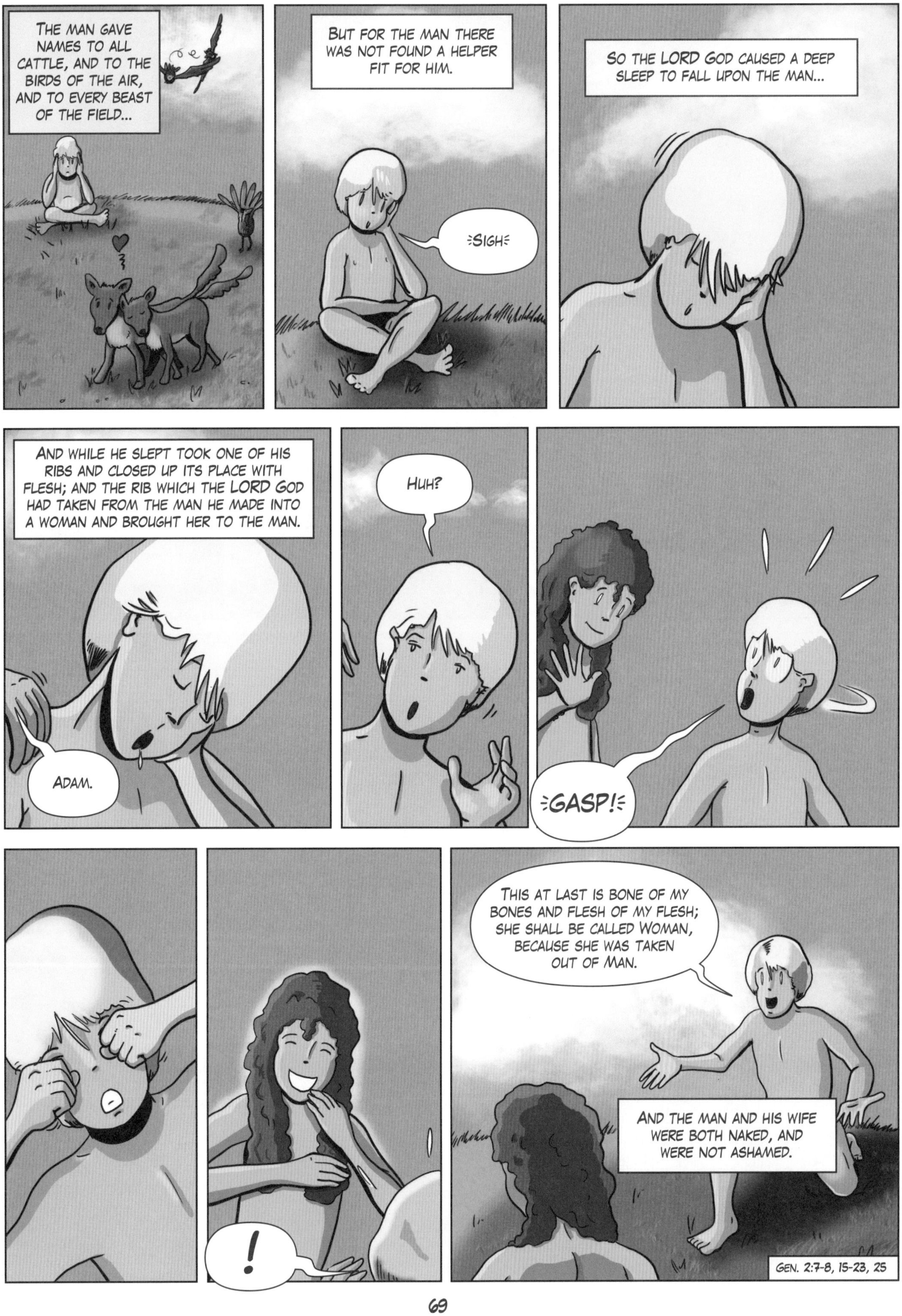
THE MAN GAVE NAMES TO ALL CATTLE, AND TO THE BIRDS OF THE AIR, AND TO EVERY BEAST OF THE FIELD...
BUT FOR THE MAN THERE WAS NOT FOUND A HELPER FIT FOR HIM.
SIGH
SO THE LORD GOD CAUSED A DEEP SLEEP TO FALL UPON THE MAN...
AND WHILE HE SLEPT TOOK ONE OF HIS RIBS AND CLOSED UP ITS PLACE WITH FLESH; AND THE RIB WHICH THE LORD GOD HAD TAKEN FROM THE MAN HE MADE INTO A WOMAN AND BROUGHT HER TO THE MAN.
ADAM.
HUH?
GASP!
!
THIS AT LAST IS BONE OF MY BONES AND FLESH OF MY FLESH; SHE SHALL BE CALLED WOMAN, BECAUSE SHE WAS TAKEN OUT OF MAN.
AND THE MAN AND HIS WIFE WERE BOTH NAKED, AND WERE NOT ASHAMED.
GEN. 2:7-8, 15-23, 25

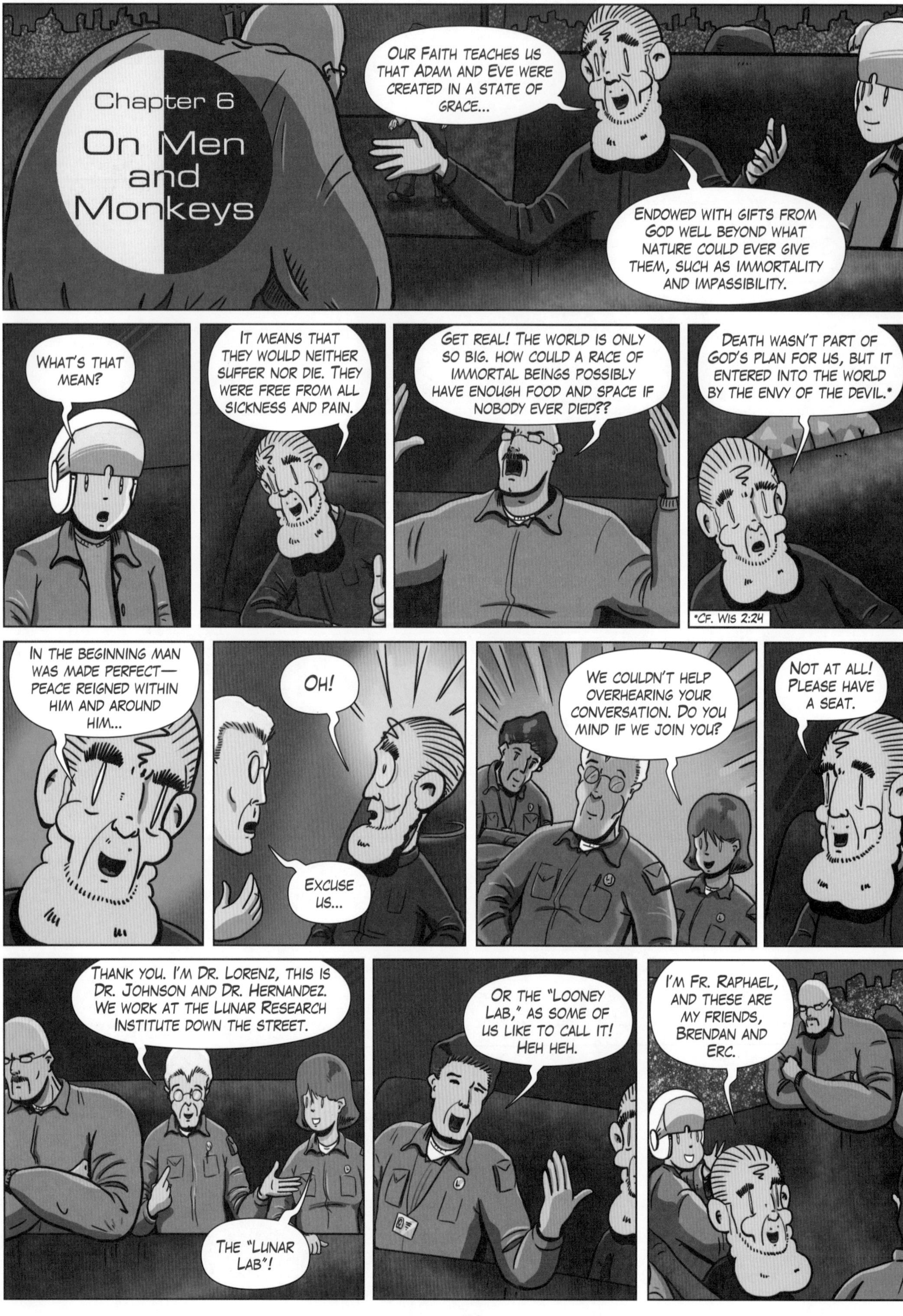

Chapter 6
On Men and Monkeys
Our Faith teaches us that Adam and Eve were created in a state of grace...
Endowed with gifts from God well beyond what nature could ever give them, such as immortality and impassibility.
What's that mean?
It means that they would neither suffer nor die. They were free from all sickness and pain.
Get real! The world is only so big. How could a race of immortal beings possibly have enough food and space if nobody ever died??
Death wasn't part of God's plan for us, but it entered into the world by the envy of the devil.*
*Cf. Wis 2:24
In the beginning man was made perfect—peace reigned within him and around him...
Oh!
Excuse us...
We couldn't help overhearing your conversation. Do you mind if we join you?
Not at all! Please have a seat.
Thank you. I'm Dr. Lorenz, this is Dr. Johnson and Dr. Hernandez. We work at the Lunar Research Institute down the street.
The "Lunar Lab"!
Or the "Looney Lab," as some of us like to call it! Heh heh.
I'm Fr. Raphael, and these are my friends, Brendan and Erc.

YOUR STORY OF EARLY MAN SOUNDS INTERESTING, BUT I'M AFRAID IT JUST DOESN'T FIT THE FACTS!

IT'S A SHAME THAT SO MANY PEOPLE MIX UP MYTHS WITH HISTORY AND CONFUSE THE MINDS OF OUR YOUTH.

THANKS TO MODERN SCIENCE, WE'RE CERTAIN THAT MAN EVOLVED FROM A LESS TO A MORE PERFECT STATE, AS DID ALL LIFE ON EARTH.

INDEED, OUR STORY BEGAN SEVERAL BILLION YEARS AGO, SHORTLY AFTER THE EARTH COOLED OFF, YET WHILE THE ATMOSPHERE STILL LACKED OXYGEN...

LIGHTNING SHOT THROUGH THE SKY, CREATING SIMPLE, ORGANIC, CHEMICAL COMPOUNDS ON THE FACE OF THE EARTH.

THESE FORMED INTO POOLS, WHICH WE CALL THE "PRIMORDIAL SOUP."

WHICH IS ANOTHER WAY OF SAYING POOLS RICH IN AMINO ACIDS—THE BUILDING BLOCKS OF LIFE!

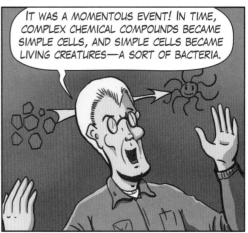

IT WAS A MOMENTOUS EVENT! IN TIME, COMPLEX CHEMICAL COMPOUNDS BECAME SIMPLE CELLS, AND SIMPLE CELLS BECAME LIVING CREATURES—A SORT OF BACTERIA.

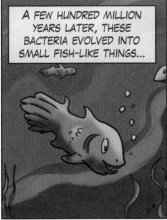

A FEW HUNDRED MILLION YEARS LATER, THESE BACTERIA EVOLVED INTO SMALL FISH-LIKE THINGS...

WHICH, IN TIME, CRAWLED ONTO DRY LAND AND BECAME THE FIRST DINOSAURS...

WHICH WERE EVENTUALLY REPLACED BY MAMMALS.

AND, FINALLY, THESE EVOLVED INTO HOMO SAPIENS, GRADUALLY BECOMING THE HUMAN BEINGS THAT DOMINATE THE EARTH TODAY!

IT'S JUST LIKE I'VE SAID, A LITTLE CHANCE AND A LOT OF TIME CAN EXPLAIN EVERYTHING!

I DON'T SEE WHY WE SHOULD THINK YOUR STORY MORE BELIEVABLE THAN THE ONE IN GENESIS.

BECAUSE IT'S SCIENTIFIC! BESIDES, EVERYONE KNOWS THAT EVOLUTION IS A FACT!

I THOUGHT IT WAS A THEORY.

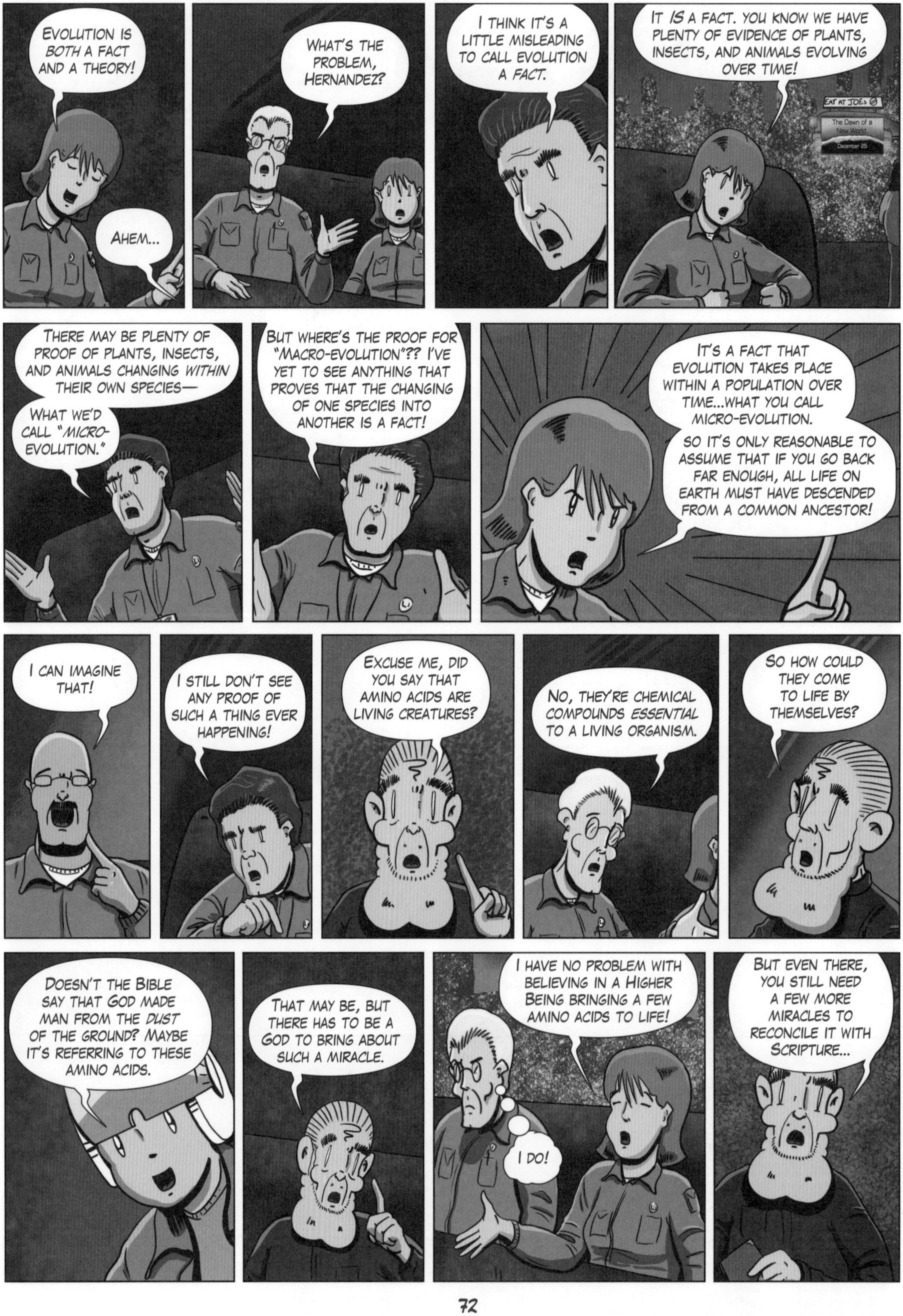
EVOLUTION IS *BOTH* A FACT AND A THEORY!
AHEM...
WHAT'S THE PROBLEM, HERNANDEZ?
I THINK IT'S A LITTLE MISLEADING TO CALL EVOLUTION A *FACT*.
IT *IS* A FACT. YOU KNOW WE HAVE PLENTY OF EVIDENCE OF PLANTS, INSECTS, AND ANIMALS EVOLVING OVER TIME!
EAT AT JOE'S
The Dawn of a New World
December 25
THERE MAY BE PLENTY OF PROOF OF PLANTS, INSECTS, AND ANIMALS CHANGING *WITHIN* THEIR OWN SPECIES—
WHAT WE'D CALL "*MICRO*-EVOLUTION."
BUT WHERE'S THE PROOF FOR "MACRO-EVOLUTION"?? I'VE YET TO SEE ANYTHING THAT PROVES THAT THE CHANGING OF ONE SPECIES INTO ANOTHER IS A FACT!
IT'S A FACT THAT EVOLUTION TAKES PLACE WITHIN A POPULATION OVER TIME...WHAT YOU CALL MICRO-EVOLUTION.
SO IT'S ONLY REASONABLE TO ASSUME THAT IF YOU GO BACK FAR ENOUGH, ALL LIFE ON EARTH MUST HAVE DESCENDED FROM A COMMON ANCESTOR!
I CAN IMAGINE THAT!
I STILL DON'T SEE ANY PROOF OF SUCH A THING EVER HAPPENING!
EXCUSE ME, DID YOU SAY THAT AMINO ACIDS ARE LIVING CREATURES?
NO, THEY'RE CHEMICAL COMPOUNDS *ESSENTIAL* TO A LIVING ORGANISM.
SO HOW COULD THEY COME TO LIFE BY THEMSELVES?
DOESN'T THE BIBLE SAY THAT GOD MADE MAN FROM THE *DUST* OF THE GROUND? MAYBE IT'S REFERRING TO THESE AMINO ACIDS.
THAT MAY BE, BUT THERE HAS TO BE A GOD TO BRING ABOUT SUCH A MIRACLE.
I HAVE NO PROBLEM WITH BELIEVING IN A HIGHER BEING BRINGING A FEW AMINO ACIDS TO LIFE!
I DO!
BUT EVEN THERE, YOU STILL NEED A FEW MORE MIRACLES TO RECONCILE IT WITH SCRIPTURE...

FOR INSTANCE, SINCE THE ENTIRE HUMAN RACE DESCENDED FROM ONLY TWO PEOPLE, THIS PROCESS COULDN'T HAVE BEEN REPEATED OVER AND OVER AGAIN.

AS WE READ, "THE MAN CALLED HIS WIFE'S NAME EVE, BECAUSE SHE WAS THE MOTHER OF ALL LIVING."*

*GEN 3:20

AND BOTH ADAM AND EVE RECEIVED THEIR SOULS *DIRECTLY* FROM GOD, WHO "BREATHED...THE BREATH OF LIFE; AND MAN BECAME A LIVING BEING."*

*GEN 2:7

BESIDES, POPE LEO XIII, SUMMING UP CATHOLIC TRADITION, TAUGHT THAT EVE WAS MIRACULOUSLY CREATED FROM THE SIDE OF ADAM.*

SO EVEN IF EVOLUTION WERE A FACT, YOU STILL NEED FAITH IN GOD'S MIRACULOUS INTERVENTIONS!

*ARCUM DIVINAE SAPIENTIAE

SPEAKING OF MIRACLES, HAS ANYONE EVER OBSERVED AMINO ACIDS FORMING OUTSIDE A LIVING BODY?

YES! STANLEY MILLER DID IN 1953, WHEN HE CREATED AMINO ACIDS USING ELECTRICITY AND AN ENVIRONMENT BASED ON A PRIMITIVE EARTH'S ATMOSPHERE.

ACTUALLY, THE "PRIMITIVE EARTH" ATMOSPHERE THAT MILLER USED TURNED OUT TO BE COMPLETELY INACCURATE!

MOST EXPERTS THINK THAT THE EARLY EARTH HAD AN ATMOSPHERE THAT INCLUDED *WATER VAPOR*, WHICH WOULD MAKE THE FORMATION OF AMINO ACIDS IMPOSSIBLE.

AND EVEN IF THEY DID FORM, HOW LONG COULD THEY SURVIVE? MILLER'S EXPERIMENT WAS DONE IN A LAB, WITH THE INTENTION TO CREATE AMINO ACIDS AND PRESERVE THEM...

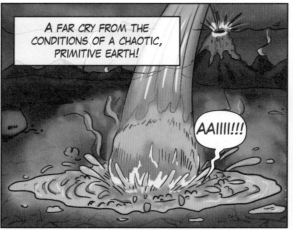
A FAR CRY FROM THE CONDITIONS OF A CHAOTIC, PRIMITIVE EARTH!

AAIIII!!!

ALL RIGHT, SO NOBODY REALLY KNOWS HOW THE FIRST LIVING THINGS APPEARED ON EARTH, BUT THAT DOESN'T MEAN EVOLUTION'S WRONG, DOES IT?

IT'S TRUE! THERE'S PLENTY OF PROOF FOR EVOLUTION FROM PALEONTOLOGY, BIOLOGY, HOMOLOGY, GENETICS...

REALLY?

SURE! LOOK AT THIS PICTURE, LITTLE BOY!

. . . LITTLE BOY??

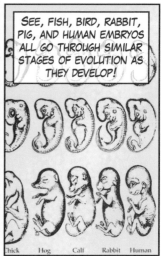
SEE, FISH, BIRD, RABBIT, PIG, AND HUMAN EMBRYOS ALL GO THROUGH SIMILAR STAGES OF EVOLUTION AS THEY DEVELOP!

Chick   Hog   Calf   Rabbit   Human

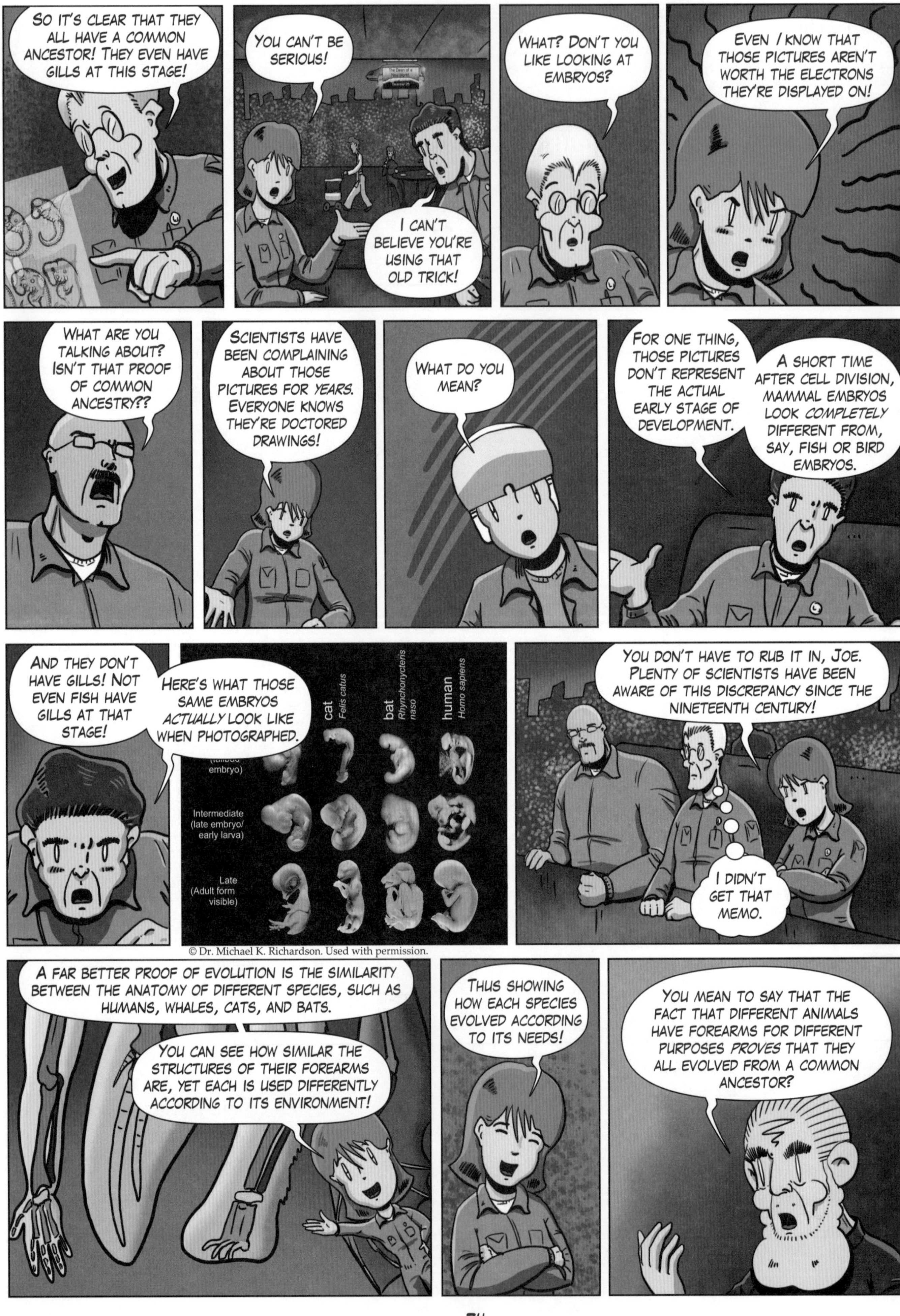

SO IT'S CLEAR THAT THEY ALL HAVE A COMMON ANCESTOR! THEY EVEN HAVE GILLS AT THIS STAGE!
YOU CAN'T BE SERIOUS!
I CAN'T BELIEVE YOU'RE USING THAT OLD TRICK!
WHAT? DON'T YOU LIKE LOOKING AT EMBRYOS?
EVEN I KNOW THAT THOSE PICTURES AREN'T WORTH THE ELECTRONS THEY'RE DISPLAYED ON!
WHAT ARE YOU TALKING ABOUT? ISN'T THAT PROOF OF COMMON ANCESTRY??
SCIENTISTS HAVE BEEN COMPLAINING ABOUT THOSE PICTURES FOR YEARS. EVERYONE KNOWS THEY'RE DOCTORED DRAWINGS!
WHAT DO YOU MEAN?
FOR ONE THING, THOSE PICTURES DON'T REPRESENT THE ACTUAL EARLY STAGE OF DEVELOPMENT.
A SHORT TIME AFTER CELL DIVISION, MAMMAL EMBRYOS LOOK COMPLETELY DIFFERENT FROM, SAY, FISH OR BIRD EMBRYOS.
AND THEY DON'T HAVE GILLS! NOT EVEN FISH HAVE GILLS AT THAT STAGE!
HERE'S WHAT THOSE SAME EMBRYOS ACTUALLY LOOK LIKE WHEN PHOTOGRAPHED.
cat
Felis catus
bat
Rhynchonycteris naso
human
Homo sapiens
embryo)
Intermediate (late embryo/ early larva)
Late (Adult form visible)
YOU DON'T HAVE TO RUB IT IN, JOE. PLENTY OF SCIENTISTS HAVE BEEN AWARE OF THIS DISCREPANCY SINCE THE NINETEENTH CENTURY!
I DIDN'T GET THAT MEMO.
A FAR BETTER PROOF OF EVOLUTION IS THE SIMILARITY BETWEEN THE ANATOMY OF DIFFERENT SPECIES, SUCH AS HUMANS, WHALES, CATS, AND BATS.
YOU CAN SEE HOW SIMILAR THE STRUCTURES OF THEIR FOREARMS ARE, YET EACH IS USED DIFFERENTLY ACCORDING TO ITS ENVIRONMENT!
THUS SHOWING HOW EACH SPECIES EVOLVED ACCORDING TO ITS NEEDS!
YOU MEAN TO SAY THAT THE FACT THAT DIFFERENT ANIMALS HAVE FOREARMS FOR DIFFERENT PURPOSES PROVES THAT THEY ALL EVOLVED FROM A COMMON ANCESTOR?

© Dr. Michael K. Richardson. Used with permission.

YES, SIMILAR SKELETAL COMPONENTS USED FOR DIFFERENT PURPOSES SHOWS THAT THEY MUST HAVE EVOLVED FROM A COMMON ANCESTOR!

WOULDN'T IT BE MORE TRUE TO SAY THAT THEIR SIMILARITIES POINT TO A COMMON *CREATOR?*

IT SOUNDS AS IF YOU'RE STARTING WITH THE *ASSUMPTION* THAT THESE ANIMALS EVOLVED AND THEN POINTING TO THEIR SIMILARITIES AS PROOF...

LIKE SAYING THAT VARIOUS UTENSILS EVOLVED FROM A COMMON ANCESTOR, BECAUSE THEY HAVE SIMILAR HANDLES.

BUT, IN FACT, THEIR SIMILARITY COMES FROM BEING DESIGNED BY THE SAME *MIND!*

WITH ALL DUE RESPECT, FATHER, THERE'S MORE TO IT THAN THAT.

HE'S RIGHT! SIMILARITY BETWEEN GROUPS OF THINGS DOESN'T EXPLAIN HOW THAT SIMILARITY CAME ABOUT!

AND BESIDES, IF SIMILARITY PROVED THAT ONE THING EVOLVED FROM ANOTHER, WHY NOT LOOK AT THE HEART OF A PIG AND A MAN—BOTH ARE HOMOLOGOUS!

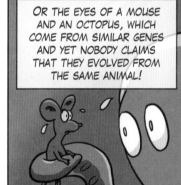

OR THE EYES OF A MOUSE AND AN OCTOPUS, WHICH COME FROM SIMILAR GENES AND YET NOBODY CLAIMS THAT THEY EVOLVED FROM THE SAME ANIMAL!

OH? WHAT ABOUT VESTIGIAL ORGANS?

DIGITAL ORGANS?

VESTIGIAL! THESE ARE USELESS ORGANS IN HUMANS AND OTHER ANIMALS THAT PROVE THEY EVOLVED FROM A LESS TO A MORE PERFECT FORM!

FOR INSTANCE, THE HUMAN APPENDIX MAY HAVE ONCE BEEN A SECOND STOMACH THAT WAS NO LONGER NEEDED AS MAN EVOLVED!

MOO?

HA! THAT'S WHAT THEY SAID ABOUT TONSILS BEFORE THEY DISCOVERED *THEIR* USEFULNESS!

NOW IT'S WELL KNOWN THAT TONSILS ARE ACTUALLY VERY USEFUL IN PROTECTING THE BODY AGAINST DISEASE!

JUST BECAUSE YOU DON'T KNOW WHAT A THING DOES, DOESN'T MAKE IT USELESS!

ALL THE SAME, THE BEST PROOF FOR EVOLUTION COMES FROM THE FOSSIL RECORD.

JUST AS DARWIN PREDICTED, THE EVOLUTION OF ONE SPECIES INTO ANOTHER IS EASILY VERIFIABLE BY THE MANY FOSSILS FOUND SHOWING VARIOUS TRANSITIONAL FORMS.

YES, THIS REPTILE-BIRD IS A PERFECT EXAMPLE OF THE EVOLUTION OF ONE SPECIES INTO ANOTHER!

≥GASP!≤ A DINOSAUR-BIRD!

NO, JUST AN ANCIENT BIRD, CALLED THE ARCHAEOPTERYX.

YET EVEN IF IT WERE HALF REPTILE, HALF BIRD, THAT HARDLY MAKES IT A MISSING LINK! LOOK AT THE BAT OR THE PLATYPUS!

BY THAT LOGIC, BATS MUST HAVE EVOLVED FROM MICE, AND DUCKS FROM PLATYPUSES!

BUT NOBODY THINKS SUCH NONSENSE!

AND IF ARCHAEOPTERYX IS THE TRANSITIONAL FORM OF REPTILES BECOMING BIRDS, HOW DO YOU EXPLAIN PROTOAVIS, WHICH IS 65 TO 75 MILLION YEARS OLDER AND YET MORE BIRDLIKE?

SO MUCH FOR YOUR MISSING LINK!

FAR FROM IT! LOOK AT THE THOUSANDS OF FOSSILS THAT SHOW THE EVOLUTION OF HUMANS FROM HOMINIDS.

HOW DO YOU KNOW THAT MAN EVOLVED FROM THESE "HOMINIDS"?

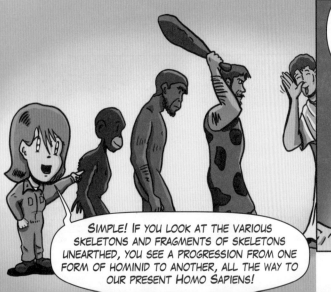

SIMPLE! IF YOU LOOK AT THE VARIOUS SKELETONS AND FRAGMENTS OF SKELETONS UNEARTHED, YOU SEE A PROGRESSION FROM ONE FORM OF HOMINID TO ANOTHER, ALL THE WAY TO OUR PRESENT HOMO SAPIENS!

BUT SURELY YOU CAN'T UNEARTH THE ONE THING THAT MAKES ANY OF THESE SKELETONS HUMAN, AND NOT ANIMAL...

THE FACT THAT THEY HAD REASON!

BESIDES, AS SOMEONE POINTED OUT, SCIENTISTS SEEM TO KNOW EVERYTHING ABOUT THE MISSING LINK EXCEPT THE FACT THAT IT'S MISSING!

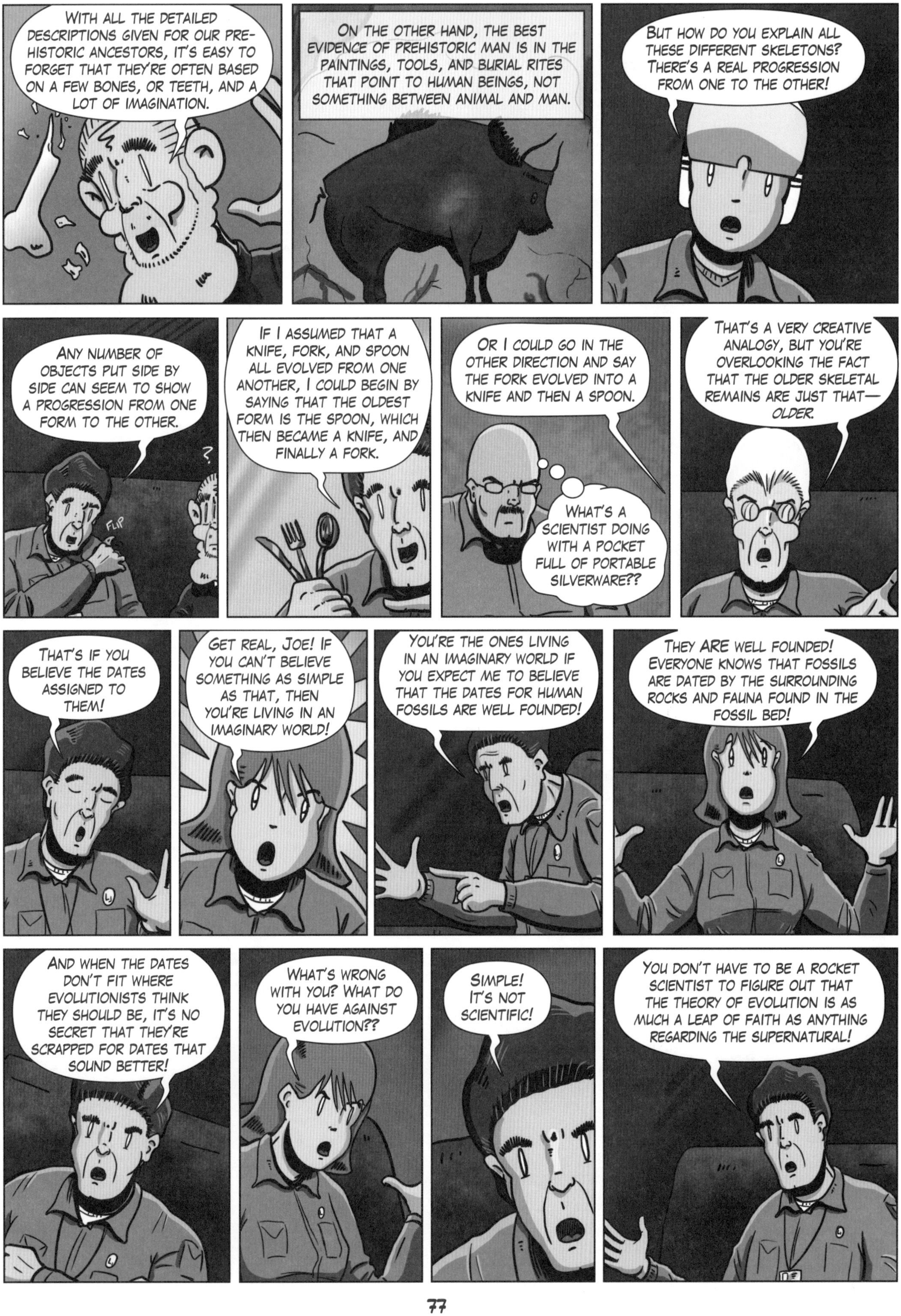
WITH ALL THE DETAILED DESCRIPTIONS GIVEN FOR OUR PREHISTORIC ANCESTORS, IT'S EASY TO FORGET THAT THEY'RE OFTEN BASED ON A FEW BONES, OR TEETH, AND A LOT OF IMAGINATION.
ON THE OTHER HAND, THE BEST EVIDENCE OF PREHISTORIC MAN IS IN THE PAINTINGS, TOOLS, AND BURIAL RITES THAT POINT TO HUMAN BEINGS, NOT SOMETHING BETWEEN ANIMAL AND MAN.
BUT HOW DO YOU EXPLAIN ALL THESE DIFFERENT SKELETONS? THERE'S A REAL PROGRESSION FROM ONE TO THE OTHER!
ANY NUMBER OF OBJECTS PUT SIDE BY SIDE CAN SEEM TO SHOW A PROGRESSION FROM ONE FORM TO THE OTHER.
?
FLIP
IF I ASSUMED THAT A KNIFE, FORK, AND SPOON ALL EVOLVED FROM ONE ANOTHER, I COULD BEGIN BY SAYING THAT THE OLDEST FORM IS THE SPOON, WHICH THEN BECAME A KNIFE, AND FINALLY A FORK.
OR I COULD GO IN THE OTHER DIRECTION AND SAY THE FORK EVOLVED INTO A KNIFE AND THEN A SPOON.
WHAT'S A SCIENTIST DOING WITH A POCKET FULL OF PORTABLE SILVERWARE??
THAT'S A VERY CREATIVE ANALOGY, BUT YOU'RE OVERLOOKING THE FACT THAT THE OLDER SKELETAL REMAINS ARE JUST THAT—*OLDER*.
THAT'S IF YOU BELIEVE THE DATES ASSIGNED TO THEM!
GET REAL, JOE! IF YOU CAN'T BELIEVE SOMETHING AS SIMPLE AS THAT, THEN YOU'RE LIVING IN AN IMAGINARY WORLD!
YOU'RE THE ONES LIVING IN AN IMAGINARY WORLD IF YOU EXPECT ME TO BELIEVE THAT THE DATES FOR HUMAN FOSSILS ARE WELL FOUNDED!
THEY **ARE** WELL FOUNDED! EVERYONE KNOWS THAT FOSSILS ARE DATED BY THE SURROUNDING ROCKS AND FAUNA FOUND IN THE FOSSIL BED!
AND WHEN THE DATES DON'T FIT WHERE EVOLUTIONISTS THINK THEY SHOULD BE, IT'S NO SECRET THAT THEY'RE SCRAPPED FOR DATES THAT SOUND BETTER!
WHAT'S WRONG WITH YOU? WHAT DO YOU HAVE AGAINST EVOLUTION??
SIMPLE! IT'S NOT SCIENTIFIC!
YOU DON'T HAVE TO BE A ROCKET SCIENTIST TO FIGURE OUT THAT THE THEORY OF EVOLUTION IS AS MUCH A LEAP OF FAITH AS ANYTHING REGARDING THE SUPERNATURAL!

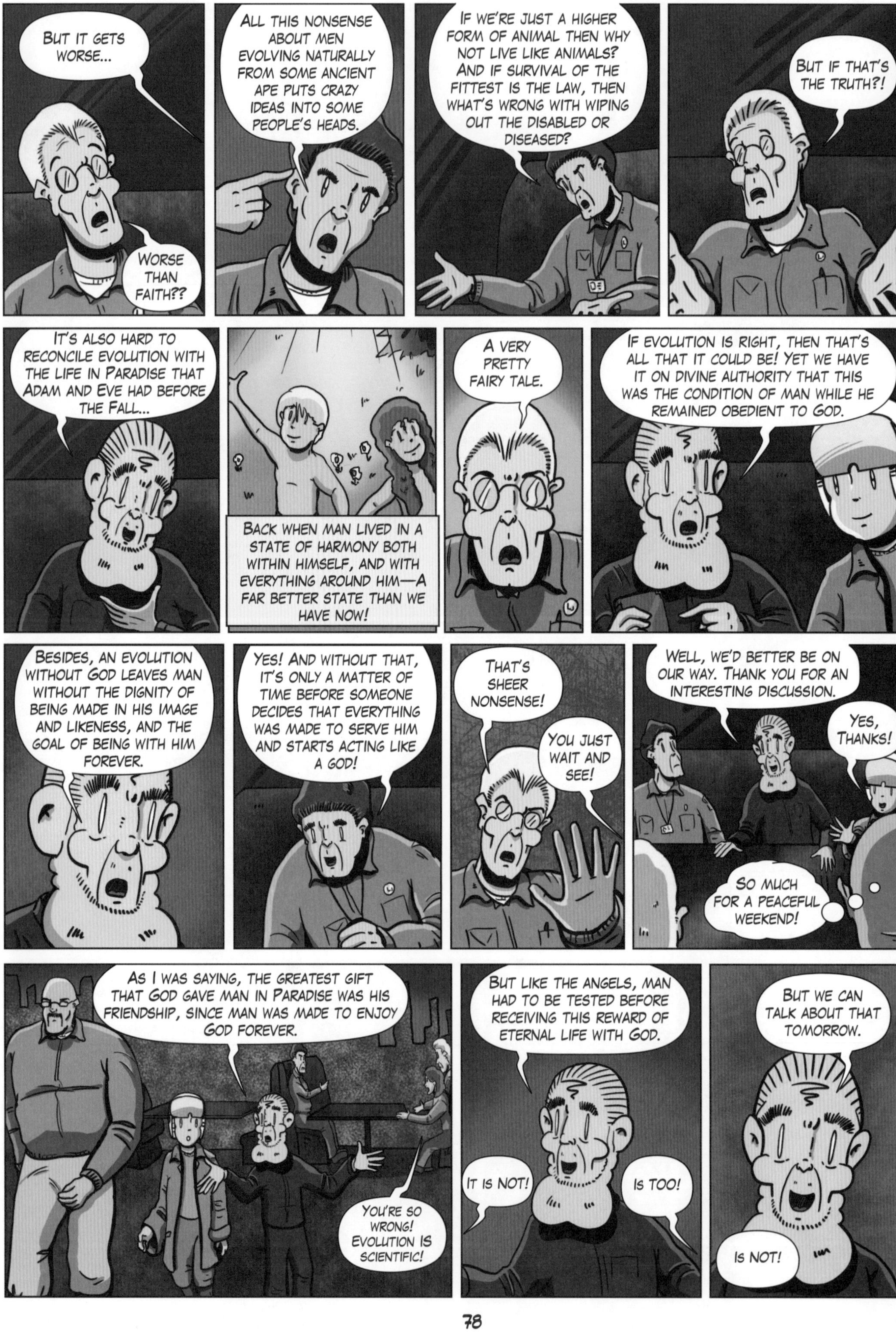
BUT IT GETS WORSE...
WORSE THAN FAITH??
ALL THIS NONSENSE ABOUT MEN EVOLVING NATURALLY FROM SOME ANCIENT APE PUTS CRAZY IDEAS INTO SOME PEOPLE'S HEADS.
IF WE'RE JUST A HIGHER FORM OF ANIMAL THEN WHY NOT LIVE LIKE ANIMALS? AND IF SURVIVAL OF THE FITTEST IS THE LAW, THEN WHAT'S WRONG WITH WIPING OUT THE DISABLED OR DISEASED?
BUT IF THAT'S THE TRUTH?!
IT'S ALSO HARD TO RECONCILE EVOLUTION WITH THE LIFE IN PARADISE THAT ADAM AND EVE HAD BEFORE THE FALL...
BACK WHEN MAN LIVED IN A STATE OF HARMONY BOTH WITHIN HIMSELF, AND WITH EVERYTHING AROUND HIM—A FAR BETTER STATE THAN WE HAVE NOW!
A VERY PRETTY FAIRY TALE.
IF EVOLUTION IS RIGHT, THEN THAT'S ALL THAT IT COULD BE! YET WE HAVE IT ON DIVINE AUTHORITY THAT THIS WAS THE CONDITION OF MAN WHILE HE REMAINED OBEDIENT TO GOD.
BESIDES, AN EVOLUTION WITHOUT GOD LEAVES MAN WITHOUT THE DIGNITY OF BEING MADE IN HIS IMAGE AND LIKENESS, AND THE GOAL OF BEING WITH HIM FOREVER.
YES! AND WITHOUT THAT, IT'S ONLY A MATTER OF TIME BEFORE SOMEONE DECIDES THAT EVERYTHING WAS MADE TO SERVE HIM AND STARTS ACTING LIKE A GOD!
THAT'S SHEER NONSENSE!
YOU JUST WAIT AND SEE!
WELL, WE'D BETTER BE ON OUR WAY. THANK YOU FOR AN INTERESTING DISCUSSION.
YES, THANKS!
SO MUCH FOR A PEACEFUL WEEKEND!
AS I WAS SAYING, THE GREATEST GIFT THAT GOD GAVE MAN IN PARADISE WAS HIS FRIENDSHIP, SINCE MAN WAS MADE TO ENJOY GOD FOREVER.
YOU'RE SO WRONG! EVOLUTION IS SCIENTIFIC!
BUT LIKE THE ANGELS, MAN HAD TO BE TESTED BEFORE RECEIVING THIS REWARD OF ETERNAL LIFE WITH GOD.
IT IS NOT!
IS TOO!
BUT WE CAN TALK ABOUT THAT TOMORROW.
IS NOT!

PART IV:
THE FALL AND THE
PROMISE

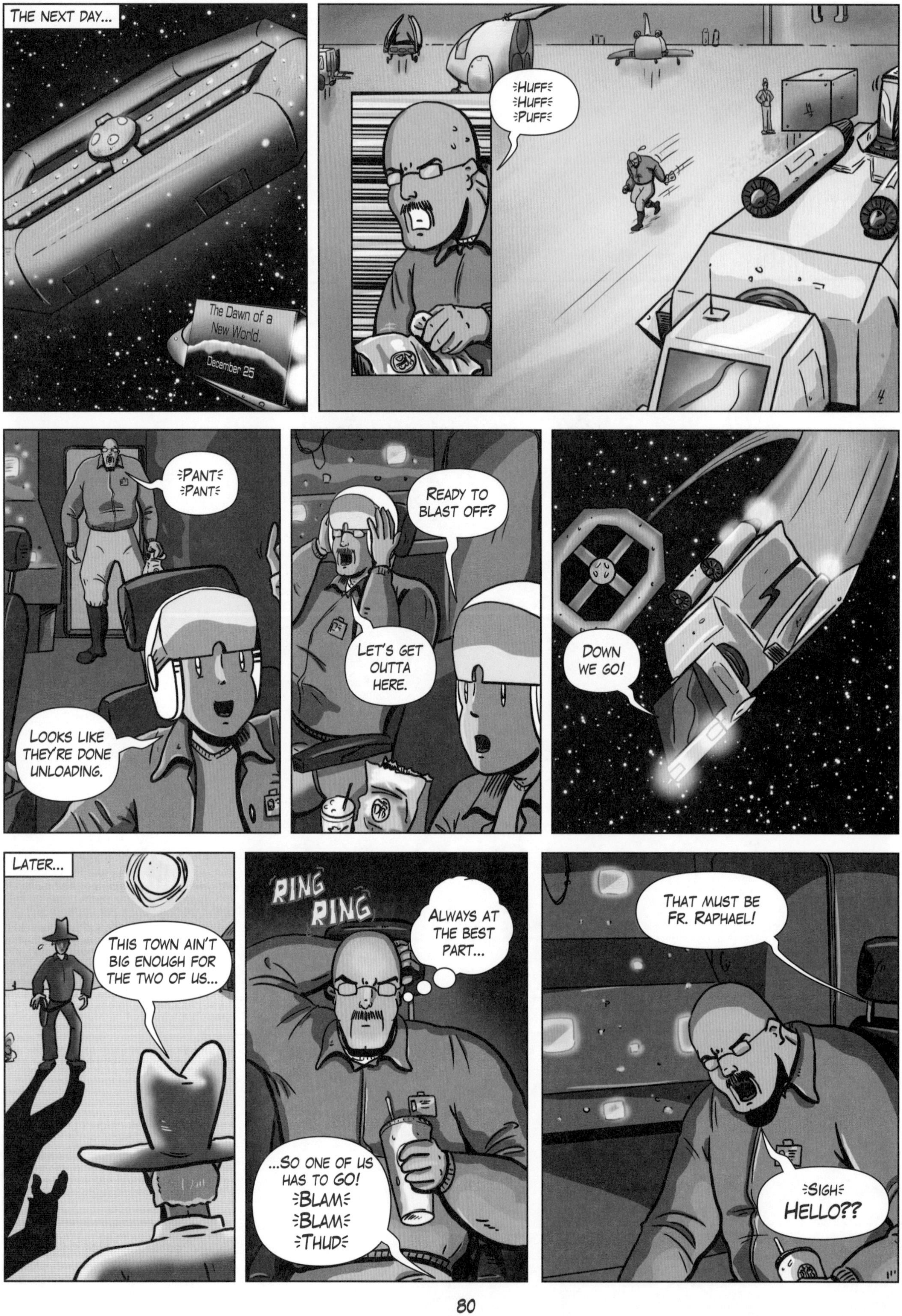

The next day...
The Dawn of a New World.
December 25
Huff
Huff
Puff
Pant
Pant
Looks like they're done unloading.
Ready to blast off?
Let's get outta here.
Down we go!
Later...
This town ain't big enough for the two of us...
Ring
Ring
Always at the best part...
...So one of us has to go!
Blam
Blam
Thud
That must be Fr. Raphael!
Sigh
Hello??

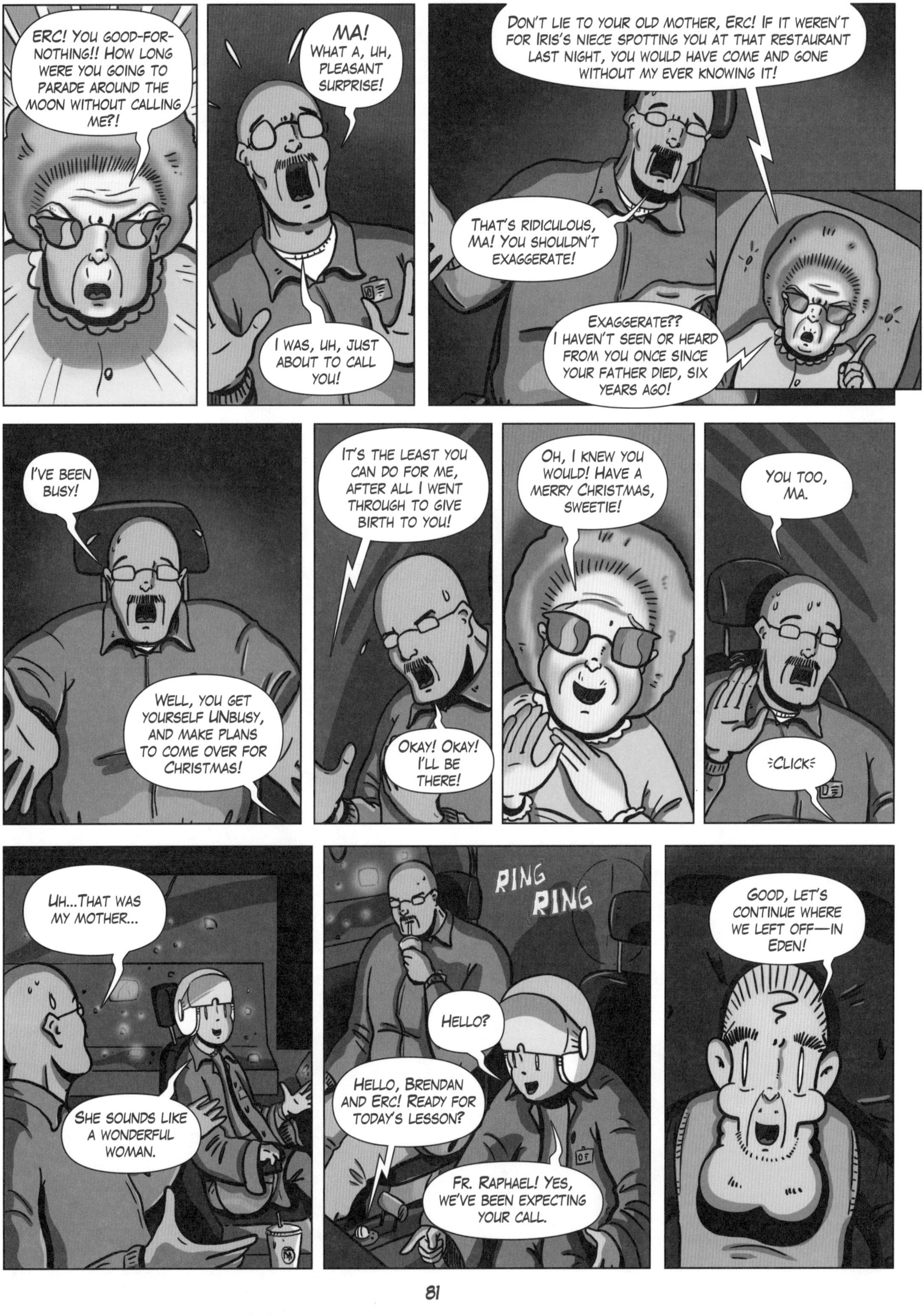
ERC! YOU GOOD-FOR-NOTHING!! HOW LONG WERE YOU GOING TO PARADE AROUND THE MOON WITHOUT CALLING ME?!
MA! WHAT A, UH, PLEASANT SURPRISE!
I WAS, UH, JUST ABOUT TO CALL YOU!
DON'T LIE TO YOUR OLD MOTHER, ERC! IF IT WEREN'T FOR IRIS'S NIECE SPOTTING YOU AT THAT RESTAURANT LAST NIGHT, YOU WOULD HAVE COME AND GONE WITHOUT MY EVER KNOWING IT!
THAT'S RIDICULOUS, MA! YOU SHOULDN'T EXAGGERATE!
EXAGGERATE?? I HAVEN'T SEEN OR HEARD FROM YOU ONCE SINCE YOUR FATHER DIED, SIX YEARS AGO!
I'VE BEEN BUSY!
WELL, YOU GET YOURSELF UNBUSY, AND MAKE PLANS TO COME OVER FOR CHRISTMAS!
IT'S THE LEAST YOU CAN DO FOR ME, AFTER ALL I WENT THROUGH TO GIVE BIRTH TO YOU!
OKAY! OKAY! I'LL BE THERE!
OH, I KNEW YOU WOULD! HAVE A MERRY CHRISTMAS, SWEETIE!
YOU TOO, MA.
CLICK
UH...THAT WAS MY MOTHER...
SHE SOUNDS LIKE A WONDERFUL WOMAN.
RING RING
HELLO?
HELLO, BRENDAN AND ERC! READY FOR TODAY'S LESSON?
FR. RAPHAEL! YES, WE'VE BEEN EXPECTING YOUR CALL.
GOOD, LET'S CONTINUE WHERE WE LEFT OFF—IN EDEN!

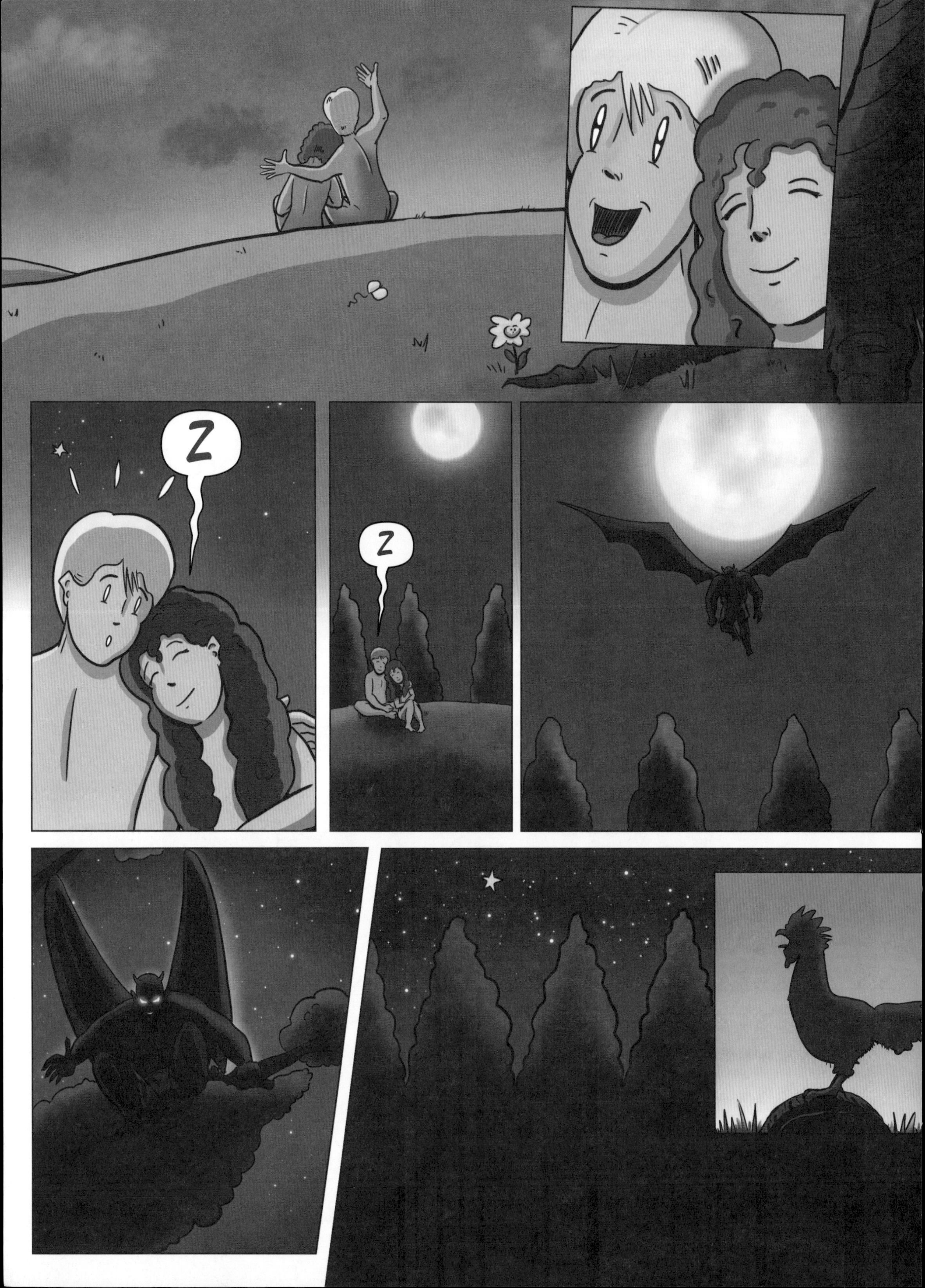
Z
Z

NOW THE SERPENT WAS MORE SUBTLE THAN ANY OTHER WILD CREATURE THAT THE LORD GOD HAD MADE...

DID GOD SAY, "YOU SHALL NOT EAT OF ANY TREE OF THE GARDEN"?

WE MAY EAT OF THE FRUIT OF THE TREES OF THE GARDEN...

BUT GOD SAID, "YOU SHALL NOT EAT OF THE FRUIT OF THE TREE WHICH IS IN THE MIDST OF THE GARDEN, NEITHER SHALL YOU TOUCH IT, LEST YOU DIE."

YOU WILL NOT DIE. FOR GOD KNOWS THAT WHEN YOU EAT OF IT YOUR EYES WILL BE OPENED, AND YOU WILL BE LIKE GOD, KNOWING GOOD AND EVIL.

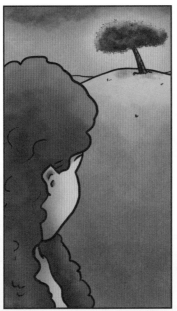

SO WHEN THE WOMAN SAW THAT THE TREE WAS GOOD FOR FOOD, AND THAT IT WAS A DELIGHT TO THE EYES...

AND THAT THE TREE WAS TO BE DESIRED TO MAKE ONE WISE, SHE TOOK OF ITS FRUIT AND ATE.

AND SHE ALSO GAVE SOME TO HER HUSBAND, AND HE ATE.

THEN THE EYES OF BOTH WERE OPENED, AND THEY KNEW THAT THEY WERE NAKED...

AND THEY SEWED FIG LEAVES TOGETHER AND MADE THEMSELVES APRONS. AND THEY HEARD THE SOUND OF THE LORD GOD WALKING IN THE GARDEN IN THE COOL OF THE DAY.

AND THE MAN AND HIS WIFE HID THEMSELVES FROM THE PRESENCE OF THE LORD GOD AMONG THE TREES OF THE GARDEN.

ADAM, WHERE ARE YOU?

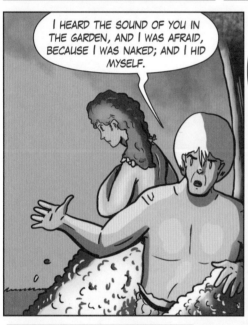

I HEARD THE SOUND OF YOU IN THE GARDEN, AND I WAS AFRAID, BECAUSE I WAS NAKED; AND I HID MYSELF.

WHO TOLD YOU THAT YOU WERE NAKED? HAVE YOU EATEN OF THE TREE OF WHICH I COMMANDED YOU NOT TO EAT?

THE WOMAN WHOM YOU GAVE TO BE WITH ME, SHE GAVE ME FRUIT OF THE TREE, AND I ATE.

THE SERPENT TRICKED ME INTO IT, SO I ATE IT.

BECAUSE YOU HAVE DONE THIS, CURSED ARE YOU... UPON YOUR BELLY YOU SHALL GO, AND DUST YOU SHALL EAT ALL THE DAYS OF YOUR LIFE.

⋕HISS⋕

I WILL PUT ENMITY BETWEEN YOU AND THE WOMAN, AND BETWEEN YOUR SEED AND HER SEED; HE SHALL BRUISE YOUR HEAD, AND YOU SHALL BRUISE HIS HEEL.

I WILL GREATLY MULTIPLY YOUR PAIN IN CHILDBEARING; IN PAIN YOU SHALL BRING FORTH CHILDREN, YET YOUR DESIRE SHALL BE FOR YOUR HUSBAND, AND HE SHALL RULE OVER YOU.

BECAUSE YOU HAVE LISTENED TO THE VOICE OF YOUR WIFE, AND HAVE EATEN OF THE TREE... IN THE SWEAT OF YOUR FACE YOU SHALL EAT BREAD TILL YOU RETURN TO THE GROUND, FOR OUT OF IT YOU WERE TAKEN; YOU ARE DUST, AND TO DUST YOU SHALL RETURN.

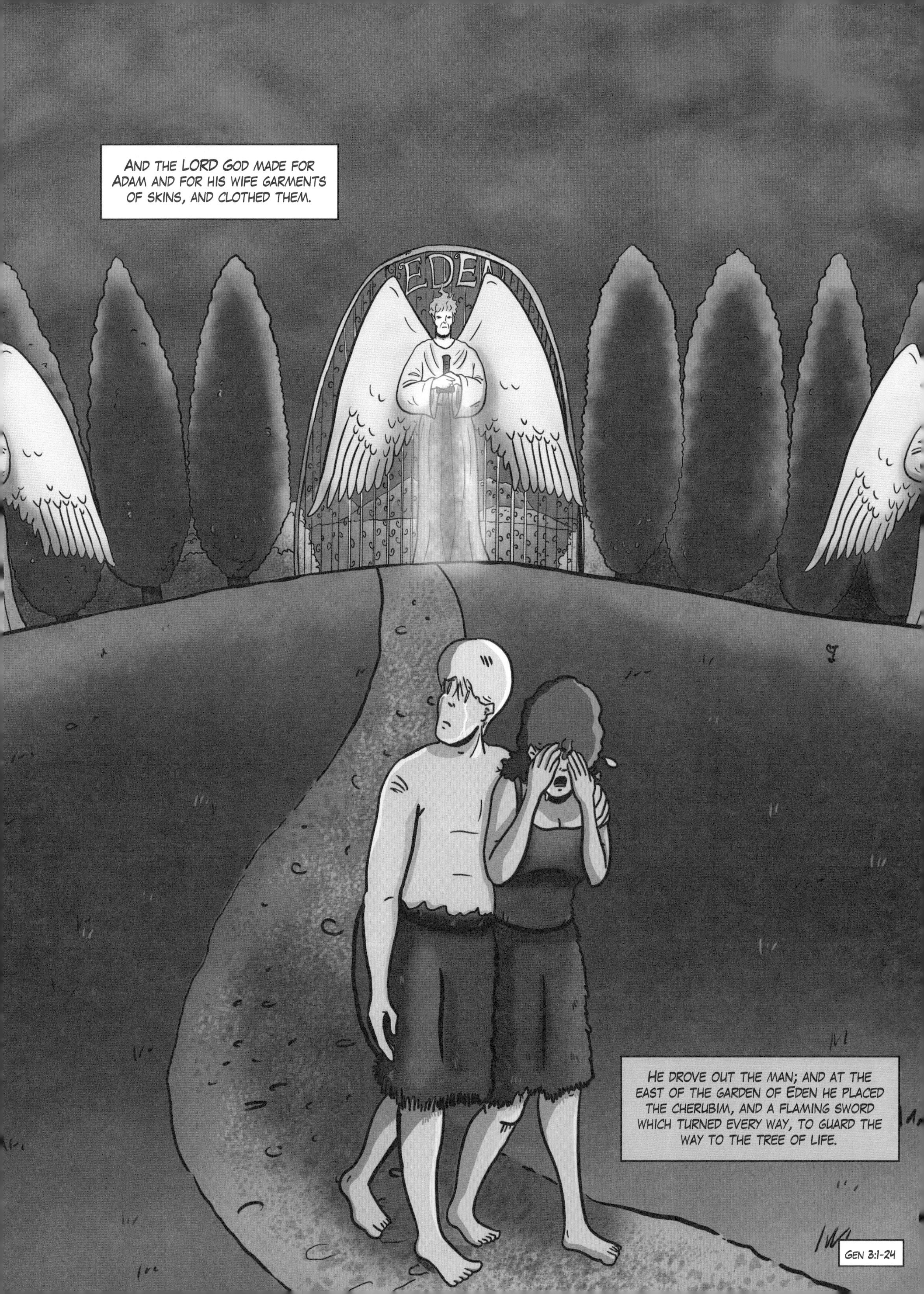
AND THE LORD GOD MADE FOR ADAM AND FOR HIS WIFE GARMENTS OF SKINS, AND CLOTHED THEM.
EDEN
HE DROVE OUT THE MAN; AND AT THE EAST OF THE GARDEN OF EDEN HE PLACED THE CHERUBIM, AND A FLAMING SWORD WHICH TURNED EVERY WAY, TO GUARD THE WAY TO THE TREE OF LIFE.
GEN 3:1-24

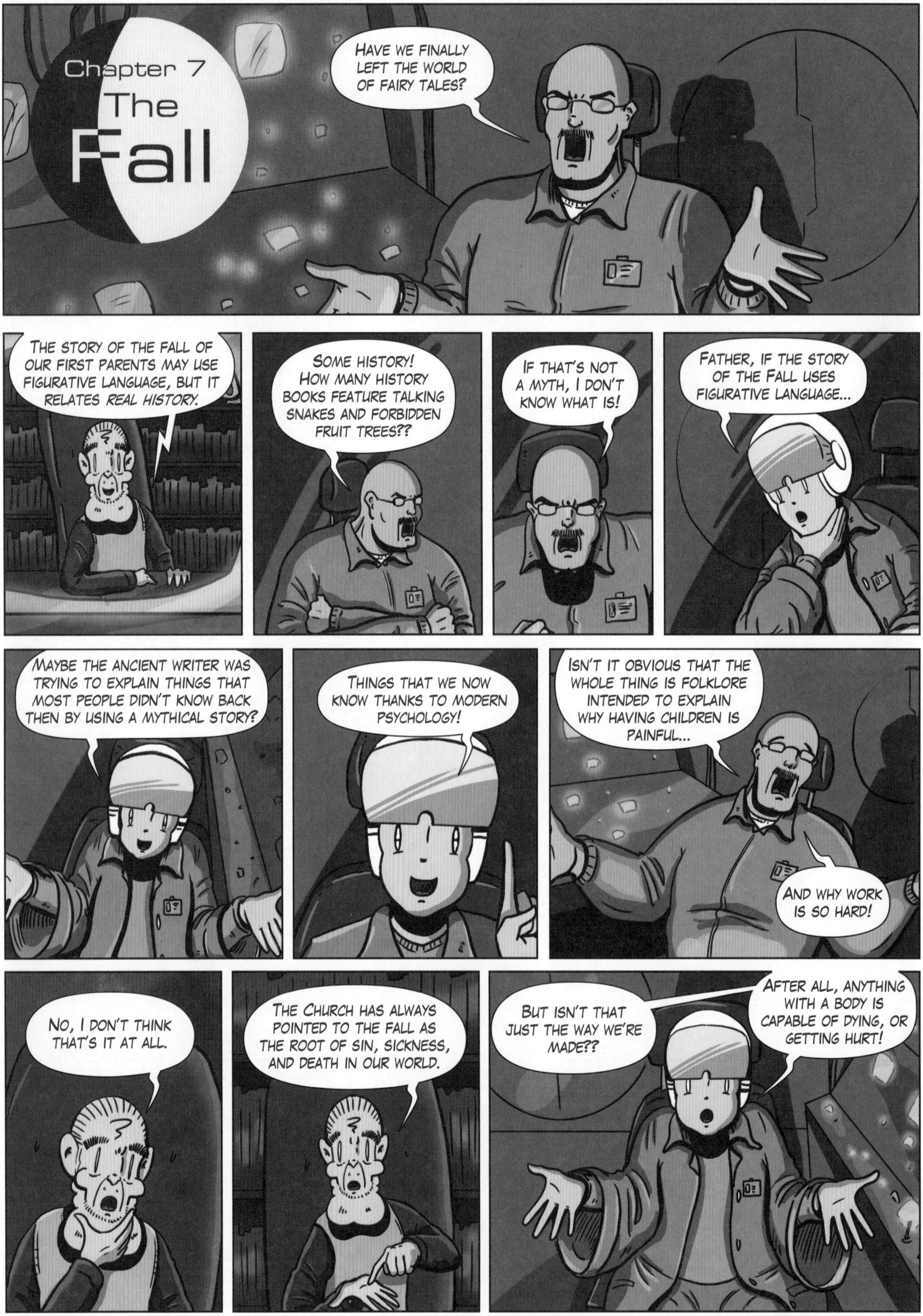
Chapter 7
The Fall
Have we finally left the world of fairy tales?
The story of the fall of our first parents may use figurative language, but it relates *real history*.
Some history! How many history books feature talking snakes and forbidden fruit trees??
If that's not a myth, I don't know what is!
Father, if the story of the Fall uses figurative language...
Maybe the ancient writer was trying to explain things that most people didn't know back then by using a mythical story?
Things that we now know thanks to modern psychology!
Isn't it obvious that the whole thing is folklore intended to explain why having children is painful...
And why work is so hard!
No, I don't think that's it at all.
The Church has always pointed to the Fall as the root of sin, sickness, and death in our world.
But isn't that just the way we're made??
After all, anything with a body is capable of dying, or getting hurt!

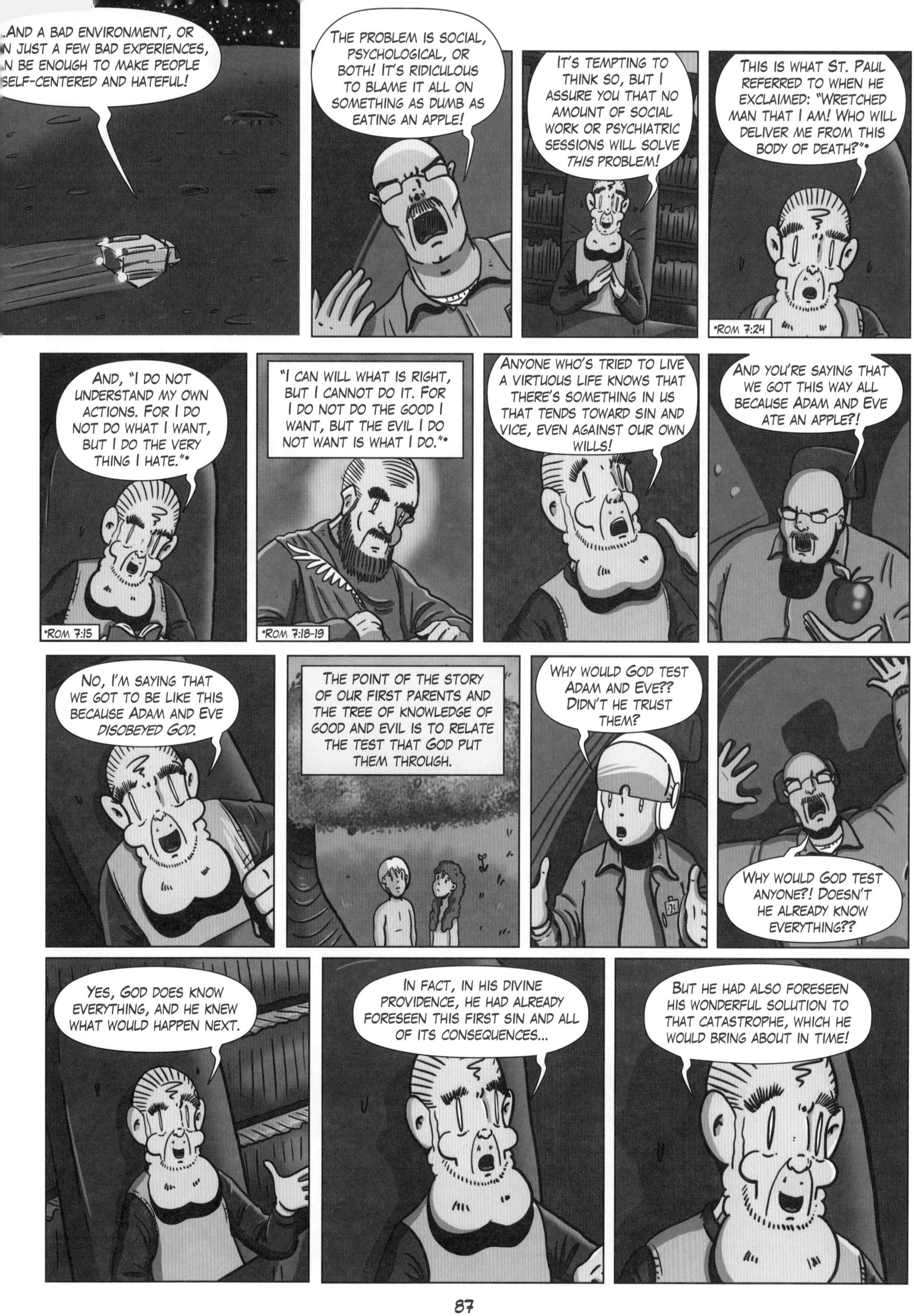
.AND A BAD ENVIRONMENT, OR
N JUST A FEW BAD EXPERIENCES,
N BE ENOUGH TO MAKE PEOPLE
SELF-CENTERED AND HATEFUL!
THE PROBLEM IS SOCIAL, PSYCHOLOGICAL, OR BOTH! IT'S RIDICULOUS TO BLAME IT ALL ON SOMETHING AS DUMB AS EATING AN APPLE!
IT'S TEMPTING TO THINK SO, BUT I ASSURE YOU THAT NO AMOUNT OF SOCIAL WORK OR PSYCHIATRIC SESSIONS WILL SOLVE THIS PROBLEM!
THIS IS WHAT ST. PAUL REFERRED TO WHEN HE EXCLAIMED: "WRETCHED MAN THAT I AM! WHO WILL DELIVER ME FROM THIS BODY OF DEATH?"*
*ROM 7:24
AND, "I DO NOT UNDERSTAND MY OWN ACTIONS. FOR I DO NOT DO WHAT I WANT, BUT I DO THE VERY THING I HATE."*
*ROM 7:15
"I CAN WILL WHAT IS RIGHT, BUT I CANNOT DO IT. FOR I DO NOT DO THE GOOD I WANT, BUT THE EVIL I DO NOT WANT IS WHAT I DO."*
*ROM 7:18-19
ANYONE WHO'S TRIED TO LIVE A VIRTUOUS LIFE KNOWS THAT THERE'S SOMETHING IN US THAT TENDS TOWARD SIN AND VICE, EVEN AGAINST OUR OWN WILLS!
AND YOU'RE SAYING THAT WE GOT THIS WAY ALL BECAUSE ADAM AND EVE ATE AN APPLE?!
NO, I'M SAYING THAT WE GOT TO BE LIKE THIS BECAUSE ADAM AND EVE DISOBEYED GOD.
THE POINT OF THE STORY OF OUR FIRST PARENTS AND THE TREE OF KNOWLEDGE OF GOOD AND EVIL IS TO RELATE THE TEST THAT GOD PUT THEM THROUGH.
WHY WOULD GOD TEST ADAM AND EVE?? DIDN'T HE TRUST THEM?
WHY WOULD GOD TEST ANYONE?! DOESN'T HE ALREADY KNOW EVERYTHING??
YES, GOD DOES KNOW EVERYTHING, AND HE KNEW WHAT WOULD HAPPEN NEXT.
IN FACT, IN HIS DIVINE PROVIDENCE, HE HAD ALREADY FORESEEN THIS FIRST SIN AND ALL OF ITS CONSEQUENCES...
BUT HE HAD ALSO FORESEEN HIS WONDERFUL SOLUTION TO THAT CATASTROPHE, WHICH HE WOULD BRING ABOUT IN TIME!

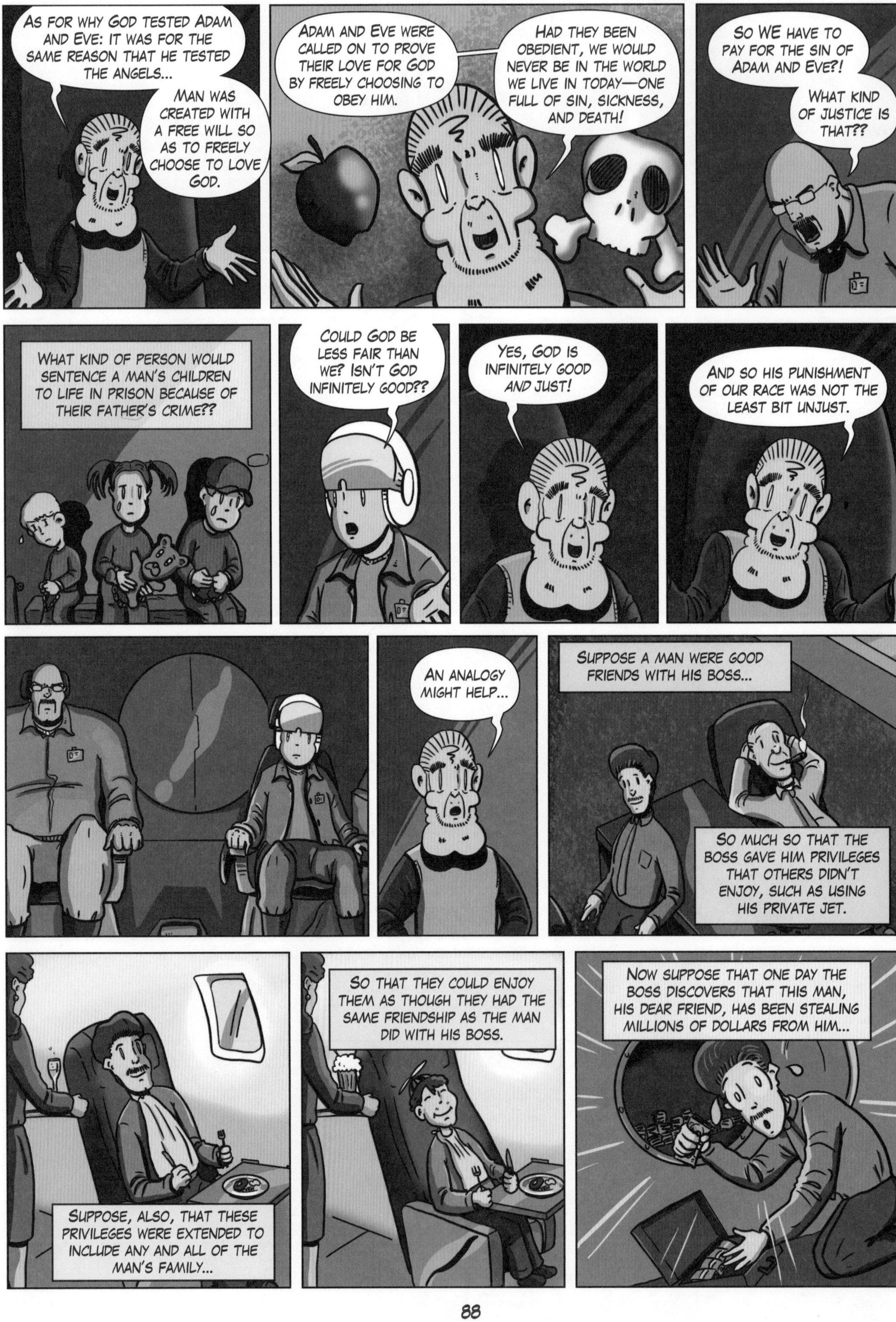
As for why God tested Adam and Eve: it was for the same reason that he tested the angels...
Man was created with a free will so as to freely choose to love God.
Adam and Eve were called on to prove their love for God by freely choosing to obey him.
Had they been obedient, we would never be in the world we live in today—one full of sin, sickness, and death!
So WE have to pay for the sin of Adam and Eve?!
What kind of justice is that??
What kind of person would sentence a man's children to life in prison because of their father's crime??
Could God be less fair than we? Isn't God infinitely good??
Yes, God is infinitely good and just!
And so his punishment of our race was not the least bit unjust.
An analogy might help...
Suppose a man were good friends with his boss...
So much so that the boss gave him privileges that others didn't enjoy, such as using his private jet.
Suppose, also, that these privileges were extended to include any and all of the man's family...
So that they could enjoy them as though they had the same friendship as the man did with his boss.
Now suppose that one day the boss discovers that this man, his dear friend, has been stealing millions of dollars from him...

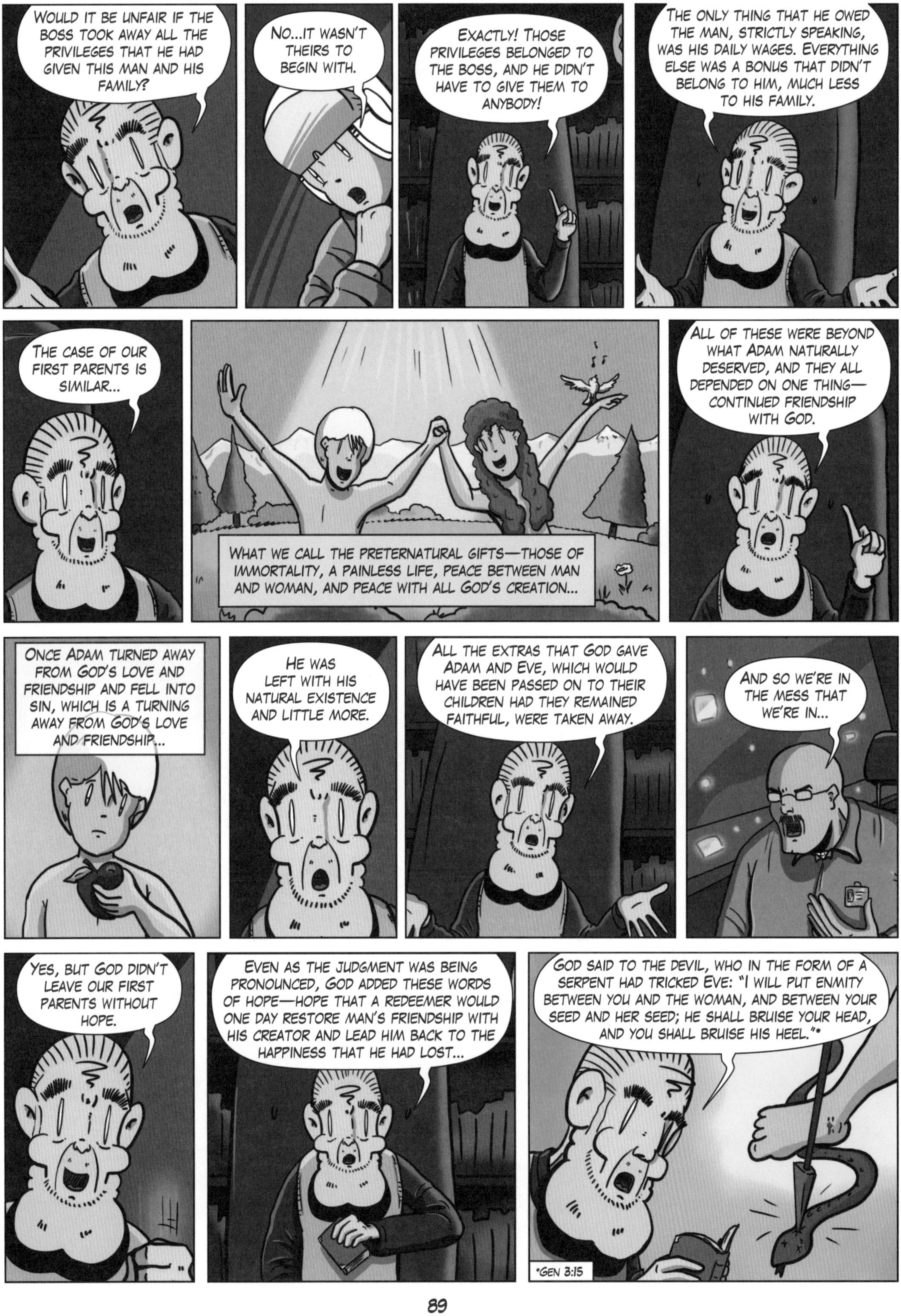

Would it be unfair if the boss took away all the privileges that he had given this man and his family?
No...it wasn't theirs to begin with.
Exactly! Those privileges belonged to the boss, and he didn't have to give them to anybody!
The only thing that he owed the man, strictly speaking, was his daily wages. Everything else was a bonus that didn't belong to him, much less to his family.
The case of our first parents is similar...
What we call the preternatural gifts—those of immortality, a painless life, peace between man and woman, and peace with all God's creation...
All of these were beyond what Adam naturally deserved, and they all depended on one thing—continued friendship with God.
Once Adam turned away from God's love and friendship and fell into sin, which is a turning away from God's love and friendship...
He was left with his natural existence and little more.
All the extras that God gave Adam and Eve, which would have been passed on to their children had they remained faithful, were taken away.
And so we're in the mess that we're in...
Yes, but God didn't leave our first parents without hope.
Even as the judgment was being pronounced, God added these words of hope—hope that a redeemer would one day restore man's friendship with his creator and lead him back to the happiness that he had lost...
God said to the devil, who in the form of a serpent had tricked Eve: "I will put enmity between you and the woman, and between your seed and her seed; he shall bruise your head, and you shall bruise his heel."*
*Gen 3:15

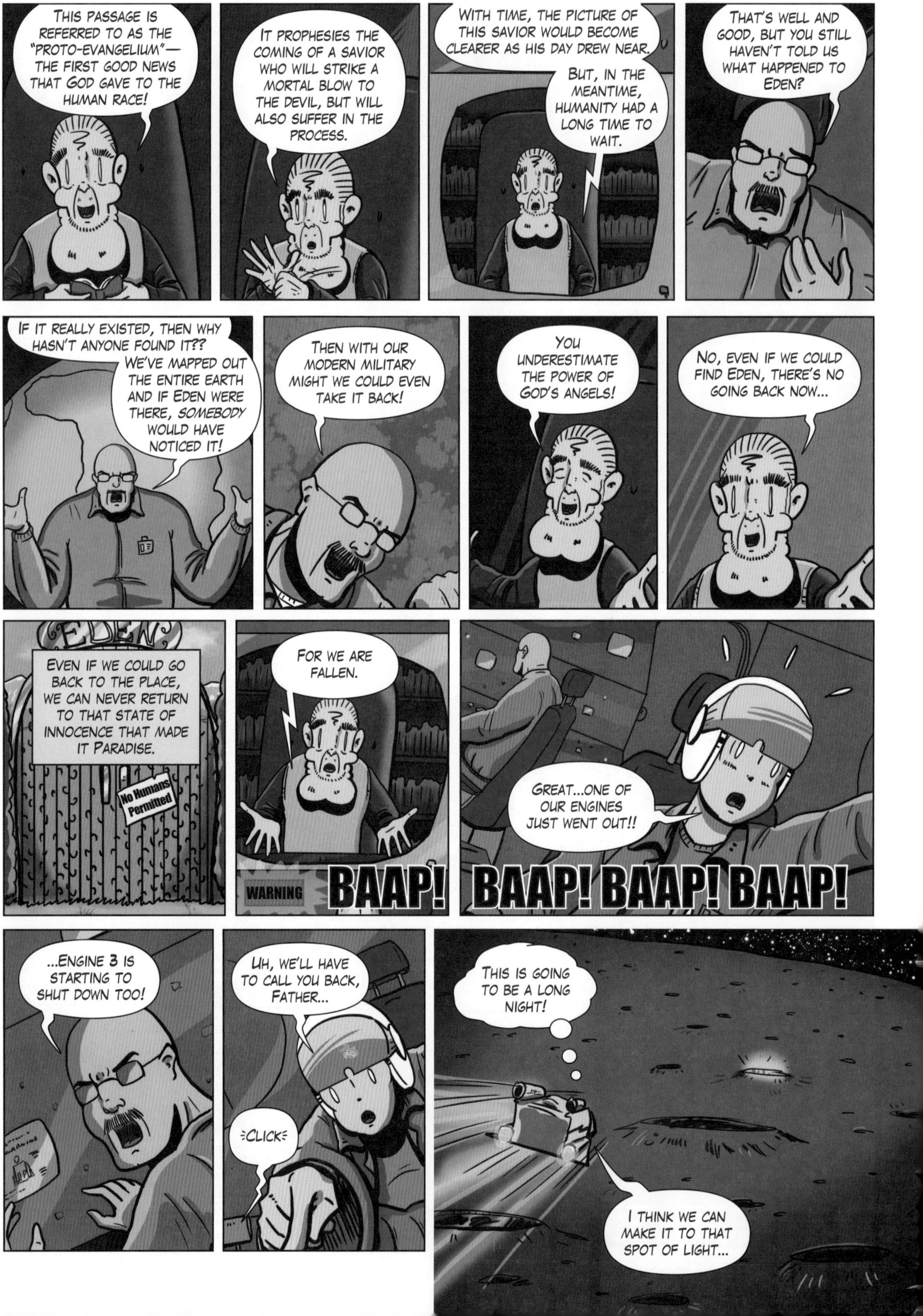

This passage is referred to as the "proto-evangelium"—the first good news that God gave to the human race!
It prophesies the coming of a savior who will strike a mortal blow to the devil, but will also suffer in the process.
With time, the picture of this savior would become clearer as his day drew near.
But, in the meantime, humanity had a long time to wait.
That's well and good, but you still haven't told us what happened to Eden?
If it really existed, then why hasn't anyone found it??
We've mapped out the entire earth and if Eden were there, *somebody* would have noticed it!
Then with our modern military might we could even take it back!
You underestimate the power of God's angels!
No, even if we could find Eden, there's no going back now...
EDEN
Even if we could go back to the place, we can never return to that state of innocence that made it Paradise.
No Humans Permitted
For we are fallen.
Great...one of our engines just went out!!
WARNING
BAAP! BAAP! BAAP! BAAP!
...Engine 3 is starting to shut down too!
Uh, we'll have to call you back, Father...
CLICK
This is going to be a long night!
I think we can make it to that spot of light...

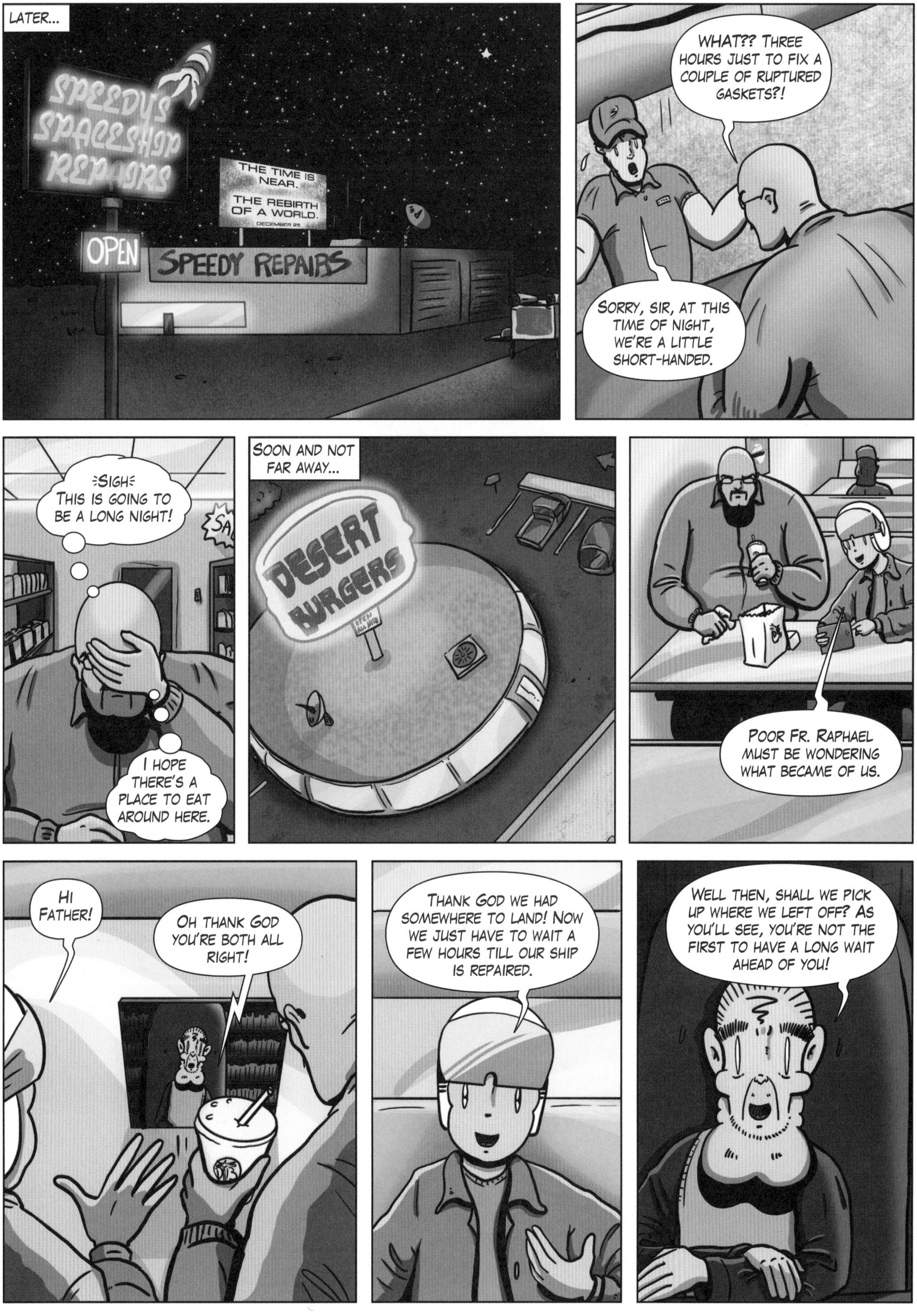

LATER...
SPEEDY'S SPACESHIP REPAIRS
THE TIME IS NEAR. THE REBIRTH OF A WORLD. DECEMBER 25
OPEN
SPEEDY REPAIRS
WHAT?? THREE HOURS JUST TO FIX A COUPLE OF RUPTURED GASKETS?!
SORRY, SIR, AT THIS TIME OF NIGHT, WE'RE A LITTLE SHORT-HANDED.
SIGH
THIS IS GOING TO BE A LONG NIGHT!
I HOPE THERE'S A PLACE TO EAT AROUND HERE.
SOON AND NOT FAR AWAY...
DESERT BURGERS
POOR FR. RAPHAEL MUST BE WONDERING WHAT BECAME OF US.
HI FATHER!
OH THANK GOD YOU'RE BOTH ALL RIGHT!
THANK GOD WE HAD SOMEWHERE TO LAND! NOW WE JUST HAVE TO WAIT A FEW HOURS TILL OUR SHIP IS REPAIRED.
WELL THEN, SHALL WE PICK UP WHERE WE LEFT OFF? AS YOU'LL SEE, YOU'RE NOT THE FIRST TO HAVE A LONG WAIT AHEAD OF YOU!

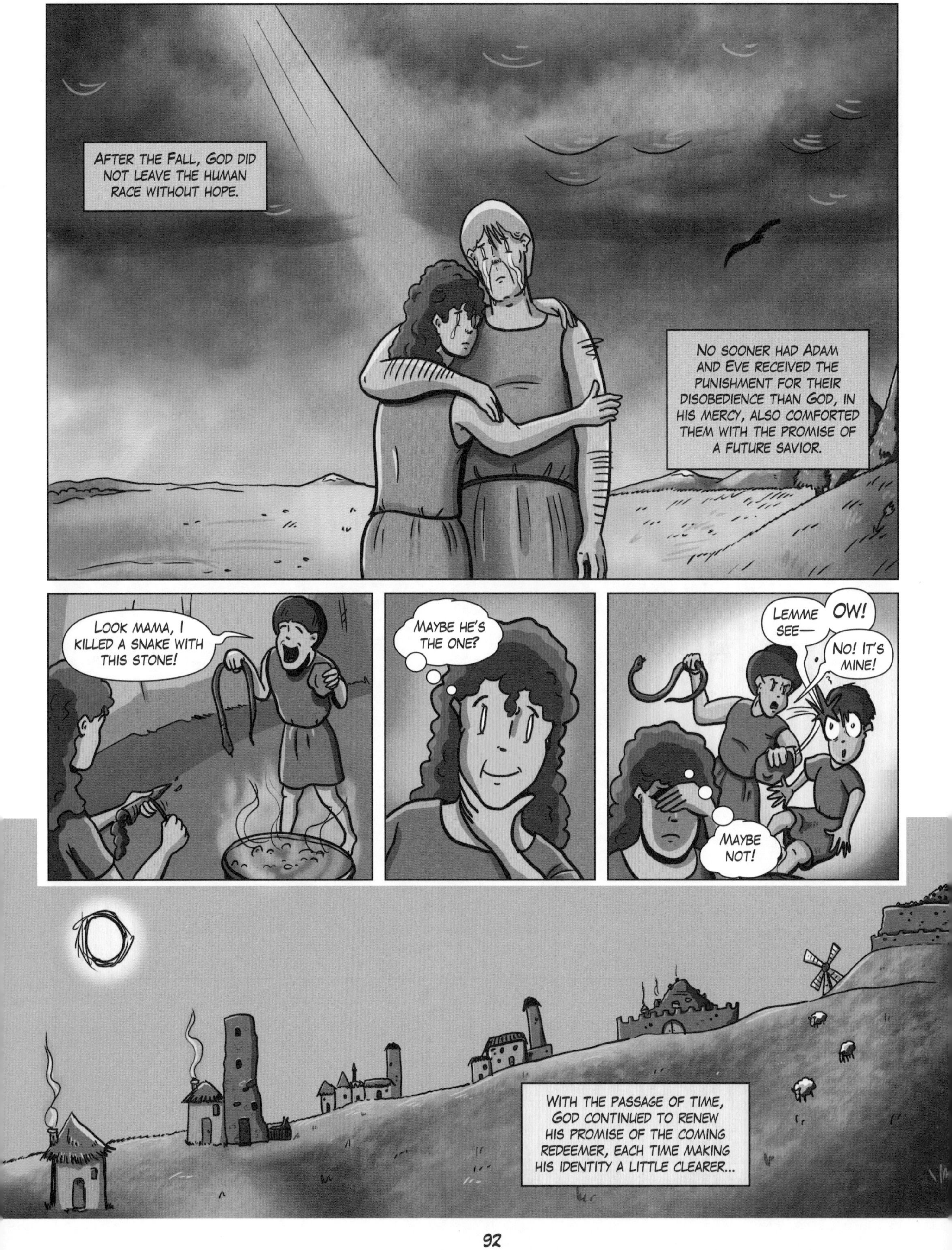
AFTER THE FALL, GOD DID NOT LEAVE THE HUMAN RACE WITHOUT HOPE.
NO SOONER HAD ADAM AND EVE RECEIVED THE PUNISHMENT FOR THEIR DISOBEDIENCE THAN GOD, IN HIS MERCY, ALSO COMFORTED THEM WITH THE PROMISE OF A FUTURE SAVIOR.
LOOK MAMA, I KILLED A SNAKE WITH THIS STONE!
MAYBE HE'S THE ONE?
LEMME SEE—
OW!
NO! IT'S MINE!
MAYBE NOT!
WITH THE PASSAGE OF TIME, GOD CONTINUED TO RENEW HIS PROMISE OF THE COMING REDEEMER, EACH TIME MAKING HIS IDENTITY A LITTLE CLEARER...

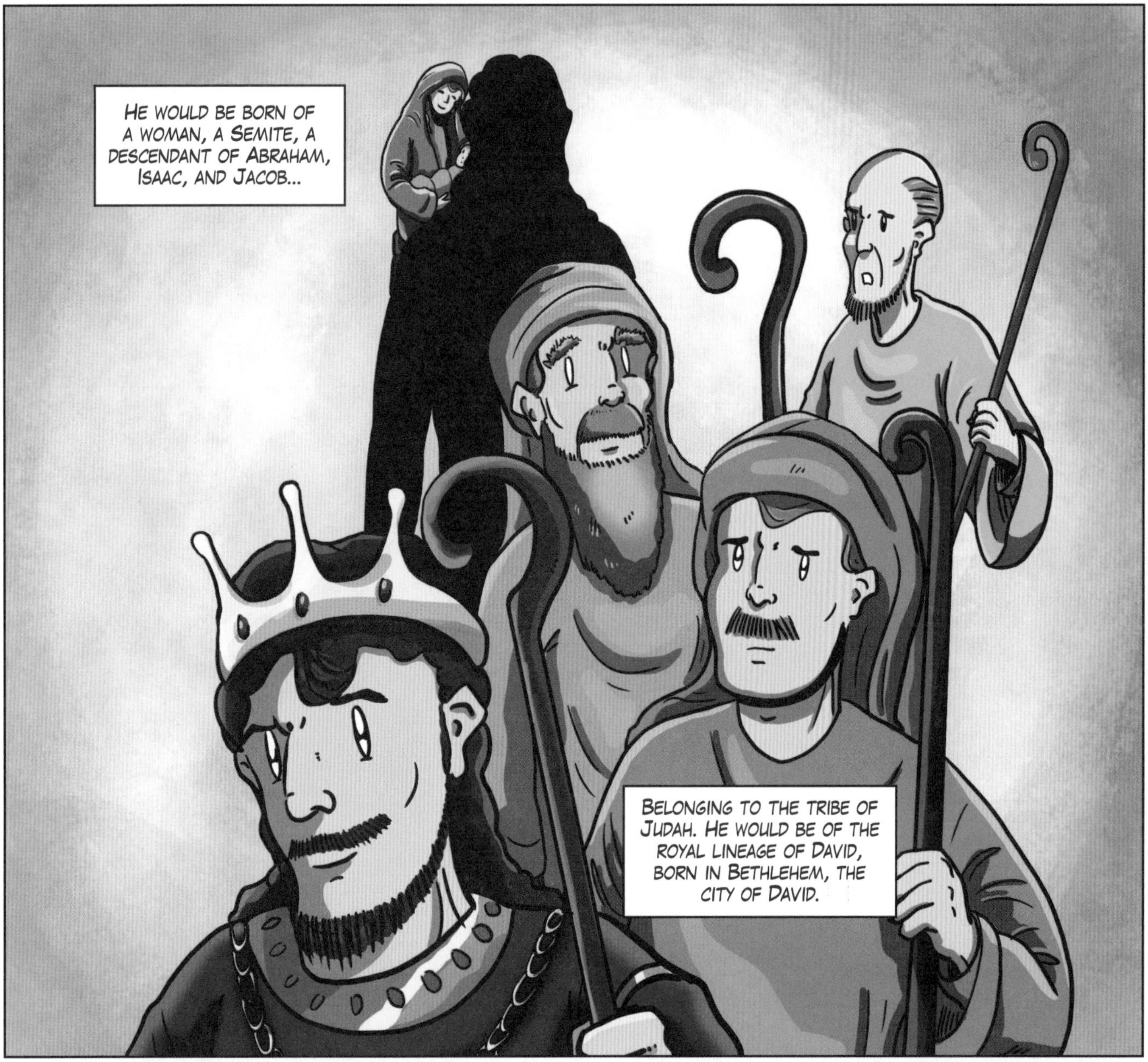
HE WOULD BE BORN OF A WOMAN, A SEMITE, A DESCENDANT OF ABRAHAM, ISAAC, AND JACOB...
BELONGING TO THE TRIBE OF JUDAH. HE WOULD BE OF THE ROYAL LINEAGE OF DAVID, BORN IN BETHLEHEM, THE CITY OF DAVID.

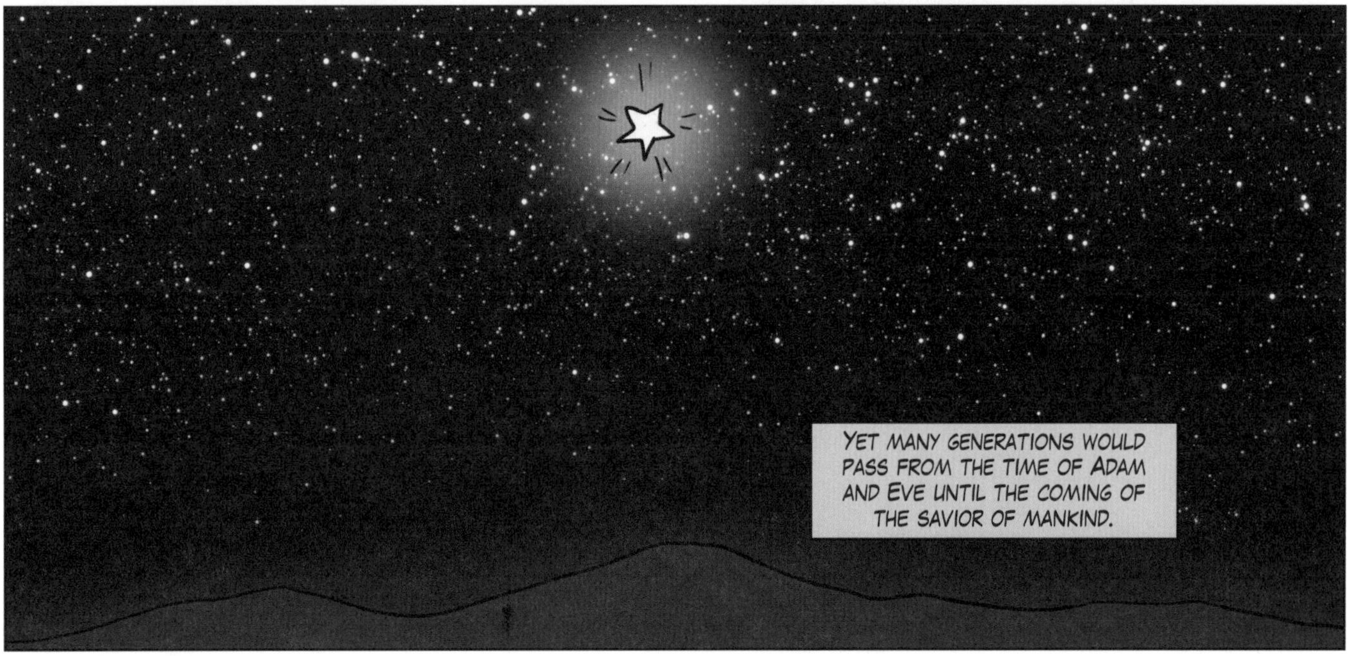
YET MANY GENERATIONS WOULD PASS FROM THE TIME OF ADAM AND EVE UNTIL THE COMING OF THE SAVIOR OF MANKIND.

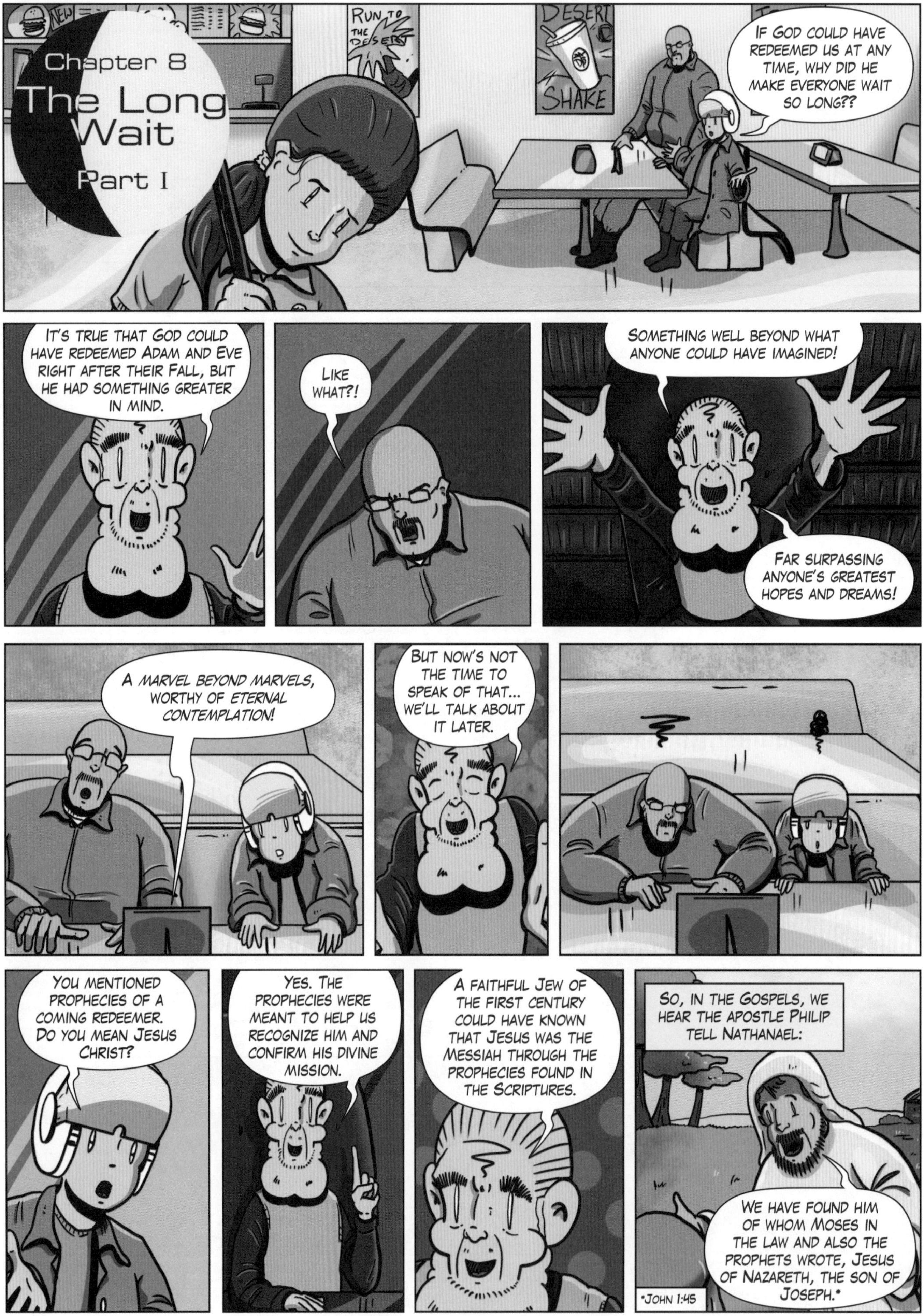
Chapter 8
The Long Wait
Part I
RUN TO THE DESERT
DESERT SHAKE
IF GOD COULD HAVE REDEEMED US AT ANY TIME, WHY DID HE MAKE EVERYONE WAIT SO LONG??
IT'S TRUE THAT GOD COULD HAVE REDEEMED ADAM AND EVE RIGHT AFTER THEIR FALL, BUT HE HAD SOMETHING GREATER IN MIND.
LIKE WHAT?!
SOMETHING WELL BEYOND WHAT ANYONE COULD HAVE IMAGINED!
FAR SURPASSING ANYONE'S GREATEST HOPES AND DREAMS!
A *MARVEL BEYOND MARVELS*, WORTHY OF *ETERNAL CONTEMPLATION!*
BUT NOW'S NOT THE TIME TO SPEAK OF THAT... WE'LL TALK ABOUT IT LATER.
YOU MENTIONED PROPHECIES OF A COMING REDEEMER. DO YOU MEAN JESUS CHRIST?
YES. THE PROPHECIES WERE MEANT TO HELP US RECOGNIZE HIM AND CONFIRM HIS DIVINE MISSION.
A FAITHFUL JEW OF THE FIRST CENTURY COULD HAVE KNOWN THAT JESUS WAS THE MESSIAH THROUGH THE PROPHECIES FOUND IN THE SCRIPTURES.
SO, IN THE GOSPELS, WE HEAR THE APOSTLE PHILIP TELL NATHANAEL:
WE HAVE FOUND HIM OF WHOM MOSES IN THE LAW AND ALSO THE PROPHETS WROTE, JESUS OF NAZARETH, THE SON OF JOSEPH.*
*JOHN 1:45

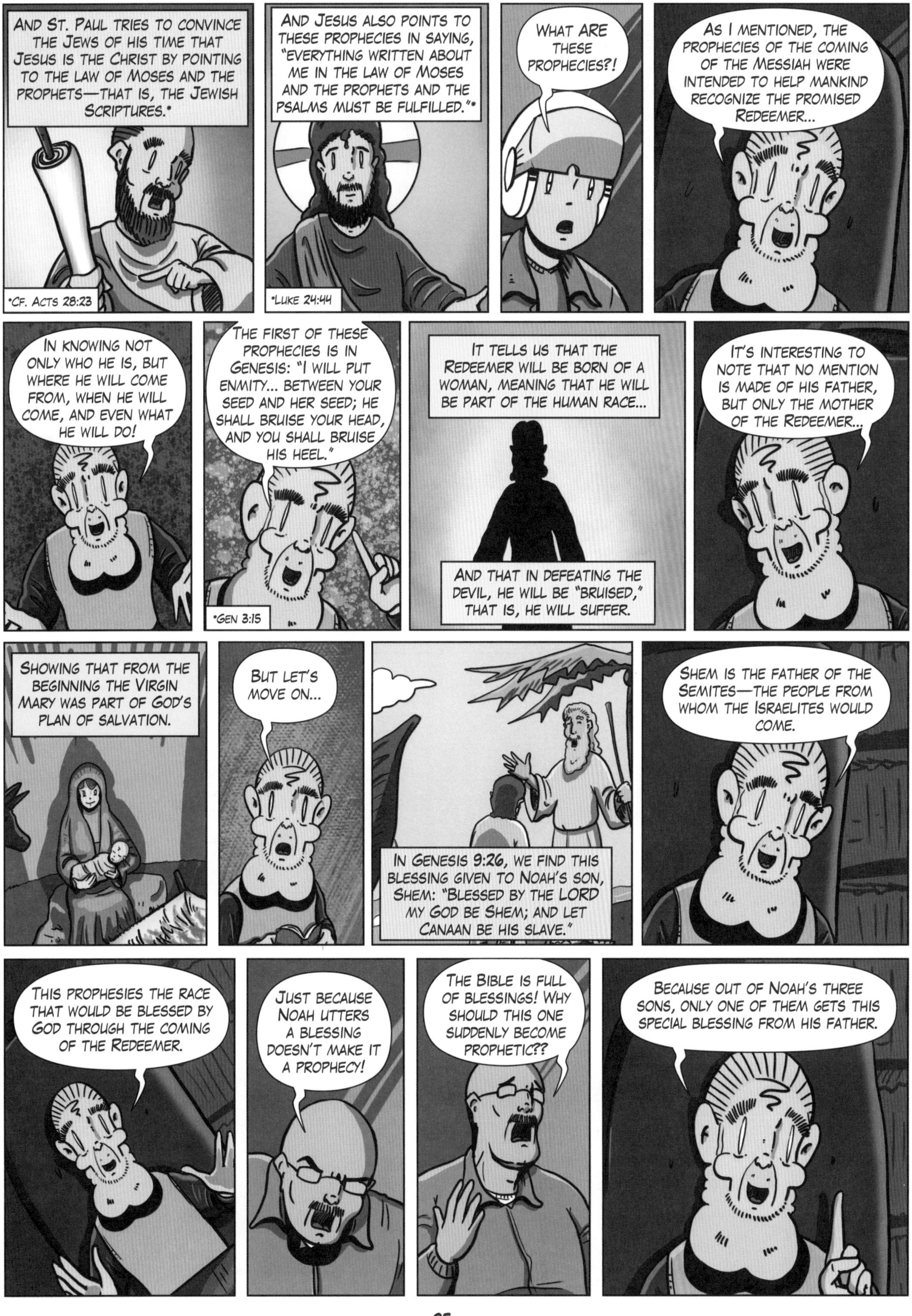

And St. Paul tries to convince the Jews of his time that Jesus is the Christ by pointing to the law of Moses and the prophets—that is, the Jewish Scriptures.*
*Cf. Acts 28:23
And Jesus also points to these prophecies in saying, "Everything written about me in the law of Moses and the prophets and the psalms must be fulfilled."*
*Luke 24:44
What ARE these prophecies?!
As I mentioned, the prophecies of the coming of the Messiah were intended to help mankind recognize the promised Redeemer...
In knowing not only who he is, but where he will come from, when he will come, and even what he will do!
The first of these prophecies is in Genesis: "I will put enmity... between your seed and her seed; he shall bruise your head, and you shall bruise his heel."
*Gen 3:15
It tells us that the Redeemer will be born of a woman, meaning that he will be part of the human race...
And that in defeating the devil, he will be "bruised," that is, he will suffer.
It's interesting to note that no mention is made of his father, but only the mother of the Redeemer...
Showing that from the beginning the Virgin Mary was part of God's plan of salvation.
But let's move on...
In Genesis 9:26, we find this blessing given to Noah's son, Shem: "Blessed by the LORD my God be Shem; and let Canaan be his slave."
Shem is the father of the Semites—the people from whom the Israelites would come.
This prophesies the race that would be blessed by God through the coming of the Redeemer.
Just because Noah utters a blessing doesn't make it a prophecy!
The Bible is full of blessings! Why should this one suddenly become prophetic??
Because out of Noah's three sons, only one of them gets this special blessing from his father.

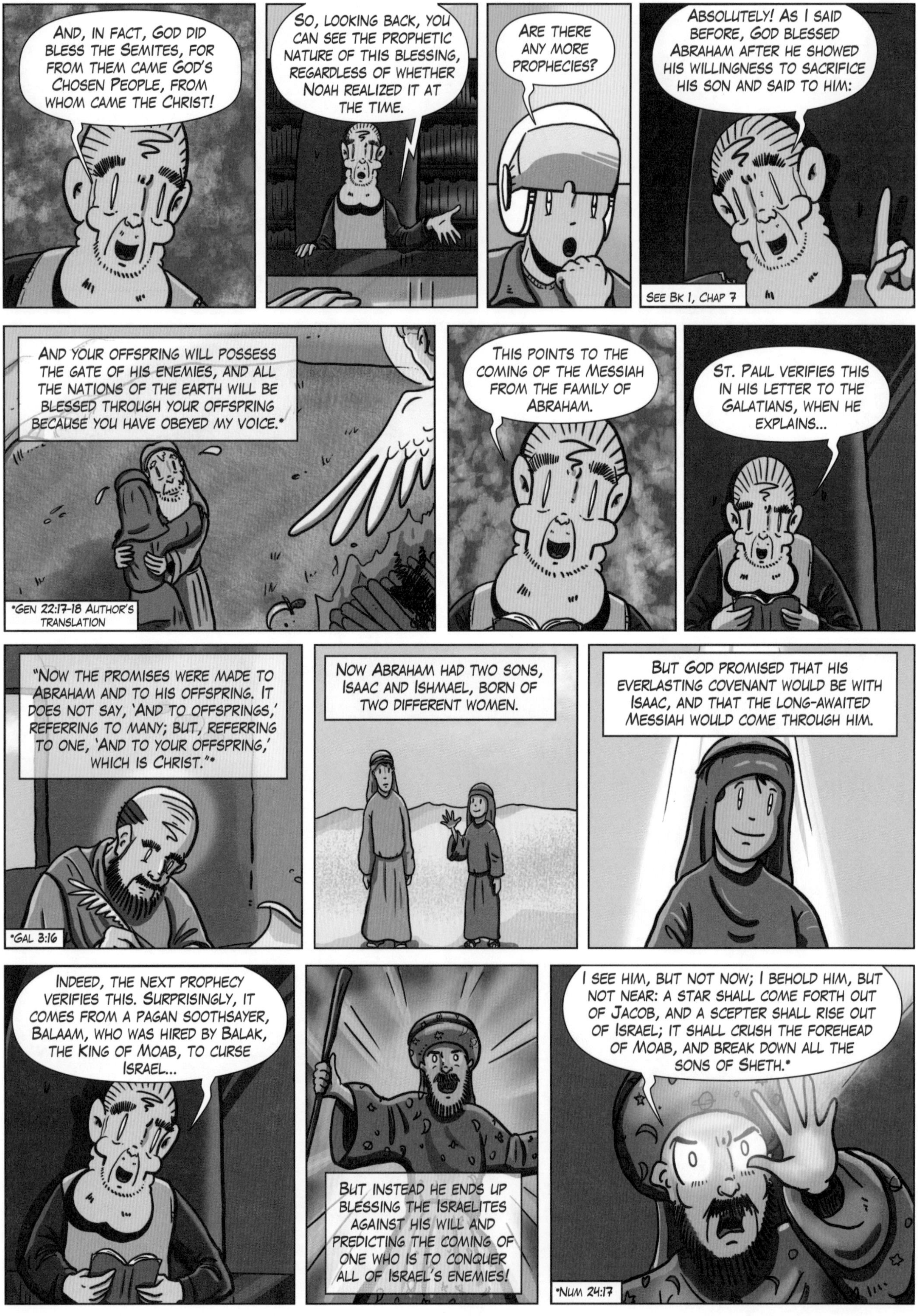

AND, IN FACT, GOD DID BLESS THE SEMITES, FOR FROM THEM CAME GOD'S CHOSEN PEOPLE, FROM WHOM CAME THE CHRIST!
SO, LOOKING BACK, YOU CAN SEE THE PROPHETIC NATURE OF THIS BLESSING, REGARDLESS OF WHETHER NOAH REALIZED IT AT THE TIME.
ARE THERE ANY MORE PROPHECIES?
ABSOLUTELY! AS I SAID BEFORE, GOD BLESSED ABRAHAM AFTER HE SHOWED HIS WILLINGNESS TO SACRIFICE HIS SON AND SAID TO HIM:
SEE BK 1, CHAP 7
AND YOUR OFFSPRING WILL POSSESS THE GATE OF HIS ENEMIES, AND ALL THE NATIONS OF THE EARTH WILL BE BLESSED THROUGH YOUR OFFSPRING BECAUSE YOU HAVE OBEYED MY VOICE.*
*GEN 22:17-18 AUTHOR'S TRANSLATION
THIS POINTS TO THE COMING OF THE MESSIAH FROM THE FAMILY OF ABRAHAM.
ST. PAUL VERIFIES THIS IN HIS LETTER TO THE GALATIANS, WHEN HE EXPLAINS...
"NOW THE PROMISES WERE MADE TO ABRAHAM AND TO HIS OFFSPRING. IT DOES NOT SAY, 'AND TO OFFSPRINGS,' REFERRING TO MANY; BUT, REFERRING TO ONE, 'AND TO YOUR OFFSPRING,' WHICH IS CHRIST."*
*GAL 3:16
NOW ABRAHAM HAD TWO SONS, ISAAC AND ISHMAEL, BORN OF TWO DIFFERENT WOMEN.
BUT GOD PROMISED THAT HIS EVERLASTING COVENANT WOULD BE WITH ISAAC, AND THAT THE LONG-AWAITED MESSIAH WOULD COME THROUGH HIM.
INDEED, THE NEXT PROPHECY VERIFIES THIS. SURPRISINGLY, IT COMES FROM A PAGAN SOOTHSAYER, BALAAM, WHO WAS HIRED BY BALAK, THE KING OF MOAB, TO CURSE ISRAEL...
BUT INSTEAD HE ENDS UP BLESSING THE ISRAELITES AGAINST HIS WILL AND PREDICTING THE COMING OF ONE WHO IS TO CONQUER ALL OF ISRAEL'S ENEMIES!
I SEE HIM, BUT NOT NOW; I BEHOLD HIM, BUT NOT NEAR: A STAR SHALL COME FORTH OUT OF JACOB, AND A SCEPTER SHALL RISE OUT OF ISRAEL; IT SHALL CRUSH THE FOREHEAD OF MOAB, AND BREAK DOWN ALL THE SONS OF SHETH.*
*NUM 24:17

HA! SO MUCH FOR PROPHECIES!

CHRIST WAS A PEACEMAKER, NOT A WARRIOR!

IT'S TRUE THAT CHRIST NEVER LED HUMAN ARMIES, BUT HE FOUGHT AGAINST THE TRUE ENEMIES OF MANKIND, THE DEMONS AND OTHER CAUSES OF SIN...

THINGS THAT DESTROY THE VERY SOUL OF MAN!

ISRAEL

ALL OF THESE ARE REPRESENTED IN THE PROPHECIES BY THE NAMES OF THE ENEMIES OF ISRAEL.

TO EGYPT

EDOM

YET KNOWING THAT THE MESSIAH WOULD COME FROM JACOB DOESN'T NARROW IT DOWN *ENOUGH*, SINCE JACOB HAD TWELVE SONS.

LEAH JACOB RACHEL

FROM WHICH OF THESE WOULD THE MESSIAH COME?

UM, THE FIRST!

ACTUALLY IT WAS THE FOURTH...

IN THE BOOK OF GENESIS, JUST BEFORE JACOB DIES, HE CALLS HIS TWELVE SONS TOGETHER AND SAYS:

GATHER YOURSELVES TOGETHER, THAT I MAY TELL YOU WHAT SHALL BEFALL YOU IN DAYS TO COME.*

*GEN 49:1

THEN HE PROPHESIES TO JUDAH, "JUDAH, YOUR BROTHERS SHALL PRAISE YOU; YOUR HAND SHALL BE ON THE NECK OF YOUR ENEMIES; YOUR FATHER'S SONS SHALL BOW DOWN BEFORE YOU."

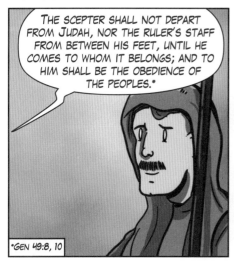

THE SCEPTER SHALL NOT DEPART FROM JUDAH, NOR THE RULER'S STAFF FROM BETWEEN HIS FEET, UNTIL HE COMES TO WHOM IT BELONGS; AND TO HIM SHALL BE THE OBEDIENCE OF THE PEOPLES.*

*GEN 49:8, 10

IN THIS WAY GOD REVEALED BOTH THE TRIBE AND THE *TIME* OF THE MESSIAH. BUT WE CAN GET BACK TO THAT LATER.

LASTLY, CENTURIES LATER, GOD REVEALS THAT THE MESSIAH WOULD COME FROM THE FAMILY OF DAVID, OF THE TRIBE OF JUDAH.

HE REVEALED THIS THROUGH THE PROPHET NATHAN, WHO ANNOUNCED THESE WORDS TO KING DAVID:

WHEN YOUR DAYS ARE FULFILLED AND YOU LIE DOWN WITH YOUR FATHERS, I WILL RAISE UP YOUR OFFSPRING AFTER YOU, WHO SHALL COME FORTH FROM YOUR BODY...

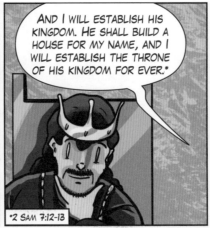

AND I WILL ESTABLISH HIS KINGDOM. HE SHALL BUILD A HOUSE FOR MY NAME, AND I WILL ESTABLISH THE THRONE OF HIS KINGDOM FOR EVER.*

*2 SAM 7:12-13

I DON'T BELIEVE IT!

EVERY ONE OF THESE SO-CALLED PROPHECIES COULD REFER TO SOMETHING THAT TOOK PLACE IN THAT VERY TIME AND HAD NOTHING TO DO WITH JESUS CHRIST!

FOR INSTANCE, WASN'T IT KING DAVID'S SON, SOLOMON, WHO BUILT A HOUSE FOR GOD??*

*1 KGS 5:5

YES, THAT'S RIGHT.

THERE'S NOTHING THAT PREVENTS THESE PROPHECIES FROM HAVING SOME FULFILLMENT AROUND THE TIME THAT THEY WERE UTTERED.

YET THEIR COMPLETE FULFILLMENT COMES ABOUT ONLY WITH THE COMING OF THE MESSIAH.

SO ALTHOUGH THIS PROPHECY FOUND SOME FULFILLMENT IN SOLOMON, WHO BUILT THE FIRST TEMPLE, IT WASN'T PERFECTLY FULFILLED IN HIM...

SINCE NEITHER SOLOMON'S REIGN NOR HIS DYNASTY ENDURED FOREVER.

SO THE PROPHECY MUST BE POINTING TO SOMETHING MORE! TO SOMEONE GREATER THAN SOLOMON!

LOOK AT PSALM 89, WHICH ALSO PROPHESIES THAT THE MESSIAH WILL COME FROM THE FAMILY OF DAVID:

"I WILL ESTABLISH HIS LINE FOR EVER AND HIS THRONE AS THE DAYS OF THE HEAVENS."*

*V. 29

CLEARLY THIS NEVER HAPPENED IN ANCIENT ISRAEL. BY THE FIRST CENTURY, THE HOUSE OF DAVID HAD LONG SINCE CEASED TO RULE!

HMPH!

AND PSALM 2 HINTS THAT THE CHRIST WOULD BE MORE THAN A MERE MAN: "I WILL TELL OF THE DECREE OF THE LORD: HE SAID TO ME, "YOU ARE MY SON, TODAY I HAVE BEGOTTEN YOU."*

*V. 7

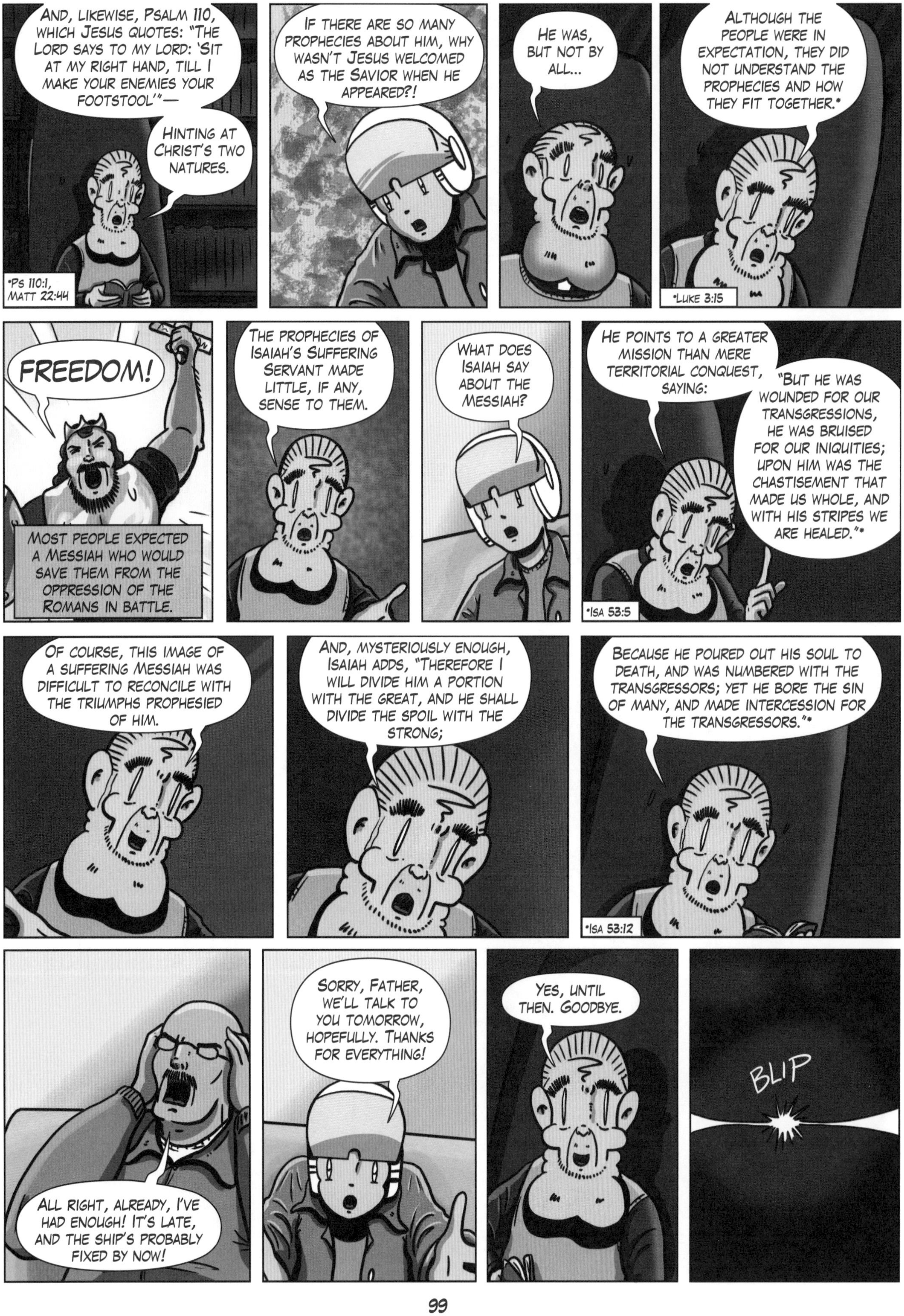

And, likewise, Psalm 110, which Jesus quotes: "The Lord says to my lord: 'Sit at my right hand, till I make your enemies your footstool'"—
Hinting at Christ's two natures.
*Ps 110:1, Matt 22:44
If there are so many prophecies about him, why wasn't Jesus welcomed as the Savior when he appeared?!
He was, but not by all...
Although the people were in expectation, they did not understand the prophecies and how they fit together.*
*Luke 3:15
FREEDOM!
Most people expected a Messiah who would save them from the oppression of the Romans in battle.
The prophecies of Isaiah's Suffering Servant made little, if any, sense to them.
What does Isaiah say about the Messiah?
He points to a greater mission than mere territorial conquest, saying:
"But he was wounded for our transgressions, he was bruised for our iniquities; upon him was the chastisement that made us whole, and with his stripes we are healed."*
*Isa 53:5
Of course, this image of a suffering Messiah was difficult to reconcile with the triumphs prophesied of him.
And, mysteriously enough, Isaiah adds, "Therefore I will divide him a portion with the great, and he shall divide the spoil with the strong;
Because he poured out his soul to death, and was numbered with the transgressors; yet he bore the sin of many, and made intercession for the transgressors."*
*Isa 53:12
All right, already, I've had enough! It's late, and the ship's probably fixed by now!
Sorry, Father, we'll talk to you tomorrow, hopefully. Thanks for everything!
Yes, until then. Goodbye.
BLIP

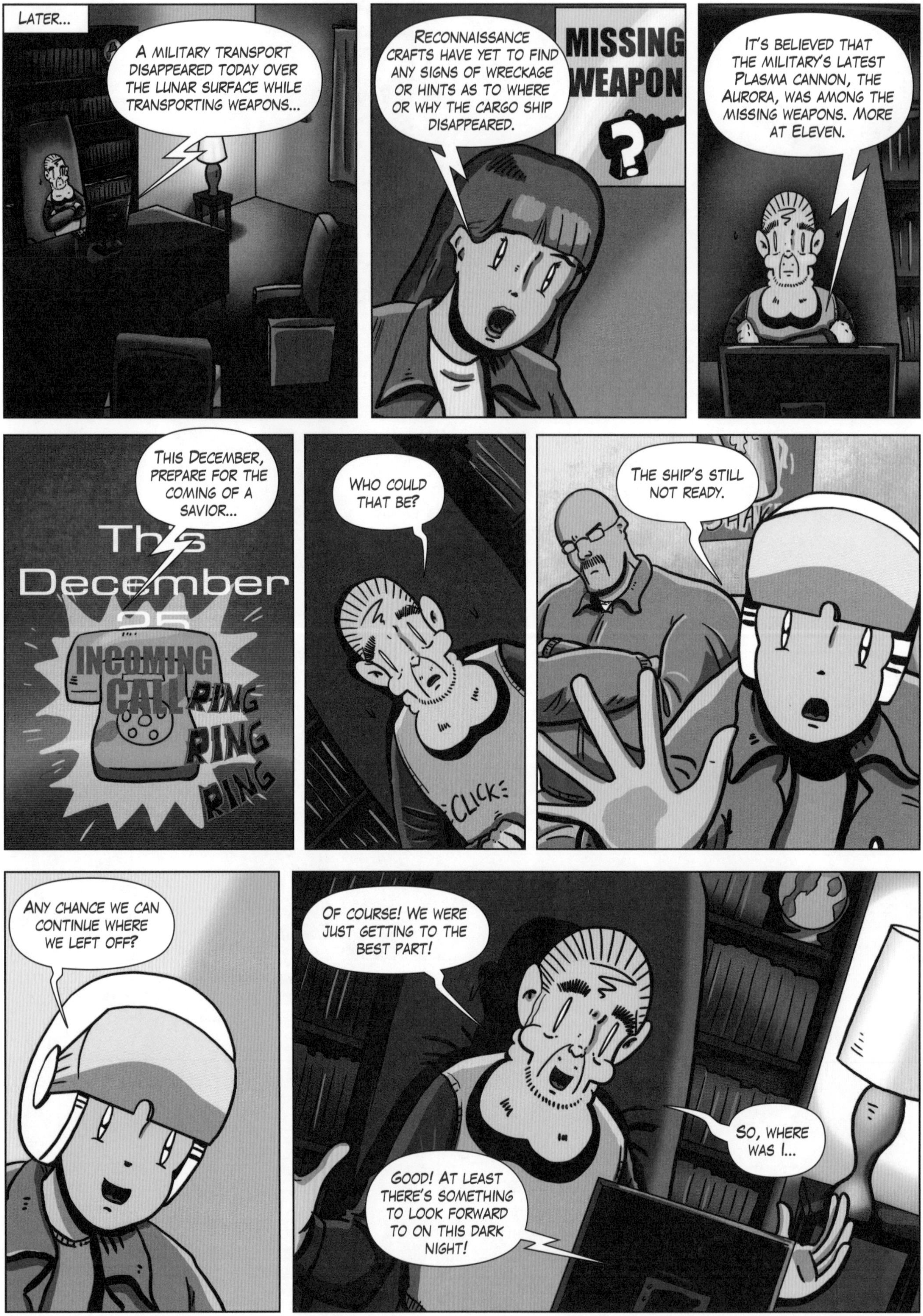
LATER...
A MILITARY TRANSPORT DISAPPEARED TODAY OVER THE LUNAR SURFACE WHILE TRANSPORTING WEAPONS...
RECONNAISSANCE CRAFTS HAVE YET TO FIND ANY SIGNS OF WRECKAGE OR HINTS AS TO WHERE OR WHY THE CARGO SHIP DISAPPEARED.
MISSING WEAPON
IT'S BELIEVED THAT THE MILITARY'S LATEST PLASMA CANNON, THE AURORA, WAS AMONG THE MISSING WEAPONS. MORE AT ELEVEN.
THIS DECEMBER, PREPARE FOR THE COMING OF A SAVIOR...
This December 25
INCOMING CALL
RING RING RING
WHO COULD THAT BE?
CLICK
THE SHIP'S STILL NOT READY.
ANY CHANCE WE CAN CONTINUE WHERE WE LEFT OFF?
OF COURSE! WE WERE JUST GETTING TO THE BEST PART!
SO, WHERE WAS I...
GOOD! AT LEAST THERE'S SOMETHING TO LOOK FORWARD TO ON THIS DARK NIGHT!

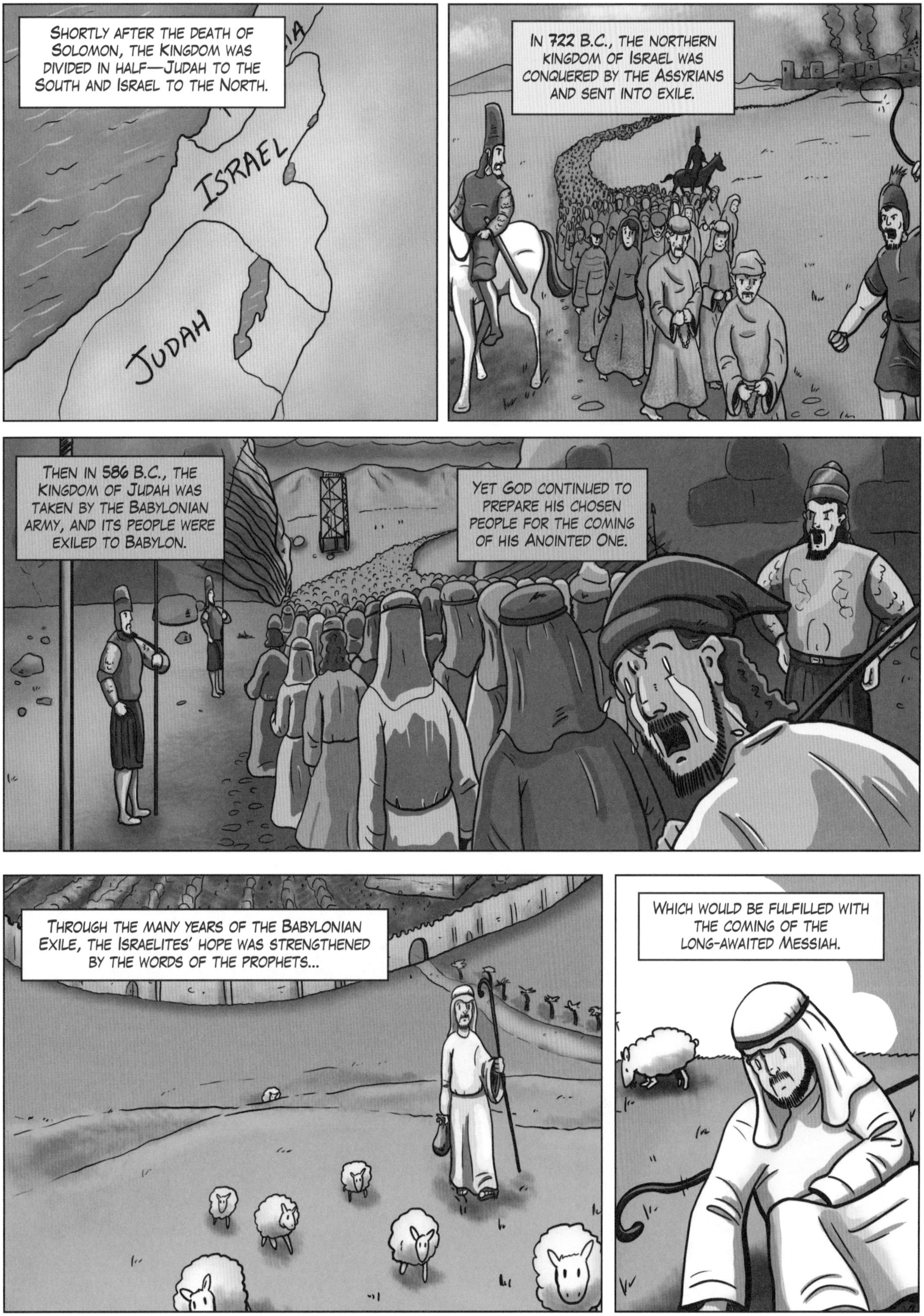

Shortly after the death of Solomon, the Kingdom was divided in half—Judah to the South and Israel to the North.
Israel
Judah
In 722 B.C., the northern kingdom of Israel was conquered by the Assyrians and sent into exile.
Then in 586 B.C., the Kingdom of Judah was taken by the Babylonian army, and its people were exiled to Babylon.
Yet God continued to prepare his chosen people for the coming of his Anointed One.
Through the many years of the Babylonian Exile, the Israelites' hope was strengthened by the words of the prophets...
Which would be fulfilled with the coming of the long-awaited Messiah.

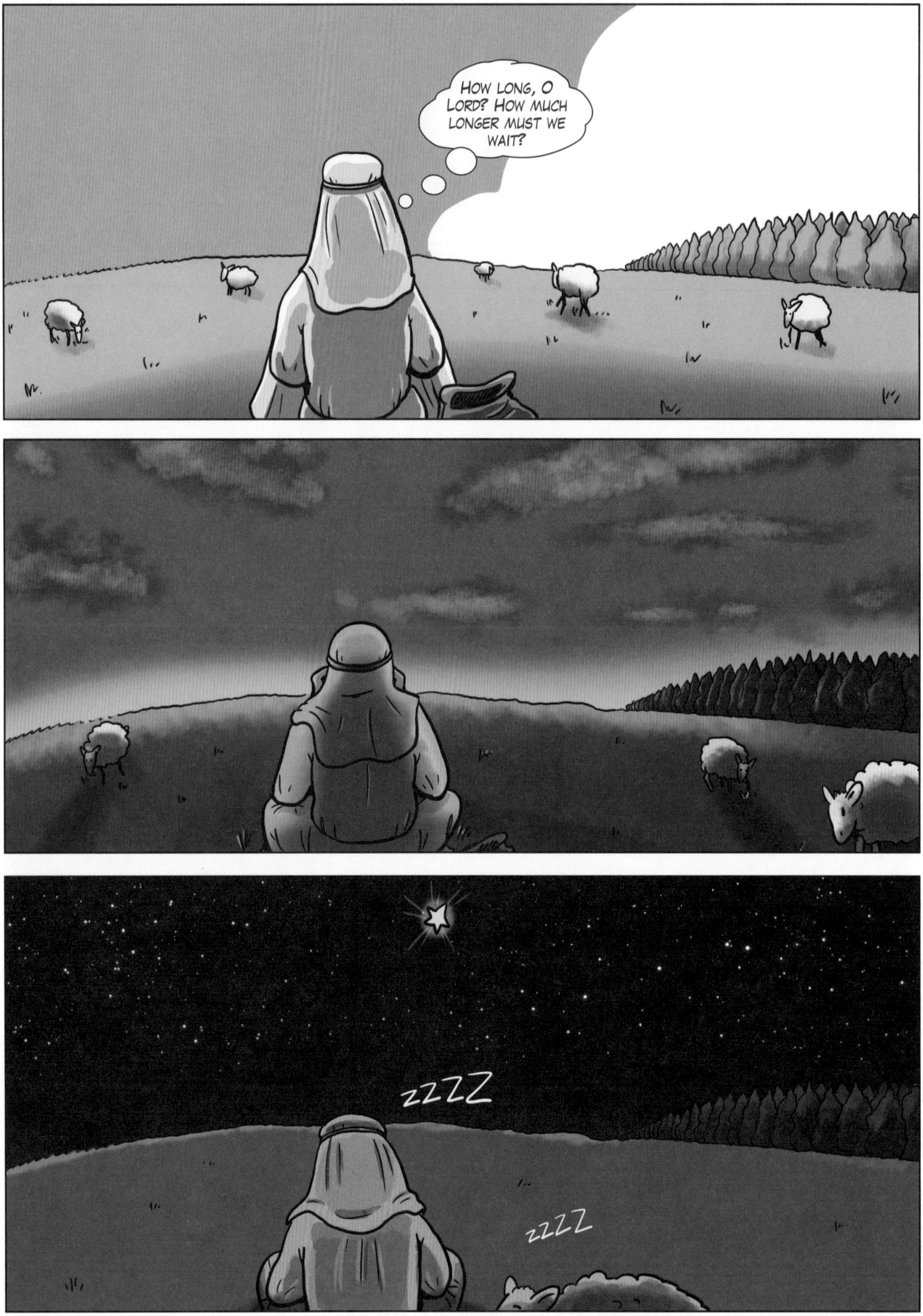
HOW LONG, O LORD? HOW MUCH LONGER MUST WE WAIT?
ZZZZ
ZZZZ

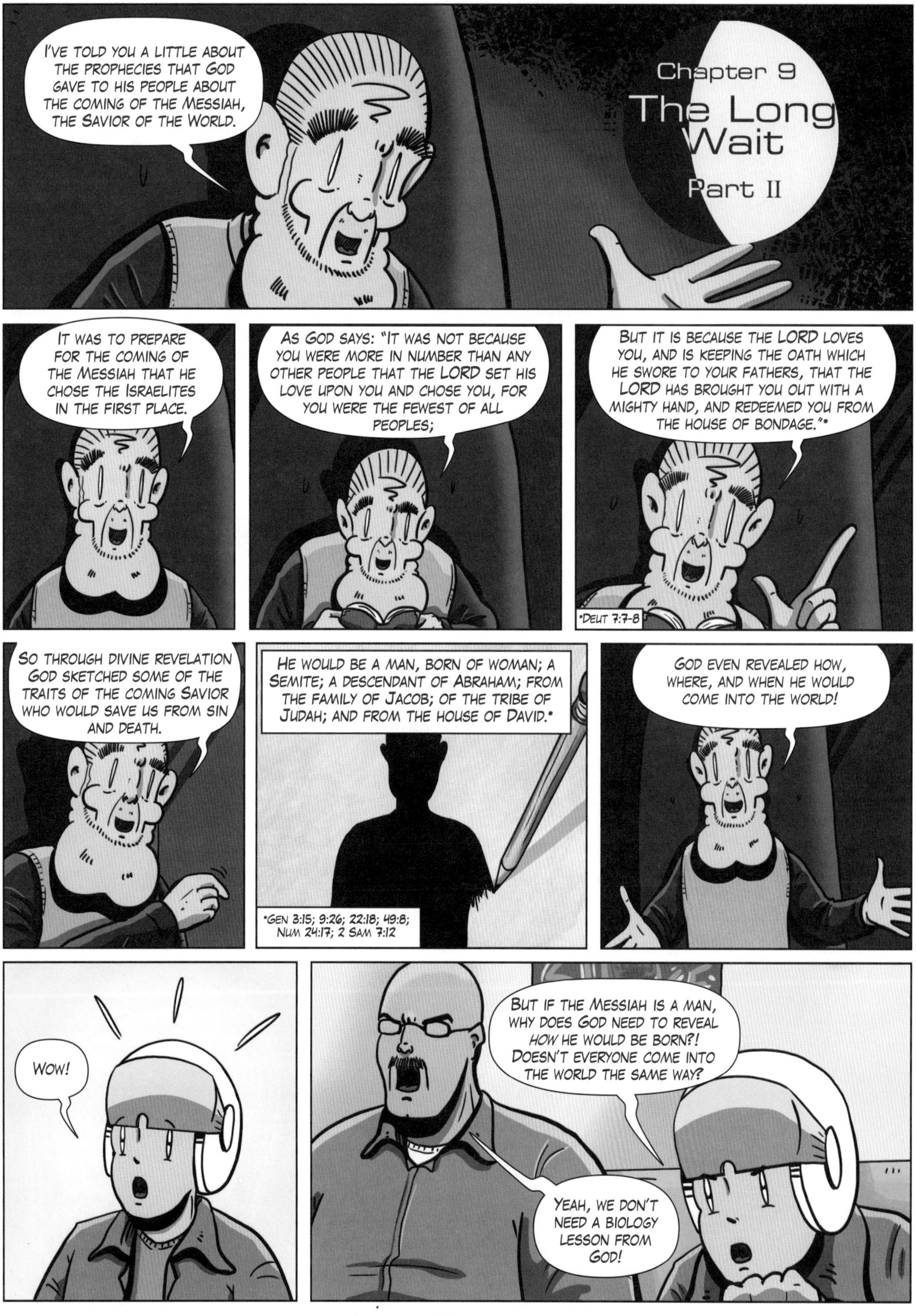
I'VE TOLD YOU A LITTLE ABOUT THE PROPHECIES THAT GOD GAVE TO HIS PEOPLE ABOUT THE COMING OF THE MESSIAH, THE SAVIOR OF THE WORLD.
Chapter 9
The Long Wait
Part II
IT WAS TO PREPARE FOR THE COMING OF THE MESSIAH THAT HE CHOSE THE ISRAELITES IN THE FIRST PLACE.
AS GOD SAYS: "IT WAS NOT BECAUSE YOU WERE MORE IN NUMBER THAN ANY OTHER PEOPLE THAT THE LORD SET HIS LOVE UPON YOU AND CHOSE YOU, FOR YOU WERE THE FEWEST OF ALL PEOPLES;
BUT IT IS BECAUSE THE LORD LOVES YOU, AND IS KEEPING THE OATH WHICH HE SWORE TO YOUR FATHERS, THAT THE LORD HAS BROUGHT YOU OUT WITH A MIGHTY HAND, AND REDEEMED YOU FROM THE HOUSE OF BONDAGE."*
*DEUT 7:7-8
SO THROUGH DIVINE REVELATION GOD SKETCHED SOME OF THE TRAITS OF THE COMING SAVIOR WHO WOULD SAVE US FROM SIN AND DEATH.
HE WOULD BE A MAN, BORN OF WOMAN; A SEMITE; A DESCENDANT OF ABRAHAM; FROM THE FAMILY OF JACOB; OF THE TRIBE OF JUDAH; AND FROM THE HOUSE OF DAVID.*
*GEN 3:15; 9:26; 22:18; 49:8; NUM 24:17; 2 SAM 7:12
GOD EVEN REVEALED HOW, WHERE, AND WHEN HE WOULD COME INTO THE WORLD!
WOW!
BUT IF THE MESSIAH IS A MAN, WHY DOES GOD NEED TO REVEAL *HOW* HE WOULD BE BORN?! DOESN'T EVERYONE COME INTO THE WORLD THE SAME WAY?
YEAH, WE DON'T NEED A BIOLOGY LESSON FROM GOD!

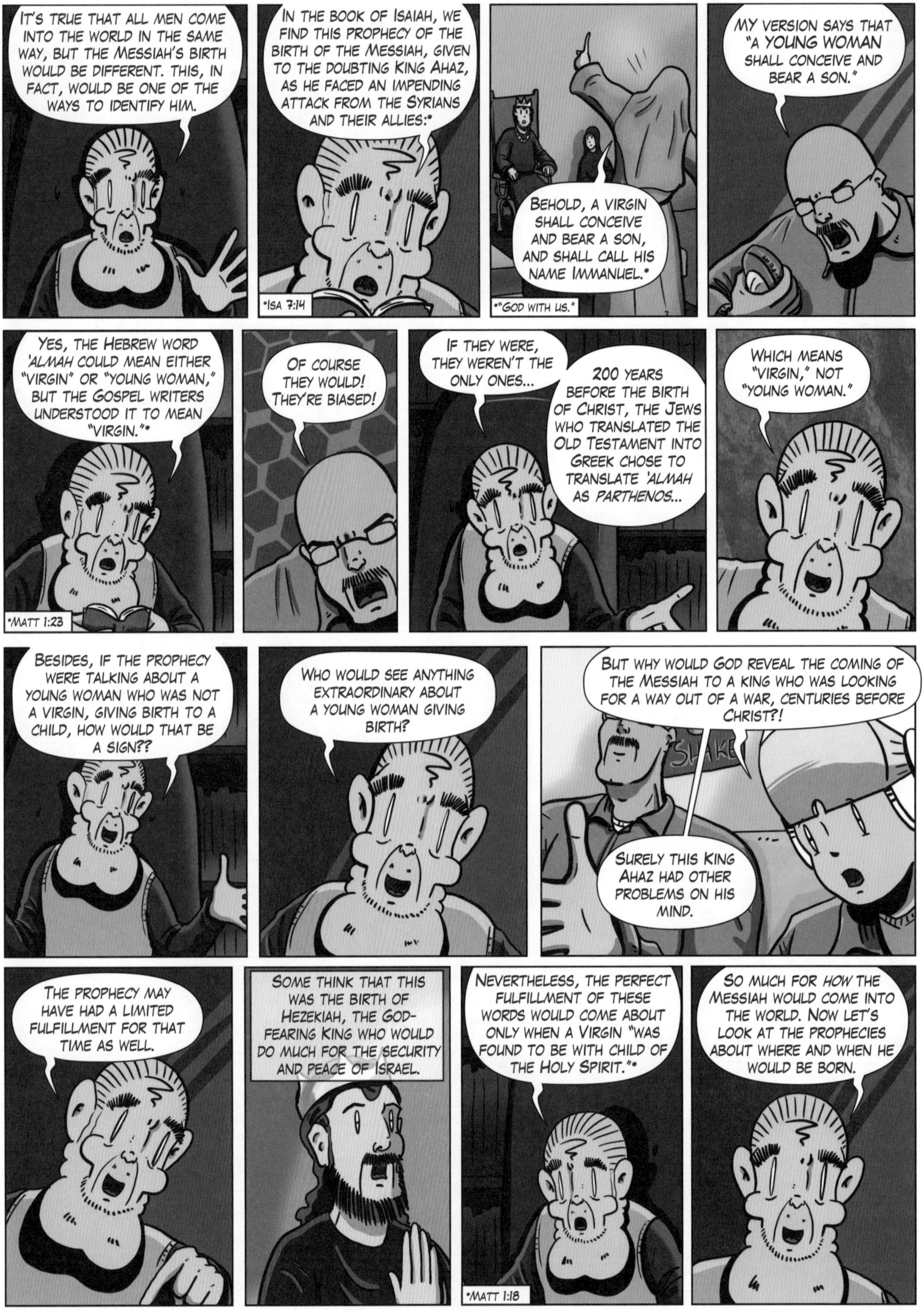
It's true that all men come into the world in the same way, but the Messiah's birth would be different. This, in fact, would be one of the ways to identify him.
In the book of Isaiah, we find this prophecy of the birth of the Messiah, given to the doubting King Ahaz, as he faced an impending attack from the Syrians and their allies:*
*Isa 7:14
Behold, a virgin shall conceive and bear a son, and shall call his name Immanuel.*
*"God with us."
My version says that "a young woman shall conceive and bear a son."
Yes, the Hebrew word 'almah could mean either "virgin" or "young woman," but the Gospel writers understood it to mean "virgin."*
*Matt 1:23
Of course they would! They're biased!
If they were, they weren't the only ones...
200 years before the birth of Christ, the Jews who translated the Old Testament into Greek chose to translate 'almah as parthenos...
Which means "virgin," not "young woman."
Besides, if the prophecy were talking about a young woman who was not a virgin, giving birth to a child, how would that be a sign??
Who would see anything extraordinary about a young woman giving birth?
But why would God reveal the coming of the Messiah to a king who was looking for a way out of a war, centuries before Christ?!
Surely this King Ahaz had other problems on his mind.
The prophecy may have had a limited fulfillment for that time as well.
Some think that this was the birth of Hezekiah, the God-fearing King who would do much for the security and peace of Israel.
Nevertheless, the perfect fulfillment of these words would come about only when a Virgin "was found to be with child of the Holy Spirit."*
*Matt 1:18
So much for how the Messiah would come into the world. Now let's look at the prophecies about where and when he would be born.

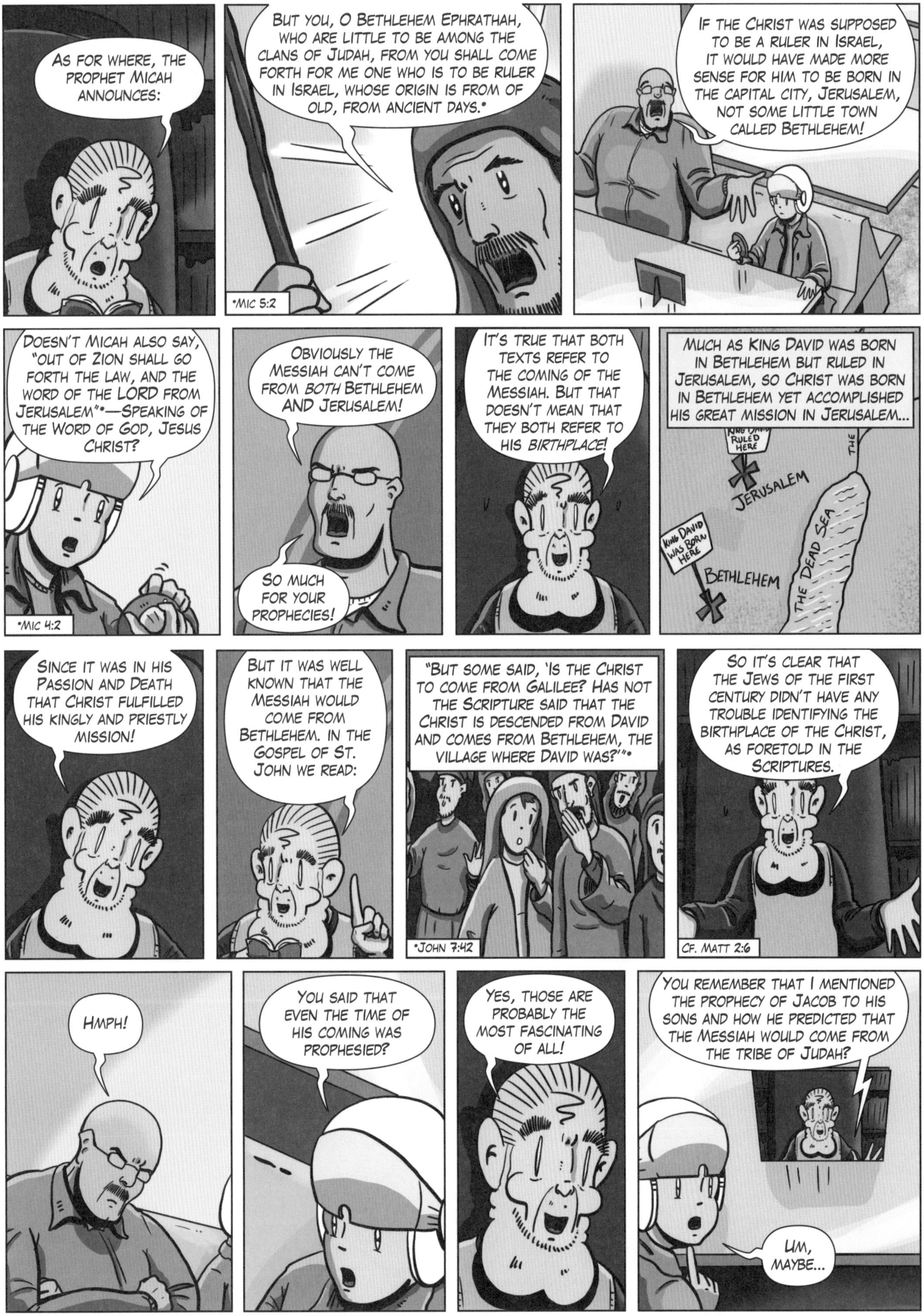
As for where, the prophet Micah announces:
But you, O Bethlehem Ephrathah, who are little to be among the clans of Judah, from you shall come forth for me one who is to be ruler in Israel, whose origin is from of old, from ancient days.*
*Mic 5:2
If the Christ was supposed to be a ruler in Israel, it would have made more sense for him to be born in the capital city, Jerusalem, not some little town called Bethlehem!
Doesn't Micah also say, "out of Zion shall go forth the law, and the word of the LORD from Jerusalem"*—Speaking of the Word of God, Jesus Christ?
*Mic 4:2
Obviously the Messiah can't come from both Bethlehem AND Jerusalem!
So much for your prophecies!
It's true that both texts refer to the coming of the Messiah. But that doesn't mean that they both refer to his birthplace!
Much as King David was born in Bethlehem but ruled in Jerusalem, so Christ was born in Bethlehem yet accomplished his great mission in Jerusalem...
Ruled here
Jerusalem
King David was born here
Bethlehem
The Dead Sea
Since it was in his Passion and Death that Christ fulfilled his kingly and priestly mission!
But it was well known that the Messiah would come from Bethlehem. In the Gospel of St. John we read:
"But some said, 'Is the Christ to come from Galilee? Has not the Scripture said that the Christ is descended from David and comes from Bethlehem, the village where David was?'"*
*John 7:42
So it's clear that the Jews of the first century didn't have any trouble identifying the birthplace of the Christ, as foretold in the Scriptures.
Cf. Matt 2:6
Hmph!
You said that even the time of his coming was prophesied?
Yes, those are probably the most fascinating of all!
You remember that I mentioned the prophecy of Jacob to his sons and how he predicted that the Messiah would come from the tribe of Judah?
Um, maybe...

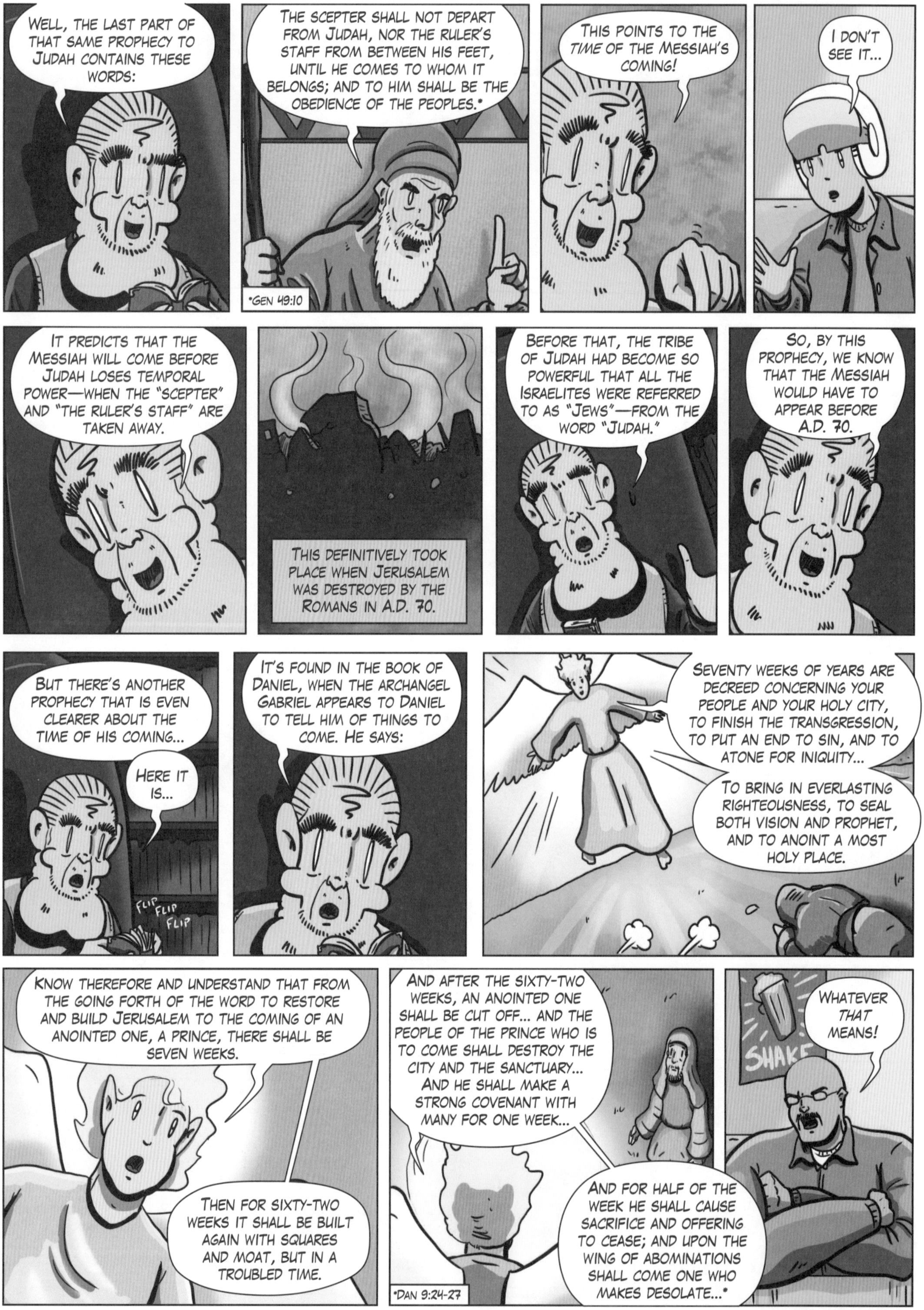
WELL, THE LAST PART OF THAT SAME PROPHECY TO JUDAH CONTAINS THESE WORDS:
THE SCEPTER SHALL NOT DEPART FROM JUDAH, NOR THE RULER'S STAFF FROM BETWEEN HIS FEET, UNTIL HE COMES TO WHOM IT BELONGS; AND TO HIM SHALL BE THE OBEDIENCE OF THE PEOPLES.*
*GEN 49:10
THIS POINTS TO THE *TIME* OF THE MESSIAH'S COMING!
I DON'T SEE IT...
IT PREDICTS THAT THE MESSIAH WILL COME BEFORE JUDAH LOSES TEMPORAL POWER—WHEN THE "SCEPTER" AND "THE RULER'S STAFF" ARE TAKEN AWAY.
THIS DEFINITIVELY TOOK PLACE WHEN JERUSALEM WAS DESTROYED BY THE ROMANS IN A.D. 70.
BEFORE THAT, THE TRIBE OF JUDAH HAD BECOME SO POWERFUL THAT ALL THE ISRAELITES WERE REFERRED TO AS "JEWS"—FROM THE WORD "JUDAH."
SO, BY THIS PROPHECY, WE KNOW THAT THE MESSIAH WOULD HAVE TO APPEAR BEFORE A.D. 70.
BUT THERE'S ANOTHER PROPHECY THAT IS EVEN CLEARER ABOUT THE TIME OF HIS COMING...
HERE IT IS...
FLIP FLIP FLIP
IT'S FOUND IN THE BOOK OF DANIEL, WHEN THE ARCHANGEL GABRIEL APPEARS TO DANIEL TO TELL HIM OF THINGS TO COME. HE SAYS:
SEVENTY WEEKS OF YEARS ARE DECREED CONCERNING YOUR PEOPLE AND YOUR HOLY CITY, TO FINISH THE TRANSGRESSION, TO PUT AN END TO SIN, AND TO ATONE FOR INIQUITY...
TO BRING IN EVERLASTING RIGHTEOUSNESS, TO SEAL BOTH VISION AND PROPHET, AND TO ANOINT A MOST HOLY PLACE.
KNOW THEREFORE AND UNDERSTAND THAT FROM THE GOING FORTH OF THE WORD TO RESTORE AND BUILD JERUSALEM TO THE COMING OF AN ANOINTED ONE, A PRINCE, THERE SHALL BE SEVEN WEEKS.
THEN FOR SIXTY-TWO WEEKS IT SHALL BE BUILT AGAIN WITH SQUARES AND MOAT, BUT IN A TROUBLED TIME.
AND AFTER THE SIXTY-TWO WEEKS, AN ANOINTED ONE SHALL BE CUT OFF... AND THE PEOPLE OF THE PRINCE WHO IS TO COME SHALL DESTROY THE CITY AND THE SANCTUARY... AND HE SHALL MAKE A STRONG COVENANT WITH MANY FOR ONE WEEK...
AND FOR HALF OF THE WEEK HE SHALL CAUSE SACRIFICE AND OFFERING TO CEASE; AND UPON THE WING OF ABOMINATIONS SHALL COME ONE WHO MAKES DESOLATE...*
*DAN 9:24-27
SHAKE
WHATEVER *THAT* MEANS!

THE HEBREW WORD *SHABUA*, WHICH IS TRANSLATED AS "WEEKS OF YEARS," REFERS TO ANY MEASURE OF SEVEN, MUCH AS "DOZEN" CAN REFER TO ANY MEASURE OF TWELVE.

SO IN THE PROPHECY, THE ARCHANGEL TALKS ABOUT A GREAT EVENT TAKING PLACE AFTER "SEVENTY WEEKS OF YEARS," OR SEVENTY TIMES SEVEN MEASURES...

WHICH WILL PUT AN END TO SIN, ATONE FOR INIQUITY, AND FULFILL THE PROPHECIES CONCERNING THE COMING ANOINTED ONE, OR CHRIST.

THESE 490 YEARS BEGIN WITH "THE GOING FORTH OF THE WORD TO RESTORE AND BUILD JERUSALEM."—PREDICTING THE DECREE OF THE KING, ARTAXERXES, AROUND 457 B.C....

ALLOWING THE JEWS TO RETURN TO ISRAEL AND REBUILD JERUSALEM, AFTER THEIR LONG EXILE IN BABYLON.

*CF. NEH 2:1-8

SO 490 YEARS FROM 457 B.C. PUTS US IN A.D. 33, AROUND THE YEAR OF CHRIST'S CRUCIFIXION, WHICH TAKES AWAY OUR SINS. THIS IS ALSO THE MEANING OF THE FIRST "SEVEN WEEKS," WHERE EACH "WEEK" IS A DECADE.

THEN GABRIEL SPEAKS OF SIXTY-TWO WEEKS OF YEARS...

THAT IS 434 YEARS, AFTER THE DECREE FROM ARTAXERXES TO REBUILD JERUSALEM.

CONSIDERING THAT ACTUAL CONSTRUCTION BEGAN AROUND 444 B.C. AND LASTED THROUGH "A TROUBLED TIME" OF 434 YEARS, THIS PROPHECY ACCURATELY DESCRIBES THE TIME IT TOOK TO REBUILD JERUSALEM AND THE TEMPLE,

ENDING IN 10 B.C. WITH THE PEACE OF ROMAN DOMINION.

THE LAST "WEEK" OF THE PROPHECY, WHICH MOST OF THE CHURCH FATHERS SAW AS A "WEEK" OF DECADES, OR SEVENTY YEARS, IS THE TIME OF THE ANOINTED ONE, THE CHRIST...

HIS LIFE, WORK, AND DEATH AS WELL AS THE ESTABLISHMENT OF HIS CHURCH.

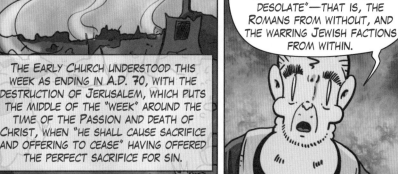
THE EARLY CHURCH UNDERSTOOD THIS WEEK AS ENDING IN A.D. 70, WITH THE DESTRUCTION OF JERUSALEM, WHICH PUTS THE MIDDLE OF THE "WEEK" AROUND THE TIME OF THE PASSION AND DEATH OF CHRIST, WHEN "HE SHALL CAUSE SACRIFICE AND OFFERING TO CEASE" HAVING OFFERED THE PERFECT SACRIFICE FOR SIN.

THE DESTRUCTION OF JERUSALEM AND THE TEMPLE WOULD COME ABOUT BY "ONE WHO MAKES DESOLATE"—THAT IS, THE ROMANS FROM WITHOUT, AND THE WARRING JEWISH FACTIONS FROM WITHIN.

THE WHOLE PROPHECY CORRESPONDS WITH STARTLING ACCURACY TO THE EVENTS THAT LED UP TO, AND FOLLOWED, THE COMING OF CHRIST!

⁼YAWN!⁼

I DON'T BUY IT!

NEVERTHELESS, THERE'S NO DENYING THAT THE FIRST-CENTURY JEWS WERE ANTICIPATING THE COMING OF THE CHRIST,* AND THIS PROPHECY MAY PARTLY EXPLAIN WHY.

*LUKE 2:15

GOD, IN HIS PROVIDENCE, MADE SURE THAT AN EVENT AS GREAT AS THE COMING OF THE SAVIOR OF THE HUMAN RACE WAS ANTICIPATED AND ACCURATELY PREDICTED...

SO THAT WHEN THE TIME CAME, HE COULD BE EASILY RECOGNIZED.

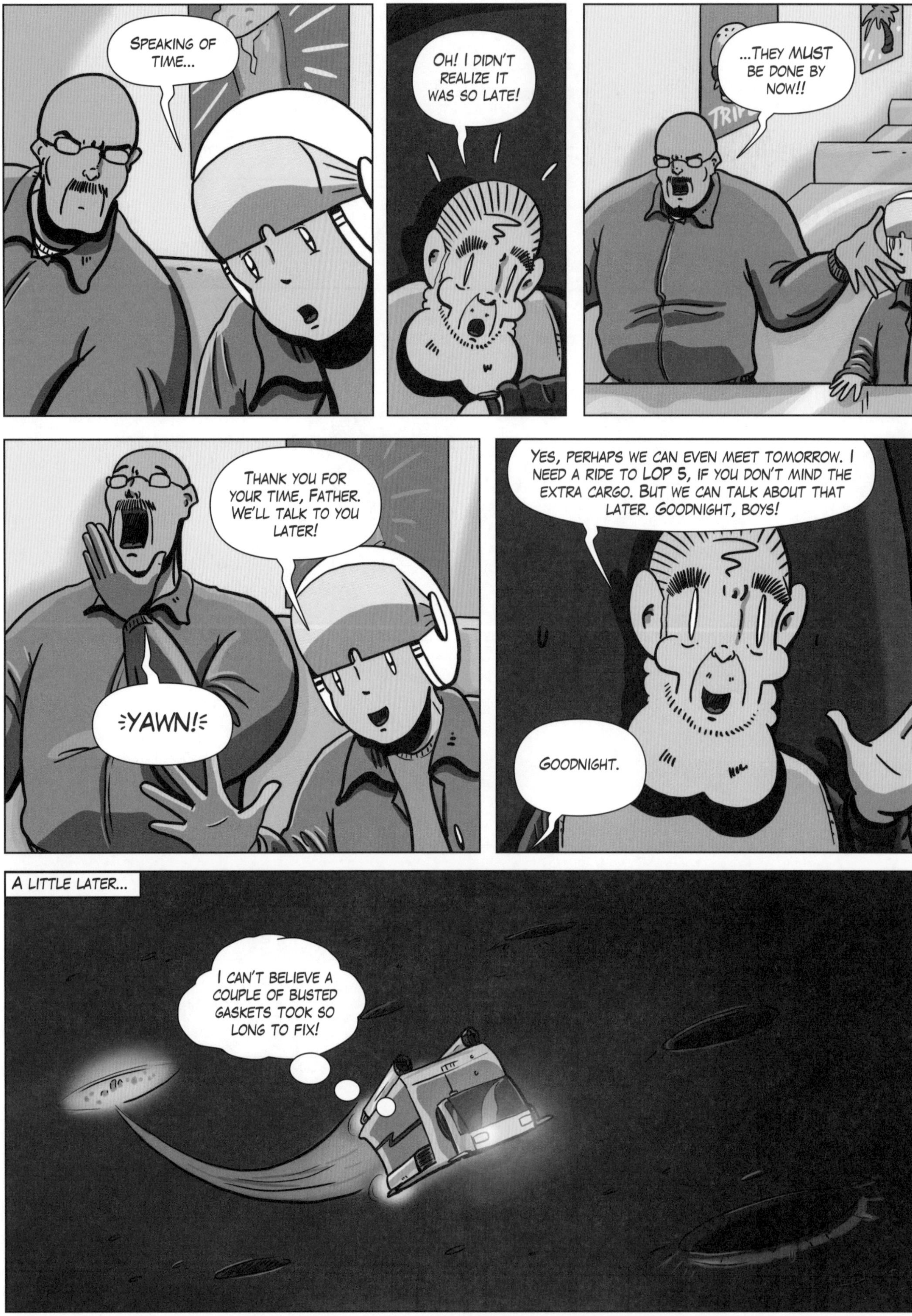
SPEAKING OF TIME...
OH! I DIDN'T REALIZE IT WAS SO LATE!
...THEY MUST BE DONE BY NOW!!
THANK YOU FOR YOUR TIME, FATHER. WE'LL TALK TO YOU LATER!
YAWN!
YES, PERHAPS WE CAN EVEN MEET TOMORROW. I NEED A RIDE TO LOP 5, IF YOU DON'T MIND THE EXTRA CARGO. BUT WE CAN TALK ABOUT THAT LATER. GOODNIGHT, BOYS!
GOODNIGHT.
A LITTLE LATER...
I CAN'T BELIEVE A COUPLE OF BUSTED GASKETS TOOK SO LONG TO FIX!

PART V:
DAWN OF THE REDEEMER

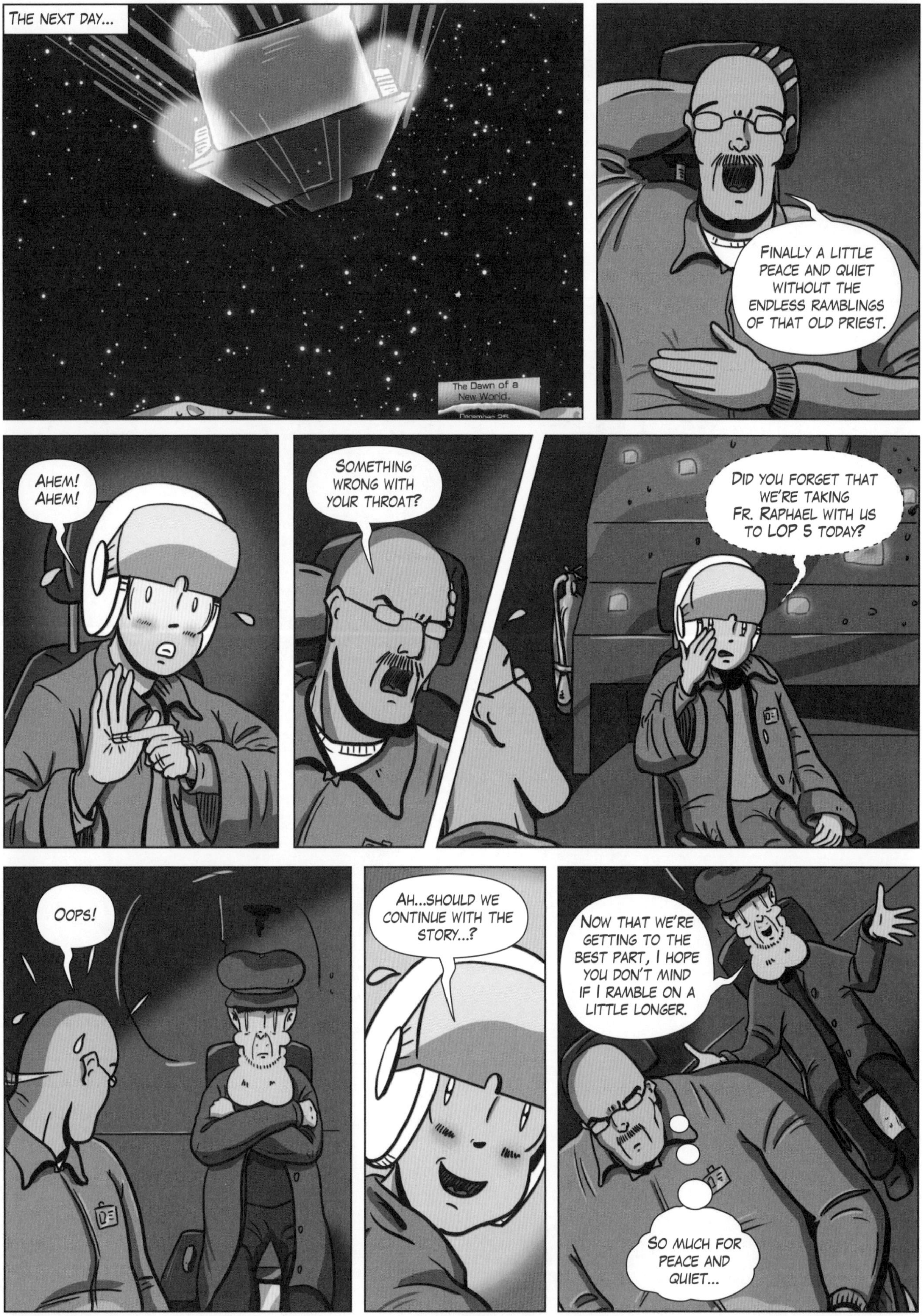
THE NEXT DAY...
The Dawn of a New World.
FINALLY A LITTLE PEACE AND QUIET WITHOUT THE ENDLESS RAMBLINGS OF THAT OLD PRIEST.
AHEM! AHEM!
SOMETHING WRONG WITH YOUR THROAT?
DID YOU FORGET THAT WE'RE TAKING FR. RAPHAEL WITH US TO LOP 5 TODAY?
OOPS!
AH...SHOULD WE CONTINUE WITH THE STORY...?
NOW THAT WE'RE GETTING TO THE BEST PART, I HOPE YOU DON'T MIND IF I RAMBLE ON A LITTLE LONGER.
SO MUCH FOR PEACE AND QUIET...

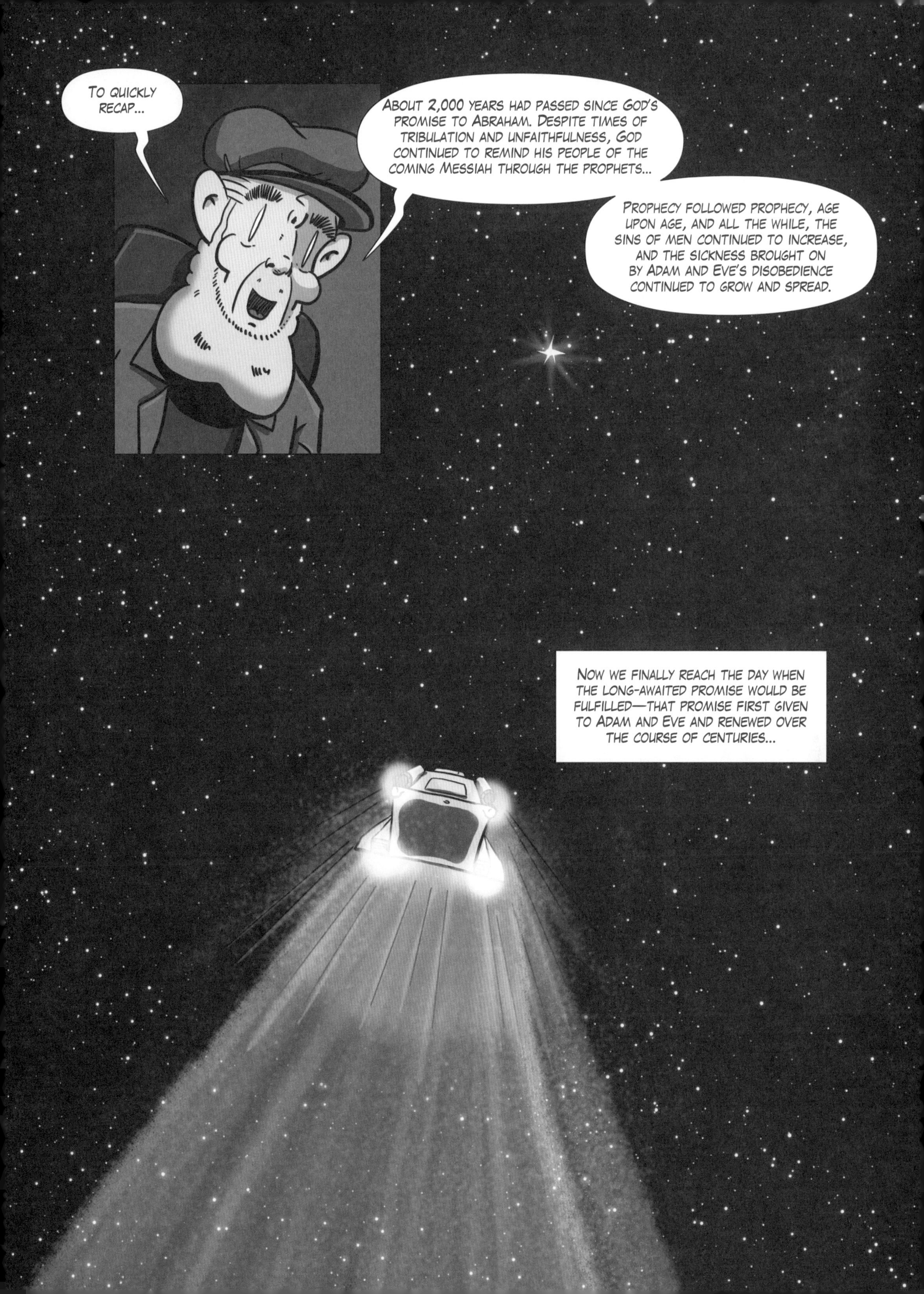
To quickly recap...
About 2,000 years had passed since God's promise to Abraham. Despite times of tribulation and unfaithfulness, God continued to remind his people of the coming Messiah through the prophets...
Prophecy followed prophecy, age upon age, and all the while, the sins of men continued to increase, and the sickness brought on by Adam and Eve's disobedience continued to grow and spread.
Now we finally reach the day when the long-awaited promise would be fulfilled—that promise first given to Adam and Eve and renewed over the course of centuries...

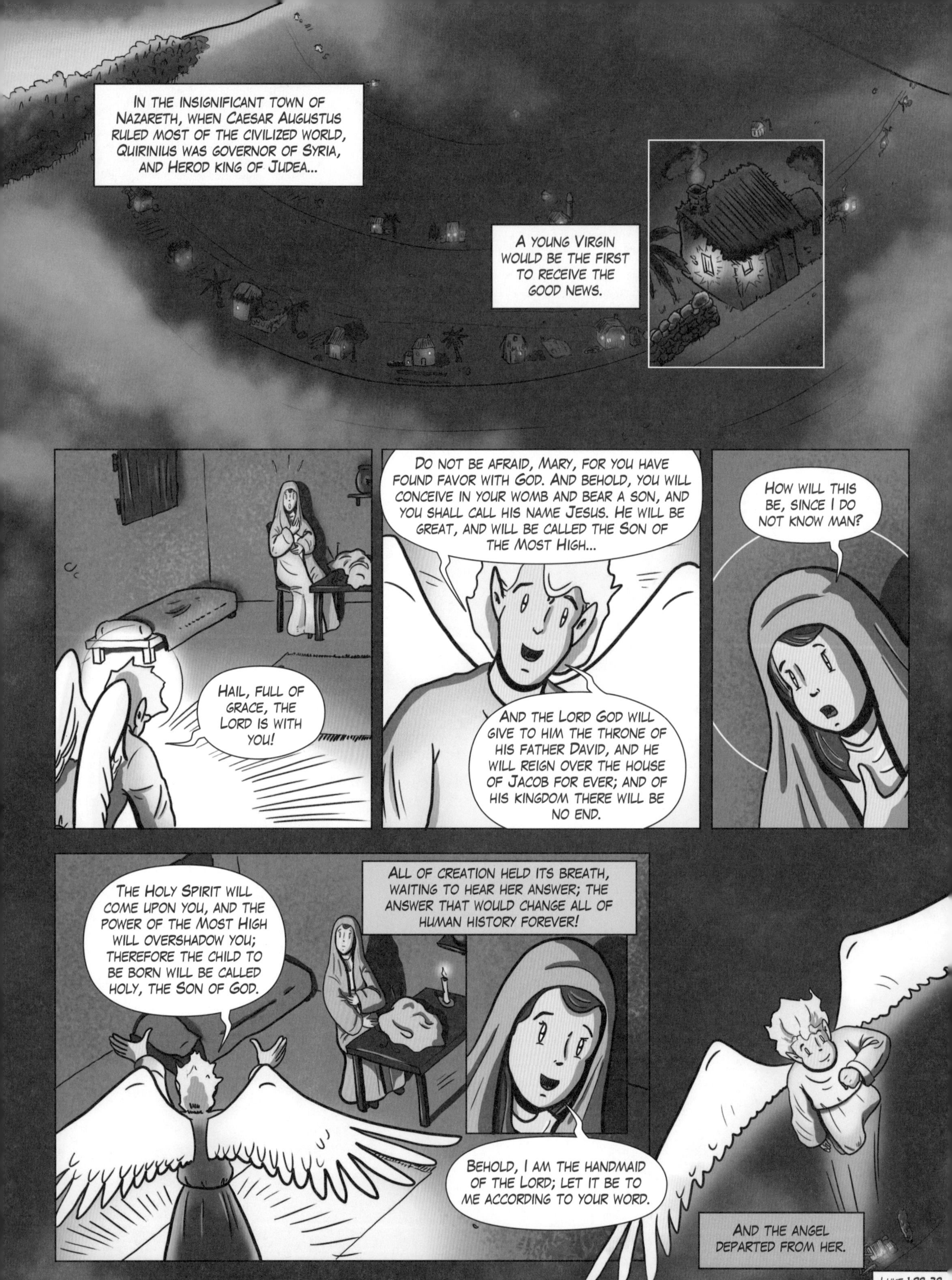

In the insignificant town of Nazareth, when Caesar Augustus ruled most of the civilized world, Quirinius was governor of Syria, and Herod king of Judea...
A young Virgin would be the first to receive the good news.
Hail, full of grace, the Lord is with you!
Do not be afraid, Mary, for you have found favor with God. And behold, you will conceive in your womb and bear a son, and you shall call his name Jesus. He will be great, and will be called the Son of the Most High...
And the Lord God will give to him the throne of his father David, and he will reign over the house of Jacob for ever; and of his kingdom there will be no end.
How will this be, since I do not know man?
The Holy Spirit will come upon you, and the power of the Most High will overshadow you; therefore the child to be born will be called holy, the Son of God.
All of creation held its breath, waiting to hear her answer; the answer that would change all of human history forever!
Behold, I am the handmaid of the Lord; let it be to me according to your word.
And the angel departed from her.

Luke 1:28-38

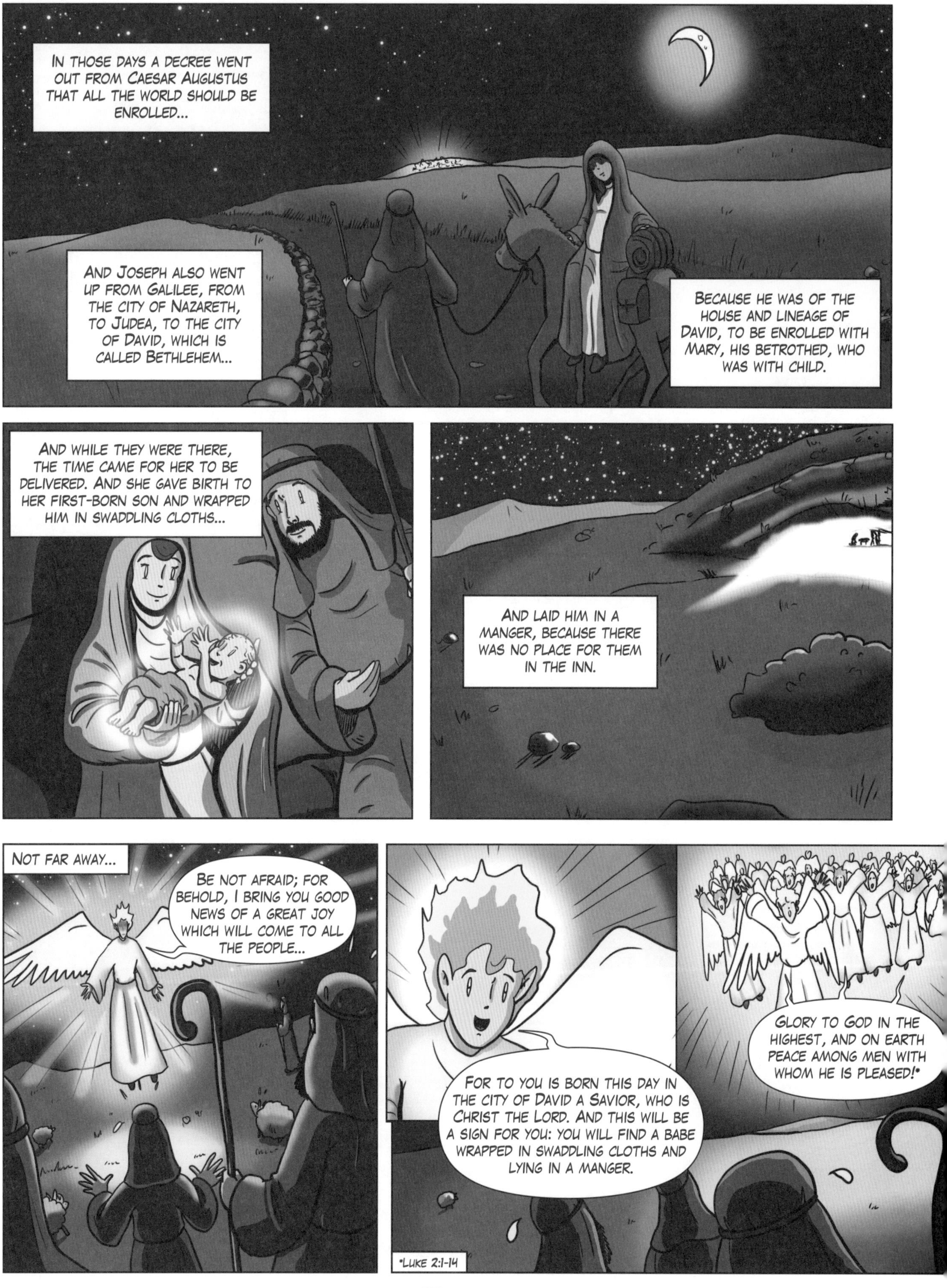

IN THOSE DAYS A DECREE WENT OUT FROM CAESAR AUGUSTUS THAT ALL THE WORLD SHOULD BE ENROLLED...
AND JOSEPH ALSO WENT UP FROM GALILEE, FROM THE CITY OF NAZARETH, TO JUDEA, TO THE CITY OF DAVID, WHICH IS CALLED BETHLEHEM...
BECAUSE HE WAS OF THE HOUSE AND LINEAGE OF DAVID, TO BE ENROLLED WITH MARY, HIS BETROTHED, WHO WAS WITH CHILD.
AND WHILE THEY WERE THERE, THE TIME CAME FOR HER TO BE DELIVERED. AND SHE GAVE BIRTH TO HER FIRST-BORN SON AND WRAPPED HIM IN SWADDLING CLOTHS...
AND LAID HIM IN A MANGER, BECAUSE THERE WAS NO PLACE FOR THEM IN THE INN.
NOT FAR AWAY...
BE NOT AFRAID; FOR BEHOLD, I BRING YOU GOOD NEWS OF A GREAT JOY WHICH WILL COME TO ALL THE PEOPLE...
FOR TO YOU IS BORN THIS DAY IN THE CITY OF DAVID A SAVIOR, WHO IS CHRIST THE LORD. AND THIS WILL BE A SIGN FOR YOU: YOU WILL FIND A BABE WRAPPED IN SWADDLING CLOTHS AND LYING IN A MANGER.
GLORY TO GOD IN THE HIGHEST, AND ON EARTH PEACE AMONG MEN WITH WHOM HE IS PLEASED!*
*LUKE 2:1-14

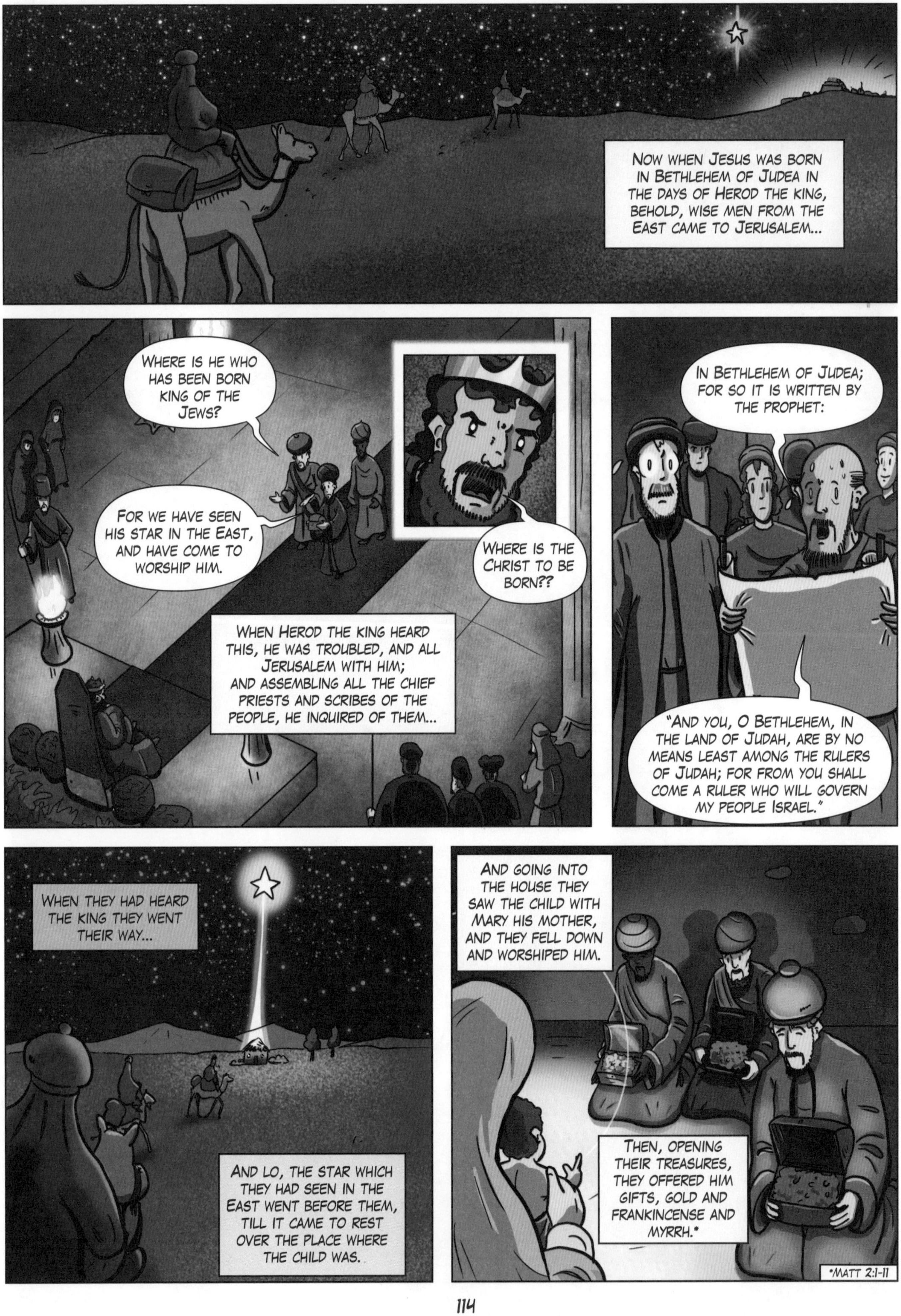

NOW WHEN JESUS WAS BORN IN BETHLEHEM OF JUDEA IN THE DAYS OF HEROD THE KING, BEHOLD, WISE MEN FROM THE EAST CAME TO JERUSALEM...
WHERE IS HE WHO HAS BEEN BORN KING OF THE JEWS?
FOR WE HAVE SEEN HIS STAR IN THE EAST, AND HAVE COME TO WORSHIP HIM.
WHERE IS THE CHRIST TO BE BORN??
WHEN HEROD THE KING HEARD THIS, HE WAS TROUBLED, AND ALL JERUSALEM WITH HIM; AND ASSEMBLING ALL THE CHIEF PRIESTS AND SCRIBES OF THE PEOPLE, HE INQUIRED OF THEM...
IN BETHLEHEM OF JUDEA; FOR SO IT IS WRITTEN BY THE PROPHET:
"AND YOU, O BETHLEHEM, IN THE LAND OF JUDAH, ARE BY NO MEANS LEAST AMONG THE RULERS OF JUDAH; FOR FROM YOU SHALL COME A RULER WHO WILL GOVERN MY PEOPLE ISRAEL."
WHEN THEY HAD HEARD THE KING THEY WENT THEIR WAY...
AND LO, THE STAR WHICH THEY HAD SEEN IN THE EAST WENT BEFORE THEM, TILL IT CAME TO REST OVER THE PLACE WHERE THE CHILD WAS.
AND GOING INTO THE HOUSE THEY SAW THE CHILD WITH MARY HIS MOTHER, AND THEY FELL DOWN AND WORSHIPED HIM.
THEN, OPENING THEIR TREASURES, THEY OFFERED HIM GIFTS, GOLD AND FRANKINCENSE AND MYRRH.*
*MATT 2:1-11

Chapter 10 Jesus the Christ

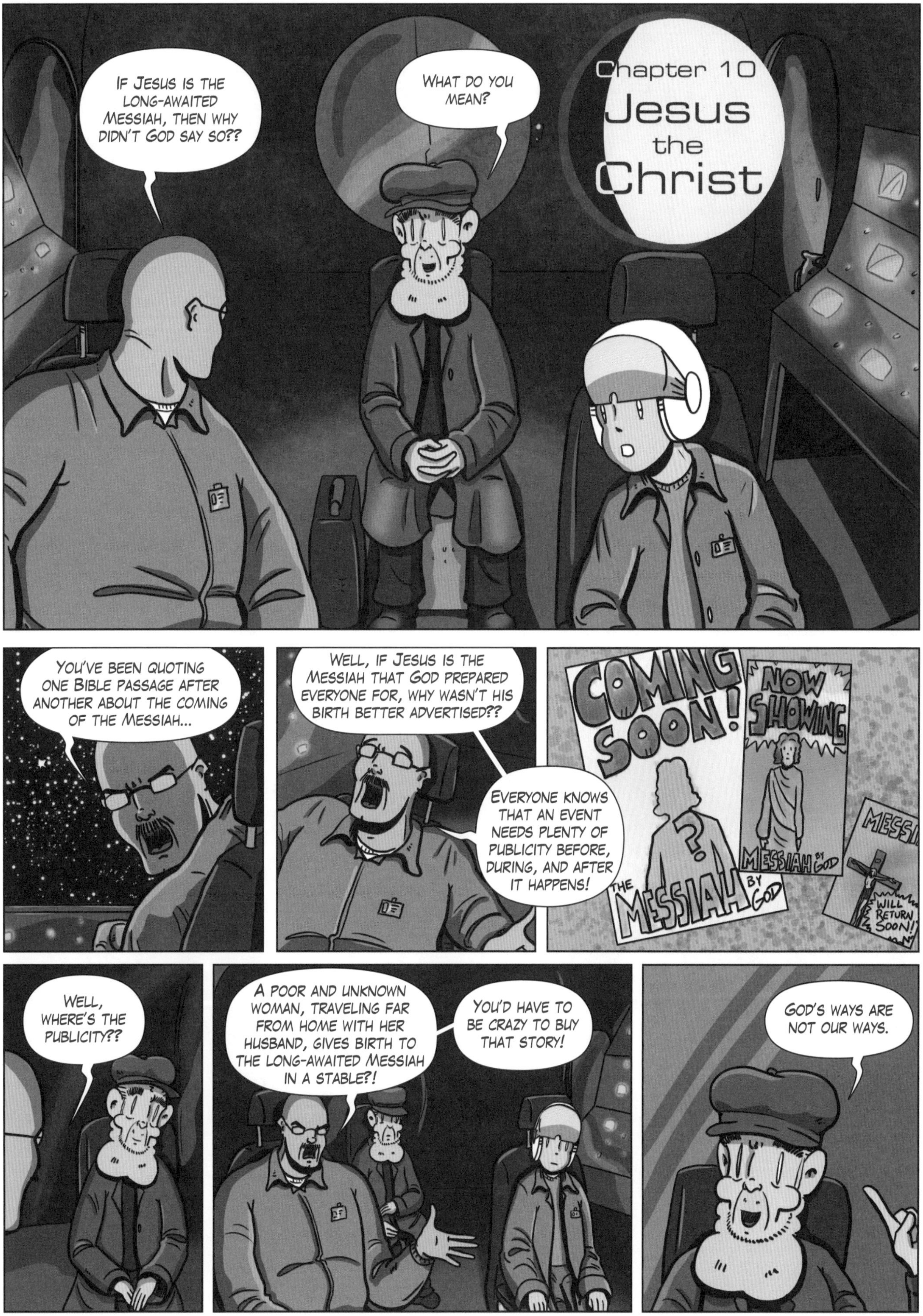

IF JESUS IS THE LONG-AWAITED MESSIAH, THEN WHY DIDN'T GOD SAY SO??
WHAT DO YOU MEAN?
YOU'VE BEEN QUOTING ONE BIBLE PASSAGE AFTER ANOTHER ABOUT THE COMING OF THE MESSIAH...
WELL, IF JESUS IS THE MESSIAH THAT GOD PREPARED EVERYONE FOR, WHY WASN'T HIS BIRTH BETTER ADVERTISED??
EVERYONE KNOWS THAT AN EVENT NEEDS PLENTY OF PUBLICITY BEFORE, DURING, AND AFTER IT HAPPENS!
COMING SOON!
THE MESSIAH BY GOD
NOW SHOWING
MESSIAH BY GOD
WILL RETURN SOON!
WELL, WHERE'S THE PUBLICITY??
A POOR AND UNKNOWN WOMAN, TRAVELING FAR FROM HOME WITH HER HUSBAND, GIVES BIRTH TO THE LONG-AWAITED MESSIAH IN A STABLE?!
YOU'D HAVE TO BE CRAZY TO BUY THAT STORY!
GOD'S WAYS ARE NOT OUR WAYS.

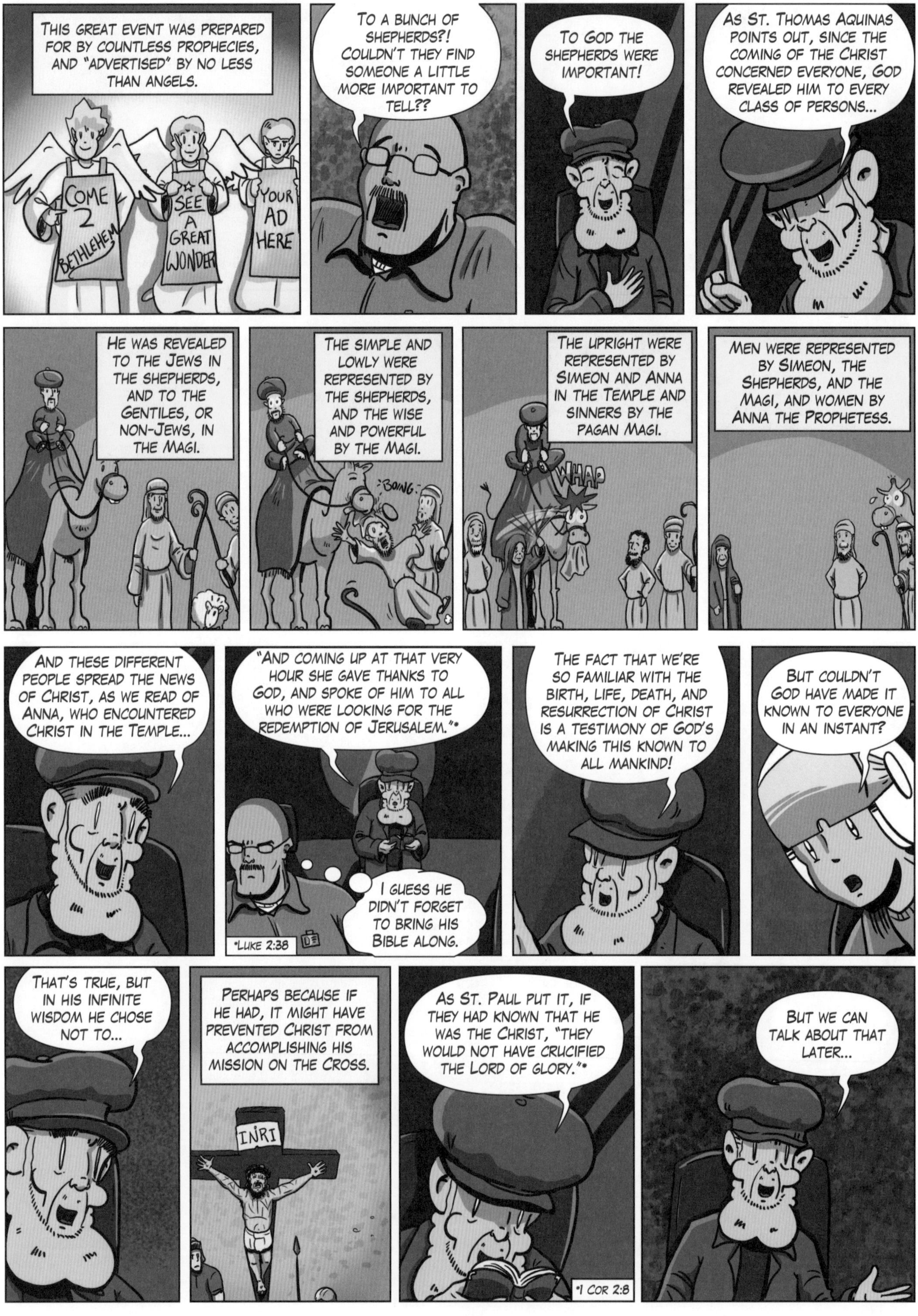
This great event was prepared for by countless prophecies, and "advertised" by no less than angels.
Come 2 Bethlehem
See a great wonder
Your ad here
To a bunch of shepherds?! Couldn't they find someone a little more important to tell??
To God the shepherds were important!
As St. Thomas Aquinas points out, since the coming of the Christ concerned everyone, God revealed him to every class of persons...
He was revealed to the Jews in the shepherds, and to the Gentiles, or non-Jews, in the Magi.
The simple and lowly were represented by the shepherds, and the wise and powerful by the Magi.
Boing
The upright were represented by Simeon and Anna in the Temple and sinners by the pagan Magi.
Whap
Men were represented by Simeon, the Shepherds, and the Magi, and women by Anna the Prophetess.
And these different people spread the news of Christ, as we read of Anna, who encountered Christ in the Temple...
"And coming up at that very hour she gave thanks to God, and spoke of him to all who were looking for the redemption of Jerusalem."*
I guess he didn't forget to bring his Bible along.
*Luke 2:38
The fact that we're so familiar with the birth, life, death, and resurrection of Christ is a testimony of God's making this known to all mankind!
But couldn't God have made it known to everyone in an instant?
That's true, but in his infinite wisdom he chose not to...
Perhaps because if he had, it might have prevented Christ from accomplishing his mission on the Cross.
INRI
As St. Paul put it, if they had known that he was the Christ, "they would not have crucified the Lord of glory."*
*1 Cor 2:8
But we can talk about that later...

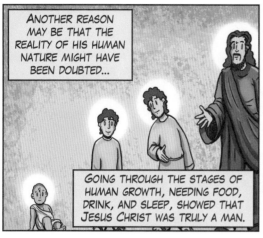

ANOTHER REASON MAY BE THAT THE REALITY OF HIS HUMAN NATURE MIGHT HAVE BEEN DOUBTED...

GOING THROUGH THE STAGES OF HUMAN GROWTH, NEEDING FOOD, DRINK, AND SLEEP, SHOWED THAT JESUS CHRIST WAS TRULY A MAN.

AFTER THE MYSTERY OF THE TRINITY, THIS IS THE GREATEST MYSTERY OF OUR FAITH—THAT IN CHRIST, GOD BECAME MAN TO SAVE THE HUMAN RACE!

THAT'S RIDICULOUS!!

WHY DO YOU SAY THAT?

JUST AS GOD BEGAN THE HUMAN RACE WITH ADAM AND EVE, SO HE CHOSE TO RE-CREATE MANKIND WITH A NEW ADAM AND A NEW EVE, JESUS AND MARY.

AND SINCE GOD CREATED ALL THINGS THROUGH HIS WORD, IT WAS FITTING THAT THE SECOND PERSON OF THE TRINITY WOULD BE THE ONE TO RE-CREATE OUR FALLEN RACE...

BECOMING LIKE US IN ALL THINGS BUT SIN.

I DON'T BELIEVE IT!

IF THE MESSIAH REALLY IS GOD, THEN WHERE'S *THAT* PROPHECY??

OBVIOUSLY THE JEWS DIDN'T KNOW OF ANY, OR THEY WOULDN'T HAVE TRIED TO KILL CHRIST FOR CLAIMING TO BE GOD!

GOD REVEALED THAT IN PROPHECY TOO, BUT IN A MORE SUBTLE WAY...

THE PROPHET ISAIAH, SPEAKING OF THE COMING MESSIAH SAYS, "HIS NAME WILL BE CALLED 'WONDERFUL COUNSELOR, MIGHTY GOD, EVERLASTING FATHER, PRINCE OF PEACE.'"*

*ISA 9:6

I THINK YOU'D AGREE THAT TITLES SUCH AS "MIGHTY GOD" AND "EVERLASTING FATHER" ARE WELL BEYOND THE MERITS OF ANY MAN, NO MATTER HOW HOLY HE MAY BE!

AND JESUS QUOTES PSALM 110, "THE LORD SAID TO MY LORD, SIT AT MY RIGHT HAND, TILL I PUT YOUR ENEMIES UNDER YOUR FEET," AND ASKS, "IF DAVID THUS CALLS HIM LORD, HOW IS HE HIS SON?"*

*MATT 22:44-45

PASSAGES LIKE THESE POINT TO THIS GREAT MYSTERY OF GOD'S INCARNATION, WHICH REQUIRES AS MUCH FAITH AS THE REVELATION OF THE TRINITY!

I'M SORRY: THAT DOESN'T REQUIRE FAITH; IT DEMANDS INSANITY!

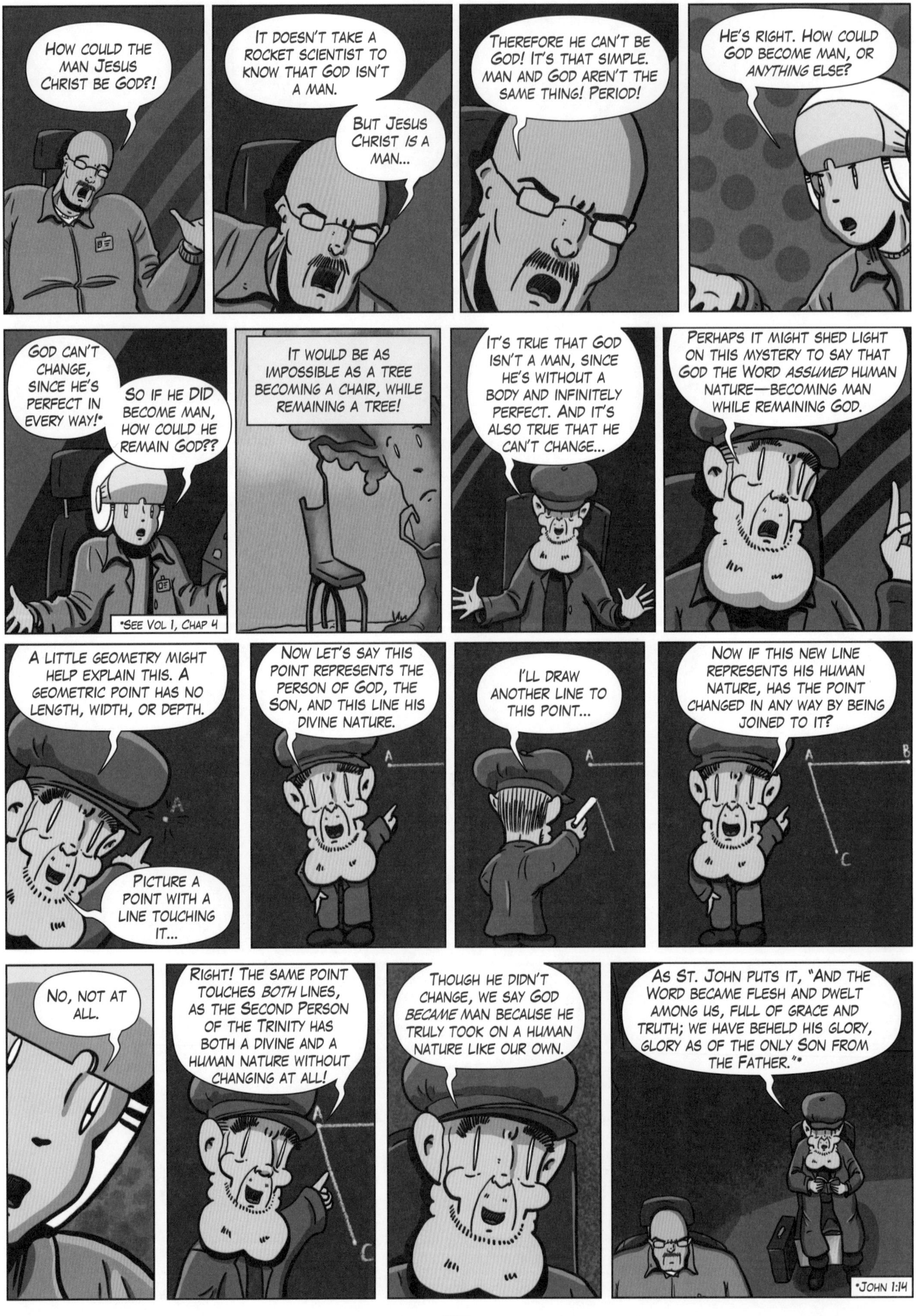
How could the man Jesus Christ be God?!
It doesn't take a rocket scientist to know that God isn't a man.
But Jesus Christ *is* a man...
Therefore he can't be God! It's that simple. Man and God aren't the same thing! Period!
He's right. How could God become man, or *anything* else?
God can't change, since he's perfect in every way!*
So if he DID become man, how could he remain God??
*See Vol 1, Chap 4
It would be as impossible as a tree becoming a chair, while remaining a tree!
It's true that God isn't a man, since he's without a body and infinitely perfect. And it's also true that he can't change...
Perhaps it might shed light on this mystery to say that God the Word *assumed* human nature—becoming man while remaining God.
A little geometry might help explain this. A geometric point has no length, width, or depth.
A
Picture a point with a line touching it...
Now let's say this point represents the person of God, the Son, and this line his divine nature.
A
I'll draw another line to this point...
A
Now if this new line represents his human nature, has the point changed in any way by being joined to it?
A
B
C
No, not at all.
Right! The same point touches *both* lines, as the Second Person of the Trinity has both a divine and a human nature without changing at all!
A
C
Though he didn't change, we say God *became* man because he truly took on a human nature like our own.
As St. John puts it, "And the Word became flesh and dwelt among us, full of grace and truth; we have beheld his glory, glory as of the only Son from the Father."*
*John 1:14

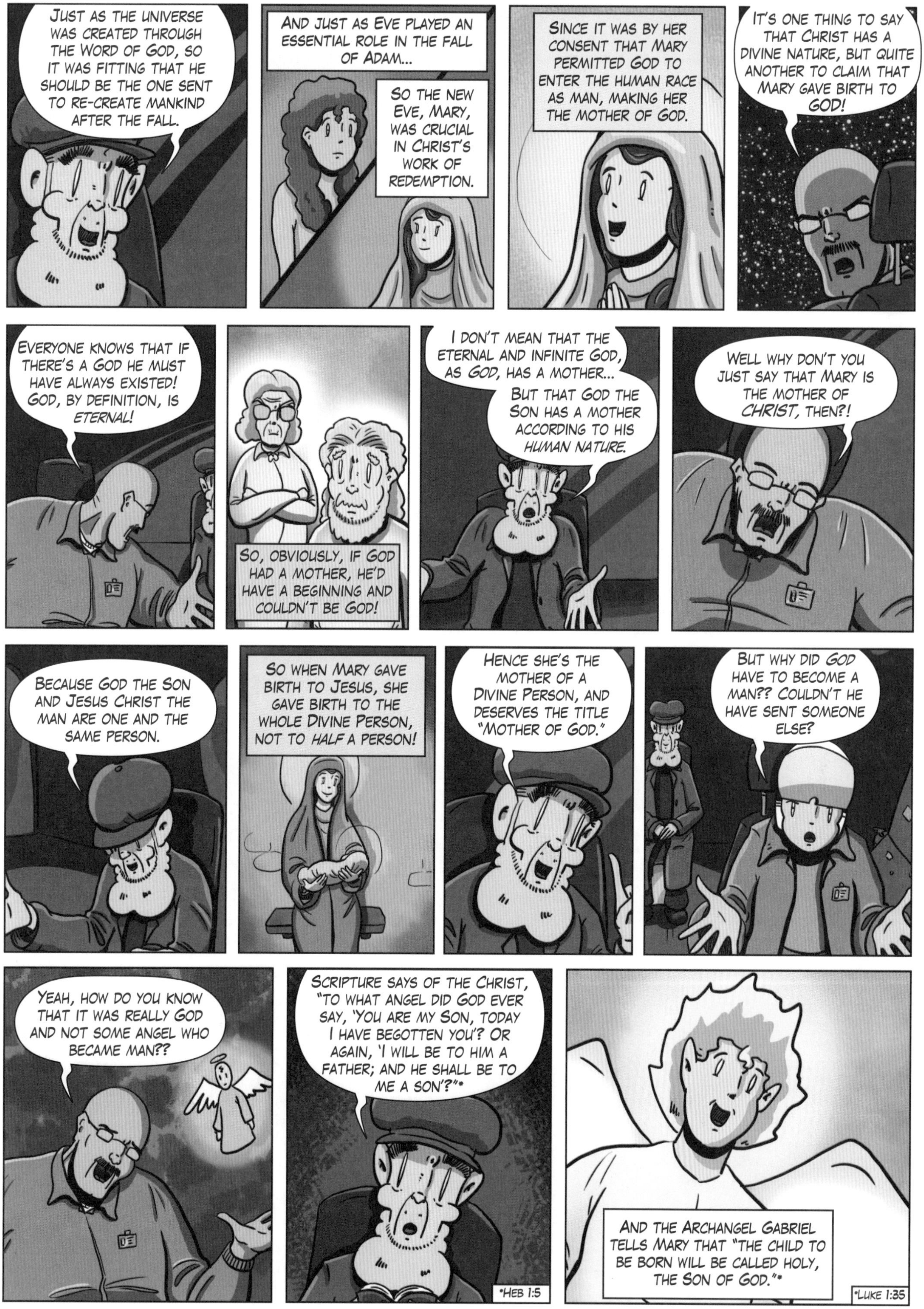
JUST AS THE UNIVERSE WAS CREATED THROUGH THE WORD OF GOD, SO IT WAS FITTING THAT HE SHOULD BE THE ONE SENT TO RE-CREATE MANKIND AFTER THE FALL.
AND JUST AS EVE PLAYED AN ESSENTIAL ROLE IN THE FALL OF ADAM...
SO THE NEW EVE, MARY, WAS CRUCIAL IN CHRIST'S WORK OF REDEMPTION.
SINCE IT WAS BY HER CONSENT THAT MARY PERMITTED GOD TO ENTER THE HUMAN RACE AS MAN, MAKING HER THE MOTHER OF GOD.
IT'S ONE THING TO SAY THAT CHRIST HAS A DIVINE NATURE, BUT QUITE ANOTHER TO CLAIM THAT MARY GAVE BIRTH TO GOD!
EVERYONE KNOWS THAT IF THERE'S A GOD HE MUST HAVE ALWAYS EXISTED! GOD, BY DEFINITION, IS ETERNAL!
SO, OBVIOUSLY, IF GOD HAD A MOTHER, HE'D HAVE A BEGINNING AND COULDN'T BE GOD!
I DON'T MEAN THAT THE ETERNAL AND INFINITE GOD, AS GOD, HAS A MOTHER...
BUT THAT GOD THE SON HAS A MOTHER ACCORDING TO HIS HUMAN NATURE.
WELL WHY DON'T YOU JUST SAY THAT MARY IS THE MOTHER OF CHRIST, THEN?!
BECAUSE GOD THE SON AND JESUS CHRIST THE MAN ARE ONE AND THE SAME PERSON.
SO WHEN MARY GAVE BIRTH TO JESUS, SHE GAVE BIRTH TO THE WHOLE DIVINE PERSON, NOT TO HALF A PERSON!
HENCE SHE'S THE MOTHER OF A DIVINE PERSON, AND DESERVES THE TITLE "MOTHER OF GOD."
BUT WHY DID GOD HAVE TO BECOME A MAN?? COULDN'T HE HAVE SENT SOMEONE ELSE?
YEAH, HOW DO YOU KNOW THAT IT WAS REALLY GOD AND NOT SOME ANGEL WHO BECAME MAN??
SCRIPTURE SAYS OF THE CHRIST, "TO WHAT ANGEL DID GOD EVER SAY, 'YOU ARE MY SON, TODAY I HAVE BEGOTTEN YOU'? OR AGAIN, 'I WILL BE TO HIM A FATHER; AND HE SHALL BE TO ME A SON'?"*
*HEB 1:5
AND THE ARCHANGEL GABRIEL TELLS MARY THAT "THE CHILD TO BE BORN WILL BE CALLED HOLY, THE SON OF GOD."*
*LUKE 1:35

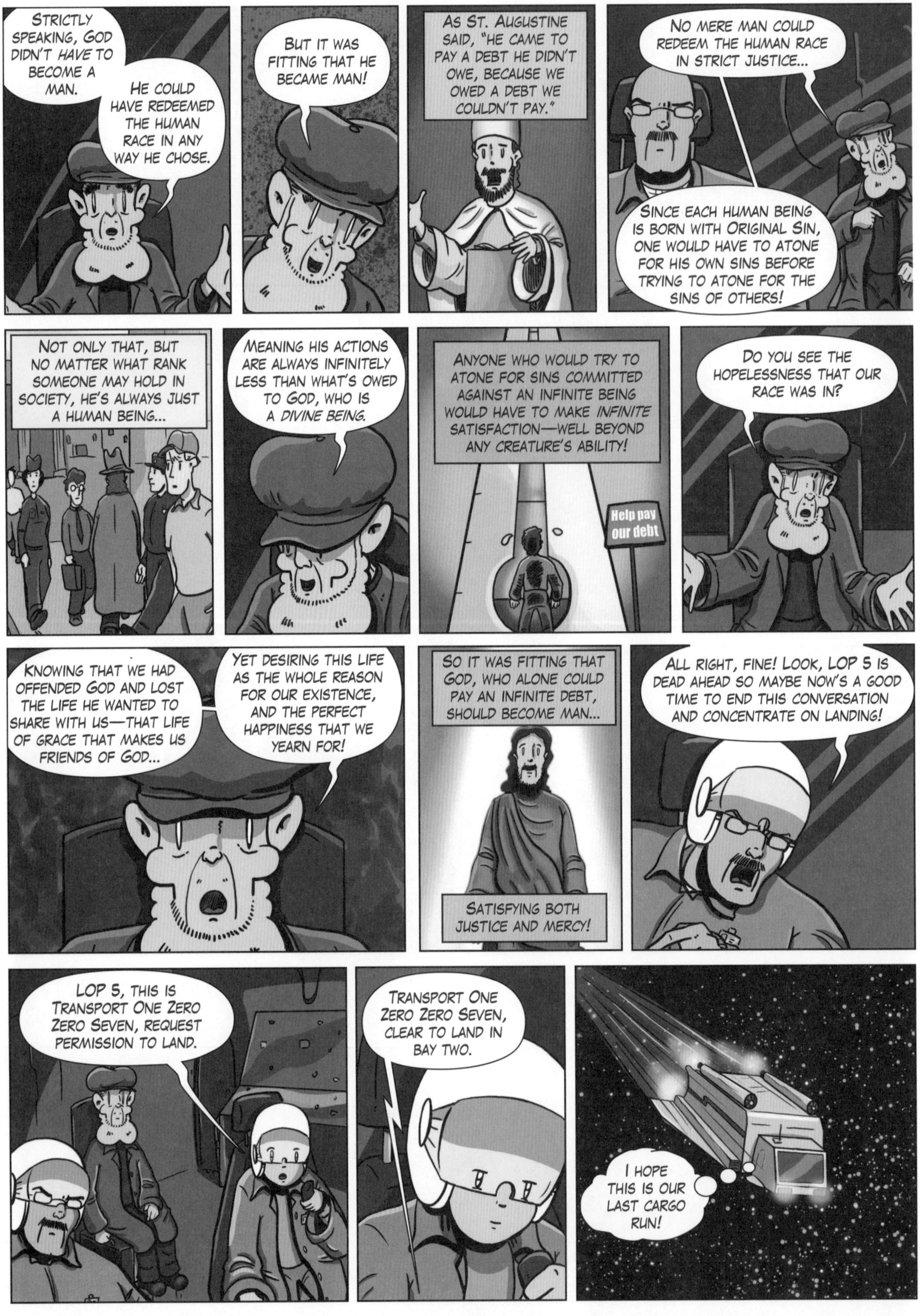
STRICTLY SPEAKING, GOD DIDN'T *HAVE* TO BECOME A MAN.
HE COULD HAVE REDEEMED THE HUMAN RACE IN ANY WAY HE CHOSE.
BUT IT WAS FITTING THAT HE BECAME MAN!
AS ST. AUGUSTINE SAID, "HE CAME TO PAY A DEBT HE DIDN'T OWE, BECAUSE WE OWED A DEBT WE COULDN'T PAY."
NO MERE MAN COULD REDEEM THE HUMAN RACE IN STRICT JUSTICE...
SINCE EACH HUMAN BEING IS BORN WITH ORIGINAL SIN, ONE WOULD HAVE TO ATONE FOR HIS OWN SINS BEFORE TRYING TO ATONE FOR THE SINS OF OTHERS!
NOT ONLY THAT, BUT NO MATTER WHAT RANK SOMEONE MAY HOLD IN SOCIETY, HE'S ALWAYS JUST A HUMAN BEING...
MEANING HIS ACTIONS ARE ALWAYS INFINITELY LESS THAN WHAT'S OWED TO GOD, WHO IS A *DIVINE BEING.*
ANYONE WHO WOULD TRY TO ATONE FOR SINS COMMITTED AGAINST AN INFINITE BEING WOULD HAVE TO MAKE *INFINITE* SATISFACTION—WELL BEYOND ANY CREATURE'S ABILITY!
Help pay our debt
DO YOU SEE THE HOPELESSNESS THAT OUR RACE WAS IN?
KNOWING THAT WE HAD OFFENDED GOD AND LOST THE LIFE HE WANTED TO SHARE WITH US—THAT LIFE OF GRACE THAT MAKES US FRIENDS OF GOD...
YET DESIRING THIS LIFE AS THE WHOLE REASON FOR OUR EXISTENCE, AND THE PERFECT HAPPINESS THAT WE YEARN FOR!
SO IT WAS FITTING THAT GOD, WHO ALONE COULD PAY AN INFINITE DEBT, SHOULD BECOME MAN...
SATISFYING BOTH JUSTICE AND MERCY!
ALL RIGHT, FINE! LOOK, LOP 5 IS DEAD AHEAD SO MAYBE NOW'S A GOOD TIME TO END THIS CONVERSATION AND CONCENTRATE ON LANDING!
LOP 5, THIS IS TRANSPORT ONE ZERO ZERO SEVEN, REQUEST PERMISSION TO LAND.
TRANSPORT ONE ZERO ZERO SEVEN, CLEAR TO LAND IN BAY TWO.
I HOPE THIS IS OUR LAST CARGO RUN!

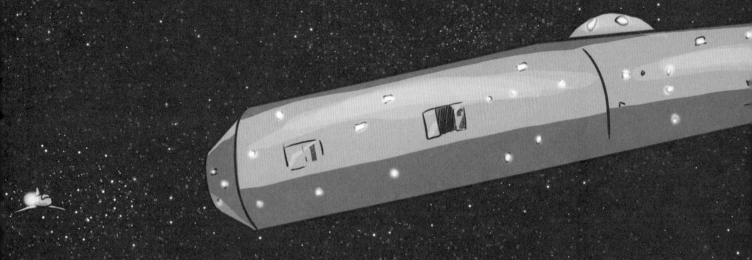

THE TIME IS
NEAR.

THE REBIRTH
OF A WORLD.

DECEMBER 25

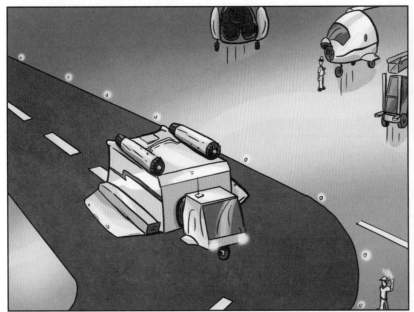

OKAY, FATHER, YOU CAN GET OFF HERE. WE'LL CATCH UP WITH YOU AFTER WE'VE UNLOADED THIS CARGO.

ALL RIGHT. HOW ABOUT WE MEET FOR COFFEE AT THE LOP 5 CAFÉ IN AN HOUR...MY TREAT.

SOUNDS GOOD!

"CLICK"

SHHHOOOP

CLAMP

TOMORROW'S CHRISTMAS EVE AND THE UNVEILING OF THE NEW FLEET. I WONDER WHAT OUR SHIP WILL BE LIKE AFTER THOSE REPAIRS?

I DON'T CARE AS LONG AS I DON'T HAVE TO FLY IN THIS BUCKET OF JUNK ANYMORE!

LATER...

ERC, WE'VE BEEN FLYING THAT STARHAWK FOR NEARLY A MONTH, AND I CAN'T SEE WHY YOU STILL DON'T LIKE IT.

SURE IT'S OBSOLETE, BUT IT'S SOLIDLY BUILT AND FLIES WELL!

YEAH, AS LONG AS THE ENGINES WORK!

BUT EVEN IF IT DOES FLY WELL, IT'S STILL A LOUSY SHIP!

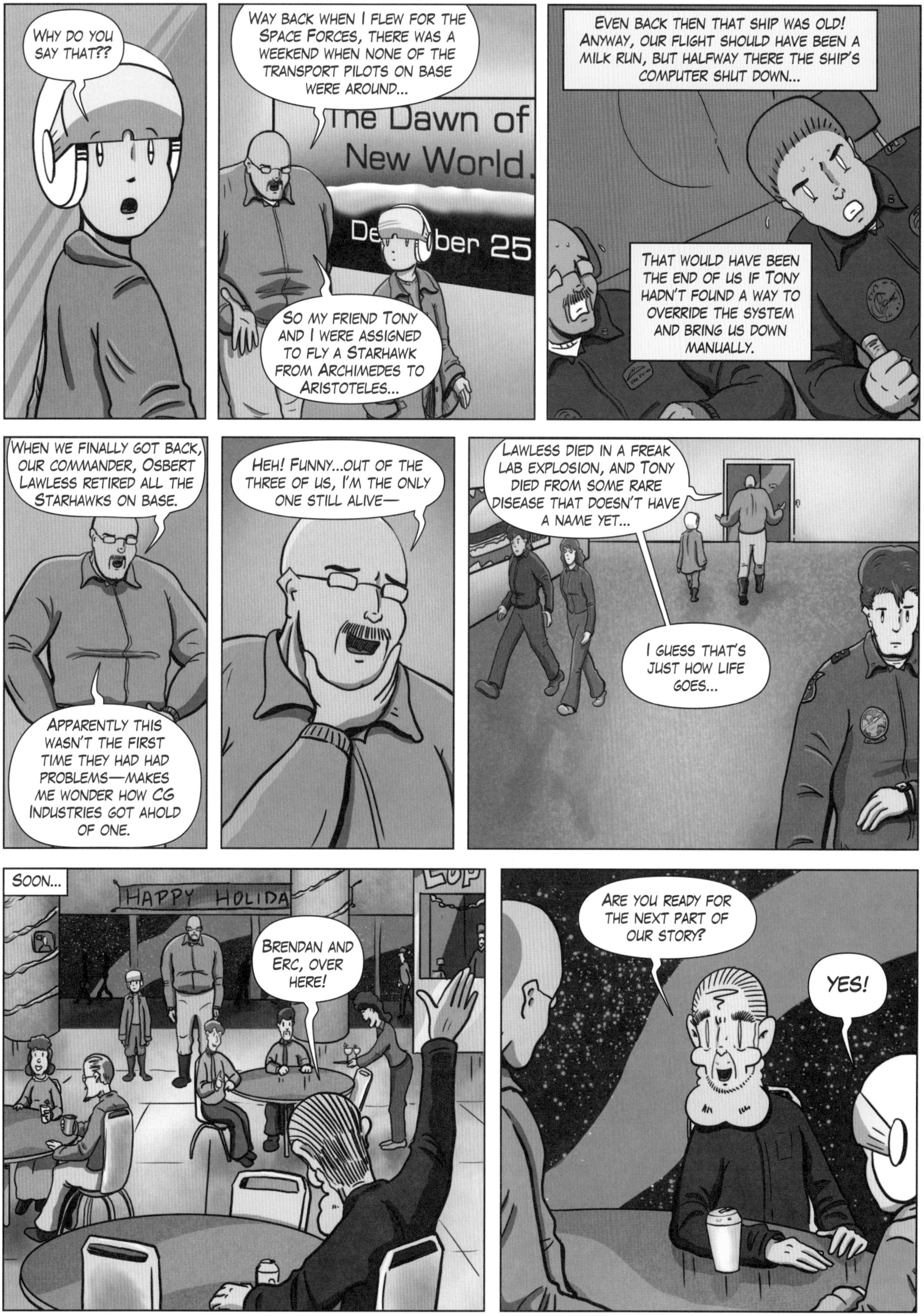
WHY DO YOU SAY THAT??
WAY BACK WHEN I FLEW FOR THE SPACE FORCES, THERE WAS A WEEKEND WHEN NONE OF THE TRANSPORT PILOTS ON BASE WERE AROUND...
The Dawn of New World.
De ber 25
SO MY FRIEND TONY AND I WERE ASSIGNED TO FLY A STARHAWK FROM ARCHIMEDES TO ARISTOTELES...
EVEN BACK THEN THAT SHIP WAS OLD! ANYWAY, OUR FLIGHT SHOULD HAVE BEEN A MILK RUN, BUT HALFWAY THERE THE SHIP'S COMPUTER SHUT DOWN...
THAT WOULD HAVE BEEN THE END OF US IF TONY HADN'T FOUND A WAY TO OVERRIDE THE SYSTEM AND BRING US DOWN MANUALLY.
WHEN WE FINALLY GOT BACK, OUR COMMANDER, OSBERT LAWLESS RETIRED ALL THE STARHAWKS ON BASE.
APPARENTLY THIS WASN'T THE FIRST TIME THEY HAD HAD PROBLEMS—MAKES ME WONDER HOW CG INDUSTRIES GOT AHOLD OF ONE.
HEH! FUNNY...OUT OF THE THREE OF US, I'M THE ONLY ONE STILL ALIVE—
LAWLESS DIED IN A FREAK LAB EXPLOSION, AND TONY DIED FROM SOME RARE DISEASE THAT DOESN'T HAVE A NAME YET...
I GUESS THAT'S JUST HOW LIFE GOES...
SOON...
HAPPY HOLIDA
BRENDAN AND ERC, OVER HERE!
ARE YOU READY FOR THE NEXT PART OF OUR STORY?
YES!

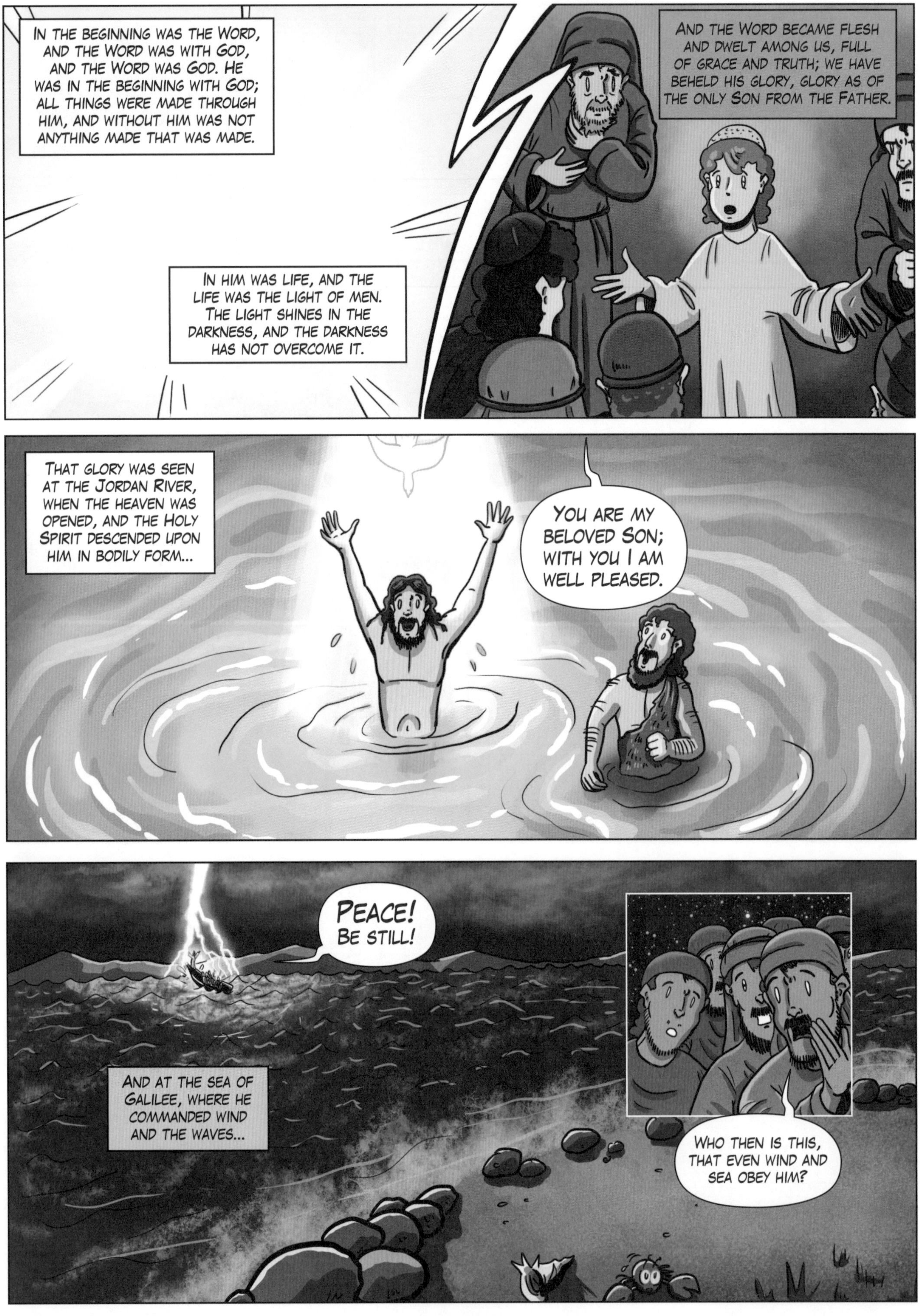
In the beginning was the Word, and the Word was with God, and the Word was God. He was in the beginning with God; all things were made through him, and without him was not anything made that was made.
In him was life, and the life was the light of men. The light shines in the darkness, and the darkness has not overcome it.
And the Word became flesh and dwelt among us, full of grace and truth; we have beheld his glory, glory as of the only Son from the Father.
That glory was seen at the Jordan River, when the heaven was opened, and the Holy Spirit descended upon him in bodily form...
You are my beloved Son; with you I am well pleased.
Peace! Be still!
And at the sea of Galilee, where he commanded wind and the waves...
Who then is this, that even wind and sea obey him?

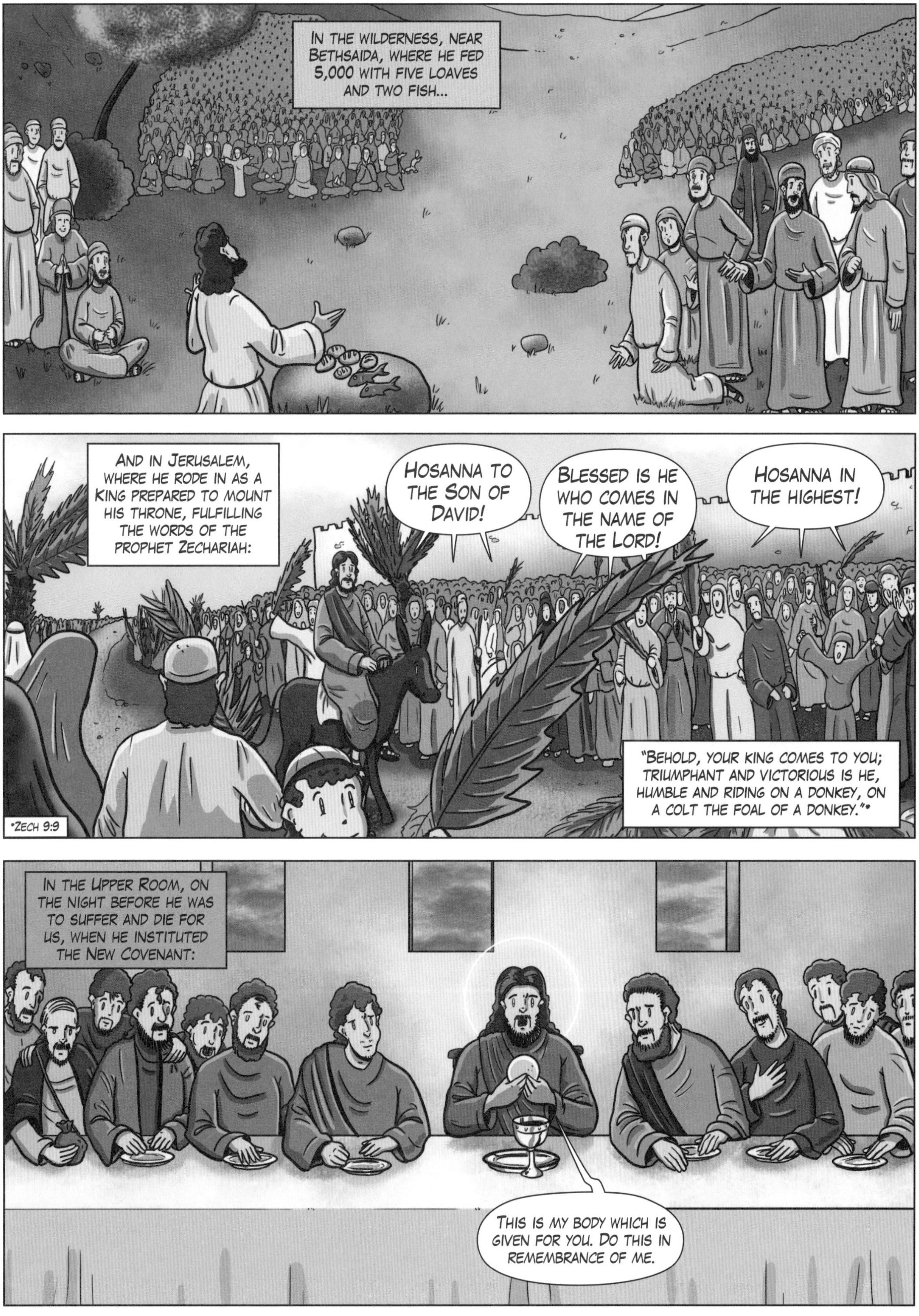
In the wilderness, near Bethsaida, where he fed 5,000 with five loaves and two fish...
And in Jerusalem, where he rode in as a King prepared to mount his throne, fulfilling the words of the prophet Zechariah:
Hosanna to the Son of David!
Blessed is he who comes in the name of the Lord!
Hosanna in the highest!
"Behold, your king comes to you; triumphant and victorious is he, humble and riding on a donkey, on a colt the foal of a donkey."*
*Zech 9:9
In the Upper Room, on the night before he was to suffer and die for us, when he instituted the New Covenant:
This is my body which is given for you. Do this in remembrance of me.

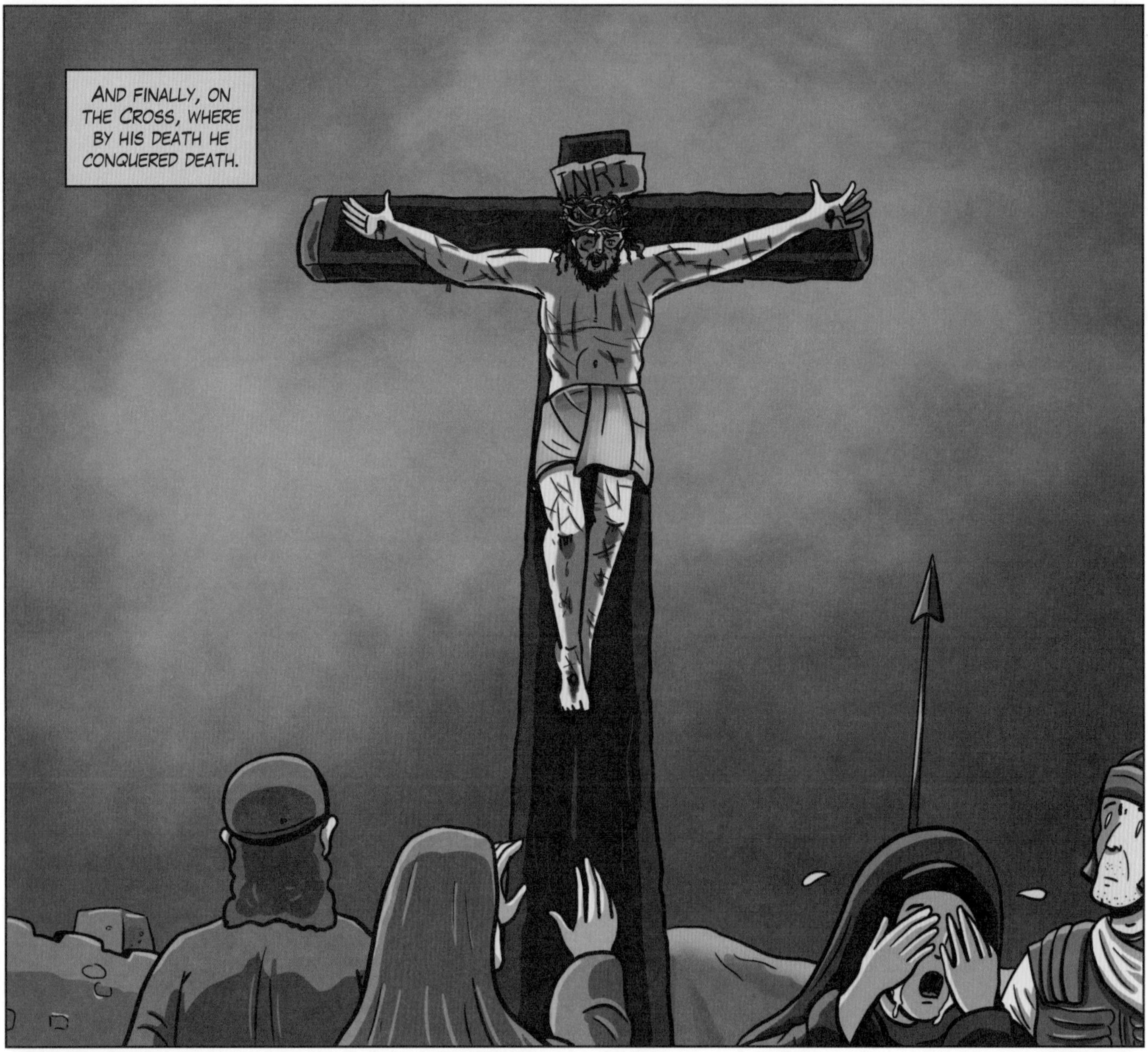
AND FINALLY, ON THE CROSS, WHERE BY HIS DEATH HE CONQUERED DEATH.
INRI

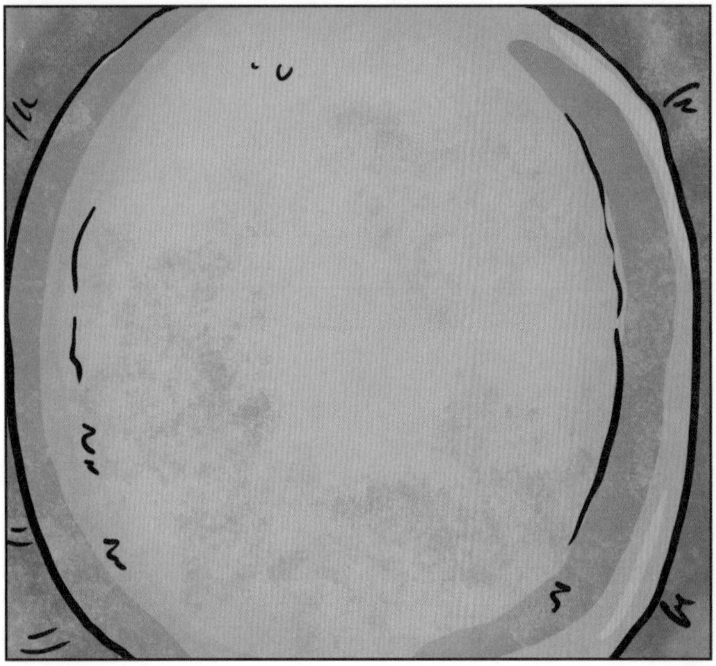

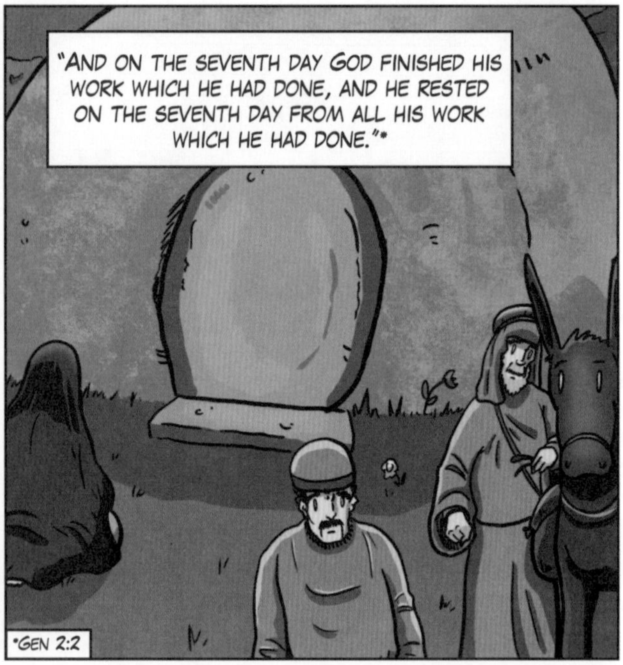
"AND ON THE SEVENTH DAY GOD FINISHED HIS WORK WHICH HE HAD DONE, AND HE RESTED ON THE SEVENTH DAY FROM ALL HIS WORK WHICH HE HAD DONE."*
*GEN 2:2

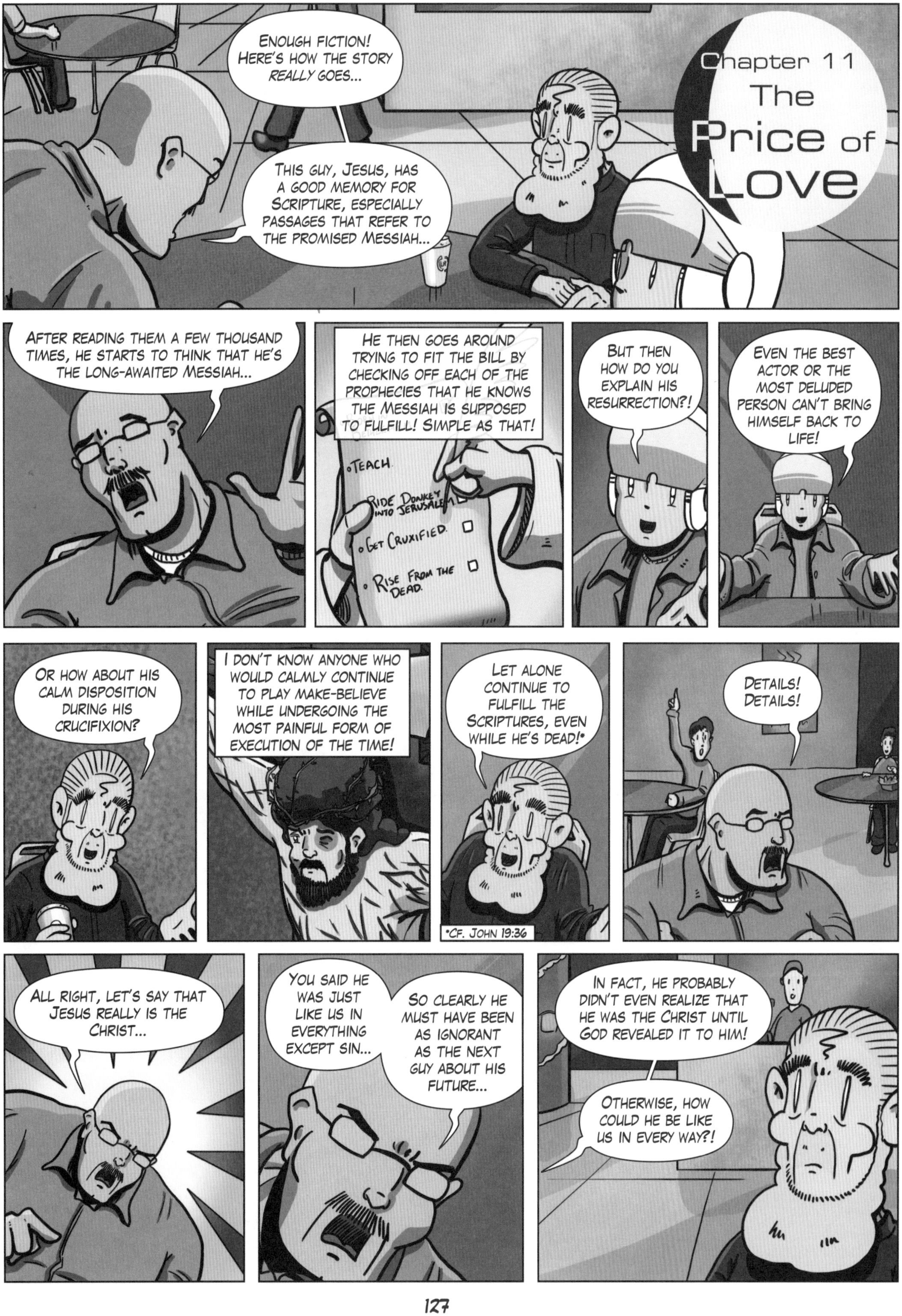
Chapter 11 The Price of Love
Enough fiction! Here's how the story really goes...
This guy, Jesus, has a good memory for Scripture, especially passages that refer to the promised Messiah...
After reading them a few thousand times, he starts to think that he's the long-awaited Messiah...
He then goes around trying to fit the bill by checking off each of the prophecies that he knows the Messiah is supposed to fulfill! Simple as that!
Teach.
Ride Donkey into Jerusalem
Get Cruxified.
Rise From the Dead.
But then how do you explain his resurrection?!
Even the best actor or the most deluded person can't bring himself back to life!
Or how about his calm disposition during his crucifixion?
I don't know anyone who would calmly continue to play make-believe while undergoing the most painful form of execution of the time!
Let alone continue to fulfill the Scriptures, even while he's dead!*
*Cf. John 19:36
Details! Details!
All right, let's say that Jesus really is the Christ...
You said he was just like us in everything except sin...
So clearly he must have been as ignorant as the next guy about his future...
In fact, he probably didn't even realize that he was the Christ until God revealed it to him!
Otherwise, how could he be like us in every way?!

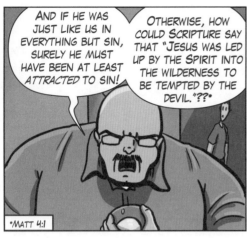

AND IF HE WAS JUST LIKE US IN EVERYTHING BUT SIN, SURELY HE MUST HAVE BEEN AT LEAST *ATTRACTED* TO SIN!

OTHERWISE, HOW COULD SCRIPTURE SAY THAT "JESUS WAS LED UP BY THE SPIRIT INTO THE WILDERNESS TO BE TEMPTED BY THE DEVIL."??*

*MATT 4:1

EVEN THE DEVIL CAN QUOTE SCRIPTURE!

WHAT'S *THAT* SUPPOSED TO MEAN?!

IT'S TRUE THAT BEING FREE FROM SIN DOESN'T MEAN YOU'RE NOT ATTRACTED TO SIN!

AND IF JESUS COULD SUFFER, THEN HE MUST HAVE HAD THE SAME FALLEN HUMAN NATURE AS WE HAVE...SINCE ADAM AND EVE DIDN'T SUFFER UNTIL AFTER THE FALL!

IT'S TRUE THAT ADAM AND EVE DIDN'T SUFFER UNTIL AFTER THE FALL, WHEN THEY LOST GOD'S GIFTS, AND THAT OUR LORD TOOK A BODY CAPABLE OF SUFFERING...

BUT THAT DOESN'T MEAN CHRIST WAS BORN WITH ORIGINAL SIN! NOR WAS HE IGNORANT JUST BECAUSE HE HAD A HUMAN NATURE, SINCE BEING IGNORANT ISN'T *ESSENTIAL* TO OUR NATURE.

IT WAS ESSENTIAL TO HIS MISSION THAT HE BE ABLE TO SUFFER SO AS TO REDEEM US...

BUT IT WASN'T NECESSARY FOR THAT MISSION TO BE IGNORANT OF WHO HE WAS EVEN FOR AN INSTANT!

AS TRUE MAN, CHRIST HAD A HUMAN KNOWLEDGE THAT COULD GROW WITH TIME AND EXPERIENCE LIKE US, BUT HE ALSO HAD AN *INFUSED* KNOWLEDGE FROM HIS UNION WITH HIS DIVINE NATURE...

WHICH GAVE HIM KNOWLEDGE OF ALL THINGS KNOWN THROUGH DIVINE REVELATION AND HUMAN SCIENCE...

INCLUDING THE THOUGHTS OF MEN!

DID YOU NEED SOMETHING?

NO THANK YOU.

OH? DOESN'T HE SAY SOMEWHERE...

"BUT OF THAT DAY OR THAT HOUR NO ONE KNOWS, NOT EVEN THE ANGELS IN HEAVEN, NOR THE SON, BUT ONLY THE FATHER"?*

YES, BUT IT DOESN'T MEAN WHAT YOU MIGHT THINK...

*MARK 13:32

IT SEEMS PRETTY OBVIOUS THAT IT MEANS HE DIDN'T KNOW SOMETHING!

AS ST. JOHN CHRYSOSTOM POINTS OUT, IF CHRIST, AS MAN, HAS THE POWER TO KNOW HOW TO JUDGE ALL PEOPLE ON THE DAY OF JUDGMENT, HOW MUCH MORE DOES HE HAVE THE POWER TO KNOW SOMETHING OF LESS IMPORTANCE SUCH AS *WHEN* THAT DAY WILL COME.*

*MATT 25:31-36

BUT THEN WHY DOES HE SAY THAT HE DOESN'T KNOW?

JESUS IS USING A WAY OF SPEAKING THAT TELLS HIS LISTENERS THAT IT'S NOT FOR THEM TO KNOW THE ANSWER.

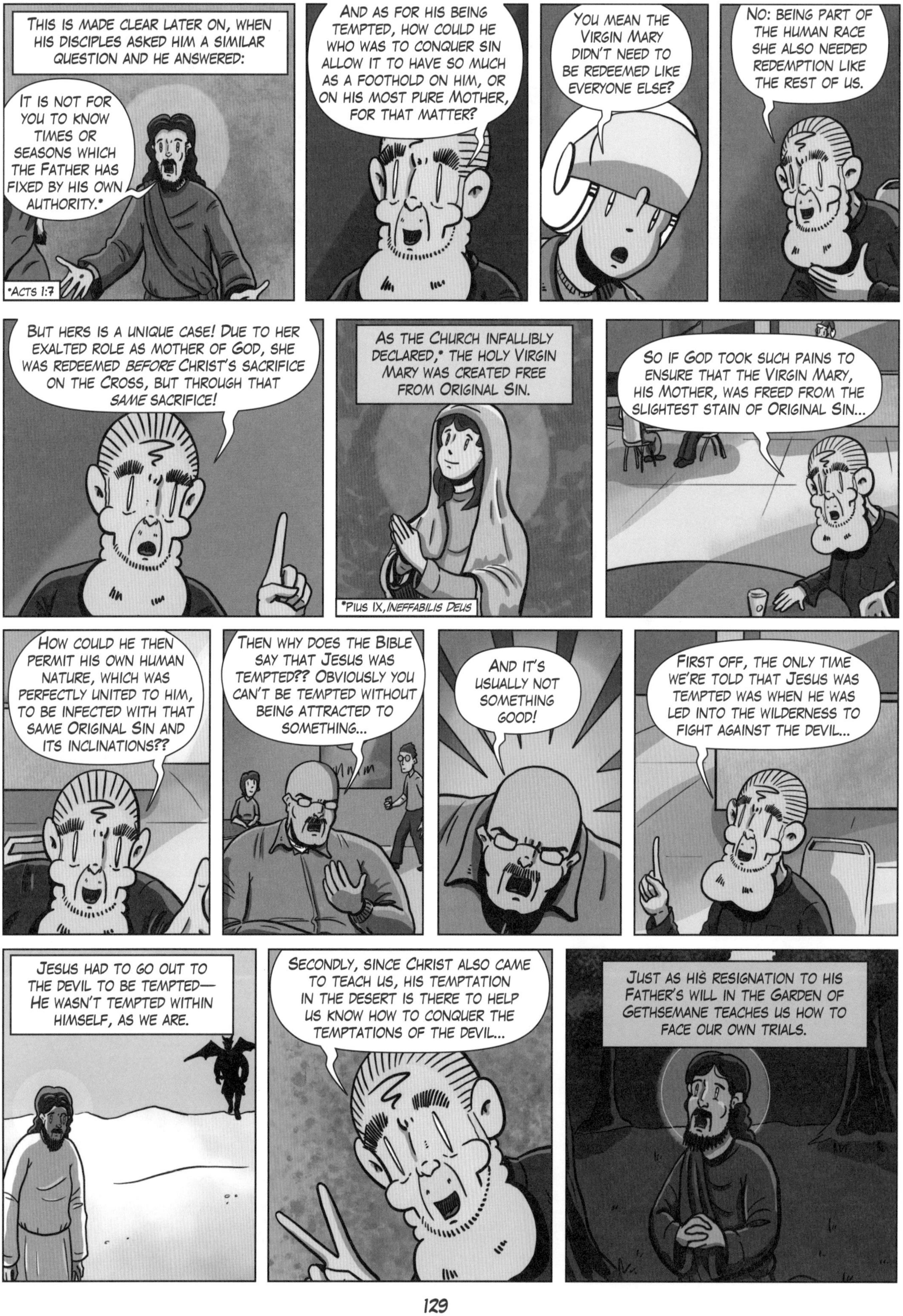

This is made clear later on, when his disciples asked him a similar question and he answered:
It is not for you to know times or seasons which the Father has fixed by his own authority.*
*Acts 1:7
And as for his being tempted, how could he who was to conquer sin allow it to have so much as a foothold on him, or on his most pure Mother, for that matter?
You mean the Virgin Mary didn't need to be redeemed like everyone else?
No: being part of the human race she also needed redemption like the rest of us.
But hers is a unique case! Due to her exalted role as mother of God, she was redeemed *before* Christ's sacrifice on the Cross, but through that *same* sacrifice!
As the Church infallibly declared,* the holy Virgin Mary was created free from Original Sin.
*Pius IX, *Ineffabilis Deus*
So if God took such pains to ensure that the Virgin Mary, his Mother, was freed from the slightest stain of Original Sin...
How could he then permit his own human nature, which was perfectly united to him, to be infected with that same Original Sin and its inclinations??
Then why does the Bible say that Jesus was tempted?? Obviously you can't be tempted without being attracted to something...
And it's usually not something good!
First off, the only time we're told that Jesus was tempted was when he was led into the wilderness to fight against the devil...
Jesus had to go out to the devil to be tempted—He wasn't tempted within himself, as we are.
Secondly, since Christ also came to teach us, his temptation in the desert is there to help us know how to conquer the temptations of the devil...
Just as his resignation to his Father's will in the Garden of Gethsemane teaches us how to face our own trials.

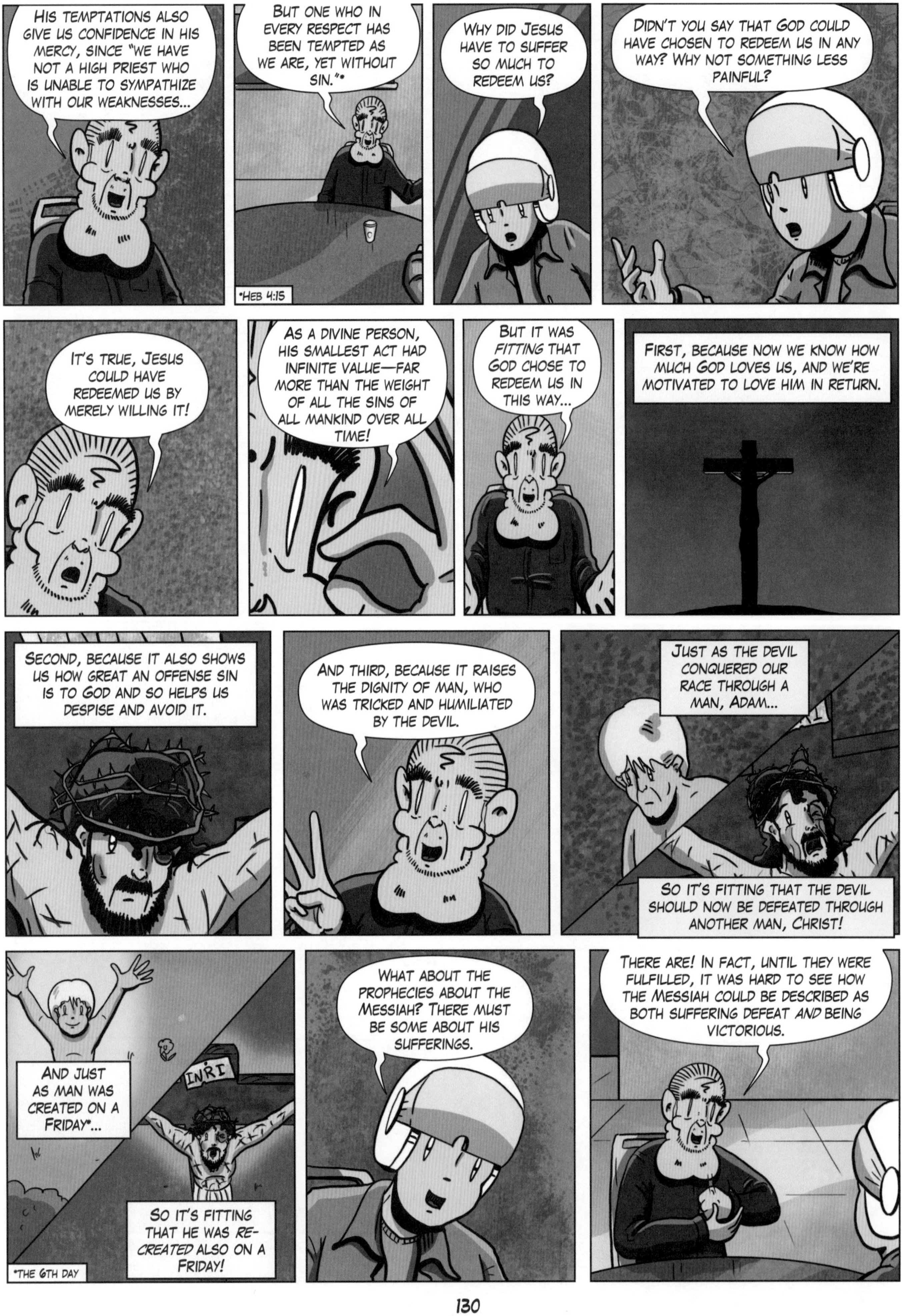

His temptations also give us confidence in his mercy, since "we have not a high priest who is unable to sympathize with our weaknesses...
But one who in every respect has been tempted as we are, yet without sin."*
*Heb 4:15
Why did Jesus have to suffer so much to redeem us?
Didn't you say that God could have chosen to redeem us in any way? Why not something less painful?
It's true, Jesus could have redeemed us by merely willing it!
As a divine person, his smallest act had infinite value—far more than the weight of all the sins of all mankind over all time!
But it was *fitting* that God chose to redeem us in this way...
First, because now we know how much God loves us, and we're motivated to love him in return.
Second, because it also shows us how great an offense sin is to God and so helps us despise and avoid it.
And third, because it raises the dignity of man, who was tricked and humiliated by the devil.
Just as the devil conquered our race through a man, Adam...
So it's fitting that the devil should now be defeated through another man, Christ!
And just as man was created on a Friday*...
INRI
So it's fitting that he was *re-created* also on a Friday!
*The 6th day
What about the prophecies about the Messiah? There must be some about his sufferings.
There are! In fact, until they were fulfilled, it was hard to see how the Messiah could be described as both suffering defeat *and* being victorious.

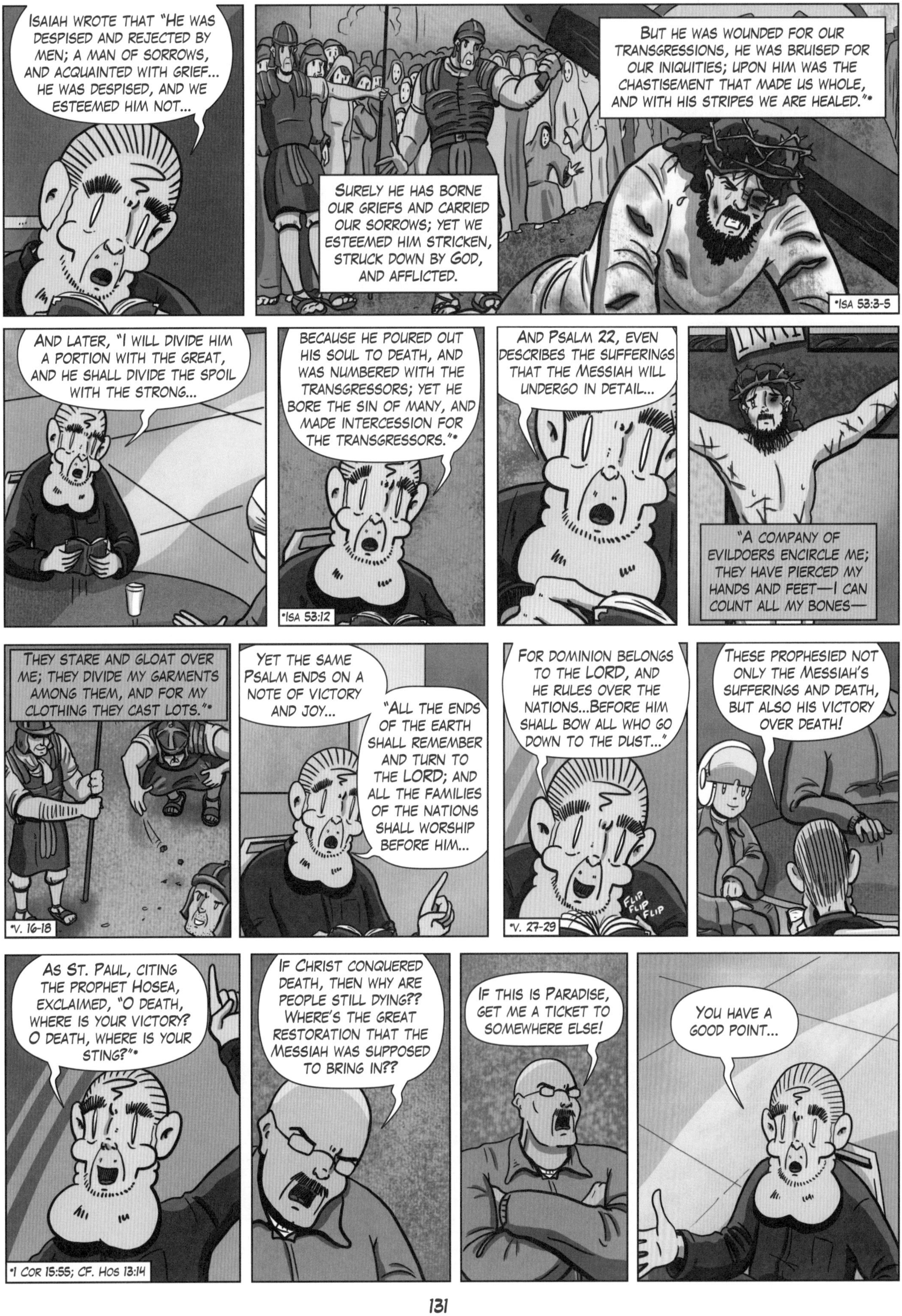

Isaiah wrote that "He was despised and rejected by men; a man of sorrows, and acquainted with grief... he was despised, and we esteemed him not...
Surely he has borne our griefs and carried our sorrows; yet we esteemed him stricken, struck down by God, and afflicted.
But he was wounded for our transgressions, he was bruised for our iniquities; upon him was the chastisement that made us whole, and with his stripes we are healed."*
*Isa 53:3-5
And later, "I will divide him a portion with the great, and he shall divide the spoil with the strong...
because he poured out his soul to death, and was numbered with the transgressors; yet he bore the sin of many, and made intercession for the transgressors."*
*Isa 53:12
And Psalm 22, even describes the sufferings that the Messiah will undergo in detail...
"A company of evildoers encircle me; they have pierced my hands and feet—I can count all my bones—
They stare and gloat over me; they divide my garments among them, and for my clothing they cast lots."*
*v. 16-18
Yet the same Psalm ends on a note of victory and joy...
"All the ends of the earth shall remember and turn to the LORD; and all the families of the nations shall worship before him...
For dominion belongs to the LORD, and he rules over the nations...Before him shall bow all who go down to the dust..."
Flip Flip Flip
*v. 27-29
These prophesied not only the Messiah's sufferings and death, but also his victory over death!
As St. Paul, citing the prophet Hosea, exclaimed, "O death, where is your victory? O death, where is your sting?"*
*1 Cor 15:55; cf. Hos 13:14
If Christ conquered death, then why are people still dying?? Where's the great restoration that the Messiah was supposed to bring in??
If this is Paradise, get me a ticket to somewhere else!
You have a good point...

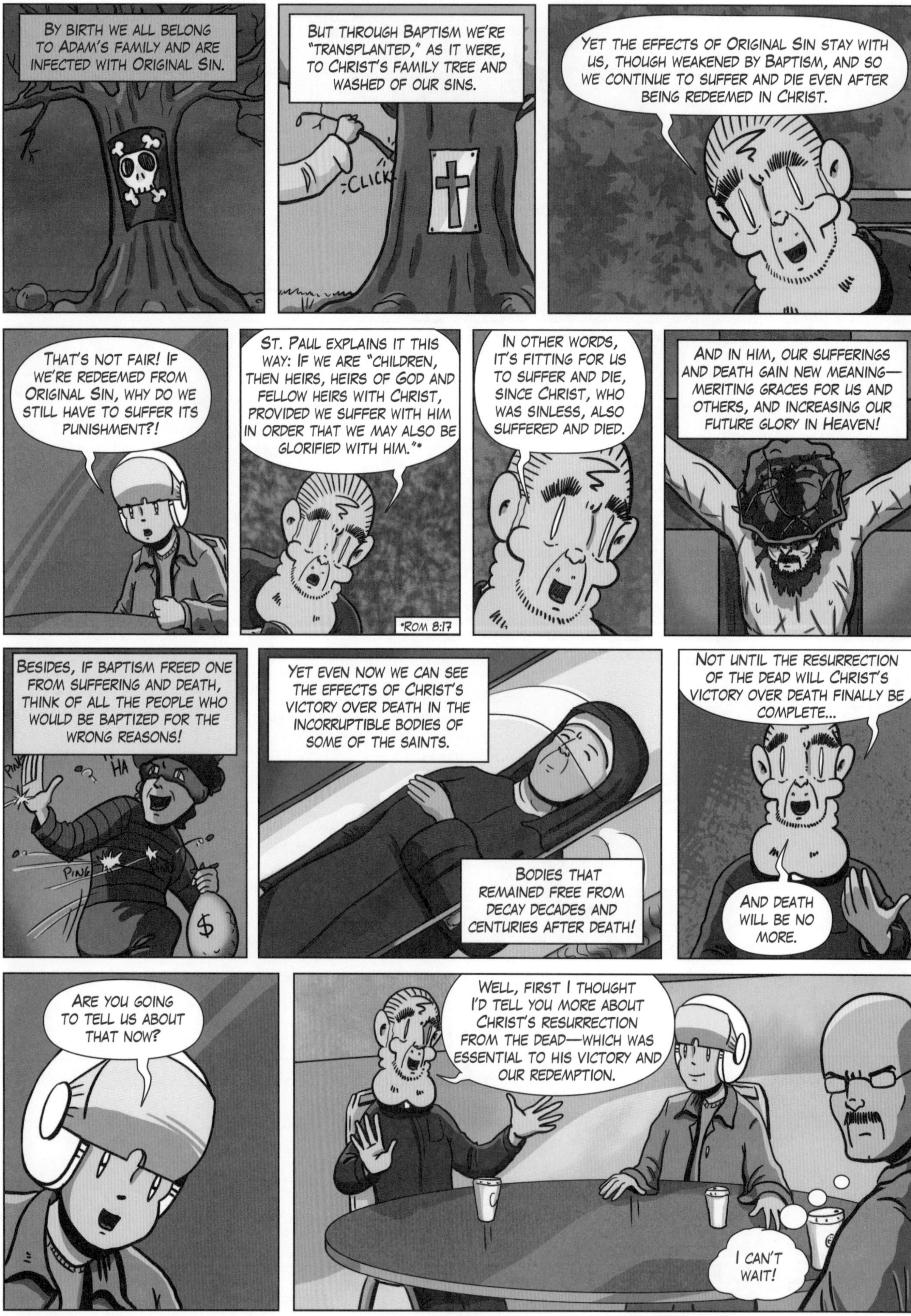
BY BIRTH WE ALL BELONG TO ADAM'S FAMILY AND ARE INFECTED WITH ORIGINAL SIN.
BUT THROUGH BAPTISM WE'RE "TRANSPLANTED," AS IT WERE, TO CHRIST'S FAMILY TREE AND WASHED OF OUR SINS.
CLICK
YET THE EFFECTS OF ORIGINAL SIN STAY WITH US, THOUGH WEAKENED BY BAPTISM, AND SO WE CONTINUE TO SUFFER AND DIE EVEN AFTER BEING REDEEMED IN CHRIST.
THAT'S NOT FAIR! IF WE'RE REDEEMED FROM ORIGINAL SIN, WHY DO WE STILL HAVE TO SUFFER ITS PUNISHMENT?!
ST. PAUL EXPLAINS IT THIS WAY: IF WE ARE "CHILDREN, THEN HEIRS, HEIRS OF GOD AND FELLOW HEIRS WITH CHRIST, PROVIDED WE SUFFER WITH HIM IN ORDER THAT WE MAY ALSO BE GLORIFIED WITH HIM."*
*ROM 8:17
IN OTHER WORDS, IT'S FITTING FOR US TO SUFFER AND DIE, SINCE CHRIST, WHO WAS SINLESS, ALSO SUFFERED AND DIED.
AND IN HIM, OUR SUFFERINGS AND DEATH GAIN NEW MEANING—MERITING GRACES FOR US AND OTHERS, AND INCREASING OUR FUTURE GLORY IN HEAVEN!
BESIDES, IF BAPTISM FREED ONE FROM SUFFERING AND DEATH, THINK OF ALL THE PEOPLE WHO WOULD BE BAPTIZED FOR THE WRONG REASONS!
HA
PING
PING
YET EVEN NOW WE CAN SEE THE EFFECTS OF CHRIST'S VICTORY OVER DEATH IN THE INCORRUPTIBLE BODIES OF SOME OF THE SAINTS.
BODIES THAT REMAINED FREE FROM DECAY DECADES AND CENTURIES AFTER DEATH!
NOT UNTIL THE RESURRECTION OF THE DEAD WILL CHRIST'S VICTORY OVER DEATH FINALLY BE COMPLETE...
AND DEATH WILL BE NO MORE.
ARE YOU GOING TO TELL US ABOUT THAT NOW?
WELL, FIRST I THOUGHT I'D TELL YOU MORE ABOUT CHRIST'S RESURRECTION FROM THE DEAD—WHICH WAS ESSENTIAL TO HIS VICTORY AND OUR REDEMPTION.
I CAN'T WAIT!

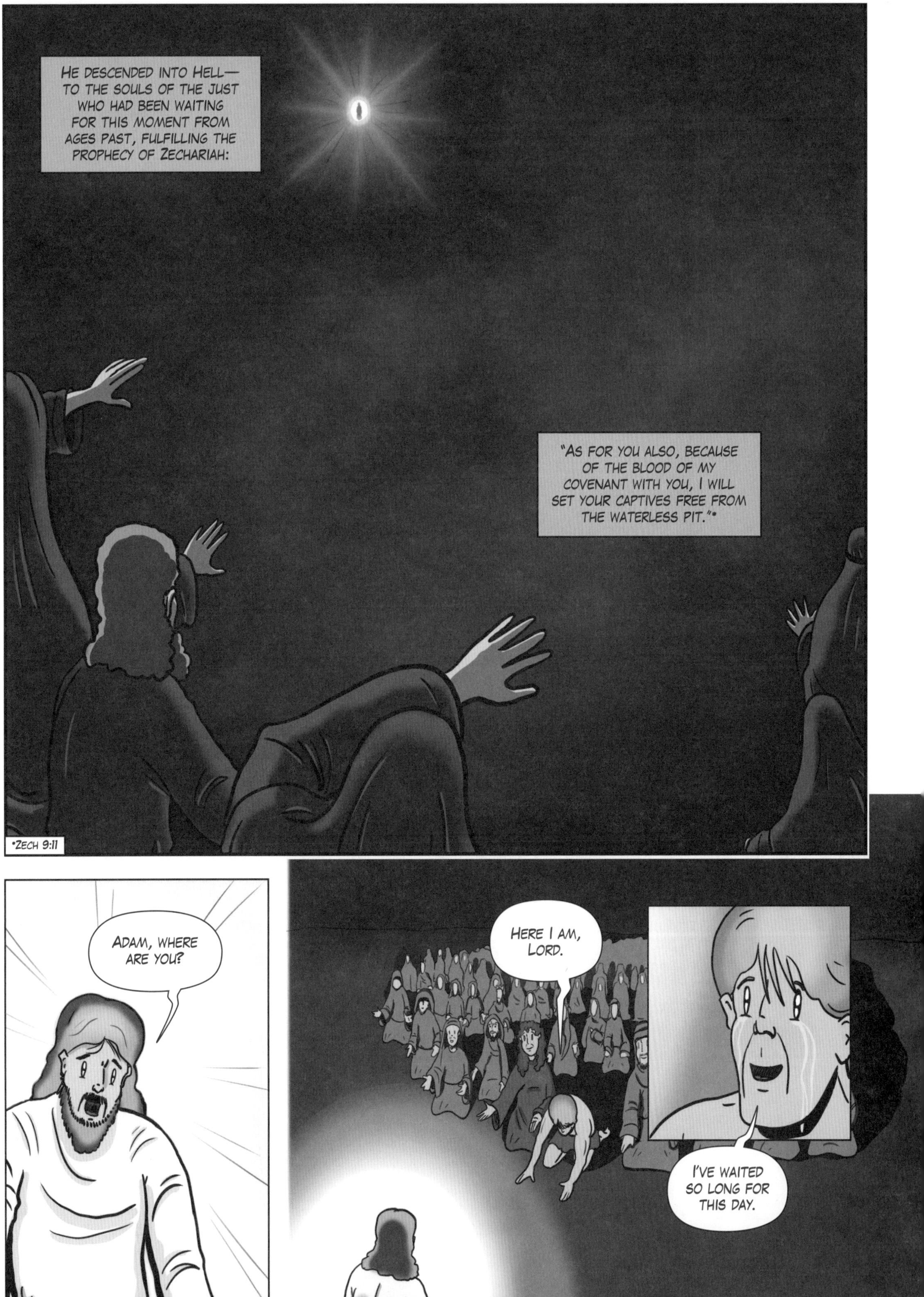
He descended into Hell—to the souls of the just who had been waiting for this moment from ages past, fulfilling the prophecy of Zechariah:
"As for you also, because of the blood of my covenant with you, I will set your captives free from the waterless pit."*
*Zech 9:11
Adam, where are you?
Here I am, Lord.
I've waited so long for this day.

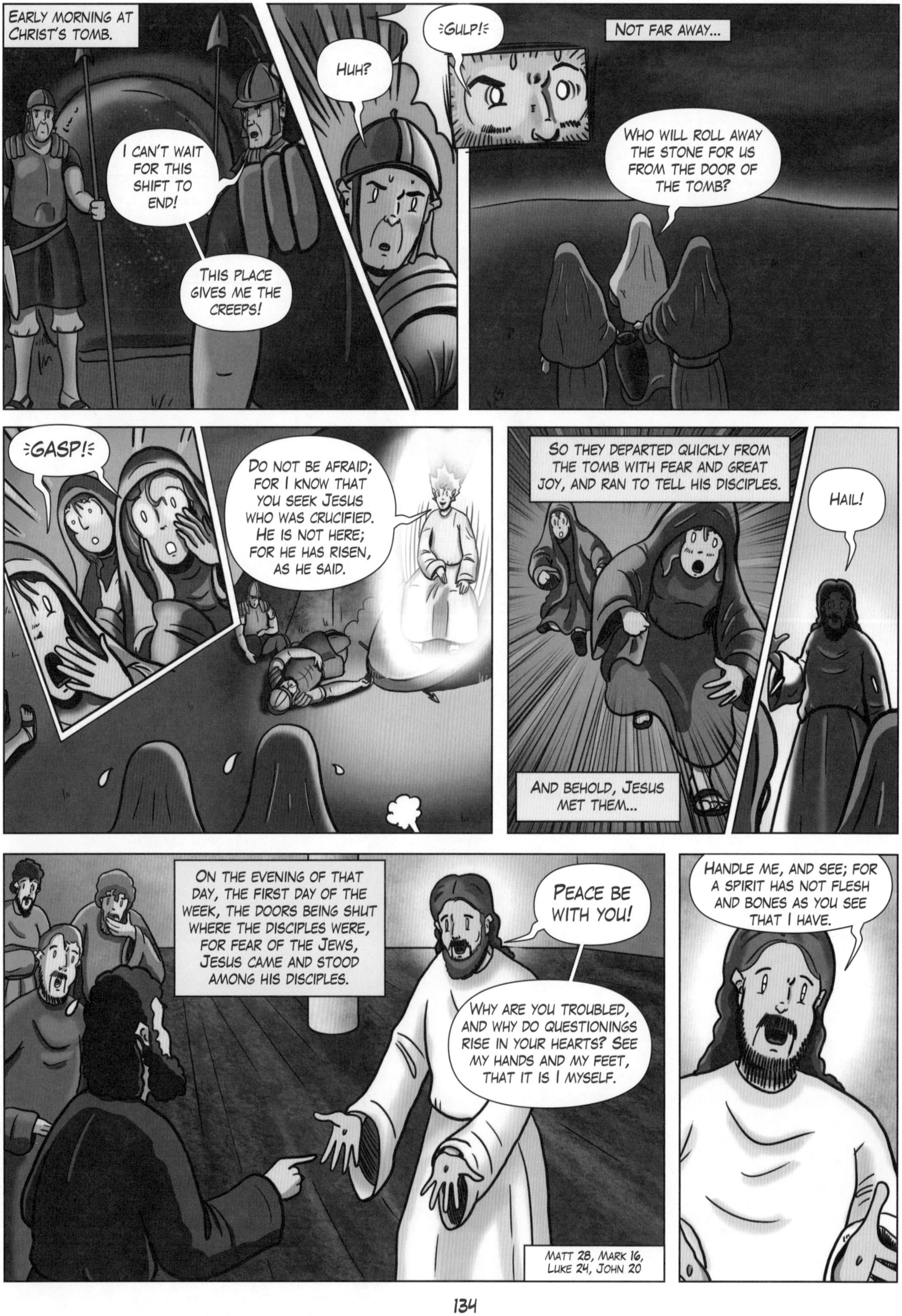
Early morning at Christ's tomb.
I can't wait for this shift to end!
This place gives me the creeps!
Huh?
Gulp!
Not far away...
Who will roll away the stone for us from the door of the tomb?
Gasp!
Do not be afraid; for I know that you seek Jesus who was crucified. He is not here; for he has risen, as he said.
So they departed quickly from the tomb with fear and great joy, and ran to tell his disciples.
And behold, Jesus met them...
Hail!
On the evening of that day, the first day of the week, the doors being shut where the disciples were, for fear of the Jews, Jesus came and stood among his disciples.
Peace be with you!
Why are you troubled, and why do questionings rise in your hearts? See my hands and my feet, that it is I myself.
Matt 28, Mark 16, Luke 24, John 20
Handle me, and see; for a spirit has not flesh and bones as you see that I have.

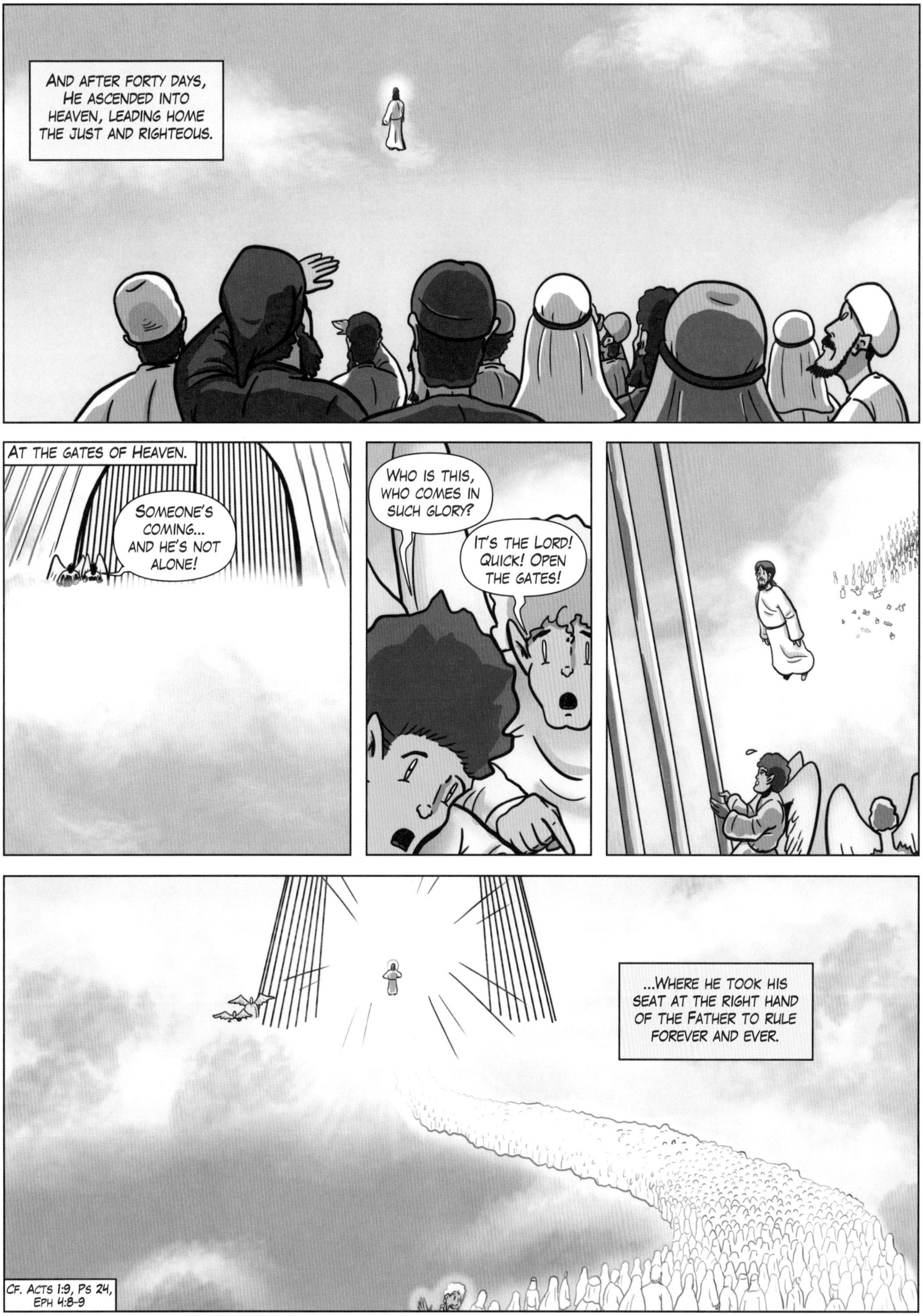

And after forty days, He ascended into heaven, leading home the just and righteous.
At the gates of Heaven.
Someone's coming... and he's not alone!
Who is this, who comes in such glory?
It's the Lord! Quick! Open the gates!
...Where he took his seat at the right hand of the Father to rule forever and ever.
Cf. Acts 1:9, Ps 24, Eph 4:8-9

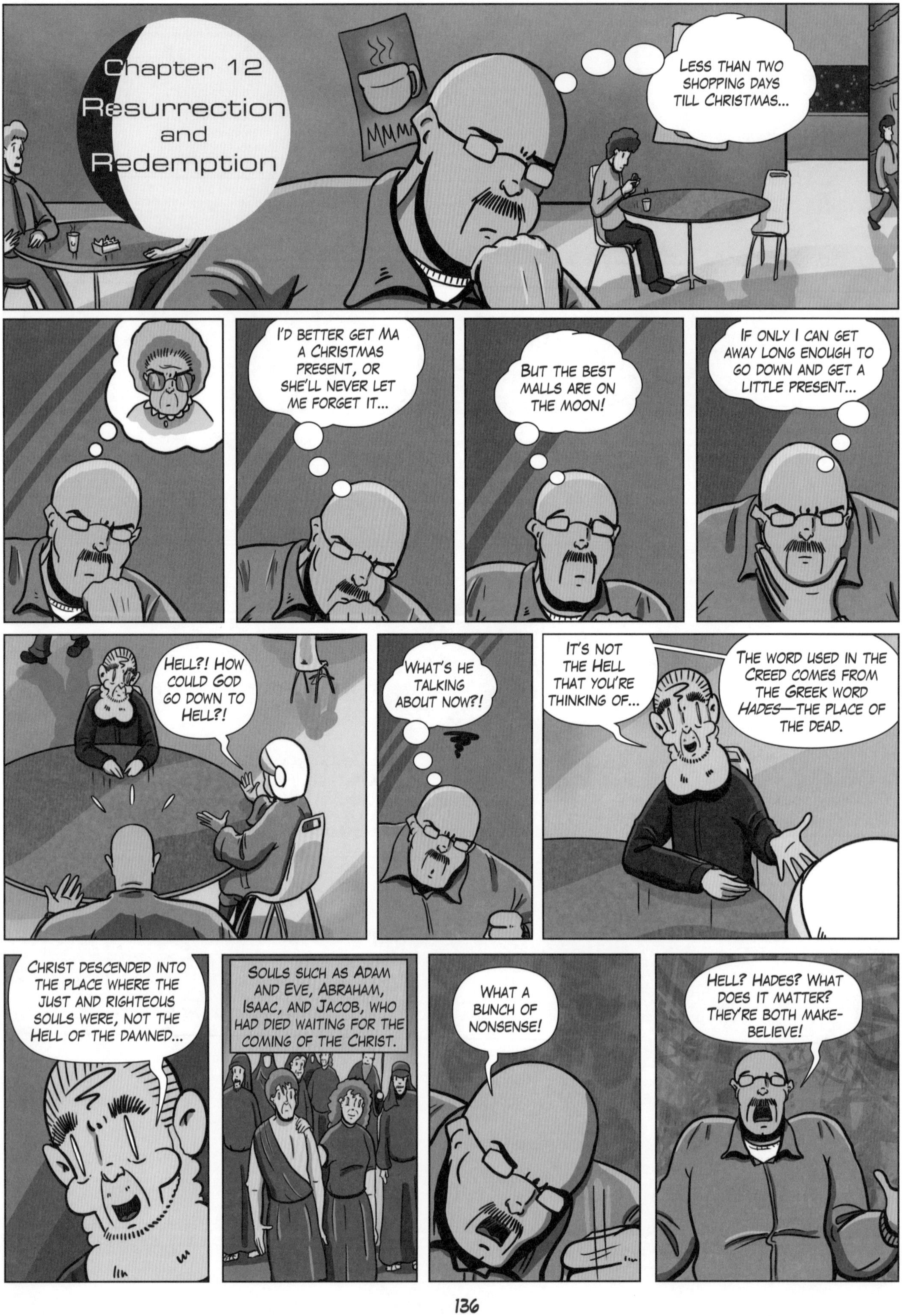

Chapter 12
Resurrection and Redemption
Less than two shopping days till Christmas...
MMM
I'd better get Ma a Christmas present, or she'll never let me forget it...
But the best malls are on the moon!
If only I can get away long enough to go down and get a little present...
Hell?! How could God go down to Hell?!
What's he talking about now?!
It's not the Hell that you're thinking of...
The word used in the Creed comes from the Greek word *Hades*—the place of the dead.
Christ descended into the place where the just and righteous souls were, not the Hell of the damned...
Souls such as Adam and Eve, Abraham, Isaac, and Jacob, who had died waiting for the coming of the Christ.
What a bunch of nonsense!
Hell? Hades? What does it matter? They're both make-believe!

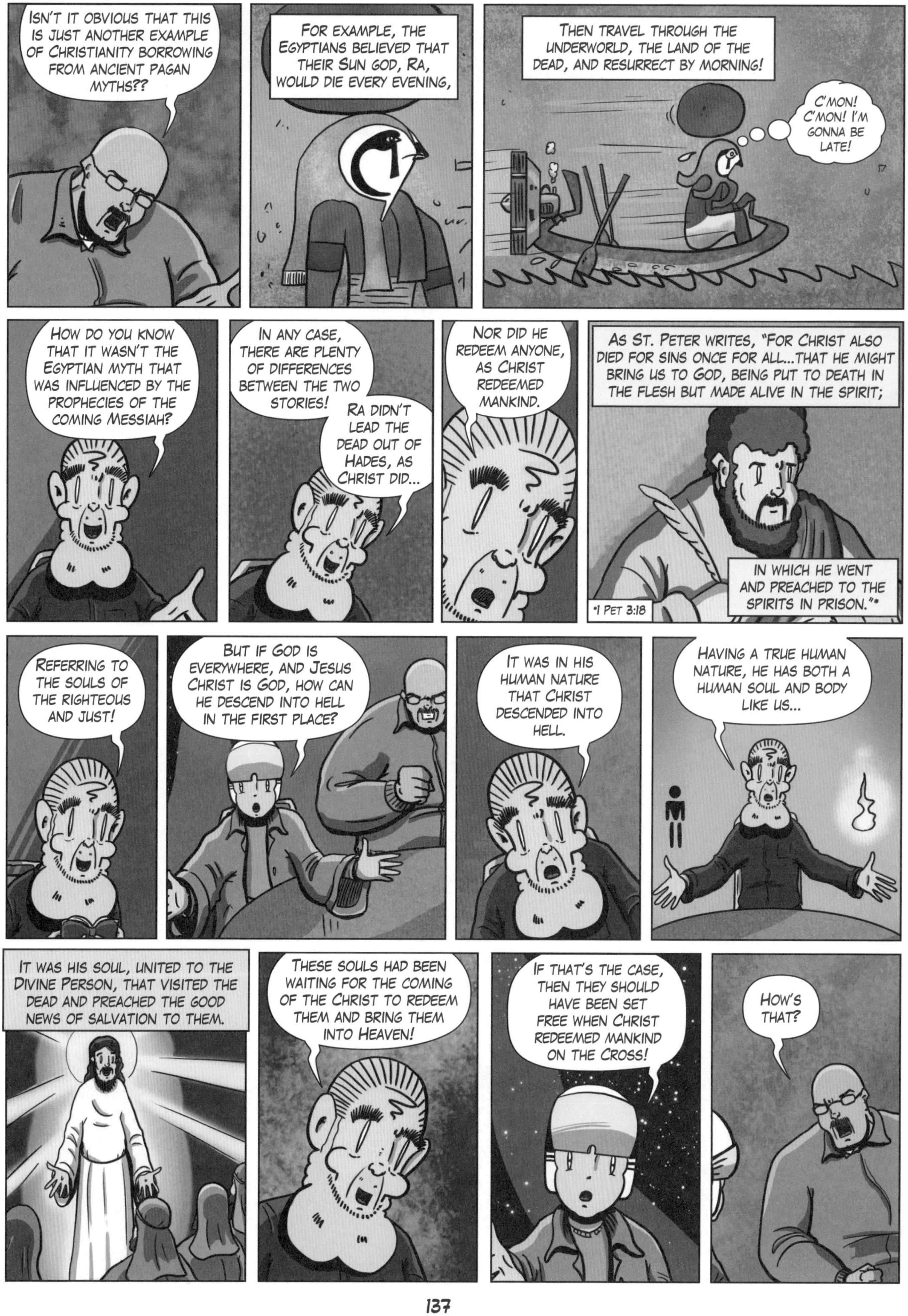
ISN'T IT OBVIOUS THAT THIS IS JUST ANOTHER EXAMPLE OF CHRISTIANITY BORROWING FROM ANCIENT PAGAN MYTHS??
FOR EXAMPLE, THE EGYPTIANS BELIEVED THAT THEIR SUN GOD, RA, WOULD DIE EVERY EVENING,
THEN TRAVEL THROUGH THE UNDERWORLD, THE LAND OF THE DEAD, AND RESURRECT BY MORNING!
C'MON! C'MON! I'M GONNA BE LATE!
HOW DO YOU KNOW THAT IT WASN'T THE EGYPTIAN MYTH THAT WAS INFLUENCED BY THE PROPHECIES OF THE COMING MESSIAH?
IN ANY CASE, THERE ARE PLENTY OF DIFFERENCES BETWEEN THE TWO STORIES!
RA DIDN'T LEAD THE DEAD OUT OF HADES, AS CHRIST DID...
NOR DID HE REDEEM ANYONE, AS CHRIST REDEEMED MANKIND.
AS ST. PETER WRITES, "FOR CHRIST ALSO DIED FOR SINS ONCE FOR ALL...THAT HE MIGHT BRING US TO GOD, BEING PUT TO DEATH IN THE FLESH BUT MADE ALIVE IN THE SPIRIT;
IN WHICH HE WENT AND PREACHED TO THE SPIRITS IN PRISON."*
*1 PET 3:18
REFERRING TO THE SOULS OF THE RIGHTEOUS AND JUST!
BUT IF GOD IS EVERYWHERE, AND JESUS CHRIST IS GOD, HOW CAN HE DESCEND INTO HELL IN THE FIRST PLACE?
IT WAS IN HIS HUMAN NATURE THAT CHRIST DESCENDED INTO HELL.
HAVING A TRUE HUMAN NATURE, HE HAS BOTH A HUMAN SOUL AND BODY LIKE US...
IT WAS HIS SOUL, UNITED TO THE DIVINE PERSON, THAT VISITED THE DEAD AND PREACHED THE GOOD NEWS OF SALVATION TO THEM.
THESE SOULS HAD BEEN WAITING FOR THE COMING OF THE CHRIST TO REDEEM THEM AND BRING THEM INTO HEAVEN!
IF THAT'S THE CASE, THEN THEY SHOULD HAVE BEEN SET FREE WHEN CHRIST REDEEMED MANKIND ON THE CROSS!
HOW'S THAT?

IF ORIGINAL SIN WAS ALL THAT KEPT THESE SOULS FROM HEAVEN, AND IT WAS TAKEN AWAY BY CHRIST'S SACRIFICE, THEN THEY SHOULD HAVE BEEN IMMEDIATELY RELEASED, RIGHT?

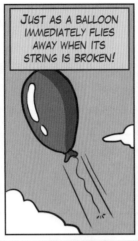

JUST AS A BALLOON IMMEDIATELY FLIES AWAY WHEN ITS STRING IS BROKEN!

TRUE, CHRIST'S PASSION WAS THE GENERAL CAUSE OF EVERYONE'S SALVATION—WHETHER LIVING OR DEAD...

BUT JUST AS IT HAS TO BE APPLIED TO EACH LIVING PERSON IN BAPTISM, SO IT HAD TO BE APPLIED TO THE DEAD BY CHRIST'S DESCENT INTO HELL.

CHRIST SPENT THREE DAYS AMONG THE DEAD, BRINGING THEM THE GOOD NEWS OF THEIR SALVATION, THEN ROSE AGAIN ON THE THIRD DAY.

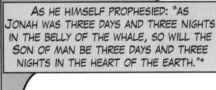

AS HE HIMSELF PROPHESIED: "AS JONAH WAS THREE DAYS AND THREE NIGHTS IN THE BELLY OF THE WHALE, SO WILL THE SON OF MAN BE THREE DAYS AND THREE NIGHTS IN THE HEART OF THE EARTH."*

SPOOT

*MATT 12:40

WAIT A MINUTE!

IF CHRIST DIED ON A FRIDAY AFTERNOON, AND ROSE AGAIN ON SUNDAY MORNING, HOW COULD HE BE THREE DAYS IN THE TOMB?!

I CAN SEE HOW HE ROSE ON THE THIRD DAY, BUT THAT'S NOT THE SAME AS THREE DAYS IN THE TOMB...

HMPH! HE MUST HAVE CUT HIS TRIP SHORT AFTER HE SAW THE PLACE!

ST. AUGUSTINE EXPLAINS IT BY UNDERSTANDING THE PART AS STANDING FOR THE WHOLE...

SO THAT FRIDAY IS TAKEN AS ONE DAY, EVEN THOUGH INCOMPLETE, SATURDAY AS A DAY AND A NIGHT, AND THE EARLY PART OF SUNDAY AS A THIRD DAY.

BESIDES, IT WAS FITTING THAT CHRIST SHOULD STAY IN THE TOMB FOR SO LONG, IN CASE ANYONE DOUBTED THAT HE REALLY DIED!

JUST AS IT WAS FITTING THAT HE ROSE AGAIN, IN CASE ANYONE DOUBTED THAT HE CONQUERED DEATH AS OUR SAVIOR!

AS HE TOLD THE TWO DISCIPLES AFTER HIS RESURRECTION, "WAS IT NOT NECESSARY THAT THE CHRIST SHOULD SUFFER THESE THINGS AND ENTER INTO HIS GLORY?"*

*LUKE 24:25

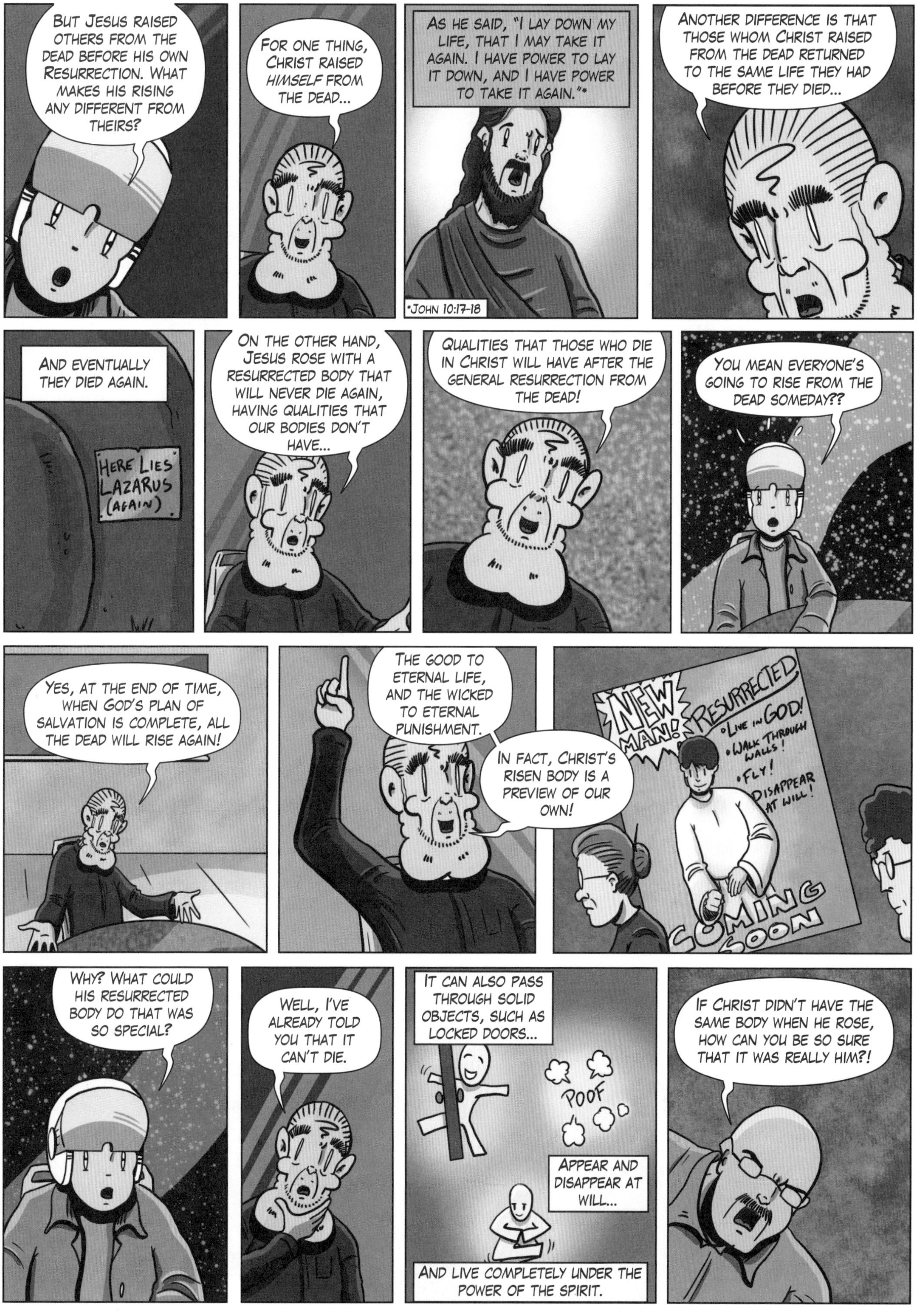
But Jesus raised others from the dead before his own Resurrection. What makes his rising any different from theirs?
For one thing, Christ raised *himself* from the dead...
As he said, "I lay down my life, that I may take it again. I have power to lay it down, and I have power to take it again."*
*John 10:17-18
Another difference is that those whom Christ raised from the dead returned to the same life they had before they died...
And eventually they died again.
Here Lies Lazarus (again)
On the other hand, Jesus rose with a resurrected body that will never die again, having qualities that our bodies don't have...
Qualities that those who die in Christ will have after the general resurrection from the dead!
You mean everyone's going to rise from the dead someday??
Yes, at the end of time, when God's plan of salvation is complete, all the dead will rise again!
The good to eternal life, and the wicked to eternal punishment.
In fact, Christ's risen body is a preview of our own!
New Man! Resurrected
•Live in God!
•Walk through walls!
•Fly!
•Disappear at will!
Coming soon
Why? What could his resurrected body do that was so special?
Well, I've already told you that it can't die.
It can also pass through solid objects, such as locked doors...
Poof
Appear and disappear at will...
And live completely under the power of the spirit.
If Christ didn't have the same body when he rose, how can you be so sure that it was really him?!

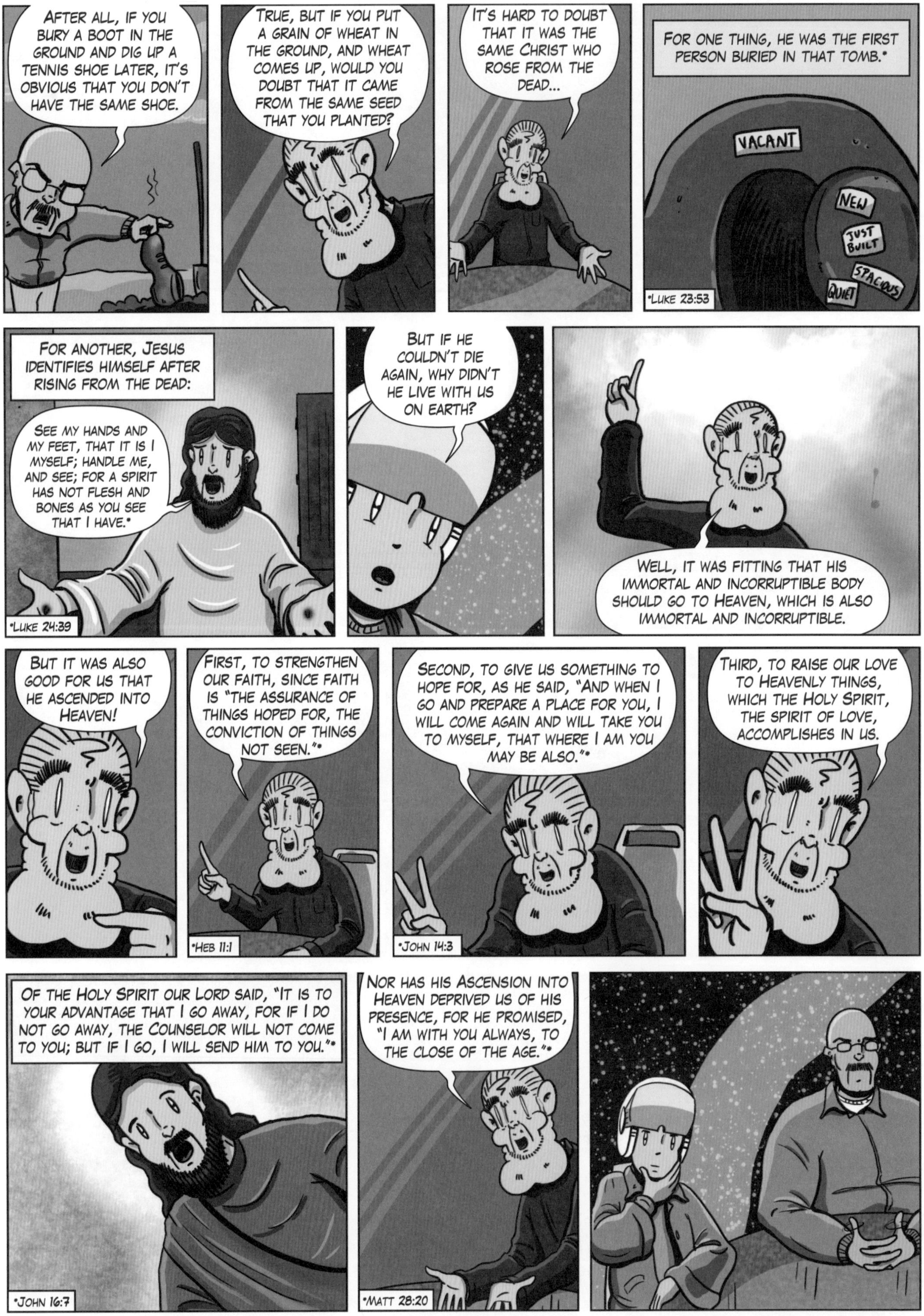

After all, if you bury a boot in the ground and dig up a tennis shoe later, it's obvious that you don't have the same shoe.
True, but if you put a grain of wheat in the ground, and wheat comes up, would you doubt that it came from the same seed that you planted?
It's hard to doubt that it was the same Christ who rose from the dead...
For one thing, he was the first person buried in that tomb.*
VACANT
NEW
JUST BUILT
SPACIOUS
QUIET
*Luke 23:53
For another, Jesus identifies himself after rising from the dead:
See my hands and my feet, that it is I myself; handle me, and see; for a spirit has not flesh and bones as you see that I have.*
*Luke 24:39
But if he couldn't die again, why didn't he live with us on earth?
Well, it was fitting that his immortal and incorruptible body should go to Heaven, which is also immortal and incorruptible.
But it was also good for us that he ascended into Heaven!
First, to strengthen our faith, since faith is "the assurance of things hoped for, the conviction of things not seen."*
*Heb 11:1
Second, to give us something to hope for, as he said, "And when I go and prepare a place for you, I will come again and will take you to myself, that where I am you may be also."*
*John 14:3
Third, to raise our love to Heavenly things, which the Holy Spirit, the spirit of love, accomplishes in us.
Of the Holy Spirit our Lord said, "It is to your advantage that I go away, for if I do not go away, the Counselor will not come to you; but if I go, I will send him to you."*
*John 16:7
Nor has his Ascension into Heaven deprived us of his presence, for he promised, "I am with you always, to the close of the age."*
*Matt 28:20

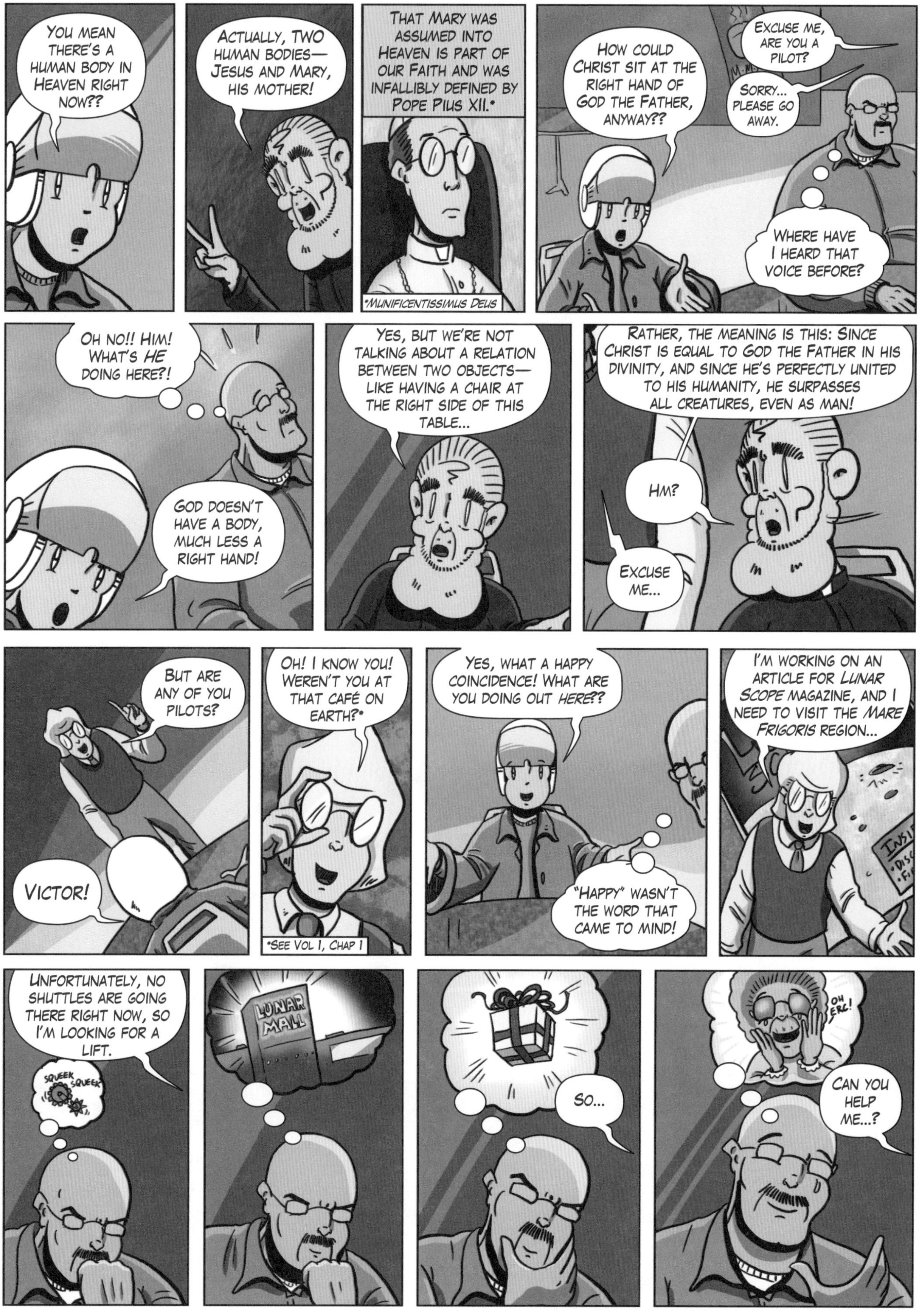

YOU MEAN THERE'S A HUMAN BODY IN HEAVEN RIGHT NOW??
ACTUALLY, TWO HUMAN BODIES—JESUS AND MARY, HIS MOTHER!
THAT MARY WAS ASSUMED INTO HEAVEN IS PART OF OUR FAITH AND WAS INFALLIBLY DEFINED BY POPE PIUS XII.*
*MUNIFICENTISSIMUS DEUS
HOW COULD CHRIST SIT AT THE RIGHT HAND OF GOD THE FATHER, ANYWAY??
EXCUSE ME, ARE YOU A PILOT?
SORRY... PLEASE GO AWAY.
WHERE HAVE I HEARD THAT VOICE BEFORE?
OH NO!! HIM! WHAT'S HE DOING HERE?!
GOD DOESN'T HAVE A BODY, MUCH LESS A RIGHT HAND!
YES, BUT WE'RE NOT TALKING ABOUT A RELATION BETWEEN TWO OBJECTS—LIKE HAVING A CHAIR AT THE RIGHT SIDE OF THIS TABLE...
RATHER, THE MEANING IS THIS: SINCE CHRIST IS EQUAL TO GOD THE FATHER IN HIS DIVINITY, AND SINCE HE'S PERFECTLY UNITED TO HIS HUMANITY, HE SURPASSES ALL CREATURES, EVEN AS MAN!
HM?
EXCUSE ME...
BUT ARE ANY OF YOU PILOTS?
VICTOR!
OH! I KNOW YOU! WEREN'T YOU AT THAT CAFÉ ON EARTH?*
*SEE VOL 1, CHAP 1
YES, WHAT A HAPPY COINCIDENCE! WHAT ARE YOU DOING OUT HERE??
"HAPPY" WASN'T THE WORD THAT CAME TO MIND!
I'M WORKING ON AN ARTICLE FOR LUNAR SCOPE MAGAZINE, AND I NEED TO VISIT THE MARE FRIGORIS REGION...
UNFORTUNATELY, NO SHUTTLES ARE GOING THERE RIGHT NOW, SO I'M LOOKING FOR A LIFT.
SQUEEK SQUEEK
LUNAR MALL
SO...
OH ERIC!
CAN YOU HELP ME...?

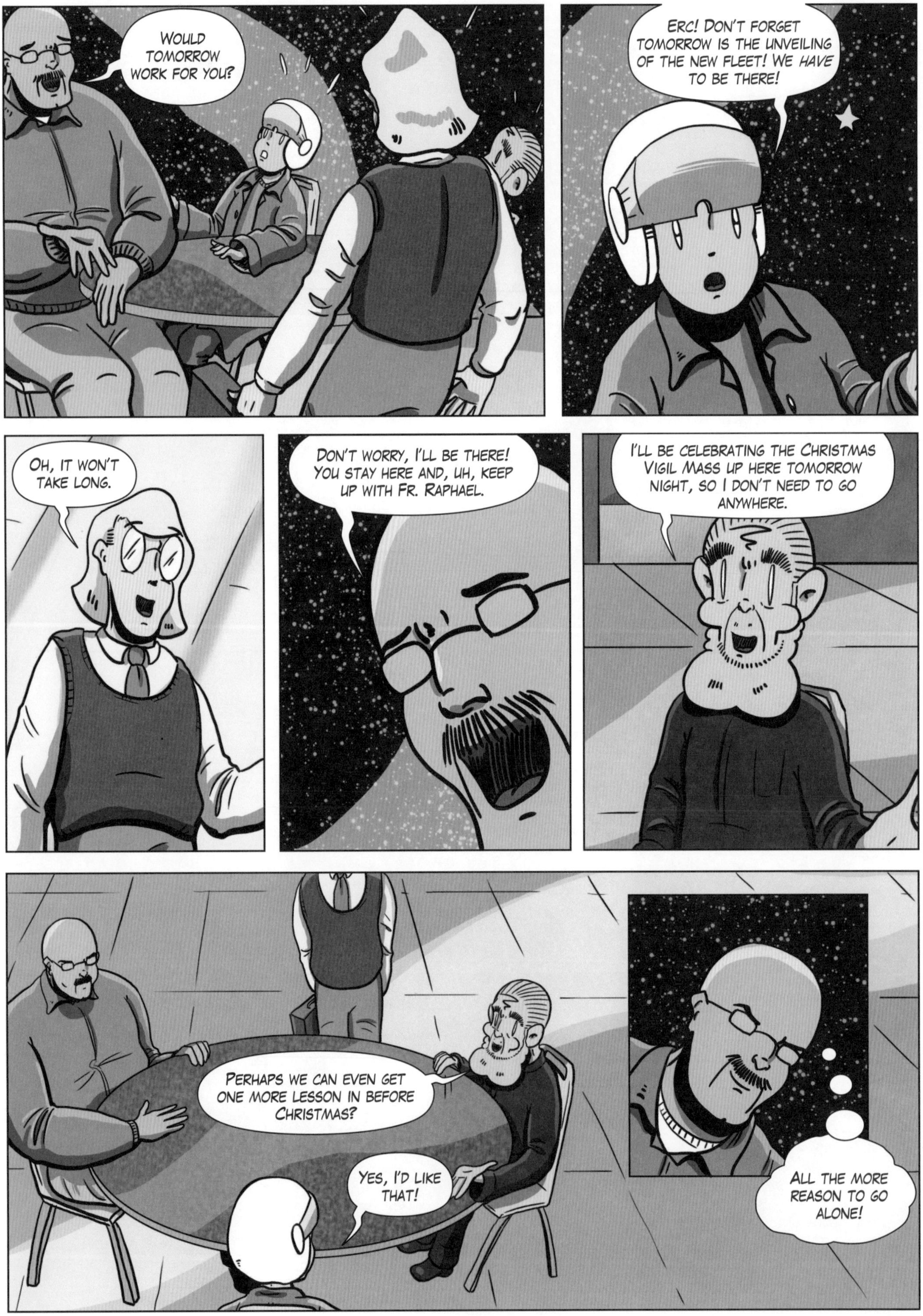

Would tomorrow work for you?
Erc! Don't forget tomorrow is the unveiling of the new fleet! We *have* to be there!
Oh, it won't take long.
Don't worry, I'll be there! You stay here and, uh, keep up with Fr. Raphael.
I'll be celebrating the Christmas Vigil Mass up here tomorrow night, so I don't need to go anywhere.
Perhaps we can even get one more lesson in before Christmas?
Yes, I'd like that!
All the more reason to go alone!

PART VI:
CONSUMMATION
AND FULFILLMENT

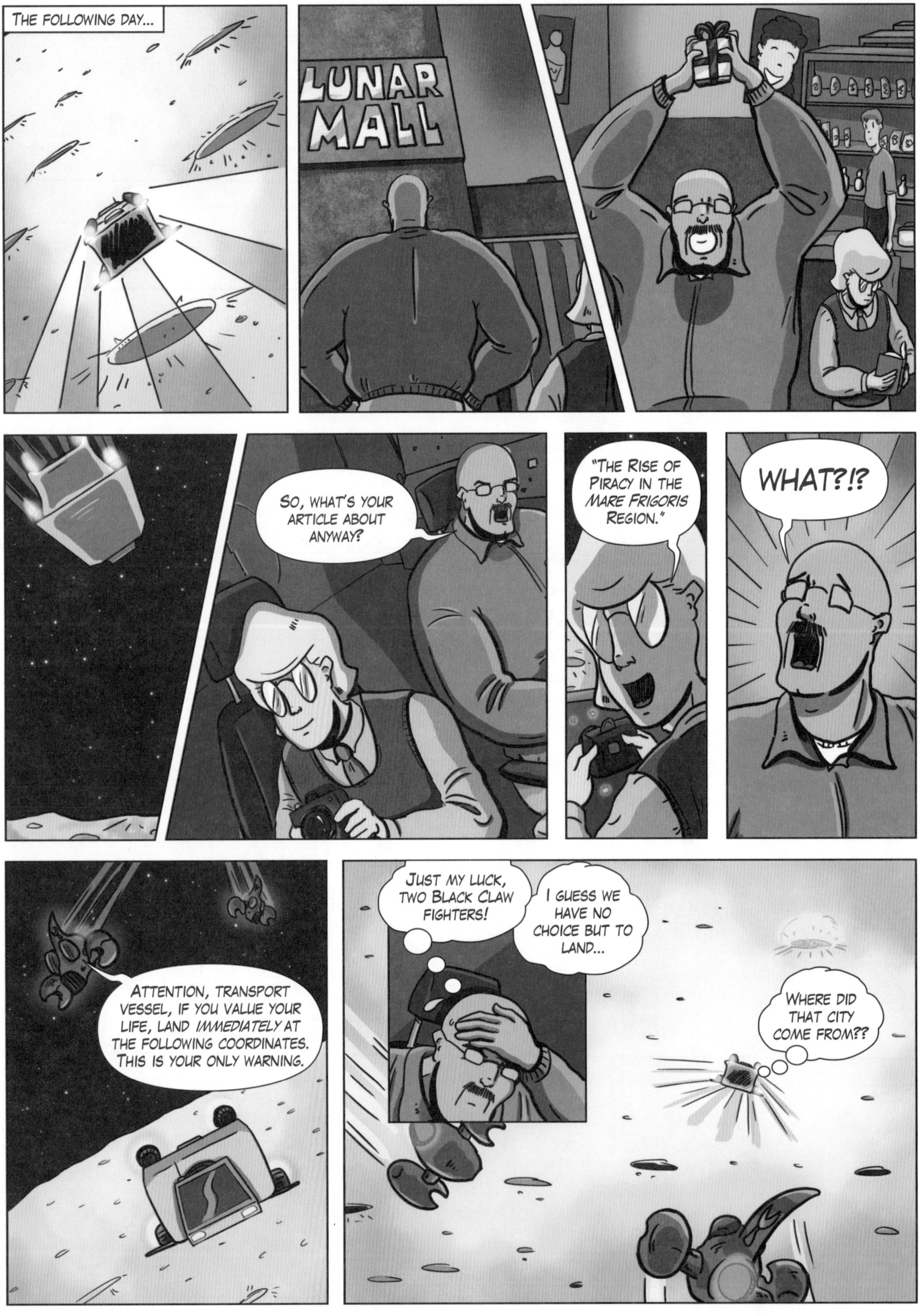

THE FOLLOWING DAY...
LUNAR MALL
SO, WHAT'S YOUR ARTICLE ABOUT ANYWAY?
"THE RISE OF PIRACY IN THE *MARE FRIGORIS* REGION."
WHAT?!?
ATTENTION, TRANSPORT VESSEL, IF YOU VALUE YOUR LIFE, LAND *IMMEDIATELY* AT THE FOLLOWING COORDINATES. THIS IS YOUR ONLY WARNING.
JUST MY LUCK, TWO BLACK CLAW FIGHTERS!
I GUESS WE HAVE NO CHOICE BUT TO LAND...
WHERE DID THAT CITY COME FROM??

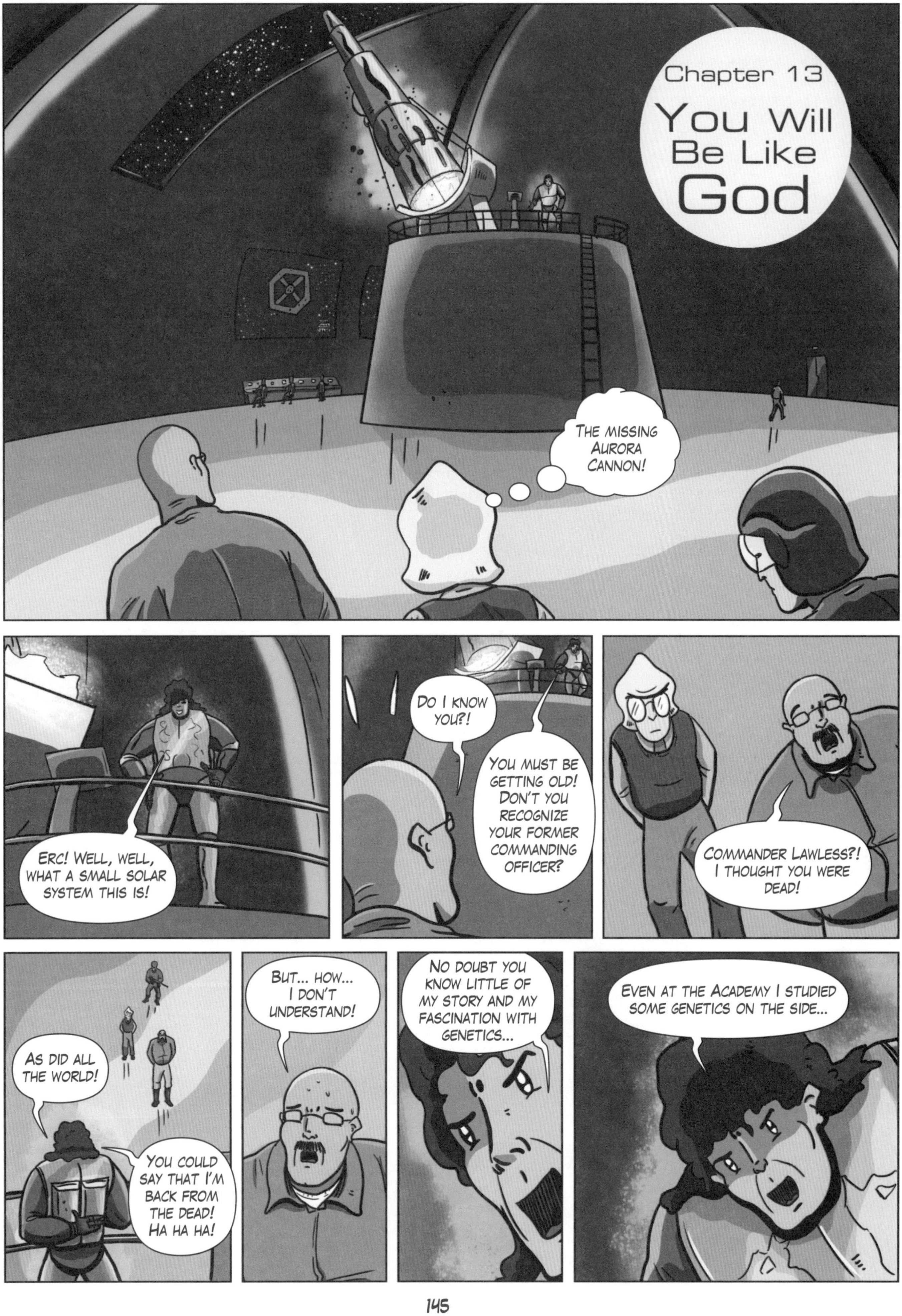
Chapter 13
You Will Be Like God
The missing Aurora Cannon!
Erc! Well, well, what a small solar system this is!
Do I know you?!
You must be getting old! Don't you recognize your former commanding officer?
Commander Lawless?! I thought you were dead!
As did all the world!
You could say that I'm back from the dead! Ha ha ha!
But... how... I don't understand!
No doubt you know little of my story and my fascination with genetics...
Even at the Academy I studied some genetics on the side...

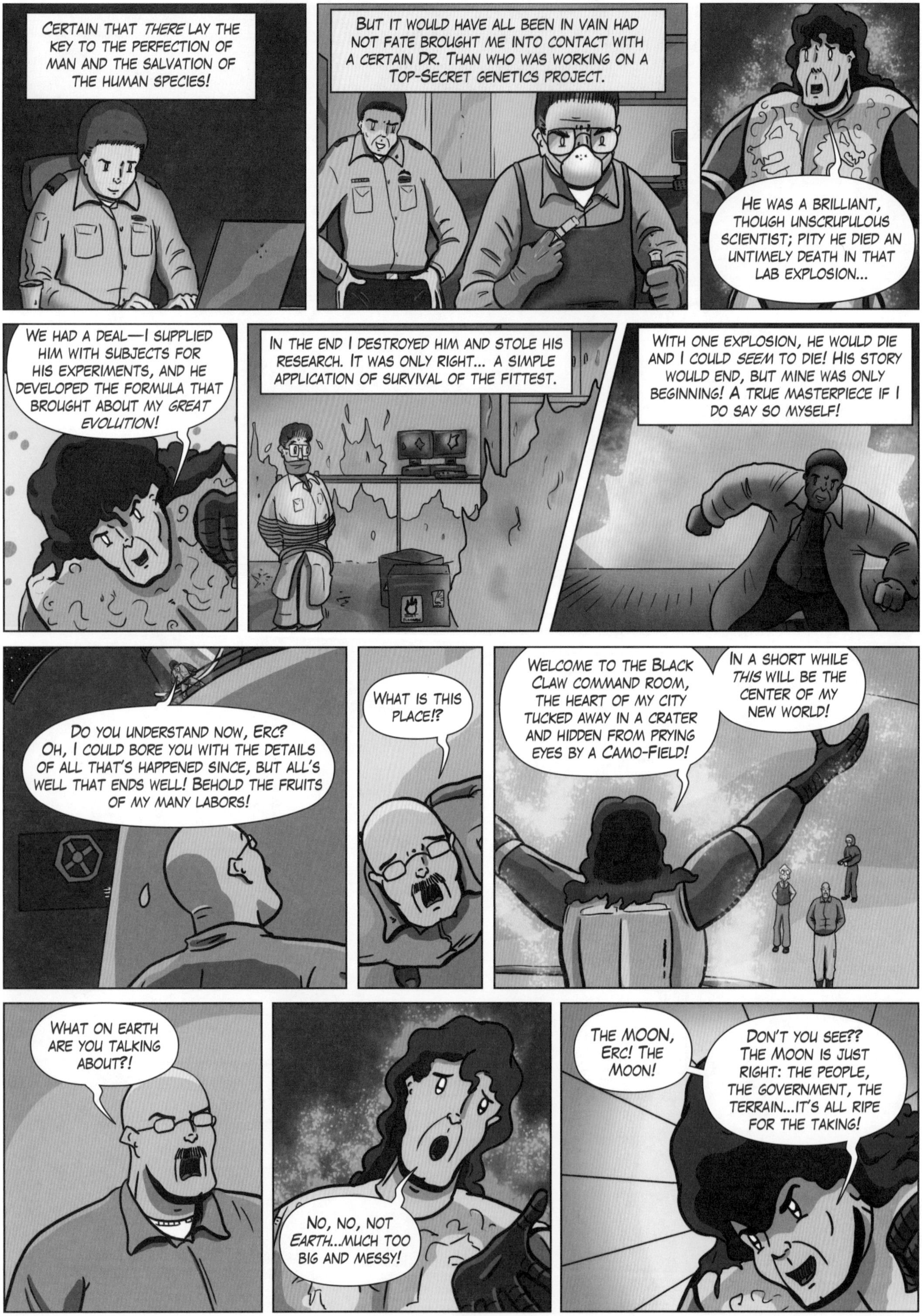

CERTAIN THAT *THERE* LAY THE KEY TO THE PERFECTION OF MAN AND THE SALVATION OF THE HUMAN SPECIES!
BUT IT WOULD HAVE ALL BEEN IN VAIN HAD NOT FATE BROUGHT ME INTO CONTACT WITH A CERTAIN DR. THAN WHO WAS WORKING ON A TOP-SECRET GENETICS PROJECT.
HE WAS A BRILLIANT, THOUGH UNSCRUPULOUS SCIENTIST; PITY HE DIED AN UNTIMELY DEATH IN THAT LAB EXPLOSION...
WE HAD A DEAL—I SUPPLIED HIM WITH SUBJECTS FOR HIS EXPERIMENTS, AND HE DEVELOPED THE FORMULA THAT BROUGHT ABOUT MY *GREAT EVOLUTION*!
IN THE END I DESTROYED HIM AND STOLE HIS RESEARCH. IT WAS ONLY RIGHT... A SIMPLE APPLICATION OF SURVIVAL OF THE FITTEST.
WITH ONE EXPLOSION, HE WOULD DIE AND I COULD *SEEM* TO DIE! HIS STORY WOULD END, BUT MINE WAS ONLY BEGINNING! A TRUE MASTERPIECE IF I DO SAY SO MYSELF!
DO YOU UNDERSTAND NOW, ERC? OH, I COULD BORE YOU WITH THE DETAILS OF ALL THAT'S HAPPENED SINCE, BUT ALL'S WELL THAT ENDS WELL! BEHOLD THE FRUITS OF MY MANY LABORS!
WHAT IS THIS PLACE!?
WELCOME TO THE BLACK CLAW COMMAND ROOM, THE HEART OF MY CITY TUCKED AWAY IN A CRATER AND HIDDEN FROM PRYING EYES BY A CAMO-FIELD!
IN A SHORT WHILE *THIS* WILL BE THE CENTER OF MY NEW WORLD!
WHAT ON EARTH ARE YOU TALKING ABOUT?!
NO, NO, NOT *EARTH*...MUCH TOO BIG AND MESSY!
THE MOON, ERC! THE MOON!
DON'T YOU SEE?? THE MOON IS JUST RIGHT: THE PEOPLE, THE GOVERNMENT, THE TERRAIN...IT'S ALL RIPE FOR THE TAKING!

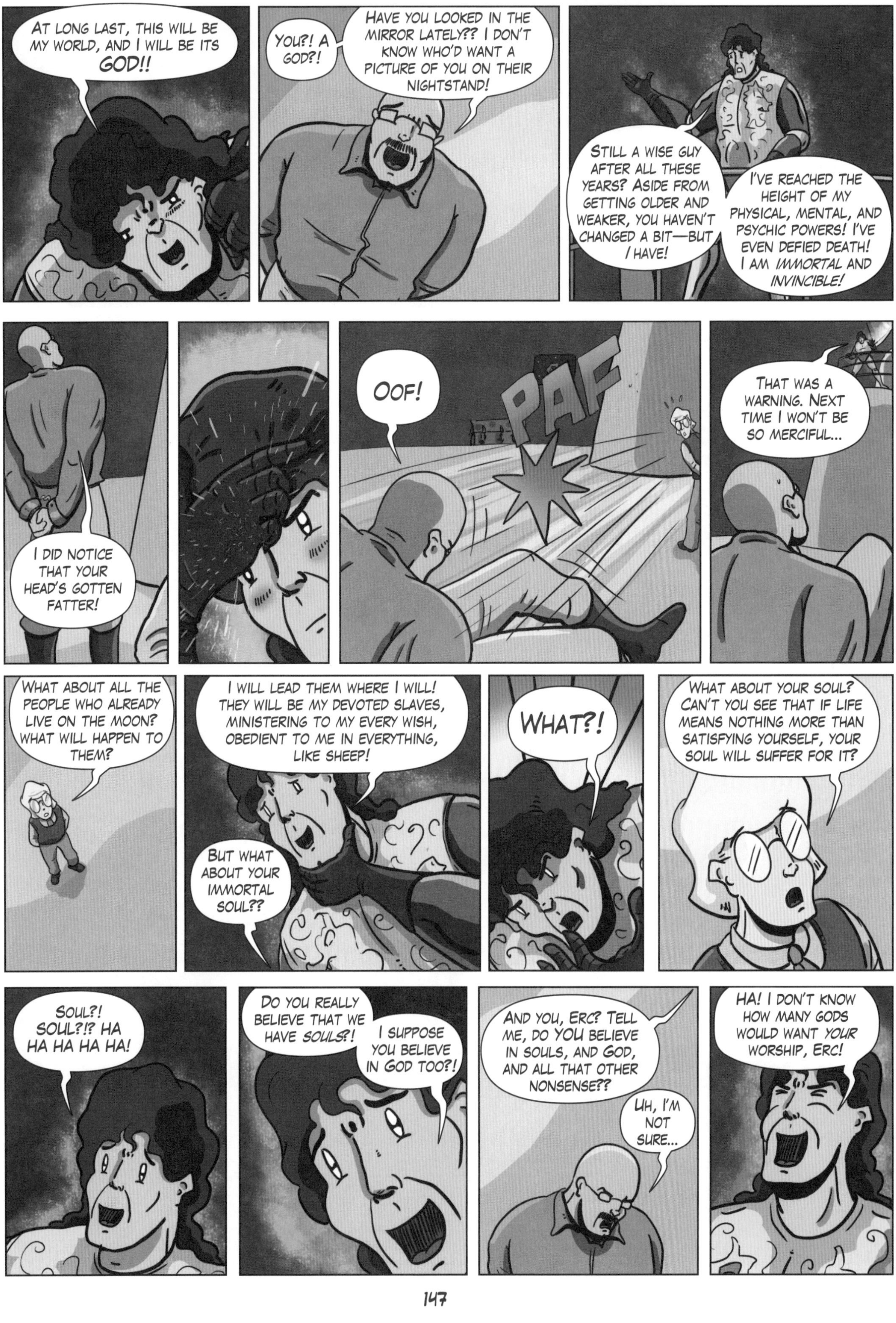

AT LONG LAST, THIS WILL BE MY WORLD, AND I WILL BE ITS GOD!!
YOU?! A GOD?!
HAVE YOU LOOKED IN THE MIRROR LATELY?? I DON'T KNOW WHO'D WANT A PICTURE OF YOU ON THEIR NIGHTSTAND!
STILL A WISE GUY AFTER ALL THESE YEARS? ASIDE FROM GETTING OLDER AND WEAKER, YOU HAVEN'T CHANGED A BIT—BUT I HAVE!
I'VE REACHED THE HEIGHT OF MY PHYSICAL, MENTAL, AND PSYCHIC POWERS! I'VE EVEN DEFIED DEATH! I AM IMMORTAL AND INVINCIBLE!
I DID NOTICE THAT YOUR HEAD'S GOTTEN FATTER!
OOF!
PAF
THAT WAS A WARNING. NEXT TIME I WON'T BE SO MERCIFUL...
WHAT ABOUT ALL THE PEOPLE WHO ALREADY LIVE ON THE MOON? WHAT WILL HAPPEN TO THEM?
I WILL LEAD THEM WHERE I WILL! THEY WILL BE MY DEVOTED SLAVES, MINISTERING TO MY EVERY WISH, OBEDIENT TO ME IN EVERYTHING, LIKE SHEEP!
BUT WHAT ABOUT YOUR IMMORTAL SOUL??
WHAT?!
WHAT ABOUT YOUR SOUL? CAN'T YOU SEE THAT IF LIFE MEANS NOTHING MORE THAN SATISFYING YOURSELF, YOUR SOUL WILL SUFFER FOR IT?
SOUL?! SOUL?!? HA HA HA HA HA!
DO YOU REALLY BELIEVE THAT WE HAVE SOULS?!
I SUPPOSE YOU BELIEVE IN GOD TOO?!
AND YOU, ERC? TELL ME, DO YOU BELIEVE IN SOULS, AND GOD, AND ALL THAT OTHER NONSENSE??
UH, I'M NOT SURE...
HA! I DON'T KNOW HOW MANY GODS WOULD WANT YOUR WORSHIP, ERC!

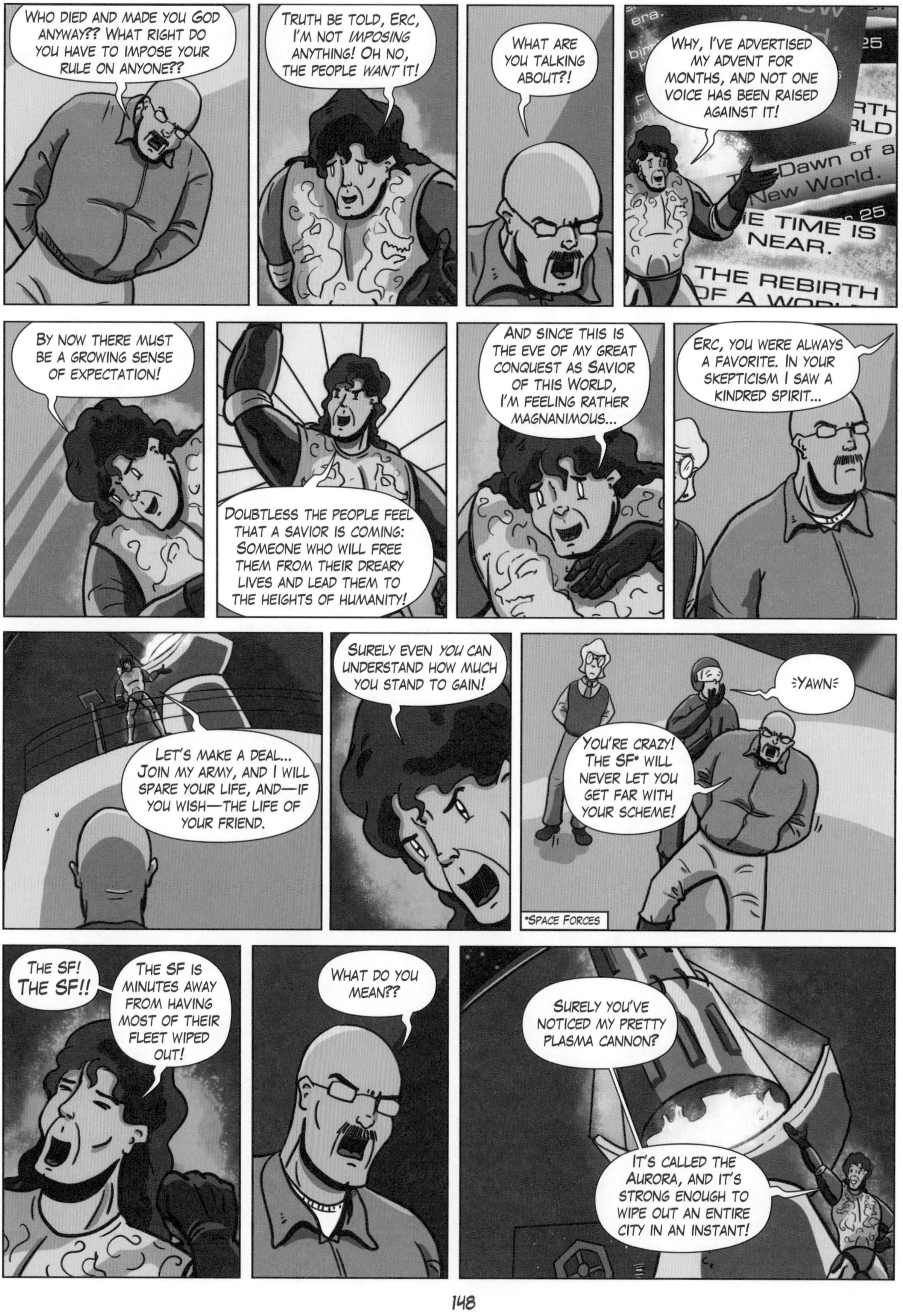

WHO DIED AND MADE YOU GOD ANYWAY?? WHAT RIGHT DO YOU HAVE TO IMPOSE YOUR RULE ON ANYONE??
TRUTH BE TOLD, ERC, I'M NOT *IMPOSING* ANYTHING! OH NO, THE PEOPLE *WANT* IT!
WHAT ARE YOU TALKING ABOUT?!
WHY, I'VE ADVERTISED MY ADVENT FOR MONTHS, AND NOT ONE VOICE HAS BEEN RAISED AGAINST IT!
Dawn of a
New World.
NEAR.
BY NOW THERE MUST BE A GROWING SENSE OF EXPECTATION!
DOUBTLESS THE PEOPLE FEEL THAT A SAVIOR IS COMING: SOMEONE WHO WILL FREE THEM FROM THEIR DREARY LIVES AND LEAD THEM TO THE HEIGHTS OF HUMANITY!
AND SINCE THIS IS THE EVE OF MY GREAT CONQUEST AS SAVIOR OF THIS WORLD, I'M FEELING RATHER MAGNANIMOUS...
ERC, YOU WERE ALWAYS A FAVORITE. IN YOUR SKEPTICISM I SAW A KINDRED SPIRIT...
LET'S MAKE A DEAL... JOIN MY ARMY, AND I WILL SPARE YOUR LIFE, AND—IF YOU WISH—THE LIFE OF YOUR FRIEND.
SURELY EVEN *YOU* CAN UNDERSTAND HOW MUCH YOU STAND TO GAIN!
YAWN
YOU'RE CRAZY! THE SF* WILL NEVER LET YOU GET FAR WITH YOUR SCHEME!
*SPACE FORCES
THE SF! THE SF!!
THE SF IS MINUTES AWAY FROM HAVING MOST OF THEIR FLEET WIPED OUT!
WHAT DO YOU MEAN??
SURELY YOU'VE NOTICED MY PRETTY PLASMA CANNON?
IT'S CALLED THE AURORA, AND IT'S STRONG ENOUGH TO WIPE OUT AN ENTIRE CITY IN AN INSTANT!

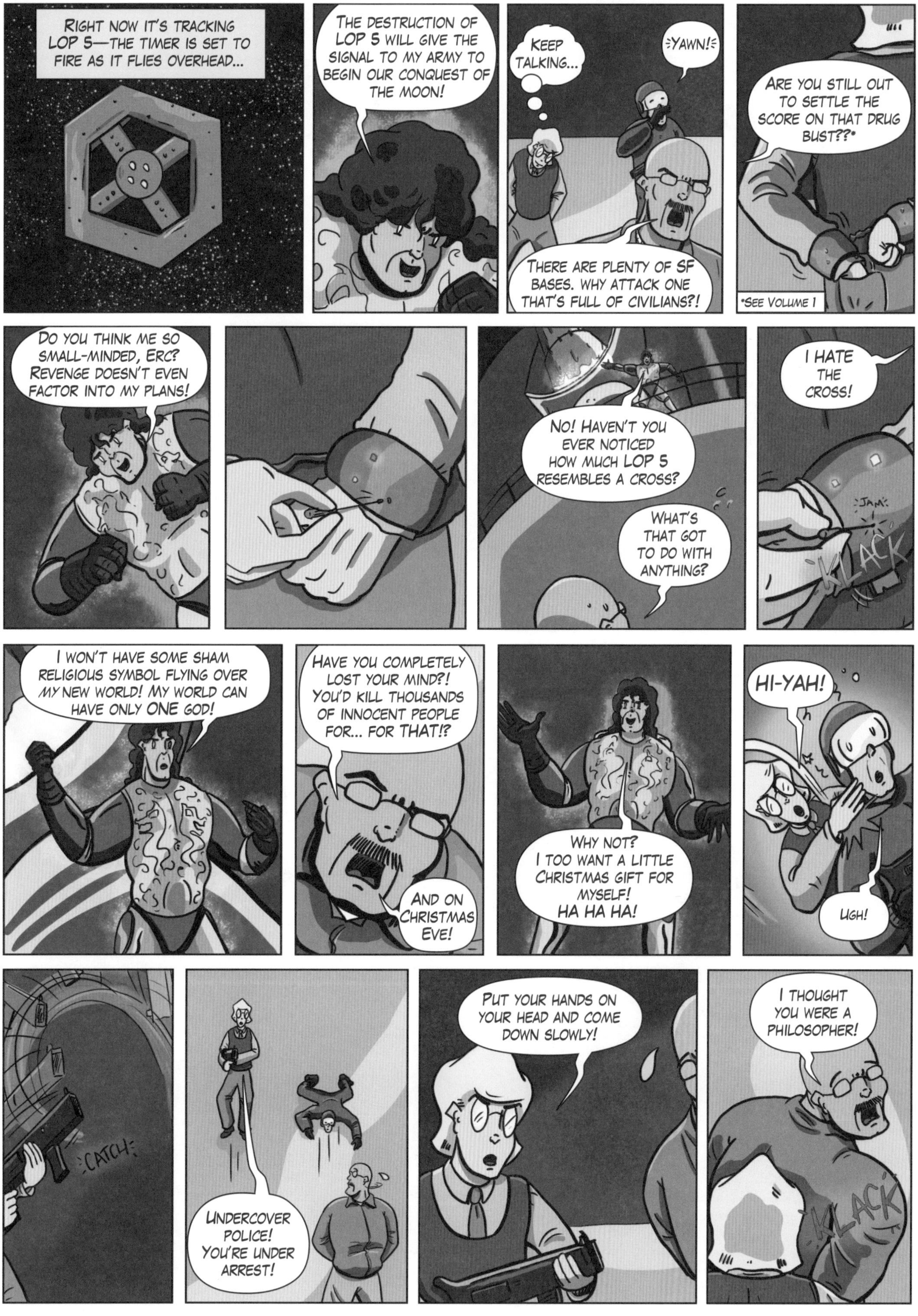

RIGHT NOW IT'S TRACKING LOP 5—THE TIMER IS SET TO FIRE AS IT FLIES OVERHEAD...
THE DESTRUCTION OF LOP 5 WILL GIVE THE SIGNAL TO MY ARMY TO BEGIN OUR CONQUEST OF THE MOON!
KEEP TALKING...
YAWN!
THERE ARE PLENTY OF SF BASES. WHY ATTACK ONE THAT'S FULL OF CIVILIANS?!
ARE YOU STILL OUT TO SETTLE THE SCORE ON THAT DRUG BUST??*
*SEE VOLUME 1
DO YOU THINK ME SO SMALL-MINDED, ERC? REVENGE DOESN'T EVEN FACTOR INTO MY PLANS!
NO! HAVEN'T YOU EVER NOTICED HOW MUCH LOP 5 RESEMBLES A CROSS?
WHAT'S THAT GOT TO DO WITH ANYTHING?
I HATE THE CROSS!
JAM
KLACK
I WON'T HAVE SOME SHAM RELIGIOUS SYMBOL FLYING OVER MY NEW WORLD! MY WORLD CAN HAVE ONLY ONE GOD!
HAVE YOU COMPLETELY LOST YOUR MIND?! YOU'D KILL THOUSANDS OF INNOCENT PEOPLE FOR... FOR THAT!?
AND ON CHRISTMAS EVE!
WHY NOT? I TOO WANT A LITTLE CHRISTMAS GIFT FOR MYSELF! HA HA HA!
HI-YAH!
UGH!
CATCH
UNDERCOVER POLICE! YOU'RE UNDER ARREST!
PUT YOUR HANDS ON YOUR HEAD AND COME DOWN SLOWLY!
I THOUGHT YOU WERE A PHILOSOPHER!
KLACK

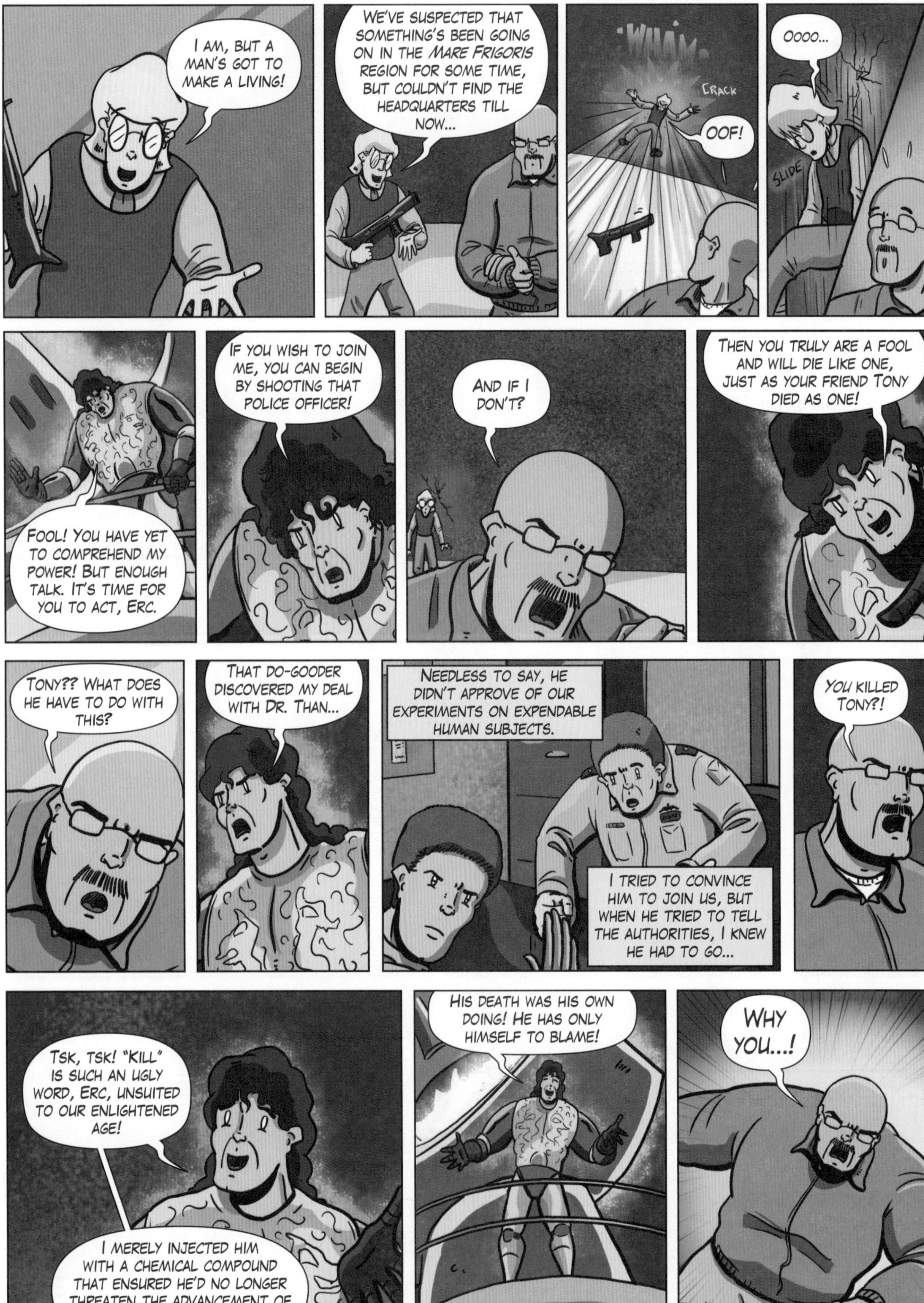
I AM, BUT A MAN'S GOT TO MAKE A LIVING!
WE'VE SUSPECTED THAT SOMETHING'S BEEN GOING ON IN THE *MARE FRIGORIS* REGION FOR SOME TIME, BUT COULDN'T FIND THE HEADQUARTERS TILL NOW...
WHAM
CRACK
OOF!
OOOO...
SLIDE
FOOL! YOU HAVE YET TO COMPREHEND MY POWER! BUT ENOUGH TALK. IT'S TIME FOR YOU TO ACT, ERC.
IF YOU WISH TO JOIN ME, YOU CAN BEGIN BY SHOOTING THAT POLICE OFFICER!
AND IF I DON'T?
THEN YOU TRULY ARE A FOOL AND WILL DIE LIKE ONE, JUST AS YOUR FRIEND TONY DIED AS ONE!
TONY?? WHAT DOES HE HAVE TO DO WITH THIS?
THAT DO-GOODER DISCOVERED MY DEAL WITH DR. THAN...
NEEDLESS TO SAY, HE DIDN'T APPROVE OF OUR EXPERIMENTS ON EXPENDABLE HUMAN SUBJECTS.
I TRIED TO CONVINCE HIM TO JOIN US, BUT WHEN HE TRIED TO TELL THE AUTHORITIES, I KNEW HE HAD TO GO...
YOU KILLED TONY?!
TSK, TSK! "KILL" IS SUCH AN UGLY WORD, ERC, UNSUITED TO OUR ENLIGHTENED AGE!
I MERELY INJECTED HIM WITH A CHEMICAL COMPOUND THAT ENSURED HE'D NO LONGER THREATEN THE ADVANCEMENT OF MAN AND TECHNOLOGY!
HIS DEATH WAS HIS OWN DOING! HE HAS ONLY HIMSELF TO BLAME!
WHY YOU...!

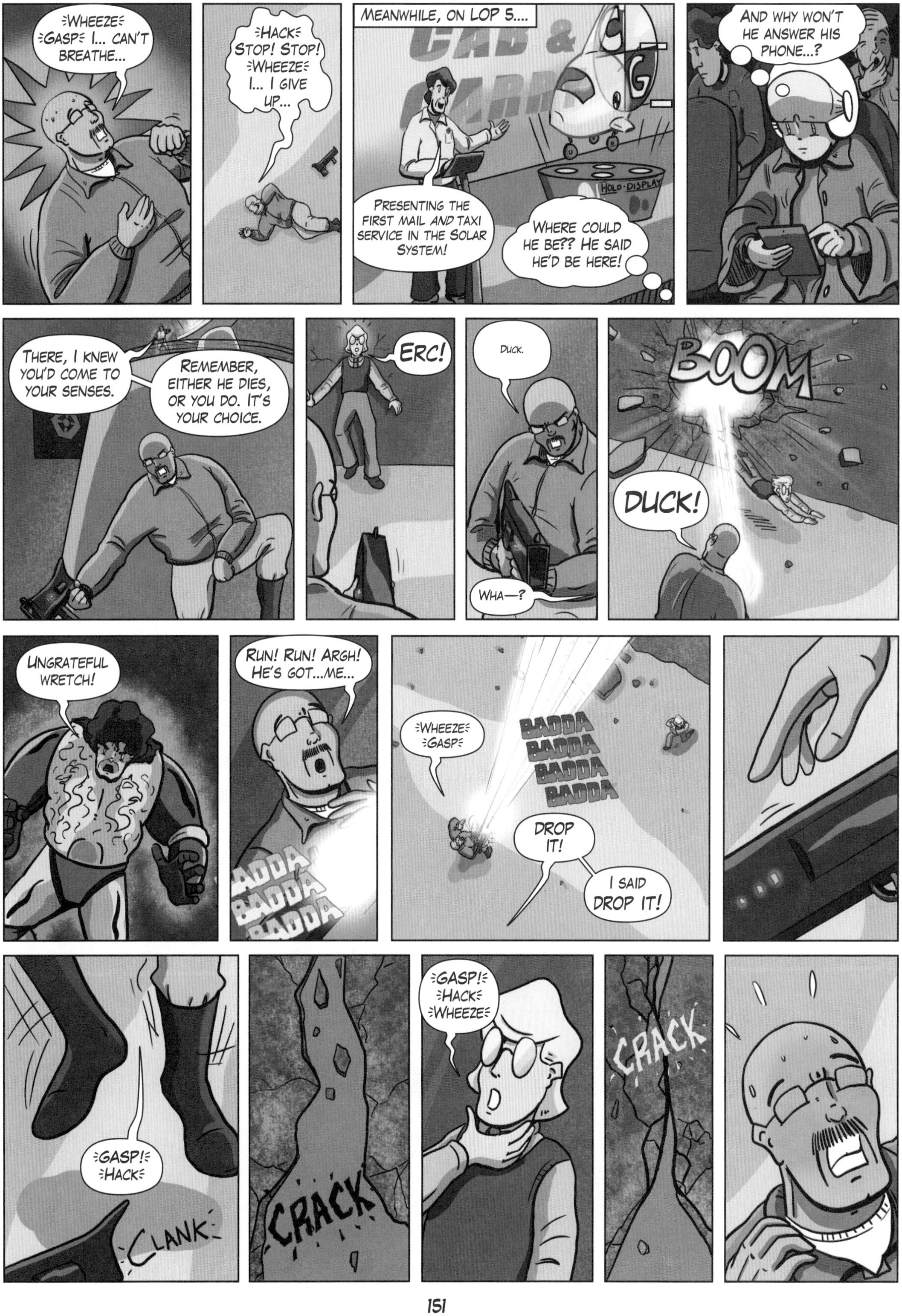
WHEEZE GASP I... CAN'T BREATHE...
HACK STOP! STOP! WHEEZE I... I GIVE UP...
MEANWHILE, ON LOP 5....
PRESENTING THE FIRST MAIL AND TAXI SERVICE IN THE SOLAR SYSTEM!
HOLO-DISPLAY
WHERE COULD HE BE?? HE SAID HE'D BE HERE!
AND WHY WON'T HE ANSWER HIS PHONE...?
THERE, I KNEW YOU'D COME TO YOUR SENSES.
REMEMBER, EITHER HE DIES, OR YOU DO. IT'S YOUR CHOICE.
ERC!
DUCK.
WHA—?
BOOM
DUCK!
UNGRATEFUL WRETCH!
RUN! RUN! ARGH! HE'S GOT...ME...
BADDA BADDA BADDA
WHEEZE GASP
BADDA BADDA BADDA BADDA
DROP IT!
I SAID DROP IT!
GASP! HACK
CLANK
CRACK
GASP! HACK WHEEZE
CRACK

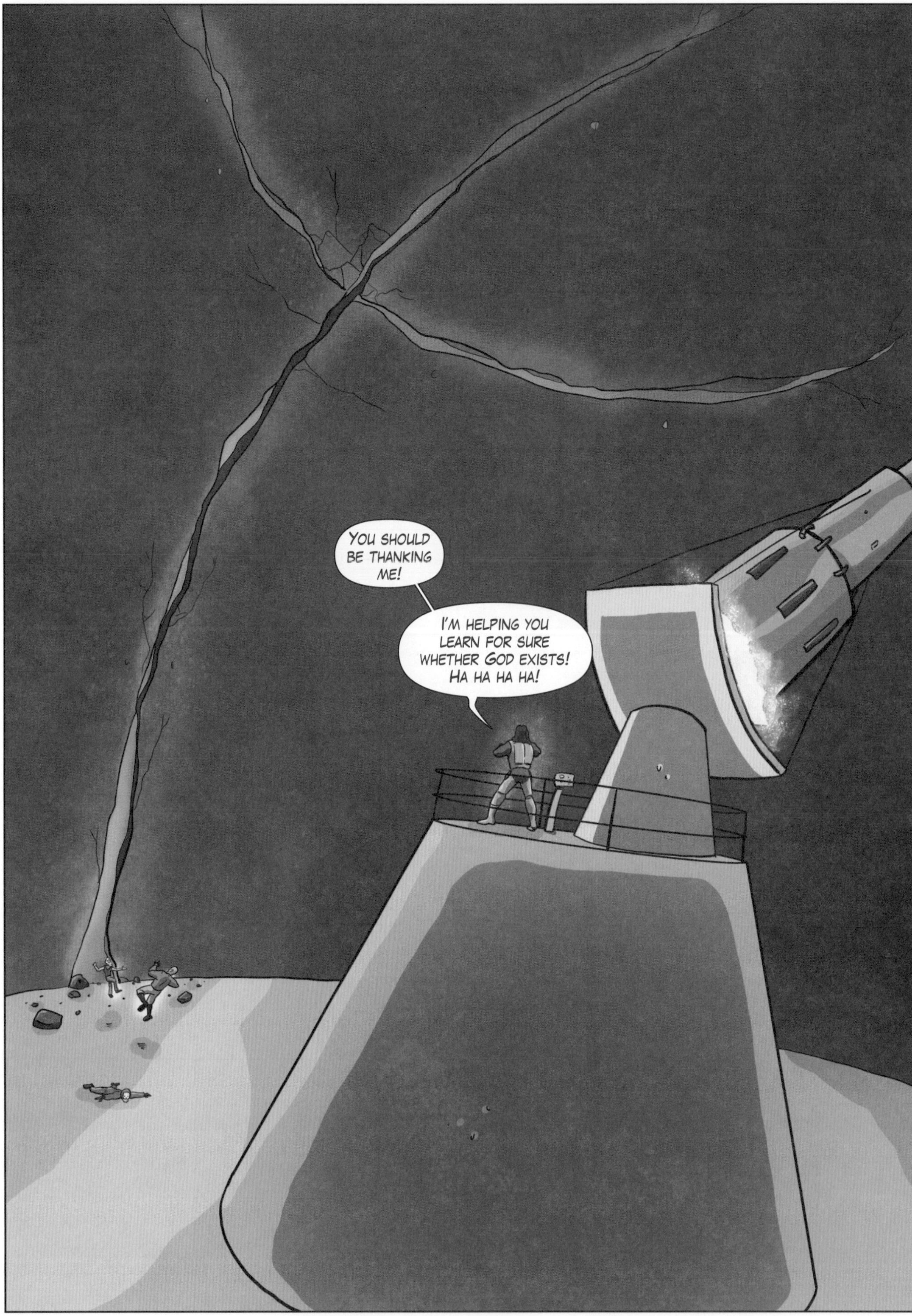
YOU SHOULD BE THANKING ME!
I'M HELPING YOU LEARN FOR SURE WHETHER GOD EXISTS! HA HA HA HA!

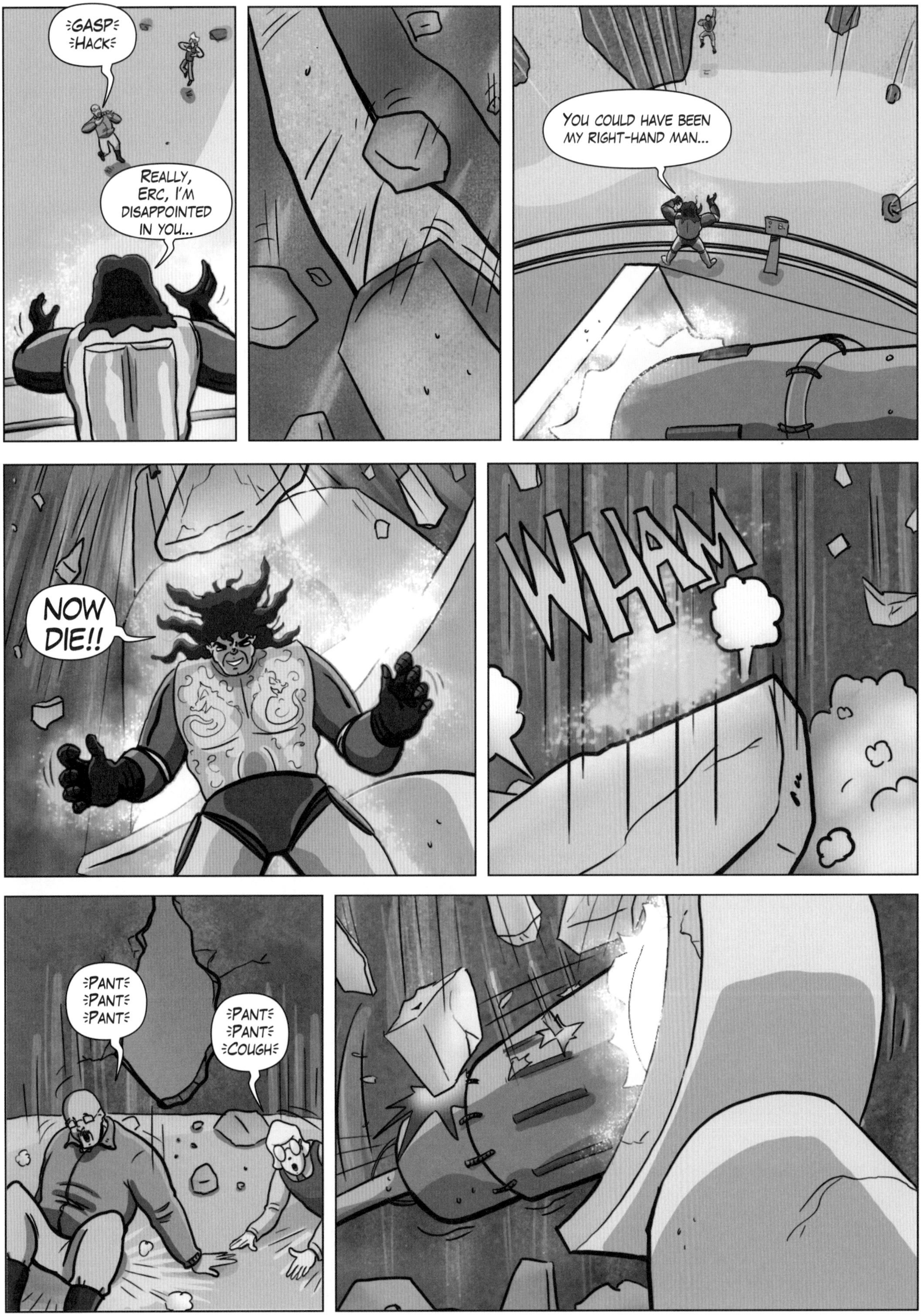
GASP
HACK
REALLY, ERC, I'M DISAPPOINTED IN YOU...
YOU COULD HAVE BEEN MY RIGHT-HAND MAN...
NOW DIE!!
WHAM
PANT PANT PANT
PANT PANT COUGH

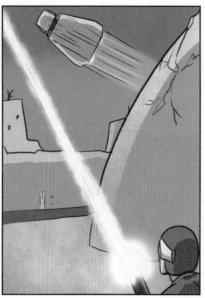

MEANWHILE, AS LOP 5 PASSES OVERHEAD...

10...9...8...7...6...

≶HUFF!≷ ALMOST FREE!

5...4...3...2...1...

≶GASP≷ THE AURORA CANNON...

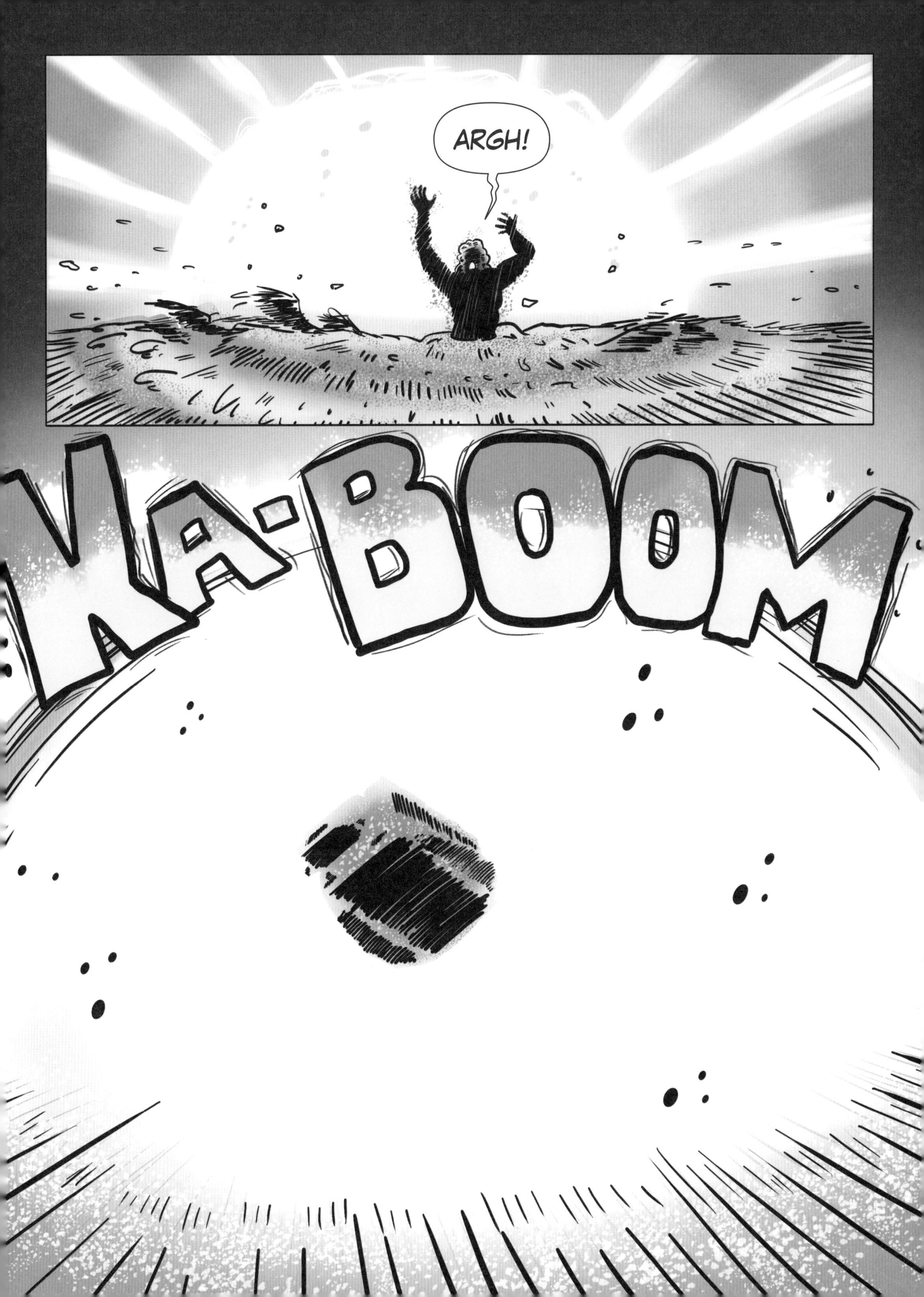
ARGH!
KA-BOOM

Chapter 14
Between Heaven and Hell

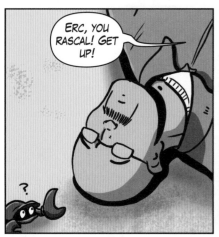

ERC, YOU RASCAL! GET UP!

THAT VOICE...

IT CAN'T BE!

TONY! WHAT ARE YOU DOING HERE?? YOU'RE SUPPOSED TO BE DEAD!

AS SHARP AS EVER, ERC! I AM DEAD, OR AT LEAST MY BODY IS!

DOES THAT MEAN...UH, AM I... UM...?

DEAD? NO, NOT YET ANYWAY.

AND FOR THAT ALONE YOU SHOULD BE THANKING GOD'S MERCY!

HMPH! WHERE WAS HIS MERCY WHEN YOU WERE DYING??

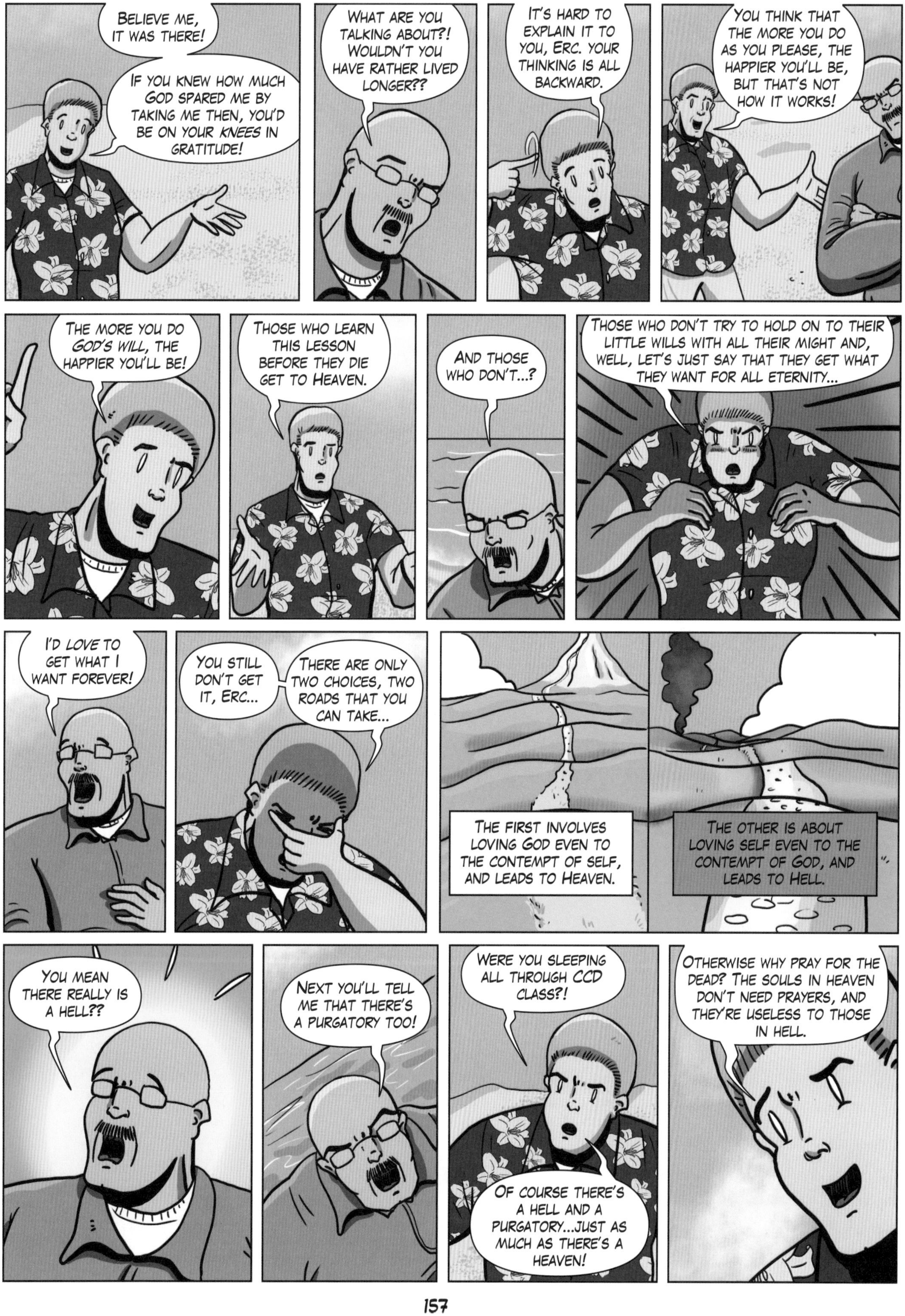
Believe me, it was there!
If you knew how much God spared me by taking me then, you'd be on your knees in gratitude!
What are you talking about?! Wouldn't you have rather lived longer??
It's hard to explain it to you, Erc. Your thinking is all backward.
You think that the more you do as you please, the happier you'll be, but that's not how it works!
The more you do God's will, the happier you'll be!
Those who learn this lesson before they die get to Heaven.
And those who don't...?
Those who don't try to hold on to their little wills with all their might and, well, let's just say that they get what they want for all eternity...
I'd love to get what I want forever!
You still don't get it, Erc...
There are only two choices, two roads that you can take...
The first involves loving God even to the contempt of self, and leads to Heaven.
The other is about loving self even to the contempt of God, and leads to Hell.
You mean there really is a hell??
Next you'll tell me that there's a purgatory too!
Were you sleeping all through CCD class?!
Of course there's a hell and a purgatory...just as much as there's a heaven!
Otherwise why pray for the dead? The souls in heaven don't need prayers, and they're useless to those in hell.

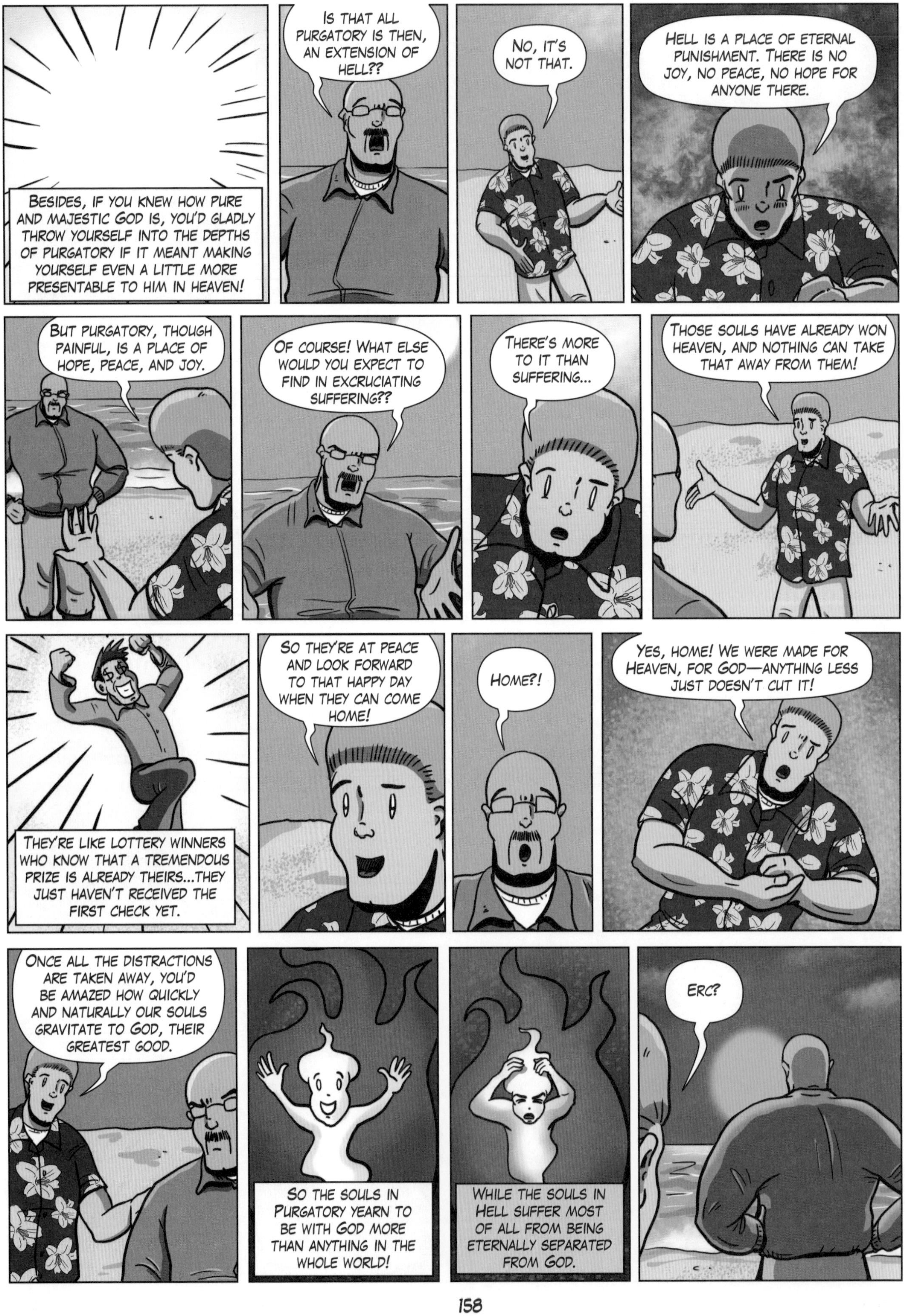
Besides, if you knew how pure and majestic God is, you'd gladly throw yourself into the depths of purgatory if it meant making yourself even a little more presentable to him in heaven!
Is that all purgatory is then, an extension of hell??
No, it's not that.
Hell is a place of eternal punishment. There is no joy, no peace, no hope for anyone there.
But purgatory, though painful, is a place of hope, peace, and joy.
Of course! What else would you expect to find in excruciating suffering??
There's more to it than suffering...
Those souls have already won heaven, and nothing can take that away from them!
They're like lottery winners who know that a tremendous prize is already theirs...they just haven't received the first check yet.
So they're at peace and look forward to that happy day when they can come home!
Home?!
Yes, home! We were made for Heaven, for God—anything less just doesn't cut it!
Once all the distractions are taken away, you'd be amazed how quickly and naturally our souls gravitate to God, their greatest good.
So the souls in Purgatory yearn to be with God more than anything in the whole world!
While the souls in Hell suffer most of all from being eternally separated from God.
Erc?

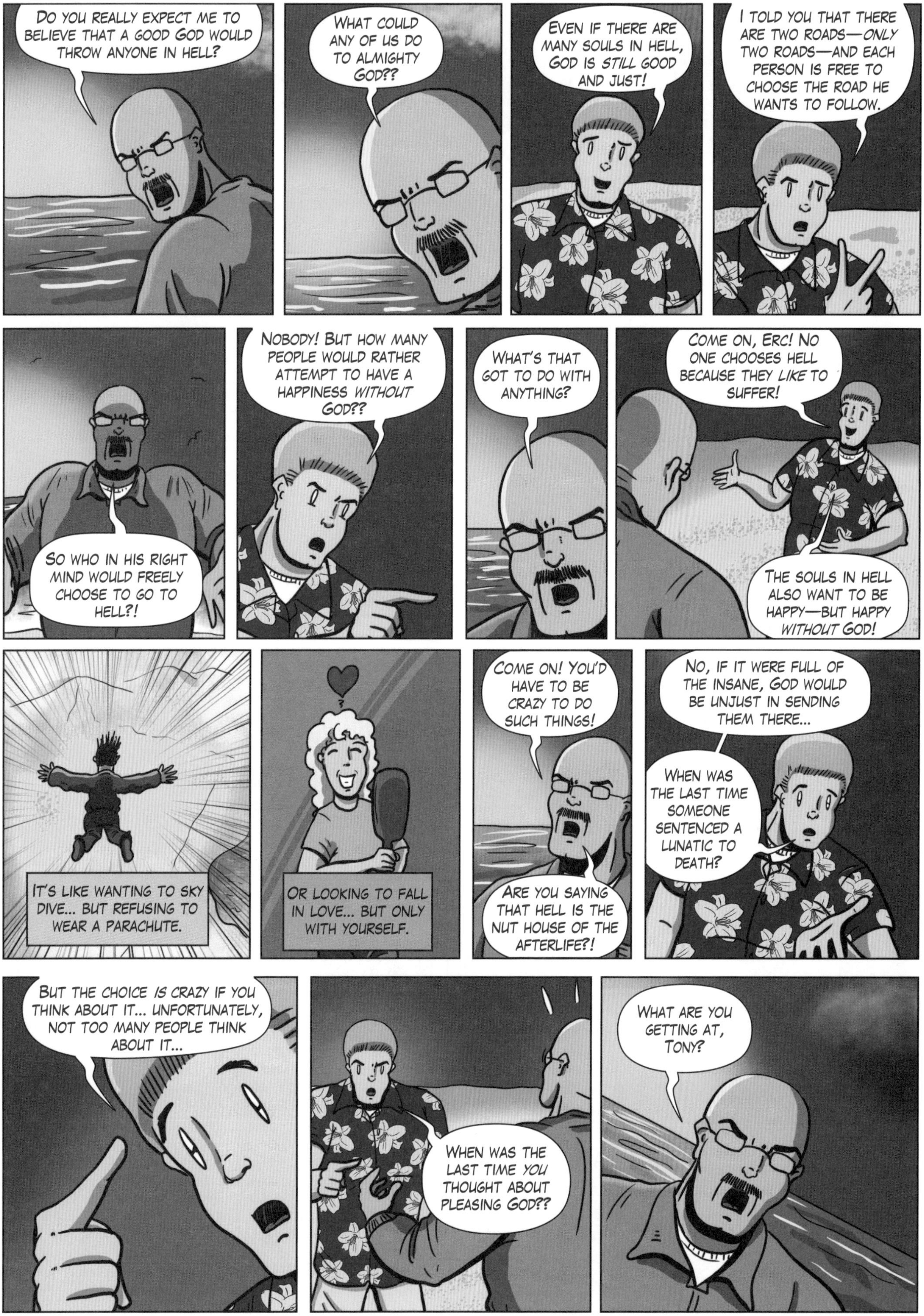

Do you really expect me to believe that a good God would throw anyone in hell?
What could any of us do to almighty God??
Even if there are many souls in hell, God is *still* good and just!
I told you that there are two roads—*only* two roads—and each person is free to choose the road he wants to follow.
So who in his right mind would freely choose to go to hell?!
Nobody! But how many people would rather attempt to have a happiness *without* God??
What's that got to do with anything?
Come on, Erc! No one chooses hell because they *like* to suffer!
The souls in hell also want to be happy—but happy *without* God!
It's like wanting to sky dive... but refusing to wear a parachute.
Or looking to fall in love... but only with yourself.
Come on! You'd have to be crazy to do such things!
Are you saying that hell is the nut house of the afterlife?!
No, if it were full of the insane, God would be unjust in sending them there...
When was the last time someone sentenced a lunatic to death?
But the choice *is* crazy if you think about it... unfortunately, not too many people think about it...
When was the last time *you* thought about pleasing God??
What are you getting at, Tony?

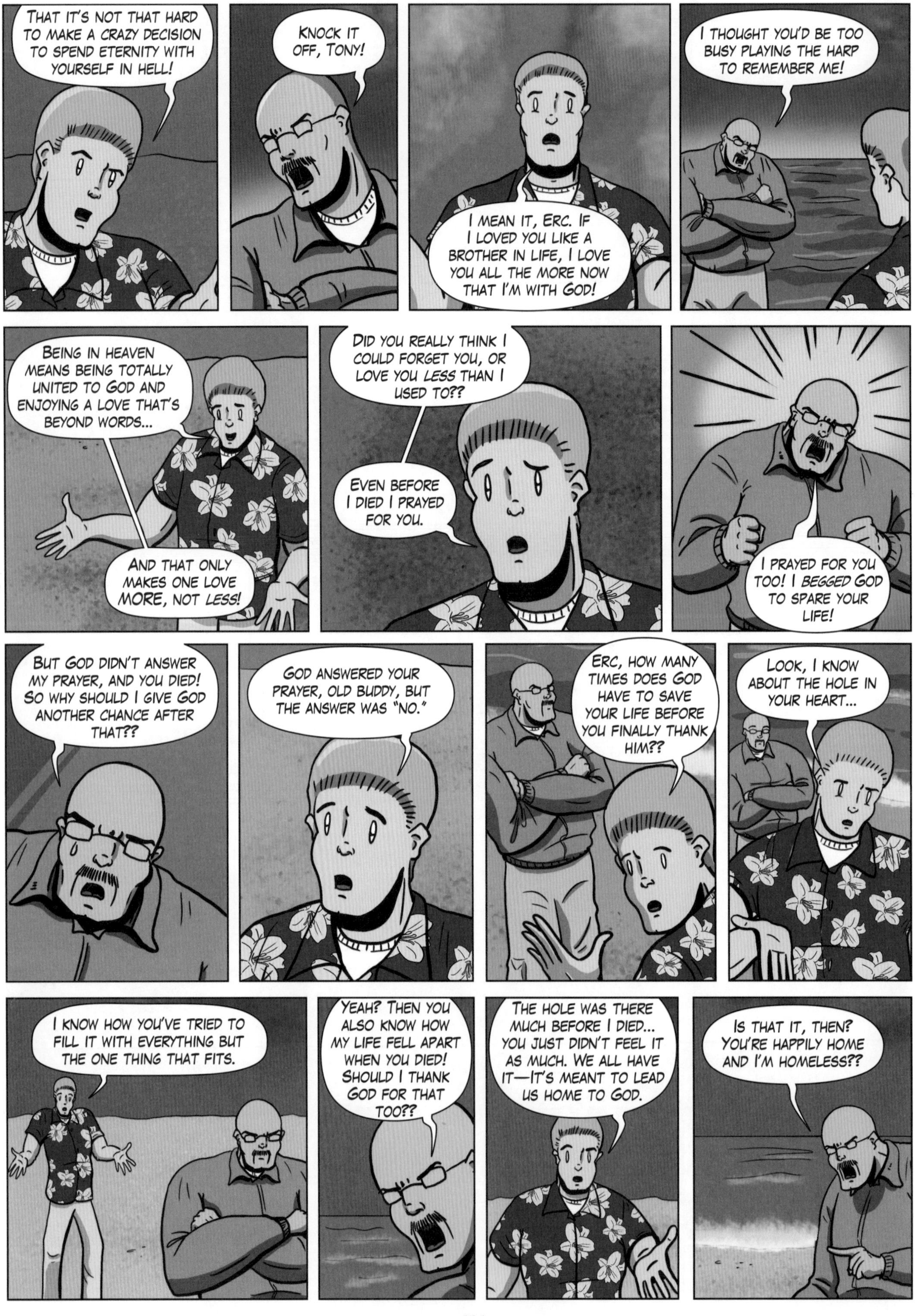
THAT IT'S NOT THAT HARD TO MAKE A CRAZY DECISION TO SPEND ETERNITY WITH YOURSELF IN HELL!
KNOCK IT OFF, TONY!
I MEAN IT, ERC. IF I LOVED YOU LIKE A BROTHER IN LIFE, I LOVE YOU ALL THE MORE NOW THAT I'M WITH GOD!
I THOUGHT YOU'D BE TOO BUSY PLAYING THE HARP TO REMEMBER ME!
BEING IN HEAVEN MEANS BEING TOTALLY UNITED TO GOD AND ENJOYING A LOVE THAT'S BEYOND WORDS...
AND THAT ONLY MAKES ONE LOVE MORE, NOT LESS!
DID YOU REALLY THINK I COULD FORGET YOU, OR LOVE YOU LESS THAN I USED TO??
EVEN BEFORE I DIED I PRAYED FOR YOU.
I PRAYED FOR YOU TOO! I BEGGED GOD TO SPARE YOUR LIFE!
BUT GOD DIDN'T ANSWER MY PRAYER, AND YOU DIED! SO WHY SHOULD I GIVE GOD ANOTHER CHANCE AFTER THAT??
GOD ANSWERED YOUR PRAYER, OLD BUDDY, BUT THE ANSWER WAS "NO."
ERC, HOW MANY TIMES DOES GOD HAVE TO SAVE YOUR LIFE BEFORE YOU FINALLY THANK HIM??
LOOK, I KNOW ABOUT THE HOLE IN YOUR HEART...
I KNOW HOW YOU'VE TRIED TO FILL IT WITH EVERYTHING BUT THE ONE THING THAT FITS.
YEAH? THEN YOU ALSO KNOW HOW MY LIFE FELL APART WHEN YOU DIED! SHOULD I THANK GOD FOR THAT TOO??
THE HOLE WAS THERE MUCH BEFORE I DIED... YOU JUST DIDN'T FEEL IT AS MUCH. WE ALL HAVE IT—IT'S MEANT TO LEAD US HOME TO GOD.
IS THAT IT, THEN? YOU'RE HAPPILY HOME AND I'M HOMELESS??

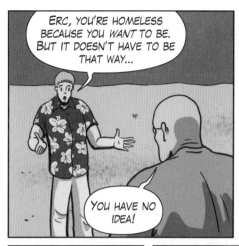

ERC, YOU'RE HOMELESS BECAUSE YOU *WANT* TO BE. BUT IT DOESN'T HAVE TO BE THAT WAY...

YOU HAVE NO IDEA!

WHEN WAS THE LAST TIME YOU FELT AT PEACE OR KNEW A DEEP JOY IN YOUR SOUL?

WHAT DOES IT MATTER? WHO CARES WHAT I FEEL OR DON'T FEEL! LIFE'S SHORT AND MISERABLE, AND THEN WE DIE!

THAT'S NOT WHAT CAPTAIN ERC USED TO THINK...

THAT ERC'S DEAD! NO THANKS TO YOU OR YOUR GOD!

I DON'T BELIEVE IT! THERE'S STILL TOO MUCH GOOD IN YOU.

YOU HAVE NO IDEA OF ALL THAT I'VE DONE SINCE YOU DIED...

THERE'S STILL HOPE...

NOT FOR ME!

AS LONG AS YOU'RE STILL BREATHING, GOD'S MERCY IS THERE FOR YOU. SO WHAT'S STOPPING YOU??

ARE YOU SET ON BEING MISERABLE AT ALL COSTS??

I...DON'T KNOW...

WAIT, TONY! WHAT'S THE RUSH? WHY DON'T WE TALK A LITTLE MORE!

MY TIME'S UP, OLD BUDDY. IT WAS GREAT TALKING WITH YOU AGAIN. I HOPE IT WON'T BE THE LAST...

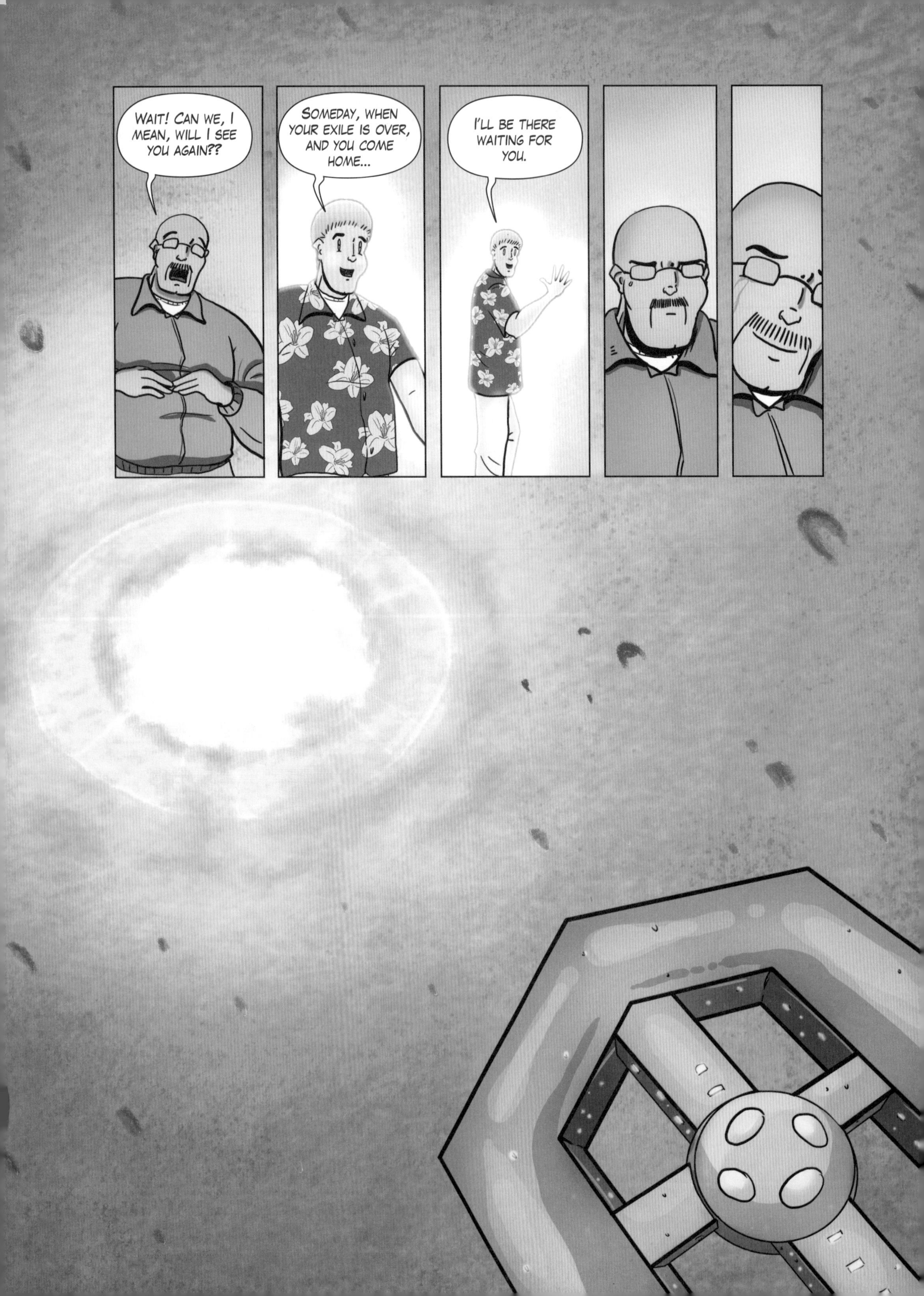
WAIT! CAN WE, I MEAN, WILL I SEE YOU AGAIN??
SOMEDAY, WHEN YOUR EXILE IS OVER, AND YOU COME HOME...
I'LL BE THERE WAITING FOR YOU.

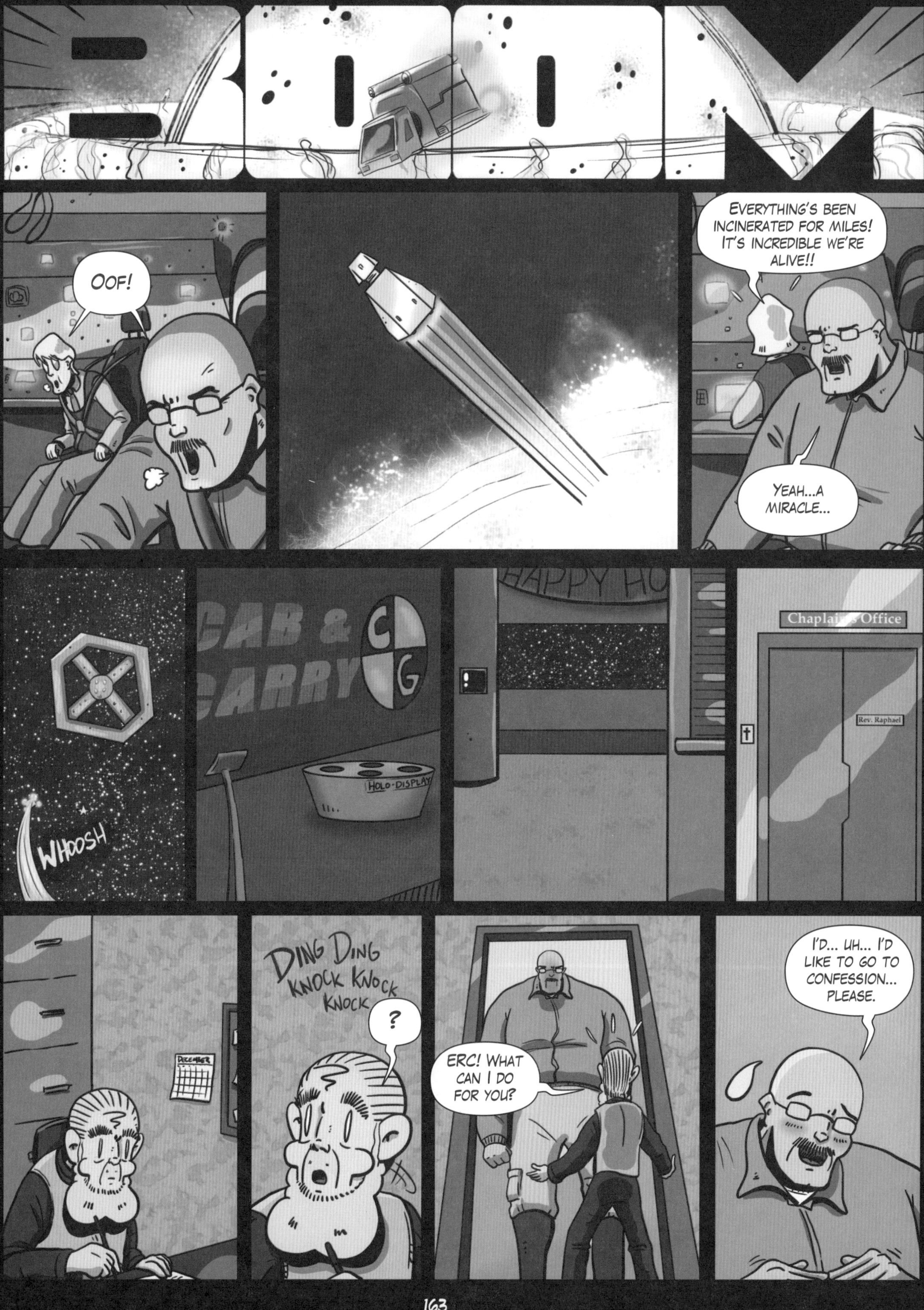
BOOOM
OOF!
EVERYTHING'S BEEN INCINERATED FOR MILES! IT'S INCREDIBLE WE'RE ALIVE!!
YEAH...A MIRACLE...
WHOOSH
CAB & CARRY
C G
HOLO-DISPLAY
HAPPY HO
Chaplain's Office
Rev. Raphael
DECEMBER
DING DING KNOCK KNOCK KNOCK
?
ERC! WHAT CAN I DO FOR YOU?
I'D... UH... I'D LIKE TO GO TO CONFESSION... PLEASE.

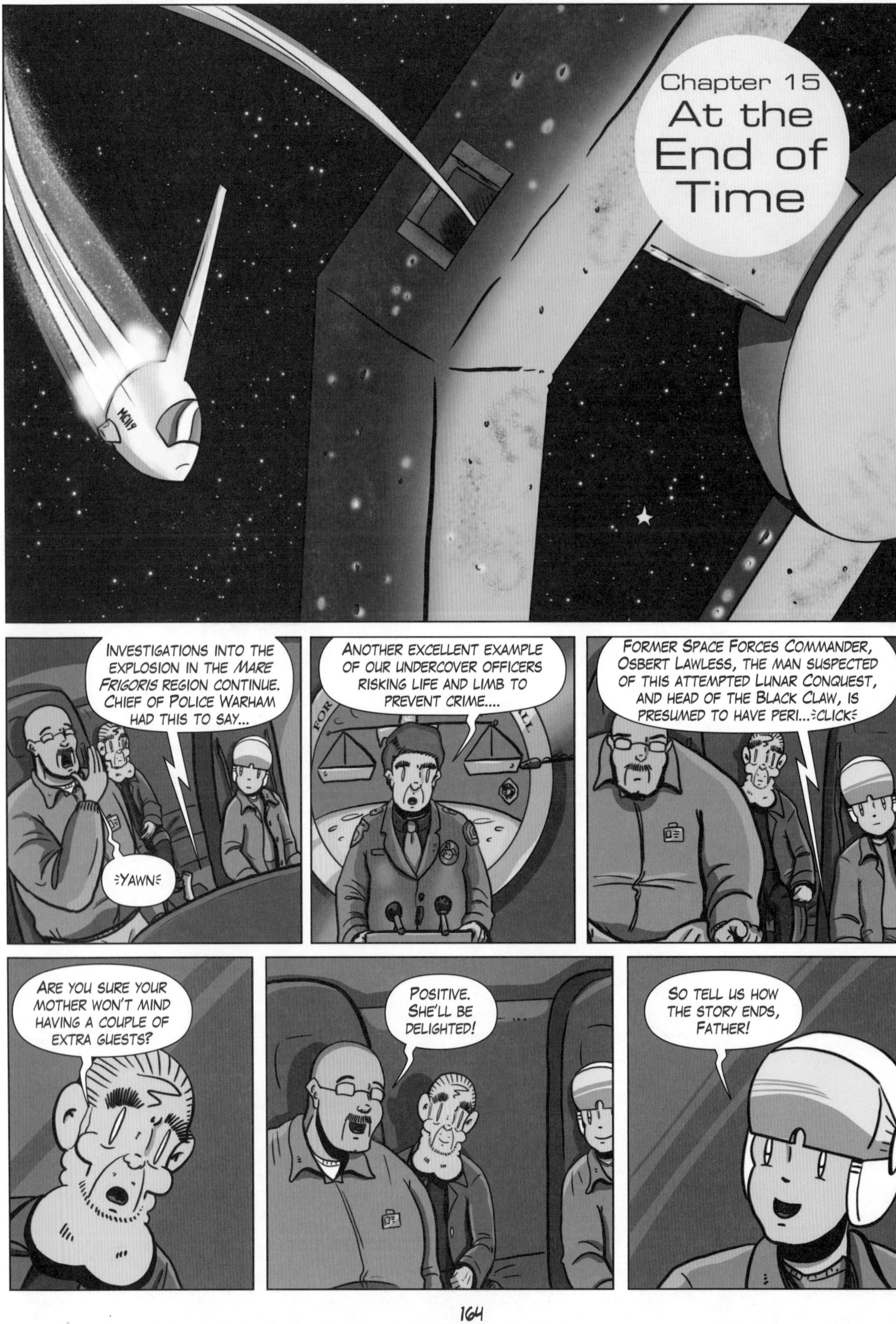
Chapter 15
At the End of Time
MCN9
INVESTIGATIONS INTO THE EXPLOSION IN THE *MARE FRIGORIS* REGION CONTINUE. CHIEF OF POLICE WARHAM HAD THIS TO SAY...
YAWN
ANOTHER EXCELLENT EXAMPLE OF OUR UNDERCOVER OFFICERS RISKING LIFE AND LIMB TO PREVENT CRIME....
FORMER SPACE FORCES COMMANDER, OSBERT LAWLESS, THE MAN SUSPECTED OF THIS ATTEMPTED LUNAR CONQUEST, AND HEAD OF THE BLACK CLAW, IS PRESUMED TO HAVE PERI...
CLICK
ARE YOU SURE YOUR MOTHER WON'T MIND HAVING A COUPLE OF EXTRA GUESTS?
POSITIVE. SHE'LL BE DELIGHTED!
SO TELL US HOW THE STORY ENDS, FATHER!

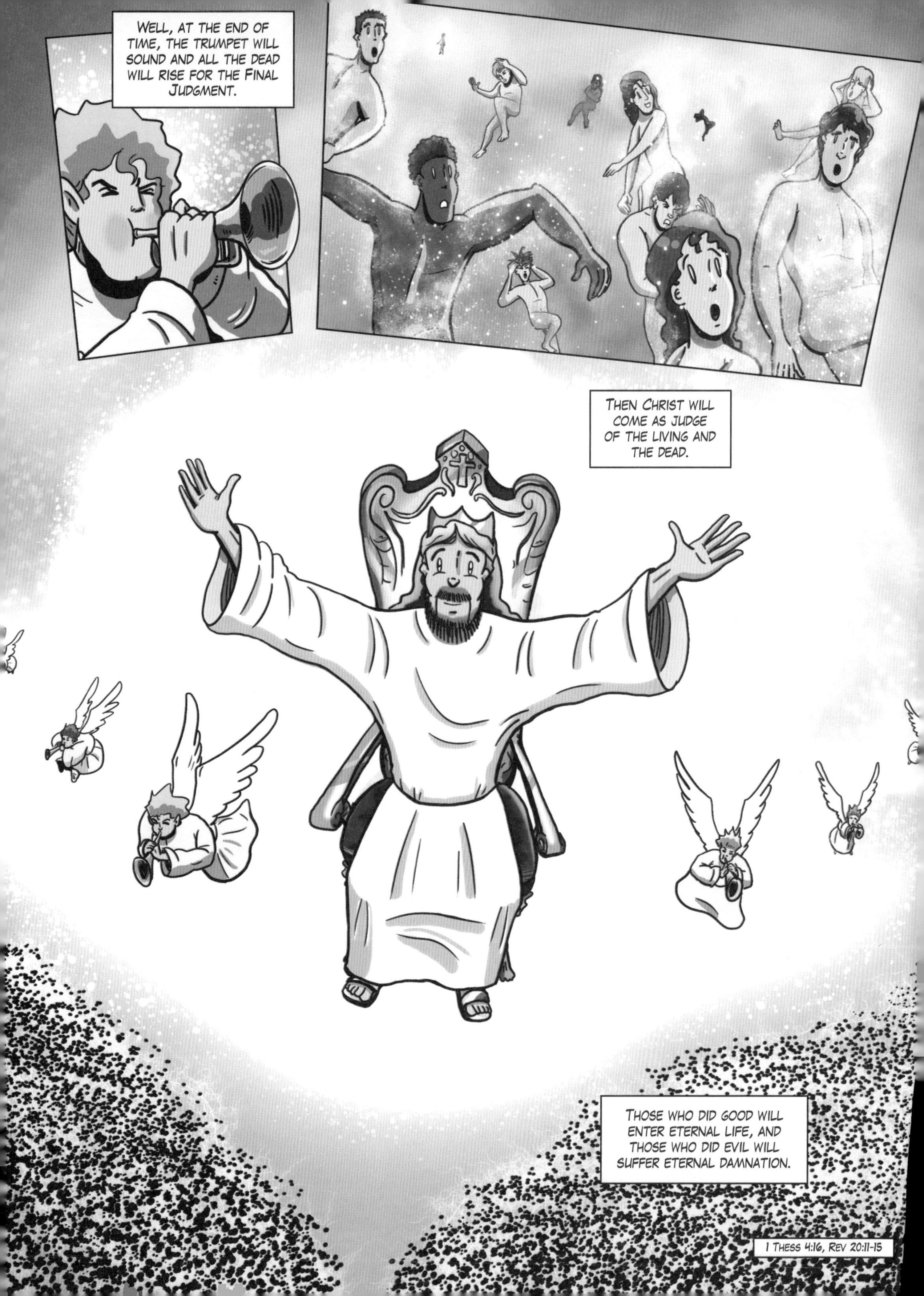
WELL, AT THE END OF TIME, THE TRUMPET WILL SOUND AND ALL THE DEAD WILL RISE FOR THE FINAL JUDGMENT.
THEN CHRIST WILL COME AS JUDGE OF THE LIVING AND THE DEAD.
THOSE WHO DID GOOD WILL ENTER ETERNAL LIFE, AND THOSE WHO DID EVIL WILL SUFFER ETERNAL DAMNATION.
1 THESS 4:16, REV 20:11-15

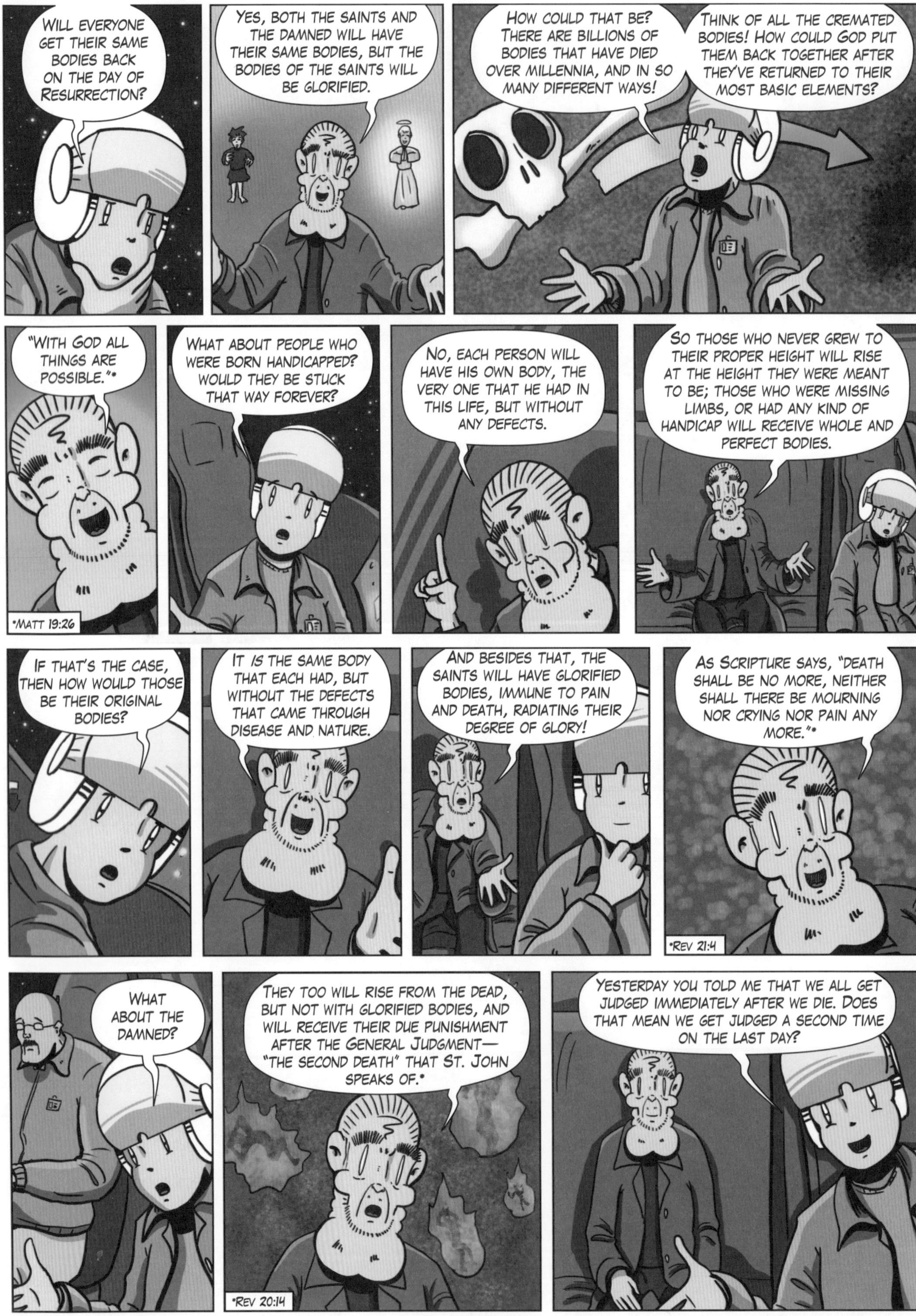

WILL EVERYONE GET THEIR SAME BODIES BACK ON THE DAY OF RESURRECTION?
YES, BOTH THE SAINTS AND THE DAMNED WILL HAVE THEIR SAME BODIES, BUT THE BODIES OF THE SAINTS WILL BE GLORIFIED.
HOW COULD THAT BE? THERE ARE BILLIONS OF BODIES THAT HAVE DIED OVER MILLENNIA, AND IN SO MANY DIFFERENT WAYS!
THINK OF ALL THE CREMATED BODIES! HOW COULD GOD PUT THEM BACK TOGETHER AFTER THEY'VE RETURNED TO THEIR MOST BASIC ELEMENTS?
"WITH GOD ALL THINGS ARE POSSIBLE."*
*MATT 19:26
WHAT ABOUT PEOPLE WHO WERE BORN HANDICAPPED? WOULD THEY BE STUCK THAT WAY FOREVER?
NO, EACH PERSON WILL HAVE HIS OWN BODY, THE VERY ONE THAT HE HAD IN THIS LIFE, BUT WITHOUT ANY DEFECTS.
SO THOSE WHO NEVER GREW TO THEIR PROPER HEIGHT WILL RISE AT THE HEIGHT THEY WERE MEANT TO BE; THOSE WHO WERE MISSING LIMBS, OR HAD ANY KIND OF HANDICAP WILL RECEIVE WHOLE AND PERFECT BODIES.
IF THAT'S THE CASE, THEN HOW WOULD THOSE BE THEIR ORIGINAL BODIES?
IT IS THE SAME BODY THAT EACH HAD, BUT WITHOUT THE DEFECTS THAT CAME THROUGH DISEASE AND NATURE.
AND BESIDES THAT, THE SAINTS WILL HAVE GLORIFIED BODIES, IMMUNE TO PAIN AND DEATH, RADIATING THEIR DEGREE OF GLORY!
AS SCRIPTURE SAYS, "DEATH SHALL BE NO MORE, NEITHER SHALL THERE BE MOURNING NOR CRYING NOR PAIN ANY MORE."*
*REV 21:4
WHAT ABOUT THE DAMNED?
THEY TOO WILL RISE FROM THE DEAD, BUT NOT WITH GLORIFIED BODIES, AND WILL RECEIVE THEIR DUE PUNISHMENT AFTER THE GENERAL JUDGMENT— "THE SECOND DEATH" THAT ST. JOHN SPEAKS OF.*
*REV 20:14
YESTERDAY YOU TOLD ME THAT WE ALL GET JUDGED IMMEDIATELY AFTER WE DIE. DOES THAT MEAN WE GET JUDGED A SECOND TIME ON THE LAST DAY?

YES, BUT NOT IN THE SENSE OF A RETRIAL.

EVERYONE IN HELL STAYS WHERE HE IS, AND EVERYONE IN HEAVEN LIKEWISE REMAINS IN HEAVEN...

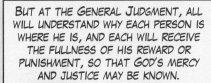
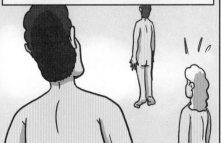

BUT AT THE GENERAL JUDGMENT, ALL WILL UNDERSTAND WHY EACH PERSON IS WHERE HE IS, AND EACH WILL RECEIVE THE FULLNESS OF HIS REWARD OR PUNISHMENT, SO THAT GOD'S MERCY AND JUSTICE MAY BE KNOWN.

SO WHAT HAPPENS NEXT? WHAT WILL EVERYONE *DO* FOR ALL OF ETERNITY?!

AH, THEY WILL REST IN GOD AND ENJOY THAT UNION WITH HIM FOREVER!

SO "LET US THEREFORE STRIVE TO ENTER THAT REST!"* WE STILL HAVE OUR PARTS TO PLAY IN THIS DRAMA OF SALVATION HISTORY.

*HEB 4:11

REMEMBER THAT THE BATTLE BETWEEN GOOD AND EVIL CONTINUES UNTIL THE LAST DAY; UNTIL CHRIST'S FINAL VICTORY OVER SIN AND DEATH...

AND THEN THE STORY *REALLY* ENDS!

HOW AMAZING TO THINK THAT WE'RE PART OF SUCH AN INCREDIBLE STORY!

INDEED IT IS! THANK GOD FOR CREATING YOU AND GIVING YOU A PART IN HIS PLAN OF SALVATION.

AFTER ALL, IF HE HADN'T, WHO'D KNOW? WHO WOULD HAVE MISSED YOU IF YOU NEVER EXISTED??

WHAT'S WRONG, ERC? YOU'VE HARDLY SAID A WORD SINCE WE LEFT LOP 5.

I'M ENJOYING SOMETHING I HAVEN'T FELT IN A LONG TIME...

WHAT'S THAT??

JOY.

THE SAVIOR IS HERE!

...YES, JOY.

167

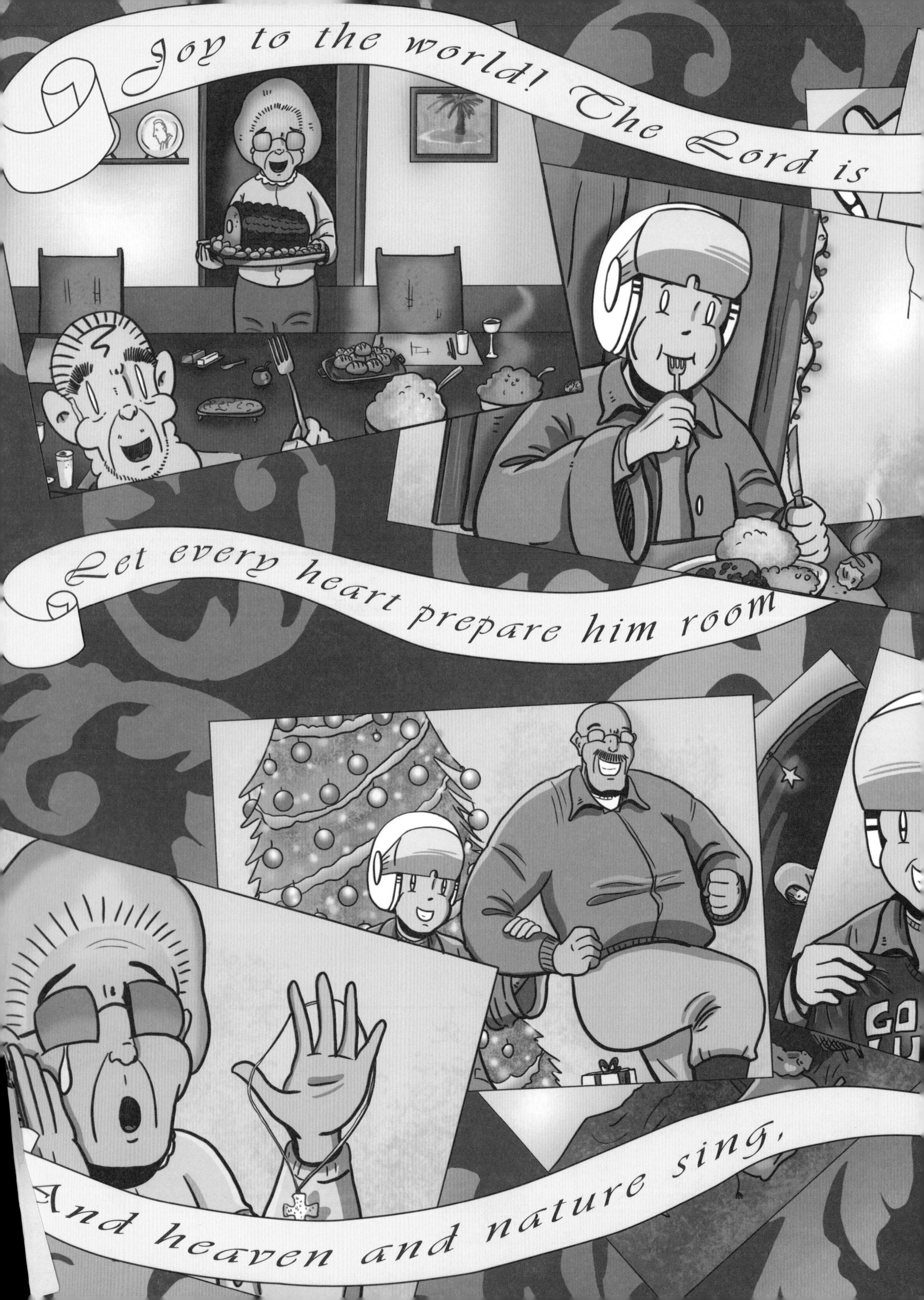
Joy to the world! The Lord is
Let every heart prepare him room
And heaven and nature sing,
GO

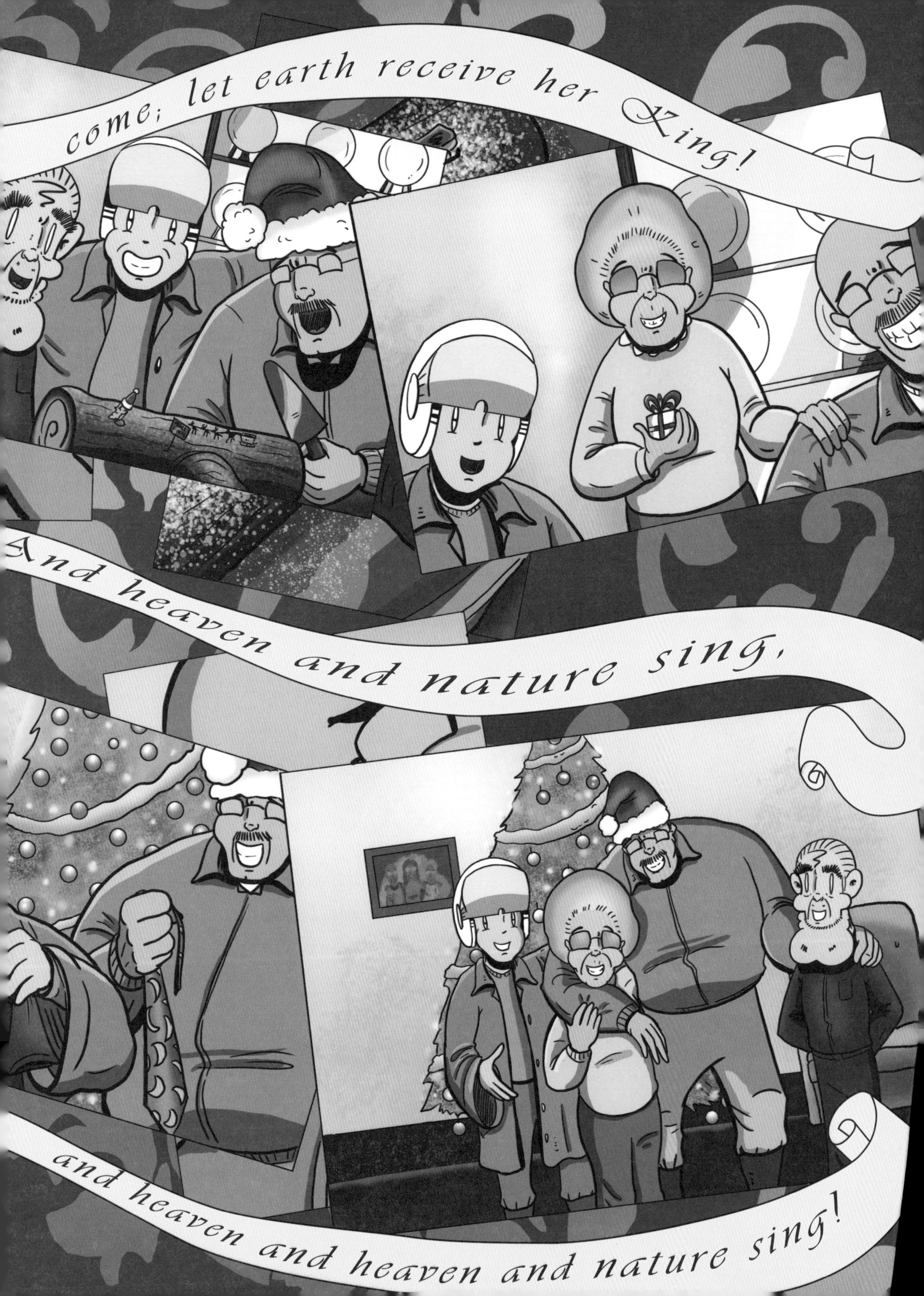
come; let earth receive her King!
And heaven and nature sing,
and heaven and heaven and nature sing!

THE END

THE PROPHECIES

THE PROTO-EVANGELIUM: GENESIS 3:15

PROPHECIES OF THE MESSIAH'S GENEALOGY:

- HE WILL BE A SEMITE: GENESIS 9:26-27
- HE WILL BE A DESCENDANT OF ABRAHAM: GENESIS 22:18 (CF. GAL 3:16)
- HE WILL BE A DESCENDANT OF JACOB: NUMBERS 24:17
- HE WILL BE OF THE TRIBE OF JUDAH: GENESIS 49:8-12 (CF. HEB 7:14)
- HE WILL BE OF THE HOUSE OF DAVID: 2 SAMUEL 7:12-16; PSALM 89:35-37; ISAIAH 11:1; JEREMIAH 23:5-6 (CF. ACTS 2:30, 2 TIM 2:8)
- HIS DIVINE NATURE: PSALM 2:7, WISDOM 2:16

PROPHECIES OF THE MESSIAH'S LIFE:

- HE WILL HAVE A FORERUNNER: MALACHI 3:1; ISAIAH 40:3 (CF. MATT 11:10)
- HE WILL BE BORN IN BETHLEHEM: MICAH 5:2 (CF. MATT 2:5-6)
- HE WILL BE BORN OF A VIRGIN: ISAIAH 7:14 (CF. MATT 1:22-23)
- HE WILL BE MEEK AND MERCIFUL: ISAIAH 42:2-3 (CF. MATT 12:18-21)
- HIS LIGHT WILL SHINE CHIEFLY ON GALILEE: ISAIAH 9:1-2 (CF. MATT 4:15-16)
- HE WILL PERFORM MIRACLES: ISAIAH 35:4-6 (CF. MATT 11:5)
- HE WILL ENTER JERUSALEM HUMBLY RIDING A DONKEY: ZECHARIAH 9:9 (CF. MATT 21:5)

PROPHECIES OF THE MESSIAH'S DEATH:

- HE WILL BE SOLD FOR THIRTY PIECES OF SILVER: ZECHARIAH 11:12-13 (CF. MATT 27:9)
- HE WILL BE FLOGGED AND SPAT UPON: ISAIAH 50:6 (CF. MATT 27:30)
- HE WILL BE CONDEMNED TO DEATH LIKE A CRIMINAL: ISAIAH 53:7, 12, WISDOM 2:20
- HIS HANDS AND FEET WILL BE PIERCED: PSALM 22:16
- HE WILL BE OFFERED VINEGAR TO DRINK: PSALM 69:21 (CF. MATT 27:48)
- HE WILL BE SHAMEFULLY MOCKED: PSALM 22:7-8 (CF. MATT 27:39-44)
- HIS CLOTHES WILL BE DIVIDED: PSALM 22:18 (CF. JOHN 19:24)
- THEY SHALL MOURN HIM: ZECHARIAH 12:10 (CF. JOHN 19:37)

PROPHECIES OF THE MESSIAH'S EXALTATION:

- THE GLORY OF HIS TOMB: ISAIAH 53:9-12
- HIS RESURRECTION: PSALM 16:9-11 (CF. ACTS 2:31)
- HIS ASCENSION: PSALM 68:18 (CF. ACTS 1:9, EPH 4:8)

FUNCTIONS OF THE MESSIAH:

- PROPHET:

  THE PROPHET: DEUTERONOMY 18:15, 18-19; ISAIAH 42:1; 55:3-4; 61:1
  THE FOUNDER OF A NEW AND UNIVERSAL COVENANT: ISAIAH 42:6; 49:8; JEREMIAH 31:31-34 (CF. ROM 11:26-27)

- PRIEST:

  HE WILL OFFER HIMSELF AS A VICTIM FOR THE SINS OF MANKIND: ISAIAH 53:4-10
  HE WILL BE A PRIEST ACCORDING TO THE ORDER OF MELCHIZEDEK: PSALM 110:4

- KING:

  PROCLAIMED AS KING: PSALM 2:6
  HIS RULE WILL BE OF JUSTICE AND PEACE: PSALM 72:4-17
  HIS WILL BE A PERPETUAL KINGDOM: PSALM 72:5, 7
  HIS WILL BE A UNIVERSAL KINGDOM: PSALM 2:8; 72:8, 11
  HE WILL COME IN HUMILITY AND PEACE: ZECHARIAH 9:9-10 (CF. MATT 21:5)

THE TIME OF HIS COMING:

- GENESIS 49:10
- DANIEL 9:24-27 (CF. NEH 2:7-8)

COMPILED (MOSTLY) FROM: DOGMATIC THEOLOGY VOL. 1: THE TRUE RELIGION BY MSGR. G. VAN NOORT.
N.B.: THIS IS NOT AN EXHAUSTIVE LIST OF MESSIANIC PROPHECIES.

SUGGESTED READING

- Catechism of the Catholic Church
- Dawn of the Messiah: The Coming of Christ in Scripture by Edward Sri
- Walking with God: A Journey through the Bible by Tim Gray & Jeff Cavins
- Bones of Contention by Marvin L. Lubenow
- The Everlasting Man by G.K. Chesterton
- The Mystery of Israel and the Church, Vol. 1: Figure and Fulfillment by Lawrence Feingold
- A Father Who Keeps His Promises by Scott Hahn
- Joy to the World: How Christ's Coming Changed Everything (And Still Does) by Scott Hahn
- The Founding of Christendom: A History of Christendom Vol. 1 by Warren H. Carroll
- Theology & Sanity by Frank Sheed
- Jesus of Nazareth: The Infancy Narratives by Pope Benedict XVI

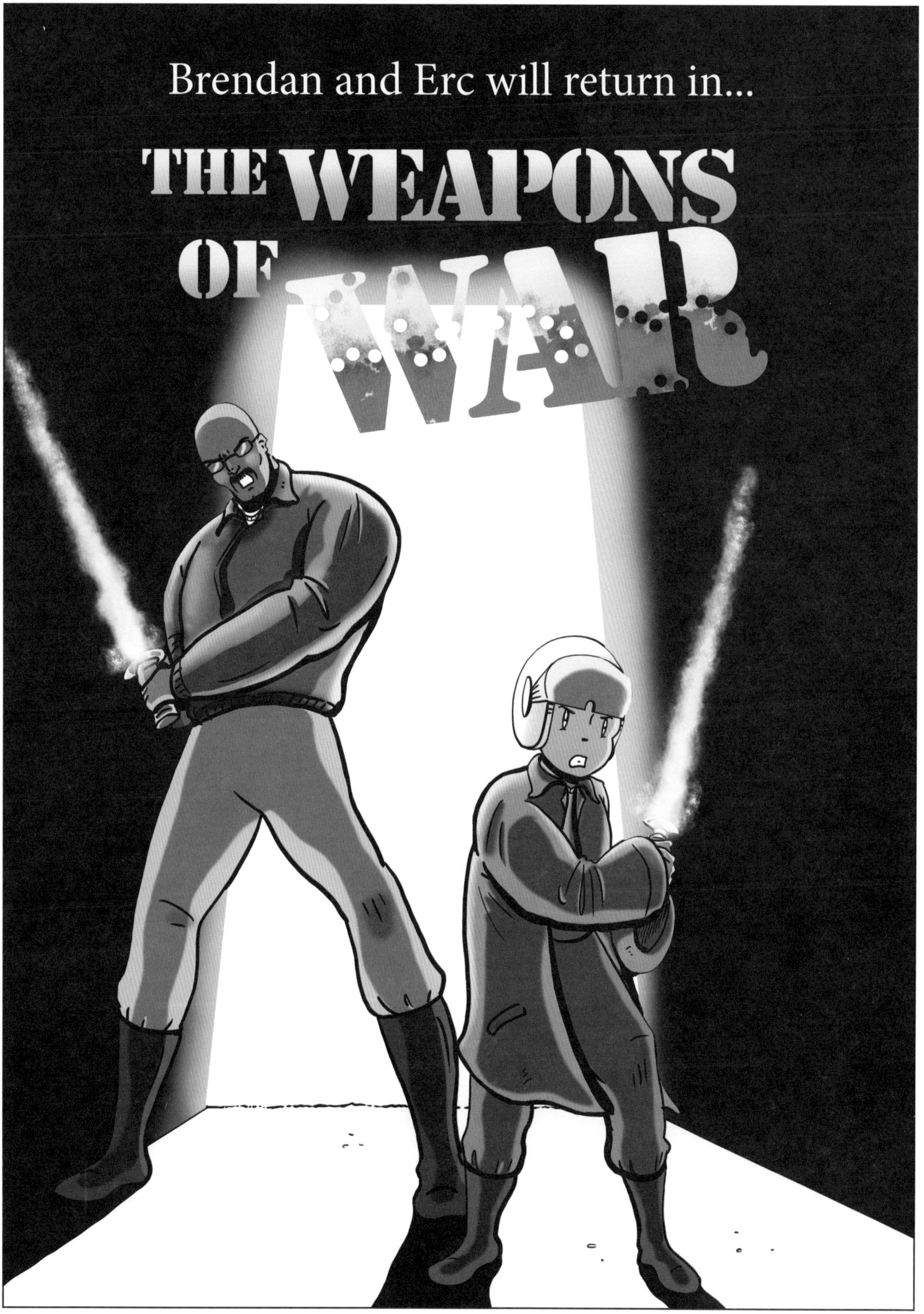
Brendan and Erc will return in...
THE WEAPONS OF WAR